CELLAR RATS

To Rob — Enjoy the flavor of So Oregon!

CJ David

CELLAR RATS

C. J. David

iUniverse, Inc.
New York Lincoln Shanghai

CELLAR RATS

Copyright © 2006 by C J David

All rights reserved. No part of this book may be used or reproduced by any means, graphic, electronic, or mechanical, including photocopying, recording, taping or by any information storage retrieval system without the written permission of the publisher except in the case of brief quotations embodied in critical articles and reviews.

iUniverse books may be ordered through booksellers or by contacting:

iUniverse
2021 Pine Lake Road, Suite 100
Lincoln, NE 68512
www.iuniverse.com
1-800-Authors (1-800-288-4677)

ISBN-13: 978-0-595-38569-0 (pbk)
ISBN-13: 978-0-595-82947-7 (ebk)
ISBN-10: 0-595-38569-9 (pbk)
ISBN-10: 0-595-82947-3 (ebk)

Printed in the United States of America

*To my very supportive family
and especially Kristen who got the ball rolling.*

PROLOGUE

The only sound emanating from the spacious building was the occasional knock-knock of the ventilation traps on the outside walls. The soft wind current caused them to open and close periodically and they echoed mournfully throughout every room to testify that something, other than the one woman working alone in her office, was still functioning. Save for that one sound, the winery was quiet.

By decree, Mountain View Winery was to be closed for at least two days, perhaps longer. It was an ultimatum handed down by the owner, who was now the only warm body in the place.

It was customary for everyone to have some time off after the particularly arduous work schedule following the annual wine festival. No one questioned the closing. The employees had received the moratorium on work with giddy acceptance of extra days with full pay. They looked forward to their hard-earned leisure. From the most reliable regular staff member to the last of the rag-tag part-time helpers, who seemed to arrive like tumbleweeds from unknown origins, they had one and all expended an exceptional amount of effort for seven days and the relief was well deserved. No one would be expected to report to work at the winery until further notified.

But for Kara Tower there would be no respite. Now she would have to dig into the unwanted and unfinished details of her winery's business.

This was a complete departure from the usual workplace hustle on a Monday morning. It seemed odd with no one there, but at the same time it was a welcome relief. Undisturbed, she silently worked away at the monumental numbers of accounts, reports, and inventories. She was saddened to think that soon, very soon, the responsibility of keeping abreast of wine production would pass to other hands.

Page by page, the piles of paper were decreasing as surely as her ability to cope with them. *How did I ever manage all of this?* she wondered, leaning for a moment to the back of her chair as if addressing the ceiling. Until now, there had been no question of her ability to control the intricacies of making award winning wine. She had been capable and efficient, rising to any and all occasions. But no longer. This was a new day, and she was ready to turn over her life's work to the powers that be.

As she bent again to the unwelcome task of sorting the papers on her desk for what she accepted regretfully to be the last time, she sensed that something was not right. Upstairs in her office, the air was charged. The hairs on the back of her neck and arms bristled.

What she heard was…elusive. But there! There it was again! A sound, but not a familiar one. Something different. A gentle scraping?

Before she could rise from the swivel desk chair, the growling echo in the big room where the wine was made became recognizable. One of the cargo doors was slowly being opened! Kara moved with an economy of motion from the second story office, and rounded the corner of the tasting room to tentatively peer down from the balcony to see what was going on. *No one should be here today at this hour*, she thought. *Why did I leave my car at the house?* She started to panic!

She heard more noise coming from the big room. What in God's name was going on? How could the cargo door be opened from the outside when it was supposed to be dead-bolted from the inside?

These were momentary thoughts, taking only a second of time. Kara's cunning instincts kicked in. Keep quiet old girl! Let's see what happens. It was a perverse curiosity that led her to watch instead of interfering. Feeling her heart beating, she could see the strong hands that pulled at the door…a crack, just wide enough to allow entrance.

She ducked back behind the doorjamb, trembling.

PART I

THE SET-UP

CHAPTER 1

❀

During the twenty some years that Kara Tower was the guiding hand that had nurtured and developed the Oregon winery known as Mountain View, it was appropriate to say that she had seen a few things and done a few things along the rusty dusty trail. In fact, twenty years *prior* to the time that she became a vintner were what most people would consider a reasonably full lifetime of experience. Kara Tower could not be regarded as a young woman.

It was however at an early age that the choice was made as to the direction her career interests would take. In spite of her parents' view that she should in some way follow in their footsteps, Kara traveled her own path in pursuit of her goals for the future. Her lifelong need and desire was to be productive as well as creative.

"We want you to have a well-rounded education. You must study the humanities!" She had listened to this mantra from both of her parents on so many occasions. Even when he was not speaking, the resonance of her father's baritone voice echoing her mother's position hung in the room. It was difficult to defend her own youthful ideas in the face of that unsurpassable voice that captivated thousands from the most prestigious stages of the world. But the young girl was immovable in her decision to separate herself from the career choice made by her famous parents.

She consoled them soothingly, "I do understand your reasoning as well as your feelings, but I'm just not cut out for acting."

This one last time, her argument didn't sound like the plaintive chirping of an eighteen-year-old. It took no more than five minutes, but she stated her position with the mature air of someone who had both feet on the ground, and no one had cause to ever argue with Kara over the issue again. The message was given and finally understood. Oddly enough, it was truly the finest piece of acting she remembered ever having performed.

Now, at fifty-five and looking at least ten years younger than her age, she was as agile as she was tireless. Looking back, she could even gloat a little that this career choice had provided her with such enormous enjoyment, derived from her constant activity. No doubt because of this, she was spared from the expected ravages of time.

Still stunningly attractive, she maintained an excellent rounded figure and was blessed with the kind of sympathetic face that invited confidentiality and oddly enough, credibility—an asset in any business. Thick lashes warmly darkened the soft brown eyes that flashed with amber highlights. They reflected a concern for others and a passionate concentration centering on the activity of the moment. Her full lips were capable of appearing either assertive or submissive, as the occasion demanded. A photographer's delight, her face was surrounded by an abundance of soft light brown curls glowing in warm red-gold highlights with just the hint of shocks of silver gray throughout. The full effect brought her the admiration of her peers, not to mention the envy of a quite a few women younger than herself. Never a model, that succulent face and figure had no doubt been the object of many a man's fantasy.

Hers was a thoroughly satisfying occupation as careers went. Enviable to most. With wine as the end product, every year was like giving birth as each new vintage was developed, step by step, into the bottled wines that bore the name of her winery, Mountain View. And every year Kara Leslie Renaud Tower could observe with gratification and pride, the work that had been accomplished in the previous seasons. It was an all-consuming enterprise and she met each new challenge head on.

"Kara, there's a problem with the...". And she would solve it.

"Kara, could you help me get this...". She was there to assist.

"Anybody interested in trying out the new..." Kara was the first in line to play the intrepid guinea pig.

Where else in the business world could the boss wear so many different hats. One moment she could be found mucking about in the vineyard irrigation system, while later that same day she might be expected to represent the winery, dressed for a formal setting in posh, well appointed surroundings, intellectually stimulating conversations buzzing in the air. A far cry from the mud of the field.

There were also the unseen elements in the life of Kara Tower. There were the ever mounting demands on her patience. The mysterious voids in provisions for production. Malfunctions of equipment. Issues of lost items, necessary to the operation. Personal belongings gone missing. Tiny nips and bites out the well-being of her existence. Small frustrations that added up to a curious state of instability and along with that, occasional moments of indecision and the constant specter of insolvency.

From grunt work to traveling salesman and mediator of problems, Mountain View Winery would demand immense versatility in the singular personage known as Kara Tower.

CHAPTER 2

Spring

Turner Ferguson propped up his head from a reclining position on the ground. "How do you intend to expand that facility? Not only that, but why would you?" The expression on his face was more lackadaisical than his words suggested. "Didn't I hear you say something once about being short of bucks?"

It was too much for him to contemplate on a day like this. They were resting between bouts of gathering newly cut logs and the thought of finding ways to make more work just didn't seem to be rational activity. The forest surrounding them was quiet without the angry whine of the chainsaw. The peacefulness seemed to be reaching out to comfort and moderate the ills of the world. So why did he get started talking business? He now wished he hadn't.

Kara breath had caught with his last question and she exhaled in a long sigh. "My plans were made a long time ago, my friend. With or without enough money, the wine industry is here to stay and it's my intention to grow with it. It's an ambitious challenge, but when we're successful, you know the whole area will benefit from it," she said in explanation.

Turner's current ambition took him no further than his own small firewood business. His biggest responsibility involved only maintaining his cutting tools and keeping 'Curley', his old green Ford pickup truck happy. He wished only to have enough food for the table, beer for the 'frig and gas to deliver the next load of wood. Turner had enough of ambition. He was through with that. Tired of being a department manager of a large high-power corporation in a big city, he had gladly relinquished the competitive lifestyle to return to his original home. The pace he was traveling now was the speed he wanted to maintain.

Picking his teeth mountain man style with a twig and contentedly swilling a brewski that had been teetering on the moldering log next to where he lay, Turner Ferguson looked around him, into the verdant greenery of the woods, and gestured to the sky.

"With all the bee-u-teeful scenery around here, why the hell do you want to muddy up the water with big business?" His flowing 'hills' dialect was close to perfection. Turner blended. He had also been raised in these hills and knew them backwards and forwards.

The dialogue regarding business growth had gone round and round in Kara's head. Business growth versus unblemished nature. It had been a gamble from the beginning, creating the winery, making it grow at the most advantageous rate. To have no growth in business is to shrivel and die. She couldn't let that happen. Mountain View had to see positive growth every year that it existed. And even more than this, Kara's fixation was on accomplishing her goal; to build a new and clean enterprise in an untried area!

Turner had made a good point. Big industry had no place in a setting such as this. But a winery wasn't the same as big industry, she reasoned. It was an agrarian enterprise in a deeply agrarian location. Here, there were farms and valleys, mountains and trees. The trees, deciduous and evergreen, especially held a precious beauty. At this time of year, the baby green shoots at each extremity of growth ensured the continuation of the season's cycle. It was a good omen and the portents of the land gave her strength, the vision to achieve her goals with the same unstoppable continuity of nature.

She dearly loved going out in the woods with Turner whenever possible. Besides being unadulterated exercise, it was a step back to the basics and a first hand opportunity to appreciate mother nature and her bounty. Together, they would cut up dry hardwood from fallen madrone and oak trees to be used later as firewood. Splitting the logs to usable sizes for burning, they would sweat with the work and then stack as much as the old Ford could possibly hold and still be able to make its way through the rough hand cleared road, swaying precariously with its burden back to the main highway. It was said by woodsmen that there were two benefits from gathering firewood, the warmth it created in collecting it and later…the warmth from the fire.

Resuming their work, the pile of wood in the back of the pickup grew noticeably larger. "How are you holding up?" Turner leaned on the splitting maul, watching as Kara placed two logs onto the truck bed. They had been hard at work, organizing the pieces that had been sawn into two foot lengths.

"Like I just spent two hours at the gym." She stretched out her arm muscles and wiped tendrils of wet hair away from her face with the back of her hand.

"Ready to take another break?"

"Oh yes!" her breathing was labored. She reached for the water bottle and savored a long drink.

Turner took one more swing at a large and unresponsive log. It finally gave in and broke cleanly in half.

When Kara regained her normal breath, she said quietly to get his attention, "Turner."

"Yeah?" He stopped what he was doing when he heard the inflection of hesitation in her voice. He had worked with enough people under his supervision to know that he was about to be asked for a favor.

"How would you like to be doing something besides cutting firewood for your friends?"

"I don't sell firewood to my friends. They wouldn't pay me enough to keep me in beer! I have customers! Have a little respect!" he goaded her.

"I'll rephrase that. Do you think you could spare some time for another job?"

"What have you got in mind?" he asked provocatively, giving way to his libidinous thoughts.

"Something we've started to talk about before," she reprimanded. "Do you remember when I mentioned needing a foreman for the vineyard?"

"I thought you had a foreman."

"Well, we do. But I'm not happy with the man who I hired. There's nothing specific, nothing I could put my finger on, but I know something is going on with him that I don't like."

"So you want to replace the foreman with me?" he asked incredulously.

"Not exactly."

"Are you saying this cause I look like I need a regular job?"

"Not exactly."

"Then what, exactly are you suggesting?"

She worded her proposal carefully. "I'm asking for you to come out of your 'retirement' to work as an overseer, a manager. To fill in as a coordinator and most of all, to keep an eye on the efficiency of the grounds operations. I'll have to confess that I've looked into your background and learned that for your young years, you've established an excellent record."

"You looked into my records?" Now she really had his attention.

"Yes," she said, looking him straight in the eye. "And your background will be considered private if that's what you wish."

She added as consolation, "We could make this as temporary or permanent a position as you feel is appropriate…Oh, and I should add we're going to need a great deal of help with the upcoming festival."

Kara had considered pursuing this offer for some days now, and the more she thought about it, the more sense it made. On too many occasions she had gone searching for Talbert, the current vineyard foreman, who *should* have been busy working in the field, only to find that he had ditched his job and had gone home. How was it she never saw him leave? He was sneaky, but she needed someone there who knew the place, and Talbert was somewhat familiar with the vineyard operation. As undependable as he was, he always managed to do just enough work to remind people of the importance of his position. But what Kara really needed was a diligent employee. If Turner could be persuaded, she knew he would be the perfect candidate.

"Well, Turner?" Piling it on she said with a grin, "You know there's no one else as trustworthy as you are. You're young, strong, and competent on top of everything else. Handsome guy like you could raise the morale of the distaff side of the crew. Think of it!" She warmed up to her pitch, her expressive motions held his attention. "You know you would love working out-of-doors, and we could always use a manager for the ranch." Now she gave him a big smile. "Well? Have I flattered you enough for you to accept the position?"

"God, woman. How in the hell did you ever expect me to say no?" He reluctantly raised himself from the comfort of the twisted log that sufficed for him as outback furniture. "Okay, okay! When do we start? How 'bout right now!" He sidled over to her with a grin and an outstretched hand. She reached up and shook it with a firm grip. The deal was set.

As soon as I have a talk with the bank about that long term loan, she thought, *then we get to work*! She frowned, realizing that their answer would come tomorrow if the committee has had their meeting. *All I have to do is settle this loan and the operating line of credit.* Then she laughed, glad to have settled the issue if only in her mind.

"Let's start tomorrow. I've done all m'homework m'lad, and it looks like all systems are GO!"

"I hope to God for your sake they are, Kara. You deserve it, you know." He was serious.

"Amen!"

There was a sudden appearance of a blue heron landing on the shallow bank of the nearby stream. It cast about for morsels of live food for a brief moment before elevating back into the air, its territory being usurped by human presence.

Kara Tower, born Kara Leslie Renaud had been in her early years, an avid reader. There was nothing quite as satisfying as opening the pages of a book, revealing worlds and people in their endless entanglements.

It was as close as she could get to the successful acting careers of both her mother, Caprice and her father, Tafton. These highly glamorous people were always involved with their fluctuating character portrayals and inconstant locations to accommodate their artistic outlets. They loved their child dearly, but the absurdity of having a child in tow in this ever-changing lifestyle was solved by the boarding school to which Kara was sent. Little wonder the young girl would lose herself in the arms of literature. It was a secure haven in an insecure world.

It was not until her later teenage years, when she would have been able to cope with the excitement and pressures of constant movement with her parents, that they suddenly reverted to the more solid, academic side of theatrics. There was a professorship for her father at the University of Southern California and a writing career for her mother. For Kara, this boded more freedom than she ever before experienced. Living together in their home in Brentwood, she was no longer a prisoner of the boarding school. For Kara, it was an awakening to the machinations of the outside world.

At the time of life when she, like others her age, was determining the choices for her future, she found that the world of commerce held a great fascination for her. She persuaded her parents to allow her to attend the university to study business and commerce in depth.

It was there, that she met Gregg, her future husband.

Their's was a happy marriage lasting years before Gregg contracted a debilitating and fatal illness. It was then that Kara found she was left with several debts, all of which were short term. God, why didn't he tell her? Why hadn't they converted the short term paper to long term loans before he passed away? Why did he have to die?

Since that time, her recriminations were many and all of them futile. She took note that while he was living, the lending institutions had no problems with lending monies based on the value of available assets and his eloquent persuasion. At least, Gregg found it an easy case to acquire any amount of money he needed at any time. His compelling ideas for developing their new Oregon property were a sales pitch no one would refuse.

She considered very carefully, her precarious financial position when she thought about Gregg. No one knew how close to the bone she was working. No one would know the *real* gamble she was taking. Now that Gregg was no longer in the picture, Kara was prepared to continue striving to carry out their preconceived vision. Now, her vision. She owed it to the memory of her dead husband. It should be a small matter for the banks to roll over the short-term loans into long-term lending.

Continuing what she and Gregg had started should be no trouble at all! A long-term loan is all she needed. The banks had done it for him. They would do it for her. And she would finally know for certain…tomorrow.

CHAPTER 3

❀

Howard Curry shoved his chair away from the conference table. He didn't like the flow of the conversation. A noncommittal expression was planted on his face as he listened to the head man.

"The little lady seems to have a tiger by the tail, doesn't she? Great piece of land out there in the valley. Prime, really. Nothing wrong with the collateral on that property." Chairman Carl Bradshaw directed this bit of inanity to his branch manager and the other two men in the loan directors' meeting of the Southern Valley Bank.

"She's making headway and the applications seem to be in order." The branch manager, George Holloway was bored at the moment and not at all interested in another loan request. He mouthed the words of affirmation, giving his subordinates the false idea he had, indeed looked over the papers. His normally cranky stomach was again making not-so-subtle noises, reminding him that he had missed breakfast and wanted to be out of there for an early lunch. Lunch would be with a very attractive client. Yes or no, he didn't care which way the deliberation would be concluded. He just wanted them to terminate this discussion and vote. It was that straight-laced, knit-picking Hutchins who would drag out the meeting with his interminable digging and questioning. Young Turk!

Actually, Tom Hutchins was a methodical person. The strength of that quality was what placed him in such high standing with the bank he had joined some seven years ago. "Yes, it looks like a clean application," he agreed with them. Then acting out as the devil's advocate he added, "But who *ever* would have thought of a viable winery in this area of Oregon. All the cash flow projections seem to be correct. In fact, her business scenario appears to have a very strong position. And as you say, Carl, the collateral is more than sufficient to cover any liability. But I can't keep from wondering about the product. Who is going to buy wine from this part of the country? I personally like the overview and would agree with granting this loan, but I believe I'd still like to have a closer look at the marketing strategies before the line of credit is in place."

"Tom, I know you're being paid to be skeptical. It's one of the reasons we need you here at this board meeting." Nodding his head, Bradshaw looked like a mother hen approving the flock. "Your reasoning is well-taken. However, the way I see it is that this business looks like a successful enterprise by popular demand. In other words, the timing couldn't be better. The area is growing rapidly in population and there is a marked emergence of a healthy tourist trade. We could certainly use the magnetism of a glamour industry as our mousetrap. What do you think, Howard?"

The moment he had been waiting for had come at last. Without seeming too negative, Howard Curry was now able to swing his weight in the direction he had intended all along. Some time ago the seed had been planted to give rise to questioning as to the ability of Kara Tower to follow through with her business plan. Now he would make that seed bloom.

"Well, Carl," he commenced his statement with a condescending shake of the head. "Besides being too short on capital equity, I've been following her public image. What kind of a mousetrap will it look like when the public learns that the business is going to be run by some scatter-brained woman? My staff and I have gone through the worksheets very carefully, and find it falling short. In fact, she misses by a mile. Sorry. Successful wineries are supposed to display sophistication. Dignity! Class! I can see the operation being led by a distinguished white-collar type, but not this so-called *lady*. Based on that alone, I'm afraid my vote will have to be no to any financial involvement with our bank. There are greener fields to plow than that one."

"I must say your position comes as a surprise, Howard. But now that you mention these shortcomings, I suppose I am disappointed in some of her friends as well," Bradshaw concurred, once more nodding his head sagely. His perception of the denizens of that local area was based on his scant acquaintance with the local news rags which were replete with tales of personal indiscretions. His lack of specific knowledge in Kara Tower's case was made up for in the thought that all actions of the people from that township were interchangeable.

"I'm even more concerned with the fact that the woman is a widow," Curry continued. "Of course I would never discriminate against women or widows, but looking at the statistics of the bank, seventy-five percent, a substantial number of our savings accounts, are in the names of widowed women." He paused for the effect of his words and then continued. "I know, I know," hands spread in front of him as if to ward off any opposition, "this seems like an incredibly high number. We have checked and checked again and found the figure to be correct.

"What are you getting at?" Bradshaw was very interested.

"Say we gave this woman, Kara Tower, her loan and something goes wrong. Say we have to foreclose on her property. The media usually carries everything she thinks or does. The publicity would be rampant. Now, what do you think those ladies with seventy-five percent of our savings accounts will do to a bank that forecloses on another widowed woman?"

"You've made your point. So be it! We'll advise Ms. Tower of our decision to decline her loan tomorrow morning." Bradshaw appeared to have concluded the subject and then added, "Tom, I believe that job lies in your jurisdiction."

Holloway breathed a sigh of relief. It wouldn't be his puppy!

"Yes sir." Tom said, knowing that any further arguments for the applicant would fall on deaf ears. He was fated in this case to play the part of the 'bad' guy. It had been his hope that every opportunity for success in her budding business should be accorded to Tower. From what he had heard, she was definitely bright and hard working. In spite of the objections raised by his own questions, Tom Hutchins knew without a doubt that Kara Tower would kick ass in the business world. What puzzled him was why Curry was so down on her venture. There had to be a reason.

CHAPTER 4

❦

Tom Hutchins often considered himself as somewhat dull, surreptitiously envying those people who he felt were easily spontaneous…exciting! At one time, he reached out longingly for a more inspired lifestyle, but learning that he lacked the proclivity for exploring the unknown or taking chances, he opted for a more sustainable way of living. Safer. In short, he became terribly conservative. Even the car he leased was what he considered a conservative vehicle. His contemporary condo reflected the organized environment of uncluttered living. No rough edges, but not too many exciting ones either.

It was one of those great days in April, unseasonably warm with the promise of the longer days to come. He headed home from the bank making a stop on his way at his favorite marketplace. It was one of those glossy up-scale grocery stores that made every item look like it was begging to be noticed by the artistry of its presentation. There was always pleasure in meandering though the produce section where row upon row of unblemished fruit and vegetables beckoned to him. Tom liked looking good, and kept his body fit by eating what he called his 'cuisine' planning. Not having a close family clamoring for his time allowed him to focus on his hobbies, and of those, gourmet cooking was the foremost.

Tonight, he looked forward to a light meal of fettuccini in white sauce cooked briefly (it was altogether too easy to overdo the pasta) with fresh spinach leaves and shrimp, topped by walnuts sauteed in butter and vodka. Accompanied by a crisp green salad, an excellent aromatic Pinot Noir was called for. What better time to assuage his curiosity. He found a lone bottle of the Mountain View vintage on the shelf, and again he reflected on Kara Tower's winery refinance program and expansion loan. The quandary of her loan application seemed to be following him.

The subject left him with a curious mind set. For the most part, the daily coordination of bank transactions left him free of any business concerns by the end of the day. When he left the bank, he left business behind him. However, the meeting this morning left him wondering about the involvement of his associate, Howard Curry and his disposition of the proposed winery loan. Frankly, he thought, The monies should have been made immediately available to the woman and Curry was objecting to it.

Slowly, as he made his approach to the underground parking garage of the condominium, he fastened his thoughts on the business of wines, remembering a newspaper article he had looked at some time ago. Years ago? He didn't remember. The more he considered the problem, the more his interest was sharpened. It wouldn't take long to look it up in the reference logs.

He had an epiphany. Why *not* do something a little spontaneous for a change? *Before I have that meeting with Kara Tower tomorrow*, he thought, *Think I'll just do a little research of my own.*

At the Medford Main Library just after opening time on Friday morning, Tom attacked the computer references to articles written about the newly emerging wine industry in southern Oregon. He was surprised to find the number of issues as well as events and general comments that were made on the subject.

Having filled the better part of an hour reading the absurd remarks from the so-called 'wine experts', he became aware of a growing boredom setting in. He was reading the tiresome expounding of the merits of various wines. At this point, he wanted to make a few comments of his own.

"*The 1986 Reserve Chardonnay is not as bold as its predecessor, but shows nuances of greatness in the finish!*" he read. As if this sweeping remark might send the populace stampeding to the wine shop's door. And he read on, "*The Pinot Noir of this vintage portrays the Burgundian style at its pinnacle.*" Burgundian, my ass!

This was not the target of information Tom was looking for. He rose from the computer monitor to stretch his body and shake out the cobwebs. He looked briefly around the room when an abandoned magazine on the adjacent table caught his eye.

Of course! What he had been searching for was not in the news area, but in a special supplement, like a magazine placed within the newspaper. The search continued only for a short time until he found what he was looking for.

In a back-issue, under a column headed "**New Kid in Town**—Wines of the Vines". Tom read on. The crux of the article was a glowing report of the rising popularity in wines of the local area. The writer, this 'Guru' of oenological knowledge seemed to be touting the product of one particular winery. Four years ago, Tom thought to himself, there were only four wineries in the area. He then read a quotation from the story.

"*Since my affiliation with the Braverly Wines,*" advised Howard Cottner, public relations representative of the wine distribution company, "*It has been deeply gratifying for all of us to see the need for escalated production in order to meet the needs of the growing demand for our vintages.*" The accompanying photograph to the article captured three men in the act of making a token salute with glasses held in a toast.

Tom caught his breath. The picture was distinct. What the hell? The man to the right purported to be Cottner was Howard Curry. Howard Cottner was Howard Curry!

He had read enough. So it was true! There was more to Curry's response to the loan request from Mountain View. Somewhere back in his past, Howard had been involved in the industry. We had all read over his qualifications when the Board of Directors considered him at the bank. There was nothing mentioned about this duplicity. He never once brought up the subject of having been with any winery prior to joining Southern Valley Bank. Dear old Howard was definitely burying something in his past.

With this new information, an idea was forming in Tom's mind. But first, he would have to circumvent the directive to turn down the Tower loan. Best get back to the office. Have a talk with Bradshaw. Avoid Curry.

CHAPTER 5

❀

Exiting the front door of the bank as Tom was entering, Howard Curry seemed to be hurried.

"What are you doing here so early, Hutchins? Already take care of the Tower fiasco?" His demeanor was prodding. Tom felt strongly that a clean punch in the jaw would take the smirk off Curry's ferret-like face. The reaction surprised him. What was happening here? It wasn't like him to have that kind of impulse. Especially with a fellow comrade of the bank. He stifled his desire to ask point blank about the obvious void in the documentation of Howard's previous work experience.

"Just getting to it, Howard. By the way, do you happen to have the worksheets from your committee's meeting? I'd like to package everything together before I shut down the file."

The smirk immediately faded from Curry's face. "Sure, Tom. But if it's okay with you," he hedged, "I'll get it for you on Monday. I'm booked solid with appointments all day." He seemed to be hustling out now, just to get away.

"Sure," Tom agreed, wanting to get in the door without further discussion with the man. Wouldn't you know he would bump into the last person he wanted to see.

Tom Hutchins, first assistant to the branch manager of the largest banking institution in the region, could hear the clipped sound of footfall on the ersatz marble floor as he purposefully strode across the vaulted room to the office area. The open aeries of the various department heads never ceased to amaze him. Anyone having a confidential conversation could be assured that their voices would be acoustically muted. No one else in the building would be able to hear the quiet discussions of the bankers with their clients. A real marvel of engineering! Tom appreciated the privacy this afforded his customers. This was as it should be.

"Goddamn it!" A distraught man shouted from one of the desks. So much for privacy. "I was told I would be treated right by you people! That asshole is a shark, and I will not, I repeat NOT be forced into paying twice for his services! I want to talk to Carl Bradshaw!" The tall well-dressed man in his late sixties rose from his chair, glaring at the cowering contract officer.

"Please Mr. Gillman, let me just talk this over with Mr. Bradshaw when he comes in. I feel certain we can iron out the details to your satisfaction." Flustered, he also rose deferentially to maintain his composure. Hutchins was retreating to his own desk in an effort to avoid colliding with the vociferous Mr. Gillman. Too late! Francis Gillman turned abruptly to disengage himself from the obsequious underling.

The impact nearly took Tom's breath away. He did not expect to be run over by a Mack truck, but the man inside the pale gray pinstripe Armani suit felt like he was made of iron. Knocked suddenly to the hard floor, he instinctively shielded himself from any further unexpected impact…like being kicked while he was conveniently down.

Much to his surprise, the graying man turned to help him up, making profound apologies. "I am sorry. Here, let me give you a hand." He lifted Tom's one-hundred ninety pounds of muscled body up from the floor like a weightless rag doll. "Lord, I'm beginning to hate doing business here. A lot of brainless people around and I just don't have the time or patience for it. Avoid this place if you can. That's my advice to you young man. You okay?"

"I'm quite all right, thank you." He dusted off his pants and straightened his jacket and tie. "But it would be a little difficult for me to avoid this…place, as you call it, since I work here. I take it your transactions are not going smoothly. Is there anything I can do to help?"

"Possibly. But let's get the Hell out of here first. I'm staying at the Red Baron and I'm told they make a passable Rob Roy at the bar. It's early, but a drink before lunch is in order. Least I can do. Care to join me? I could use a lift."

The one sided, rapid-fire conversation was the reflection of the big man's controlling personality.

Tom couldn't think of a better excuse to avoid the confrontation awaiting him at Mountain View Winery. It came to him at the same time, that this Gillman was indeed one of the major clients of the bank. Apparently Bradshaw had not come in as yet, so it would fall upon Tom to placate a disgruntled customer. This wouldn't be the first instance for him to take over for Bradshaw or the branch manager in a sensitive situation. He considered this a timely escape from the eventually inescapable.

Because of this deliverance, he opted to postpone talking with Kara Tower. They may have instructed him to wield the axe immediately, but now he had second and third thoughts about the viability of her requests versus the banker's intentions to cut her off at the knees. What could be wrong with making another attempt in passing through that long-term loan, he asked himself. "Later", he answered softly with no one within hearing distance.

For now, he ushered Gillman into the Taurus for the short jaunt to the hotel. It was never time wasted in Hutchins' mind, to acquaint himself with the big guns around town. He properly introduced himself, leaving nothing out with regard to his position in the bank's higher echelon.

"Dare I ask what set off that brou-ha-ha?" Tom inquired in what he hoped would be a congenial tone. "It's almost refreshing to hear more than a nickel drop for excitement in that place."

Laughing, Gillman was put at ease. He almost sounded like he was talking to himself when he said, "Well, now that the dust has settled somewhat, I'm not so sure I want to reopen any can of worms." There was a pause as he seemed to be thinking over the past few minutes. They maneuvered through the unavoidable morning traffic. No matter what time of day, it was impossible to avoid detours or traffic tie-ups in the city of Medford.

Once again, Gillman took up the conversation as though there had been no break. "However, you'll no doubt be hearing from Bradshaw about the acquisition my group was prepared to make. Frankly, I don't like being set up for a deal that falls though. It costs money and some very important time. No, I don't want to go through that one again. Once an opportunity is gone, I won't be looking for the leftover scraps. And I certainly won't pay for it twice. You can relay that message to Carl for me."

"Of course."

Apparently, Gillman must have thought Tom was party to his aborted negotiations. Not wanting to appear to be prying, Tom took a discrete stance and added nothing in the way of comment or inquiry. He swung the car into the nearest vacant carport. They started for the front entrance.

"You know, in a way, it would have been a dream fantasy come true for me." Gillman seemed to have a running conversation, more so with himself than with the listener. "Several of my associates agreed that owning a winery would be a financial asset. Tell me, Tom, have you ever had a vision of being the *Patron* of a vineyard estate?"

The question hit him like walking through a plate glass window. He didn't see it coming. It was only because they had come to open the entrance door that Tom could cover up his shock. The matter of two winery transactions in one day was a little too coincidental.

Opening the door for Gillman, he struggled for composure. "Mr. Gillman, I really must make a telephone call. May I catch up with you in the Siskiyou Room? I'll only be a moment."

"Of course, son." He turned away and made a one-man stampede for the bar.

It was obvious that Francis Gillman had taken an instant liking to Hutchins. Tom often elicited a positive response from people. It was just one more quality that made him worthy of his position at Southern Valley Bank. But Gillman was pondering the advisability of saying too much to this young man from the offices at the bank. Granted, there had been an ongoing but unspoken arrangement with the Chairman. And yes, that shrewd assistant, Curry was instigator of several of their transactions, he guessed not all of them totally aboveboard. But would this Hutchins be in on all the details? Tricky business, that. Gillman opted to hold back any explanation of the earlier outburst.

Hutchins returned to the bar shortly after the drinks were served. "Thanks for ordering."

His call had given him the extra time he needed to consolidate his game plan. Without wanting to be completely direct, he inquired, "Tell me, is there anything going on with your account that I can help straighten out?" He made no mention of any pending business deal.

"The truth is," Gillman started. Tom looked expectantly at the man as he was speaking. He anticipated anything but the truth. He had heard that opening line too often when it preceded lies. "It was only a venture that my partners and I were interested in. Nothing apparently congealed according to the contract officer, although against my better judgment some option monies had been accepted. I will discuss it with Bradshaw when he comes in, so no need to worry about it now. Bradshaw and I go back a long way. Maybe sometime we can think of something amusing to do to get even with old Carl for this last blunder."

He gave Tom a conspiratorial smile and ordered them another drink. He felt in good humor now and felt unquestionably more comfortable. No, he wouldn't share information about the set-up for the winery, but one never knew; this Tom fellow was sure to be in the position to be helpful in other ways.

The luncheon was copacetic and ended with a hardy handshake. Tom grimaced as the 'man of steel' crushed his hand as he knew he would. He left Gillman, satisfied that he had, indeed placated this customer, although there was more to learn about the dealings that had taken place. With an obsessive circling of thoughts, he returned to the office.

CHAPTER 6

❀

Kara replaced the phone on its cradle, feeling as though all functions of her body were on hold. Numb, she could virtually feel nothing of herself. The words she had received from Tom Hutchins seemed nebulous but the message was loud and clear. Setting up the loan was not going to run smoothly.

"Kara, can I talk to you now?" Shiron had just come from the wine cellar, known to all of them as the 'big room', and now the focus of concentrated activity.

Spring was the season for last year's harvest to be prepped for bottling. Digby the winemaker, who could usually be seen dazzling the crew with his footwork during 'crush', was now quietly going about the business of fining the wines and creating that aura of artisanship that is only acheived by the winemaker. With multiple projects in process, he could be seen to be issuing orders to the underlings; wine to be pumped, samples constantly taken for testing the balances, barrels to be cleaned and refilled, and new inventories to be accounted for in the monthly reports. The mysteries of lab work needed to be attended to with meticulous care.

As first assistant, Shiron was the liaison between the cellar and the office.

Kara shook off the implications of the phone call. She had learned over the years to turn away from one problem in order to properly face another situation.

"You bet! Im off the phone for a while" or maybe longer if I'm lucky she thought to herself. "By the way, the barrel tasting of Pinot Noir that Digby sent up will be lovely. Great potential. Tell him I agree with the level of oak but I need to speak with him about bottling."

"OK. But there's something else he noticed. We're not sure if there was an error in the inventory count, but it looks like we lost about three hundred gallons of the Sauvignon Blanc. He's double-checking it now. Will you be in for a while?"

Kara briefly went numb again for the second time in five minutes. Three hundred gallons?

"I'll be right down." She stuffed the papers she was holding into the desk file marked *'Pending'* and was on her way.

Passing through the tasting room, courtesy prevailed as the girl attending to the customers quickly noticed her and smilingly mentioned to them, "And this is the owner of the winery."

"You have such a beautiful place here. You must be awfully proud!" They gushed, mindless of the interruption of her activities. She met this most common and well-meaning remark with a returned smile, made a few polite comments, excused herself and left the room. From the balcony overlooking the wine cellar, the familiar sounds caressed. No particular voice could be made out, but the reverberating convergence of man, machine, and echo of bustling workers was music to her ears.

Not so many years ago she remembered how studiously involved she became in designing the building. No one thought that the untraditional placement of rooms and work areas would contribute so completely to the flow of production. But they did. And now she felt the hum of life and the winery became an extension of her own being. Just as the customers upstairs had moments ago suggested, she took an extraordinary pride in seeing the whole enterprise in operation.

As she took the staircase going downstairs to the cellar with a ruffled patter of feet, it gave her the appearance of flowing rather than bouncing to the first floor. Flash memories of childhood ballet classes returned. Did anyone else around here coordinate their feet like that? In that brief interlude, she felt an uncontrolled elation. Old age ain't gonna get me yet!

Digby cut into the moment. "Did Shiron tell you about the Sauv Blanc? I've gone through the bloody inventory three times and I know there was a backup barrel for topping off. I can't seem to find it bloody anywhere!" As was any good winemaker of his caliber, he was conscientious about keeping any air from spoiling any of the wine in the larger containers. This was done by keeping each of the vats or barrels filled to the very top at all times.

Kara's feeling of invincibility made a reverse trip and then something else clicked in her mind. A back-up barrel couldn't possibly mean three hundred gallons. "How much wine are we talking about?" she asked.

"Somewhere around thirty gallons, give or take. Like I said it was the wine we used for keeping the larger barrels filled to the brim, so we don't account for the whole barrel until it's empty. Anyway, the entire bloody thing is gone." Digby showed signs of losing it. Although he was educated for his oenological career at the University of California at Davis, probably the finest viticulture and winemaking school in the US, Digby's British background was blatantly evident to all but himself. He would swear he had no accent, while the 'bloody this' and the 'bloody that' would give him irreparably away.

"Good God! Shiron said there was three hundred gallons missing." Kara raised her arms in a signal of thanks to the gods. Then, shaking her head, she continued, "After we've solved the mystery of our missing barrel or figured out what we're going to do about it, maybe we should have a seminar for your assistants on the visible difference between thirty and three hundred gallons. In any case, Digs, I'm very relieved it isn't as much as I thought. Still, what do you think could have happened to that wine? Could it have been used in a blend?"

She was hopeful for an easy explanation. Anything to avoid the alternative; the acknowledgment of a truly mysterious disappearance of a barrel of wine. But Digby was already shaking his head.

"Believe me Kara, I would be the first one to know if anything had been added for a blend. That barrel is missing."

"Tell you what, before we pull out all the plugs and report a theft, let's take a physical count of all the small oak barrels as well as the fifty-fives." There were many dozens of the stainless steel drums that could be miscounted. The small 'oaks' could easily be hiding in among them. "Maybe it was just moved without your knowing about it."

"Will do." The troubled look on his face reflected the care he took in supervising the choreography of the winery. Digby was a perfectionist. Any misstep by the assistants, and the atmosphere of the cellar became a tactile environment. You could see and feel the descending tension. When Digby was unhappy with a situation, the hired hands were treading on eggshells. And now, the winemaker was definitely upset!

However, if Kara insisted he make a physical count, he would make the count! Her requests were his command and he would gladly do what she suggested.

While Kara returned to her office, Digby ran through the procedures of rechecking the inventory. It took only a matter of minutes, and to make doubly sure, he walked through the cellar with the manifest in hand to count the barrels that should be on the floor.

No doubt about it. One was indeed missing, and it hadn't been transferred to one of the larger barrels.

Taking the stairs two at a time, he wanted to get the bad news over with, and get on with the rest of his work. Making the finest wines in the country was his first priority. He entered the office knowing he was expected.

"There is no question about it. We have a thief among us." Reflecting on his past twenty-four hours he came to this conclusion. "Kara, I was the last one to leave the winery last night and the first to open up this morning. I don't know where the missing wine is, but I do know that it had to be removed by someone who had a key. I can't imagine anyone who could do that. They must have just walked in and very conveniently taken barrel and all!"

Kara picked up the phone without saying anything further. She was afraid that once she gave in to her fury, wrath would take over rationale. There were visions of strangling the thief, immediately buried by common sense. She dialed before saying, "Little good this will do. How can I expect anyone else to find the culprit when we haven't a clue ourselves? I trust everyone around me, or I wouldn't have them working here. My God, who could it be?"

She gave the information to the Sheriff's dispatcher and was told they would send an officer as soon as possible. Well…in any case, it would be on record so if anything turned up later at least the barrel might be recovered. Never mind the wine being lost, she thought. Somebody is going to have a great party. And they didn't even have the courtesy to invite me.

CHAPTER 7

❁

The question would often arise from people in the tasting room who were superficially interested in the winery aura. It was posed usually by customers as they waded their way through tastes of wine, wanting to make some intelligent conversation.

"When is your busiest time of year?" was the standard question.

There was no well-founded answer to the query.

No matter what the season, there was always work to be done and projects to be accomplished. Of course, fall could be construed as having the most feverish activity because of the prepping for, and the bringing in of the harvest. But the balance of the year was equally demanding. Winter months were usually filled with the involvement of processing the new wines, and commencement of pruning in the vineyard. Bottling the wines could take place at almost any time of the year, depending on when the winemaker discerned the point at which was the most auspicious moment to place the vintage in 'glass'. Fully throughout, and especially during the remainder of the year, there was marketing, marketing, and more marketing!

Promoting the wines was an ongoing and never ending activity. This was when Kara was all things to all people at all times. Aside from being commander in chief of the daily winery operations, there were distributors to attract, promotions to be made, the media given their morsels to chew, glamorous functions to attend, and oh, the festivals! The never ending festivals that took far more time than she had, and far more energy than three people could expend. The help and cooperation of her staff was crucial. Here, there were good people, dependable people. "Thank God we have a winning team," was a daily chant of gratitude she invoked.

The most concentrated activity for the biggest winery event of the year took place in the spring. At this time, the focus was on the success of the annual gathering for the wine festival, there on the grounds of Mountain View Winery.

The preparation for the fete really started much earlier in the year when the flyers were designed to herald the event. First, vendors must be contacted and advised as to the dates and hours for the occasion so they could reserve their positions along the river, where it was to take place. Every year it became a political maneuver just to please the artisans and food merchants in their respective pecking order. Everyone had to be made happy. Not easy!

This phase having been accomplished, there was still more to do. Monies for reservations transacted, latecomers dealt with, and the all-important musicians and entertainers settled upon, the nitty-gritty of getting the physical area ready to accommodate a couple of thousand people commenced in May.

"Where's Talbert?" she asked of anyone who could give her an answer. Kara had been working with two of her regular helpers, Netta and Beth, painting road signs directing visitors to the annual fest. She had her hand in every aspect of the project. Her energy level was infectious. In this pleasantly remote country, any work that could be done by the staff was accomplished 'in-house'. It was taken for granted that painting signs, as well as constructing any essential building needs, was done right there on the premises. All hands were required for general preparation and clean up. A modicum of staff would still be manning the operation of the winery, but everyone else was needed for the festival project. The place was buzzing with activity. But no one there was making an effort to answer her question.

"Talbert hasn't shown up yet? Who cares? But as you requested, Princess, I am at your service."

"To service," Turner whispered the last phrase hopefully in Kara's ear after leaping into the center of their work area for his grand entrance. When he was of a mind, Turner would arrive in such a way that everyone would know without a doubt that he was among them. She couldn't help but smile at his antics when she battered him away from her with full knowledge that his improper remarks were part of the package and not to be considered. But she was surprised and pleased by his sudden appearance. Never mind the sexual overtones that he was constantly dropping like pebbles in his conversation.

She was relieved to see that Turner was becoming her more dependable back-up help. They had arrived at a mutually beneficial situation for his employment and he was in the process of moving to the more accessible on-premise guesthouse located directly at the vineyard of Mountain View. For Turner, it was a turn for the better to be leaving his old roommate to his slovenly lifestyle. An infinitely better situation for both Turner and Kara.

She quipped, "So, who needs Talbert?"

Netta looked up from her work on a sign that declared, "FESTIVAL—JUNE 6, 7". She adjusted the chair she was using as an easel and replaced the finished placard with a blank board. She seemed to come to the conclusion reluctantly that it was all right now to make a comment. "I saw him last night at the park and he was dead drunk. I'm not surprised he isn't at work today." She commenced painting a new directional sign.

Kara took Turner by the hand and led him away from the others. Quietly she told him about the theft that was brought to her attention that morning. At length, she said, "I don't really understand it. No one who works for me could ever have done such a thing."

"Sure as hell sounds like somebody did!"

"All right, but the only one who comes to mind is Talbert. I've never been completely sure that he isn't mixed up with something underhanded. I do wonder about him."

It didn't take Turner time to wonder at all. "Come on Kara! Two and two usually adds up to four, doesn't it?" He quickly assumed the part of defender of the realm. "If you don't mind, let's be quiet about this for now and I'll just see if I can't learn something about that sonofabitch. I'm not saying that he's guilty at this point, but if anybody is likely to rip you off, it's Talbert." Even without a shred of proof, he knew who took off with the wine.

Turner turned and casually ambled back over to Netta to ask in a friendly way, "Hey, who does Talbert hang with these days? Maybe I can find him. We really will need extra help this afternoon. I know you started early today and I'll bet you could use a break." He gave her an extra long look, and a sympathetic smile. He knew she would give him the information he wanted.

Without hesitation, Turner was given three names as possible leads to locate the missing employee; plenty of help to point him in the right direction. Two of them he knew. The other, he didn't. He figured there was enough information for now.

Not wanting to miss the opportunity to be of further assistance, he asked Kara if there was anything she needed from town. Already he was thinking in terms of his new responsibilities. It occurred to him that he just might be a perfect fit for this position. He would show her that he could be indispensable and that her choice was a good one.

Right now he was hot to track down the wine thief. Turner could be an animal. He looked forward to meting out his own kind of justice before turning to the police. In his mind, he had it all worked out.

"We could use a dozen poles from the building supply. Something like two-by-twos should be good enough for the signs." Kara was grateful he had asked, giving her a sense of the mundane to balance the improbable.

"Will do." He reached forward with both hands to simply rub her arms gently up and down, knowing she was troubled even while displaying a determined facade. "I don't know exactly how long I'll be in town because of the…other thing," he referred to the theft, "but as soon as I'm finished, *'I'll be bock.'*" She smiled at his poorly delivered imitation of the famous Schwartzenegger line and returned to the work at hand.

He watched her for a beat and with vengeance on his mind, turned and headed for 'Curley'.

CHAPTER 8

❦

Cruising town was like second nature to Turner Ferguson. He was born and raised in southern Oregon and knew every nook and every mountain. Besides his inborn knowledge of the area, he was also acquainted with most of the inhabitants; known from either first or second-hand, their habits and habitats, just as they probably knew his. He was never one to ingratiate himself to the law, but unlike many of his acquaintances he was never one to be branded as a bad boy character either. Admittedly good looking with an earnest 'country-boy' smile, he seldom had trouble with endearing himself to people for his own purposes. His manners could be impeccable as they were when he worked in San Francisco, or he could be considered definitely rough around the edges. In truth, Turner was much like the chameleon, fitting his personality to the occasion.

Holding close his hot tempered attitude for anyone who would hurt Kara, he first picked up the sign poles as promised, laying them out in the back of trusty old 'Curley'. He then armed himself with a generous supply of beer and headed for one of the side streets where some of the town home-boys hung out.

"Hey Ferg, take ya long to get that firewood?" He found a happy group. They joked about the posts in the truck. "Yeah, you selling short cords these days?" They referred to the small stacks of wood, guffawing at their own humor.

He pulled over and parked. Pulling out a cold brewski and leaving the rest of the frosty half-rack in plain sight, he ambled over to the picnic bench where the group looked like they had been lollygagging the whole afternoon. They eyeballed the beer. He knew they'd treat him *nice* if they wanted any. He brought along plenty just for this purpose.

"How'ya doin?" he asked as he settled in for the time being. They all looked like this was a permanent career. Now they really liked him. Turner, he was one of them with his unwashed jeans and torn tee-shirt proclaiming 'One Tequila, Two Tequila, Three Tequila, Floor!'. And he had *all* that beer!

His illusion was to blend in. He wouldn't be making any mention of his new position at the winery.

"Man, we is dyin'!" one of the homies cried. To punctuate the statement, the others gave a communal groan, one even holding his throat. They all looked a little shaky.

"Need a little of the dog's hair this fine day, to ease the pain." The communal agreement followed.

"What's the trouble Bro?" Turner said to the one who seemed to be the leader of the pack, and thought, this was going to be too easy. The breath of five hangovers hovered in the atmosphere like the fumes of a fart that someone had made and hoped would go undetected. He stifled the urge to fan the air and instead, reached for the beer, offering one to each of them.

"Had us a whiz-bang last night," they said. "Ya should'a been around for the kegger." All nodding in agreement. One of them added with a sheepish grin, "Yeah, only it prob'ly wasn't beer." The guy looked like he was still reeling from the experience.

Bingo!

So, on to the next step in the progression of detecting. Turner was charged. Let's go find this 'kegger'. It wasn't difficult since he had been armed with the cold beer as an incentive for obtaining information. The group was easily bribed. Turner could see them out of his rearview mirror, guzzling the beer with ecstatic expressions on their idiot faces. Leave it to these jerks to confuse a wine barrel for a keg of beer.

Goddam, he was glad he wasn't caught in that rut.

At least they were amiable enough to let him know where he could find the 'keg', so he too, could partake. If nothing else, in times of plenty, these people were generous to a fault. These were the spoils of war. No one would question where the bounty came from. And never mind that it was stolen. They wanted to share!

Turner knew the place. It was a wooded area next to a secluded creek where more than a few local families were started. It was far enough from town to constitute some protection of privacy. The terrain was soft and grassy with shade trees of maple, beech, cottonwood and a scattering of conifers abounding in new spring foliage. Occasional outcropping of dogwoods punctuated the lush green with bright white blooms appearing like friendly faces in the forest.

Some of the group was still working on the barrel of wine, barely visible in the thick bushes when he pulled Curley into a clearing. Everyone was all smiles and gaiety. They looked like a gypsy band, right down to the strumming guitarist. He broke open another can of beer and guzzled the whole thing, tossed the can in the back of the truck and grabbed another, opening it as he approached the group.

"Hey, Ferg! Lay your burden down, and help yourself to some nectar of the gods." The speaker gestured toward the barrel, today he was the lord of the manor.

"Don't mind if I do." He replied. No one noticed that he didn't head directly for it, but continued to suck on the beer can. Apparently, that seemed right enough to the group, so no one gave him much more attention. Turner bided his time. He drank another beer. Socialized.

Judging from what Kara had said about the missing wine, there had been nearly thirty gallons in the container. Given the fact that it had disappeared at sometime late last night and the assholes had been drinking from it since then, say, for the last twelve hours, there may be somewhere between about ten to fifteen gallons left. They would be working on that barrel for the whole weekend.

Cellar rats! He remembered the nickname from the winery. Somehow, that label seemed to fit this bunch of freeloaders.

Enough waiting around! He had to bust a move. The revelers were now totally involved in a drinking game that they found hilariously funny. Turner ambled over to the barrel and removed the hose that was being used as a siphon. He unzipped his fly, and pointed at the hole. As he relieved himself of the building pressure, he gazed upward into the pristine forest and beyond to the promising blue sky. He mused, "That beer sure tastes great going down, but there ain't nothing to beat the feeling when you really gotta' go!"

He shook his member, zipped up his pants, replaced the hose, and walked away from the bushes. "Gotta' roll", he shouted amicably to the group. They waved good-by, still happy faced.

Through the rear-view, he watched one of the guys get up and go over to the wine barrel for a refill.

CHAPTER 9

✤

Kara came out of the barn-red service building with a clipboard in her hand. Nearly everything on the list had been checked off. From the provisions for the entrance tables that led into the festival area, down to providing electricity for those booths that would need it. The details were being taken care of. All that was required now was the posting of the road signs that would be installed on the morning before the festival, only ten days away. Progress, she thought was pretty well in hand.

The five people still finishing various projects were tidying up their tools and materials. It was then that she noticed that one of them curiously, was Talbert. When did he arrive? He certainly didn't say anything when he came in. He seemed to be carrying on as if he had been there all morning. Nice cover up!

She said nothing to him, not wanting to forewarn him of any impending problem. Turner must have missed him in town, and she needed to talk to ol' Ferg before making any waves with Talbert.

Just then, there was a scream, a splash, and much accompanying laughter. Inevitably, at the end of a project there was the traditional horseplay. Ben, one of the vineyard helpers had swung Gracia by her waist into the water. They were both soaked. She was wiggling away from him when Chris jumped in alongside, and started splashing both of them. Fully dressed, another joined in. Kara enjoyed seeing the water play until she realized that they were edging out of the river and heading for her. There was no escape! She took a running dive, clothes and all into the shallows before they could catch her. They all followed for a swim, fabric ballooning on the surface of the slow moving water.

It was golden times like these that made all the work worth while. The day had been especially warm and the cooling river was a godsend. Nobody cared that they were fully dressed. Just being in the water, acting like children gave the moment the flavor, the substance in which memories are made.

"Turner's back." Ben yelled. "Come on in fool!" cried out another.

"God knows you could use a bath, Ugly!" Someone else yelled. It was taken for granted that the banter was made in good humor. Turner Ferguson never was one to avoid the retort.

"Sure. But I never bathe with my cloths on!" He started unbuttoning his shirt and removed his boots. When he got to his belt buckle and the first button of his pants, they were all yelling for him to stop.

"Don't do it!"

"Look away from him or we'll be turned to stone!"

"OK cowards. I'm a busy man," he straightened his clothing. "See 'ya!" He headed for the service building.

"I wouldn't have turned to stone," one of the girls said plaintively. Two of them were wringing their garments and hair. "Kara, could we get a towels from the house?" Grazia was shivering. "I hate getting back in the car all wet."

"Of course. Beth, show them the shelves in the service porch. Use the shower if you'd like," she added graciously.

As Kara jumped out of the water also dripping wet, she turned her attention to other things. She realized that at some time during their frolic, Talbert had disappeared again. Before this time, it was of no importance to keep track of him. But now that his activity was circumspect, it was a different story and keeping track of him was absolutely important. She ran to catch up to Turner, shoes slogging with water as she walked.

"I was hoping you could break away from the others." He said, ignoring her condition. "I have good news and bad news. Which do you want first?"

"Turner, just tell me what happened in town," she demanded, nearly bouncing with anxious curiosity. "Did you learn anything?"

"Yeah! We got the lumber for twenty percent off. It was on sale!"

"Turner!"

"Well, for one thing, you can call the cops and tell them where the barrel is, but I would wait until later Saturday night before I asked them to confiscate it. I think we should let some people enjoy the contents first." She looked at him as though he were certifiable, but said nothing, wanting him to continue.

"Was that the good news, or the bad news?"

"The bad news is that I didn't find Talbert around. I was hoping to find him there red-handed with the stolen barrel. Good thing for him he wasn't. I would have broken his bones." She could see from his expression that he was dead serious. He really cares about this, she marveled to herself.

"Talbert just showed up here a little while ago," she told him. "I didn't speak to him, but he acted as though he had been here all day. What a sneak! I wish I knew where he went. He just did a disappearing act while we were in the river. Do you think he saw you coming in?"

"Maybe, but he doesn't know we're on to him. I'll look around and see if he's still here. Why don't you go back to the house and change. Oh, I picked up some nails too," as an afterthought.

"Thanks, Turner. You are mah HEERO!" She did a little Marilyn Monroe wiggle and made for the house.

CHAPTER 10

❀

Later that afternoon, Tom Hutchins turned into the driveway of the Mountain View Winery. Prior to his lunch with Francis Gillman, he had called to advise Kara Tower that deliberations on her proposed loan application were not completed. A slight softening of the truth. He then convinced a reluctant Carl Bradshaw to allow him to convey that the decision would be extended for a short time,…at least a few days. Bradshaw was not at all happy about it, but relented just the same.

Even on the phone, Tom was impressed with her *sang-froid* response. He had imagined several scenarios in which he would have to placate and commiserate with her. Instead, on the phone he was met head to head with her very reasonable comments. They led him to feel that further discussion would possibly be advantageous to her cause. It was not his intension at that moment to rush over to have a chat, but here he was, blazing a trail to the winery with the hope of absorbing background knowledge of the business.

He pulled in to the well-appointed driveway. His first impression was that of a recent new construction site, but he realized quickly that due to the time of year, the spring plantings were in the process of being completed. Several trees, still bundled, lay on the ground by their holes, awaiting burial. Natural cedar fence posts were lying together where someone had been laying out a walkway into the adjacent woods. A sign bespoke the project as a 'Future Nature Walk' for the tourists who one day might like to absorb the pleasantries of the area.

Tom drove into the wide driveway and parked his car. He envisioned the semi-trucks making their wide sweeping maneuvers, picking up and delivering goods to the stone and cedar-sided winery with its broad decks and balconies. He admired the careful planning of the layout and the flower gardens, newly planted, as he walked to the entrance. The sign here read 'Purveyors of Fine Wines—Since 1979', attesting to a ponderous twenty year tenure. A work of art in perpetual progress. Impressive!

"Welcome to Mountain View." Said a friendly voice from somewhere in the classic tasting room. A head bobbed up from behind the massive tasting bar. She sported the most amazing mop of curly red hair he had ever seen. It offset the stiff appearance of the starched white cuffs and collar of her dress giving an appealing contrast. Her face was florid to the point of his wondering, just what was it she was doing behind that bar?

And with a flourish, she produced a bottle of blush wine and commenced pouring a small serving in the tiny tasting glass.

"So sorry! I was just looking for something. Do try a sample of our newly released Cabernet Blush." Her manner was professional. "My name is Shiron, and if you have any questions at all, we'll be more than happy to answer them for you."

"Well, thank you. Actually, I was looking for Kara Tower. My name is Tom Hutchins. Is there any way we could let her know I'm here to see her?" Since it was late in the afternoon, he suspected that the winery would be closing soon.

"Did you have an appointment?"

"Uh, no. I'm with the Southern Valley Bank. She wasn't expecting me, but I was in the area...," he said, stretching the truth slightly.

"Of course. If you don't mind waiting for a moment, I'll call and see if she's at the house. You could talk to her there. May I pour you something else while you're waiting?"

"I've been told about your wonderful Pinot Noir. Have you any open for tasting?" He struggled not to tell her that he had bottle sitting on his wine cabinet. It was an opportunity to preview his purchase.

Smiling, she produced a bottle. "We're very proud of this wine. It is an international award winner. One of our finest, I'm sure you'll like it."

She excused herself and went to the other room. It gave Tom a moment to examine the surroundings. There was an interior alcove off the tasting room, glassed in a semicircle, something like a bay window allowing customers the full view of the cellar and working area. He could see the vintner engrossed at his work, taking samples from large stainless steel tanks. It occurred to him how new and sterile the wineries here in the United States appeared, compared with the *chais* of France with their wonderful patina of age, abundance of cobwebs, and occasional natural dirt floors.

Shiron returned with the message. "Kara is at the house and asked if you would come over." She pointed out the road leading to the residence, explaining how to get there by car.

"Can I interest you in a bottle of wine today?" Never the one to let a customer out of her sight without making a sale, she gave another bright smile, looking him over carefully. This was one good-looking man! His refined features were rescued from prettiness by the defined jaw line that carried just a hint of a five-o'clock shadow. Tall, well built and she guessed around thirty-two, thirty-three? Lucky Kara!

"How could I refuse?" he replied galantly. They made the transaction, and with three bottles of wine in hand, he headed for the house.

Tom arrived at the Pennsylvania Dutch cottage, complete with vine covered picket fence supported by stonework styles. The house was an unexpected piece of architecture for this area. It evidenced the owner as being a gardening enthusiast. Just as it was at the winery, the spring plantings looked fresh and abundant beside the established greenery. Closely planted trees and shrubs gave it the appearance of a cozy nest. He wondered if the interior would be as cuddlesome as the exterior. He took the stone walkway to the front door and rang the bell.

Bethany Chris appeared to have just gotten out of the shower. She was still dripping with a towel wrapped around her hair. Her body was hastily wrapped in a cotton robe and the cloth clung to her body here and there.

"Hi," she said, opening the door.

Tom bumbled a bit, feeling that he had interrupted the woman in her private time.

"I didn't realize you were indisposed," he apologized. "My name is Tom Hutchins from the Southern Valley Bank. The lady at the tasting room told me I could meet with you here."

She was stopped in mid-motion for a moment. The 'hunk' thought she was Kara, and he was actually blushing! Hoo-eee, she gets all the best men, Beth thought to herself, sulking inwardly. She wouldn't have minded at all if it was her own company that was being sought. Spending some time with this guy could be a definite good thing! He was gorgeous! But Beth wasn't about to carry out a charade,…although she would have liked to.

"I'm sorry," she finally said. "I'm Beth. You must be looking for Kara. I'll get her for you." She left him standing on the front step.

He peered through the open door.

Just as he suspected, the entry, and what he could see of the living room were a feminine collection of silk, lace and florals in shades of rose, soft greens, and dusty blues. The effect was enchanting, like that of a Laura Ashley show room. Crystal and bone china pieces were liberally perched atop occasional tables. A few well-placed paintings and abundant book shelves filled with gold embossed, leather bound tomes gave the impression of an English gentle-woman's residence.

Kara made her hasty entrance in a sweep of motion. She was an older woman of indeterminate age with a cascade of naturally curly hair gathered up and loosely tied on the top of her head with a wide nut-colored chiffon scarf. He had never seen hair that color before. In the sunlight it would be a striking burnished bronze. The colors interfused with her expressive brown eyes, flecked with gold. Her womanly figure was neither too heavy nor too thin. Her style seemed to fit perfectly, the ambiance of her home. She greeted her guest.

"I'm so glad you were able to come. Shiron phoned to tell me you were at the winery." No reference to Beth, as though it were all quite normal to be greeted at the door by a towel clad female. "I had no idea you were going to be here this afternoon. Please, come in." She led him past the entrance. "We just finished some work over by the river and I was about to have some tea. It's my way of spoiling myself. A reward at the end of the day." She was in a constant movement, and continued speaking as she walked from room to room finally reaching the kitchen. Was she nervous? He followed complacently without being told.

A flood of *deja vu* hit him and the illusion of other homes, of warm family gatherings and the familiar sensation of close ties became tantalizingly strong. It made him think of love at first sight and childhood infatuations. Had he recognized this feeling, it would have reminded him of the mother and father that he thought he would not miss.

Tom felt that the answer for his compelling need to follow through with the Tower file was here. It was the aura of the place…and the woman. In that instant, he wanted to know her better! He composed himself with a rejoinder to himself that he was here on business. Bank business.

"Please, let me help you." He watched the final touches being made to an exquisite tray holding a delicate tea service. It accompanied a small selection of delectable fruit biscuits. No weight watchers here, he thought.

She placed a second setting alongside her cup, and allowing him to carry the tray, led the way to the back of the house to a shaded patio table. Tom suddenly was struck by the impression that he was the butler carrying a tray for the estate's chatelaine. She was softly commanding. The impression was fleeting and soon enough he was able to provide a more proper introduction.

"We've spoken on the phone, I'm Tom Hutchins. I'm glad to finally meet you face to face. Mr. Curry has allowed me to take an interest in your expansion project."

Kara looked bewildered. "Judging by your call this morning, I was uncertain about the outcome of my request. Frankly, I'm even more surprised that you've taken the time to come here as a representative of the bank. Your Mr. Curry hasn't exactly been one of our regular visitors. Nor do I think he has been one of our adoring fans."

"I'd like the opportunity to change that, Ms. Tower."

They settled themselves on the redwood deck overlooking the vineyards and the mountains beyond.

From inside the house, Beth appeared at the open French door. "I'm leaving now. See you on Monday. Oh, and thanks for the use of the shower." She fluffed at her hair. "Bye, Mr. Hutchins…Tom." She didn't miss remembering his name.

Tom got back to their conversation as Kara poured. "Ms. Tower…" he started.

"You can call me Kara." She smiled, and he noticed it was a genuine and most agreeable smile.

"Kara." He paused, taking a moment to take a sip of tea. "First, I might tell you this is really a charming place. In fact, I am dumbfounded! Nothing on paper could prepare me for the impact of your property. The winery. Your home. Fantastic! Do you always turn your bankers into gushing admirers?" He warmed up to the casual ambiance of the surroundings.

"Mr. Hutchins…."

He promptly interrupted her. "And you can call me Tom." He returned what he felt was one of his most appealing smiles.

"Tom. We only try to bowl over the ones who are giving us the most difficulty in negotiating our business." So far the conversation had been light. Under the surface, Kara was apprehensive but she gave every appearance of being coolly confident. "I'm hoping you are here to determine a final solution to my request. I understood some kind of answer would be forthcoming today."

He noticed that at no time had she posed any questions like most of the supplicants he had worked with. Her comments were direct. This had to certainly be a very canny lady, and although he expected that she would be bright, he could see that she was far more than that. She was his idea of a quality person.

"I wanted first to meet you personally. You see, there has been a preliminary decision made, and frankly I was not at all satisfied with the outcome. But for now, and I hope you don't think I'm prying, would you mind telling me how well you know Howard Curry?"

She thought for a moment before answering.

"He was the bank officer who was given my loan application. I believe he was the one who was instrumental in carrying it through your chain of command for approval."

"And you didn't initially apply to him to do the paperwork?"

"No. I understand that he requested handling the account."

"Yes, I see. Ordinarily, it would have gone to one of the other loan officers. Why do you think he requested it?"

"I really couldn't tell you." She looked puzzled. "Why do you ask?"

"I'm not sure at this point." He also was not sure why he felt perfectly comfortable in taking this woman into his confidence. He made the decision to go ahead with his line of thought and continued, "There's just something about this man and the way he handled your loan request that doesn't sit right." Now he *was* going out on a limb. "Like not personally seeing you more often to examine the business. That would be our normal procedure."

She looked at him with a startled expression at his words.

"Actually, I never have met him face to face. He never came here."

Tom carefully contemplated his next question before asking it. He took a breath and asked, "How would you feel about doing a bit of sleuthing?" Then he added, "I'd appreciate our keeping this under wraps, however."

"My, my." Kara needed less than a moment to make up her mind. "This sounds too intriguing to miss."

He went on to tell her about the news supplement picture of the wine tasting event showing Howard Curry or his *doppleganger* under the guise of Howard Cottner. He produced a copy of the article, and placed it beside her plate.

Tentatively, Kara picked it up and started to read. From her expression, Tom could see her growing confusion.

"For one thing," she spoke at last, "I am familiar with this distribution group. We had done business together in the past. But I couldn't say whether or not the man in the picture is Howard Curry, because I've never met him in person. I have been in contact with him at the bank, but only by phone or through the mail. If it is the same person, I just can't see what he was doing in the wine industry using another name. By the way, the event they're celebrating in this news article is an annual affair. Everyone who is anyone in the business attends. It takes place at the Madrona Country Club near Medford every year in the first weekend in June."

Their eyes locked as they chimed simultaneously, "Tomorrow night!"

"But why would Curry, or Cottner, or whoever he decides he is, change his name?"

Tom was very serious now. "Why would anyone change their name? Desire, or expediency," he intoned, answering his own question.

CHAPTER 11

❈

The people arriving at the Club, as the Madrona was referred to, were festive. The reputation of the event was known to everyone. Expectantly looking forward to gourmet foods, elegant wines, music, and the camaraderie of their fellow peers, the guests were animated and smiling.

Here, in the outback of Oregon, you could expect to see a wide variation in the way of fashion. From jeans to white tie and tails, anything might be found attending the same function. There was no observable conformity of dress, yet one would still have the strong impression that everyone was rising to the same level of occasion. Perhaps it was less the apparel itself that was of importance, than the flair and panache with which it was worn.

Tom and Kara made their entrance shortly after the colorful gala had begun. In deference to the springtime occasion, she was wearing a sheer dress of gossamer chiffon in a pale green with a gored skirt that flared in a languid motion, validating her early training as a dancer. To punctuate the 'look' she had her streaked chestnut hair piled loosely high on her head with the addition of tiny flowers peeking and trailing from the tresses. Tom, in complete contrast to the dramatic picture she made, was in his usual conservative attire.

It came as no real surprise for anyone to see that Kara had a dashing companion at her elbow. Some attendees were already aware that he had accepted the invitation to be her date for the evening. It was often said that the people who worked in the industry gained the current gossip by simultaneous osmosis. This was the eternal 'grapevine' at work, and tongues were wagging.

Neither Kara or Tom had known beforehand that the occasion of the regional wine tasting would throw them together so soon. Until that day, when they confided with each other on the terrace deck of her home, they were unaware of the help they could give one another. She needed financial stability and Tom, with his growing suspicions of foul play, needed answers.

True to his sense of orderliness, he wanted to sort out this mystery before certain unalterable damage could be done. Curry did more than rub him the wrong way. He was dangerous to his employers as well as the future of Kara's winery. The more he learned about him, more out of place he seemed in the scheme of things. Tom planned to dig into any information about Curry that could be obtained…with discretion.

He was certain that Howard would be attending the affair at the Club. He remembered his loud mouth, vociferous in his comments about the wine tasting. Bragging about being an enthusiast! Oh yes! Curry would most definitely be in attendance to bestow his enlightened pronouncements on the fruit of the vine. You had to hand it to the guy, he had guts to take the chance that his dual identity would be revealed. On the other hand, maybe he just didn't give a damn. Maybe he was stupid after all.

Tom began wondering specifically, how did Curry earn such a high position at the bank in so little time? Now that wasn't so stupid. Did he know the right people? Had he something more profitable to offer than any other candidates?

With more than one reason to want to be involved, he had asked Kara if it would be convenient for him to escort her to the event on Saturday night. They agreed it would make sense for her to meet him in Medford, and the two of them could arrive together. He looked forward to that.

In the Club ballroom, music was playing gently as a soft background to encourage the low keyed conversations of the paying guests. The classical quartet was a subliminal audio-foundation that set the stage for the upper-crust of the local gentry. After all, the self-interest industry benefit was designed to showcase the finest of foods along with the finest of wines for the finest of people in the area. Refined music would of course, be in keeping with the high tone of the event.

In past years, the 'Tasting', as it had come to be known, had grown in ever greater proportions. This was mainly due to the growing numbers of *aficionados* who made the annual trek as though it were a pilgrimage. Those pioneers, coming for the first time, would succumb to the pleasure of experiencing the tempting flavors of the palate and eye. They would become the newly devout in this yearly gathering. Newcomers and sophisticates alike, would no doubt leave at the end of the evening with soaring spirits in spite of leaden bellies, with every intention of repeating the performance the following year.

In order to accommodate the crowd of people, the location was an immense ballroom, the size of a supermarket. It was the custom for this event that the tables, laden with fabulous displays of culinary art, were found in the center, creating a visual temptation. Inspired ice carvings bracketed the delicacies. Cheeses, breads, meats, seafood, and a vast array of seldom seen comestibles, would be crowned by the *piece de resistance,* the pageant of desserts.

Around the periphery of the expanse were tables, each bearing two or three varieties of wine from a specific winery. Every placement was manned by one or two distinguished looking wine stewards pouring their wines of the evening. Every table abounded with flowers, and discreetly nestled to the side were the water pitchers and rinsing containers. Those who would not deign to finish drinking what was in the glass that was their souvenir of the evening, could pour the unwanted wine into the bucket, rinsing their glass with the water or even cleansing the palate with a neutral sip along with eating a nondescript flavored cracker. The nuances of wine tasting were rigidly adhered to and provided for.

"Isn't it beautiful?" Kara felt like a tourist seeing the Trevi Fountain for the first time. "You know, I always balk at having to come to these events, but once I'm here, it's like entering into a world of luxurious scents and flavors, and dazzling people. Can you believe it? This is my work!"

Tom laughed. "Do you mean you are forced into these activities?"

"Not only forced, but duty bound! It is my responsibility. I am doomed to the tortures of the good life."

At the entrance, they had been given an etched wineglass, name tags. and a bound program, showing the names of the contributors of food and wine. At the back of the book there were blank pages inviting entries of personal comments for those who felt the need to keep an organized diary (seldom referred to again) of their tasting experiences. A small gold and purple decorator pencil was cleverly provided in a built in pocket. All very neat! All very posh!

The table reserved for Mountain View Winery was only a short distance from the congested entry. Already, couples could be seen standing with their glasses held out to the gentleman who was pouring. Kara and Tom made their way directly to the display of her wines.

"Hello. I'd like some Semillon," Kara said, opting to start the evening with a lighter, white wine. It was her custom to work up to the heavier whites before moving forward to the red wines. The only interest the blush wines held for her were to compare the varietals. Each grape would impart its own individual flavor, and it was perpetually enlightening to taste what could happen with a red grape that had been processed like a white wine. Unlike most, she would sample the rose and blush wines at the end of the evening.

The man behind the table was acquainted with Kara although he didn't work directly for the winery. He greeted her with obsequious warmth and then turned to Tom.

"Would you like to start with the Semillon? It has an especially grassy freshness and its low Brix should make an excellent intro for the evening."

"Brix?" Tom queried.

"Yes…sorry. You were with Kara and I thought you knew. The method of measuring how much sweetness is retained in the wine is referred to as degrees Brix, or residual sugar. Usually, the threshold of perceptible taste for most people is at 1.5 Brix and anything sweeter gradually has higher numbers and can be easily tasted. Your very sweet wines would be around 7 Brix, and the exceptionally heavy after dinner wines could be as high as 14."

"I understand. Fascinating! Thanks for the input." Tom took a sip as the man automatically poured wine for three other people who were taking advantage of the impromptu lesson, their glasses outstretched.

Kara informed the man whose name tag indicated he was 'Gary—Mountain View Winery', "Gary," she said, "it was nice of you to pour for us this evening. We'll make a tour of the room and get back to stand in for the PR."

Part of the so-called work for the winery included various public relations opportunities, such as this event. It was common for the primary people; winemakers or executives to be in evidence somewhere near their tables, chatting with the guests and answering the questions of the curious. A great way to absorb the pulse of the oenophiles.

"Take your time," he responded. "We'll have quite a crowd tonight and people are only just starting to arrive."

They looked toward the door, taking note of the constant flow of incoming celebrants.

Among the people arriving would also be those already involved in the industry; haughty wine-writers, restaurant owners and their immediate staff, often the all-important chefs, as well as purveyors of fine wine from specialty shops. It was the game of see and be seen. It was the grand opportunity for them to taste and make selections on future purchases for their establishments.

And lurking in every corner could be seen the distributors, who could make or break the balls of any wine-related business, be it production or consumption. Their shifty eyes never still, they would tune in on the public responses to the vintages being highlighted. One could sense their approval of the wines they represented, and just short of making public their derogatory remarks, their disapproval of *all* others. These middleman cliques were difficult to penetrate. This was the 'Good ol' Boys' network in action. In truth, they were untouchable power players.

But whether untouchable or reasonably available, players of all persuasion were convening on the ballroom. As they commenced circling the floor, Kara and Tom helped themselves to delectable finger foods as they sipped away at various wine samples. Pleasantries were exchanged with old friends and introductions were made to new. After only the first half-hour, one could discern rising decibels as conversations escalated. Even the music took on the ambiance of the crowd and departed from the sedate tempos to swing into an upbeat rhythm.

"What is this, George?" one woman was asking her husband.

"Sally, check this out, I think it's made out of radishes!"

"Well, I never saw a mushroom served up to look like an animal!"

You could hear the incredulous observations, referring to the ornately decorated hors d'oeuvres. Tom Hutchins was no different.

"Do you think we should chance it?" Tom asked, eyeing a morsel of food he couldn't name.

"Not sure. We could wait till somebody else tries it and see if *they* like it," Kara answered in his ear.

"Good call." They hid their amusement behind their wine glasses.

"Hal," a stout young woman addressed her unresponsive spouse. He was busy ogling the décolletage of a passing female. She tugged at his shoulder. "Hal! Try this!" She placed a morsel on his plate.

Inadvertently, his attention still on the girl, Hal plucked the piece from his plate and placed it in his mouth. Tom and Kara watched and waited for the reaction. It brought the eyes of every person surrounding the table to him. The look on Hal's face first registered pleasure and then immediately extreme pain. His face turned crimson and his eyes pooled with tears. A strangled noise escaped from his lips as though suffering an aneurism. He grabbed a napkin from the nearest person, who just happened to be a very surprised lady, the one with the neckline to her navel, and snorted into it, "Fuckin" horseradish!"

Kara gripped Tom's arm and guided them away from the scene.

"So much for sophistication and *savoir faire*. You don't think she did that on purpose, do you?" The facetious comment was all it took. They had a liberating if slightly hysterical laugh together and moved on for some Chardonnay.

"Tom," she said at last, "can you circulate without me for a while? I'd like to get back with Gary at the table. I have a feeling it's about time he'll be needing some help with the repeat customers." She added, "And by the way, from what I've seen of your performance here, you're no stranger to fine wines. You led me to believe you were a novice."

"I stand corrected. You have unveiled me. Actually, my middle name is Perignon."

"Right, and I'm Lady Godiva." She pivoted and gave him a saucy look over her shoulder. He caught her before she left.

"Seriously, Kara," he was compelled to let her know how he felt, "I want you to know that I'm really glad we came this evening. Now that I've had more exposure, I can say with some expertise that your wines are a knockout. Before this, I had no idea of how great they were until I compared them with others."

"Thank you, Tom. I can always use a vote of confidence." She turned away and left for the Mountain View table.

He stared after her thinking of the old litany of finding a woman who was a rich, beautiful nymphomaniac who owned a liquor store. Well, she was beautiful, and she did own a winery. Two down. He wondered how many optimistic admirers had stood in line only to be rejected by this lady.

Tom recognized several people in the room and was stopped at once by one of his bank customers, an acquaintance from town.

"Tom, so nice to see you. I want you to meet Clark Peterson from Pacific Land Development Company." They shook hands. "Clark's in from Washington, looking over some Southern Oregon features. Thought I'd show him a slice of the primitive life we live here."

"Good to meet you." Peterson extended his hand. "I was told you're with Southern Valley. Believe my partner was in your establishment this last week."

"Well, I'm glad he chose our bank for his business. Nice meeting you, too. But I've got to admit, you're not alone. This is my first experience with this 'primitive life'. Good thing it's not a daily event. My waistline couldn't take it."

They all agreed, ending the conversation by immediately making way to the nearest winery table, each of them for a refill.

Tom hesitated when he recognized Howard Curry across the room with none other than Francis Gillman, the man he had lunch with at the Red Barron. Peterson's partner? They were deep in conversation, their heads so close together their relationship may have been misconstrued.

Yet, as he watched them they appeared to have a more conspiratorial demeanor. Two tables over, they appeared to be glancing at Kara Tower from time to time. He observed their behavior patiently. Without a doubt, Curry was discussing Mountain View with this man. Curious, he made his way across the large space, and without appearing to have singled them out, casually approached the two men.

"Looks like this event drew out all the wine lovers! Mr. Gillman, nice to see you again."

Curry didn't hide his loss of composure. "You know each other?" looking from one man to the other. He acted as though he had been caught with his hand in the cookie jar.

"I guess I just didn't mention it to you, Howard. Tom and I had lunch the other day. You might say he rescued me from over-reacting at the bank. Thanks again," he acknowledged Tom. Jokingly he added, "Buy you a good glass of wine, young man? You appear to be empty, and around here you could be arrested for that!" Francis Gillman didn't wait for an answer. He strode to the nearest server and asked, "Do you happen to have a really good Cabernet?"

"Of course, Sir. Would you be interested in our latest release, or would you prefer the Barrel Select?"

"The Barrel Select if you please. For my friends and myself."

Tom noticed that while Gillman was warmly expansive, he couldn't help but sense that Curry was slightly agitated. Whatever it was they had been discussing earlier, the subject had been instantly dropped and Howard was not exactly happy about it.

Once poured, their attention focused upon the wine.

Gillman again led the conversation. "Tom…Howard…I would like to know your reaction to this vintage." He swirled his glass, causing the wine to travel up the sides of the globe in a circular motion. He squinted his eyes in concentration and took his time before taking a sip, watching to see how the others would handle the tasting.

Curry made a show of swirling, and then loudly slurping in a manner not unlike the professionals, he drank. Tom, like Gillman, took more time, warming the glass slightly to room temperature in the palms of his hands before swirling. He put his nose deep in the glass and took a long slow breath, savoring the rich aromas. He looked up directly at Gillman, met his eyes and nodded.

"Another point in favor of Oregon product," he said. "It seems to be typical in the cherry-like nose…that and the underlying fragrance of green pepper."

He took a tentative sip, breathing the wine through his teeth and over his tongue. "Nice. Well structured. I like the finish."

Not to be out-done, Curry loudly embellished, "The undercurrent of oak carries the balance just the way I like it. Good aftertaste!" he aped, then immediately commenced scribbling his comments on the blank pages of the program, underscoring the importance of his inspired ideas. "Again though, Frank," his voice took on a metallic timbre, "I say that the Mountain View Cab could have been a lot better than this…if it was handled correctly."

Apparently, the two men had not seen Tom arrive with Kara Tower. He intended to keep it that way for the time being. He could learn more from these two than he already knew, which wasn't much at this point. Sooner or later a few of the puzzle pieces would fall together connecting the bank, the winery, and Gillman's presence in the area. He was sure of it. Perhaps it would be wise to get a message to Kara. Not to let on they had arrived together, or even knew each other personally. At least for the moment. But how?

The answer came sooner than he expected.

Curry's comment on the wine did more than rub Tom the wrong way. The urge to punch this guy returned for the second time in spite of his effort to remain calm. He had to get away from this obnoxious asshole. He directed his parting words to Gillman, who's attention was focused somewhere at the bottom of his glass.

"Well, enjoy your wine. There's someone I'd like to talk to, if you'll excuse me, Sir?" His tone was deferential to the commanding, older man, with whom he believed he shared a mutual respect.

"Yes, of course," Gillman answered. "Our paths should cross a few more times this evening. I look forward to hearing more of your astute comments on the wines." They smiled at one another and Tom lifting his glass in a salute disappeared into the crowd.

When he approached the familiar face of his apartment neighbor, he was rapidly trying to piece together some subterfuge of a story in order to have her take a message to Kara without learning any of the incriminating truth. The truth being that he wasn't sure what he was doing, or why he was doing it. Not that it was underhanded in any devious way, but…okay! It *was* underhanded in a devious way! Tom had never practiced telling crooked stories, and he definitely felt uncomfortable.

"Hello, Nancy. You look ravishing tonight…I don't think I've ever seen you with your cloths on before. Very nice!"

Nancy brightened. "Before anyone gets the wrong idea, Tom, it seems to me that you're the only one I've seen around the pool who *was* wearing clothing. Didn't anyone ever tell you that it's customary for people to wear swimsuits in or around the water? Or are you always so busy with your banking that you never take time out for a little relaxation?" She stopped herself with, "Oh, forgive me. This is a bit of recreation for some of us."

"I hate to burst your bubble, my dear, but I am allowed to mix my business *with* pleasure. Are you enjoying the treats as much as I am?"

"Yes! And I include my boyfriend along with the other goodies. You haven't met Shawn yet, but I consider him as one of the delectables of the evening. I'd like to introduce him to you, but he just left for a moment to make space for more wine."

"Great!" Tom hadn't forgotten the imperative message he planned to get to Kara by this girl. "And while you're waiting for him, could I ask for the favor of a minute of your time?"

"Naturally. Anything for a handsome man. What is it?"

"Well first, Do you see the woman in the green dress standing by the Mountain View Winery table?"

"Uh huh," she confirmed when she spotted Kara.

"Well, I'm playing a joke on someone I know. Nothing serious, just a revenge thing." He kept the tone jovial. "Anyway, could you get a message to her without anyone else hearing about it?"

"Provocative...but I'm sure I could."

"Quietly, tell her you have a message from Tom. *Don't let them know we've met.*"

"That's it?"

"That's it! Okay?"

"Sure, but remember, you owe me a really, really big one!" Tom wasn't sure what she was referring to, but he went along with it, giving her an appreciative smile as she left on her mission.

Later on, as the party swung into high gear, Tom continued to make the 'rounds' of the room. He left Kara alone to attend to her adoring audience. They wouldn't leave her alone and it appeared that she genuinely enjoyed the give and take as she was accosted by the guests. He found the wines being served were delicious, and the presentations of food gave him so many inspired ideas for his own gourmet cuisine that he found himself making copious notes in his program. "*Sautéed basil...use Cointreau in the butter*," "*Chicken livers, cognac flambé w/garlic,"* and *"Ratatouille haven't done for a while—combo w/ brie and bread (French, of course!)"* were some of the entries. Practically none were related to wine.

He looked up at the sound of Howard Curry's familiar grating. The outspoken whine carried across the spaces of people. There seemed to be no avoiding this character. Tom would have preferred to distance himself from someone he disliked. For certain, it wasn't a question of following the man around just to listen to his dulcet tones, but curiosity prompted him to move closer. Hutchins could hear him saying, "Look Frank, I did a lot of preliminary work on this project. It's going to pay off in spades…I know that. You know that. And yes, it helped to have a little discrete front money, but the opportunity wasn't set in the time frame we had hoped for. Surely you can understand that the longer this takes, the more money it will cost."

The three men, Curry, Gillman and Peterson in tight formation were paying little attention to their surroundings and perhaps, what with having had a shade too much wine, they were not aware that their conversation could or would be overheard.

Swallowing his distaste for this kind of thing, Tom took up a position nearby to eavesdrop. He attempted to maintain his invisibility as he kept to himself and laboriously pretended to write comments in his book.

He listened intently.

"Howard, stop! The amount of money we agreed to was for targeting a takeover and setting up its availability. Not more, not less. I expect you to produce just what you said you could produce." Now Gillman's expression was forceful. "I will not, repeat *not* pay twice for setting up that winery acquisition. Peterson, what do you say?"

Tom could see another piece of a puzzle falling into place. It dropped like a lead weight as Tom surmised the relationship between Gillman, his partner Peterson, and the bank. High rollers indeed! He could safely guess that Curry was operating over and above the proper limitations of his banking discretion.

The *why* was obvious. He was soliciting kickbacks! The *how* was not so clear, at least not yet.

This would not be an auspicious time to be caught listening in to their conversation. He wanted to move away before being detected.

"Well, Hutchins!" Gillman more or less blustered, stopping Tom in midstride. He had an odd, quizzical expression that conveyed his concern that their conversation might have been overheard. Then he noticed that Tom had obviously been involved with his program entries, so perhaps…

"What are you up to now?" he asked. "Find anything worthy of comment?"

He would like to have seen what was being written in Tom's program. There was a flash thought of tearing the book from the bearer's hands to look at the entries, but of course, that was simply not his style. Quite the opposite, Francis Gillman never used his tremendous size for physical leverage. But unquestionably, he was interested in what Tom might have overheard. Actually, this Hutchins fellow seemed to be a decent kind of fellow. He felt more like there was an easy rapport between them, a comfortable give and take; while at the same time it was Howard Curry he was beginning to actively dislike. Yes, he thought, I'm going to keep my eye on these young men to see how they play out in the grand scheme of things.

Tom adjusted to the situation quietly, and to show he had been engrossed completely in his own activity, he confessed, "Well Mr. Gillman, I've been jotting down the names of a few of the wines I am particularly fond of. But I think you'll be a little disappointed in me."

Gillman was immediately put at ease. He did like this personable young man. He decided that Hutchins couldn't have been eavesdropping on their conversation, after all. He was only doing what half the other people around here were doing with their programs. Making notes.

Damned all! How could they be so damned careless to be talking so openly! Thank God it wasn't someone connected with Kara Tower and her winery who was listening to them. That would be a major blunder.

"Disappointed? Now, why would I be disappointed in you?" The others all but leaned forward to hear his answer.

Tom continued. "Well, My notes on the foods here are more complete than my reactions to the wines being served. I've been taking down all the new ideas I've seen in the food displays. You see, my greatest hobby is in gourmet cooking. Hope this doesn't disturb your sense of wine appreciation."

Gillman was almost visibly relieved. Apparently Hutchins was just what he said he was, a food enthusiast!

"Not at all, not at all! As a matter of fact, one of *my* favorite hobbies is gourmet food. The only difference however is that I like to eat it, not cook it. I might add that this may be the difference between your waistline and mine."

With that exchange, the others relapsed into their earlier mode of *bonhomie* introducing new comments about their various reactions to the entertainment, beverages and the crowd, all at the same time. The cover-up was a piece of work. Tom knew it was a sham.

To hell with these guys. He rearranged his thinking, contemplated the overheard conversation and digested the information over a late harvest Riesling from one of the northern wineries. Curry must have made offers he couldn't back up as yet. His clients were not happy. It sounded as though he had set up a Mountain View Winery take-over, based on the inability of Kara Tower to obtain her loan. Was Carl Bradshaw in on it? Francis, or Frank as he had heard him so boldly called, had certainly been offered something attractive for an unspecified sum, and for which he had already paid something in the form of earnest money. Interesting. But something went wrong and Curry had not produced. Clark Peterson, the out-of-town land developer must have been party to the offer.

Tom contemplated the compelling desire of the one faction, being Gillman and company to make this winery acquisition, as they put it, and paralleled the also compelling desire of Kara to obtain her much needed loan and continue with her dream. No doubt about it, this was the proverbial can of worms. Someone would win and someone would lose. Wasn't that always the way? Perhaps he should just bow out of something that wasn't his business and let things come about as they may…let things revert to the natural law of survival of the fittest without interference.

No, Tom couldn't do that. Not now. This had nothing to do with natural law. This was a question of who weighed in with more clout on the scales of power. Wouldn't it be perfectly fair for him to jump on Kara's end of the balance beam.

He thought about Kara being left alone at the tasting table and figured it was time to join her again. It was getting late and at this point, some of the crowd was thinning out. The *heavies* from the bank, as he had come to think of them, had wandered a bit and he noticed that Gillman and Peterson had bade their farewells and left. It was time for him to gather up his glamorous new friend for a final cruise of the room.

"Tom, you're back!" She was excited, and her color was high. "Your timing couldn't have been better!" She had just completed a detailed explanation regarding pruning techniques with some vineyardists. "Well…tell me about all the adventures you've had this evening. There are always surprises at this kind of event, but I didn't expect anything like that odd message you sent to me. What in the world is going on?"

"Glad you got it. I'll explain that one later. But another of those surprises is one you'll probably get to see for yourself on the Eleven O'clock News."

"What?"

"Since you've been holed up at your table, I've become a celebrity!"

"Good Heavens! Did they interview you, too?"

"What do you mean, me too? I thought the newscasters came all the way here just to hear my definitive opinion as to the success of the event. Couldn't have done it without me and all that, according to the interview."

"And I suppose you expounded all kinds of elaborate praise for everyone but Mountain View?" she asked saucily.

"Madam," he bowed formally, "the name of Mountain View was on my lips no fewer than a dozen times. Well…it was mentioned at least once…But it was a very complimentary remark!"

"I'll bet it was. At least it had better be, that is if you are looking for a ride home!" She tried to appear peevish with her hands on her hips. They burst out laughing. Both of them were enjoying the moment.

She told him about the last couple of hours. Kara had a good representation at her table. People had been encouraging and full of praise. The wines they had been pouring were considered to be excellent and often rated as the best in the room.

Still, there were one or two things that rankled. She thought about the cold shoulder she had been given by her distributors. They had asked in a curious fashion how she was doing, knowing full well they had let orders for Mountain View lapse dismally.

Did they expect to hear her say that things couldn't be greater? They should know better than anyone else, the condition of her sales.

"We've been receiving a wonderfully positive response tonight," she had told them. "My only problem was that too many people asked where our wines could be found in the stores. It seems there has been a lack of availability on the shelves. Should I send them to you for that information?" She asked so politely.

Answers were mumbled as they failed to make a straight forward response.

And that was all there was to it. They should have been more helpful. They should have given her some level of support. Instead, the big boys moved on to greener fields with no explanation for their painful treatment.

"Shall we see about a snack? Kara asked Tom. She wouldn't delve further in this depressing path of thought. "I think I'm entitled to some small indulgence."

"You have, indeed, and more than a small indulgence. I say we splurge!" And whirling them away from her position at the Mountain View table, he added, "Allow me to be your guide. I believe I've made a formidable foray of all the dishes here. I recommend you start with this." He deftly cut into an aromatic blue cheese that was made locally, placing it on a thin piece of French bread. "Simple, but simply grand! I think I must have eaten at least a half-dozen helpings. But here! You must try these." It was a seafood pate served on a greenery of crisp salad and topped with truffles. "They really are fresh! Have you any idea what it must have taken to get a hold of something like this?" He was playing his fork on the small dark pieces garnishing her food.

Kara gave him a look of caution. "Keep your hands off of my truffles" she hissed under her breath. Giggles followed.

As if in echo, there was another burst of laughter, but rather more raucous, at the other side of the room. Tom could see across the heads of others, who also were looking to see what the outburst was all about. He edged Kara closer in order to sort out the disturbance.

Much to their surprise, Howard Curry was holding forth with an audience of amused people. It was altogether too obvious that the wine had gotten the better of the man and his behavior had become not only boisterous, but vulgar. Kara's first instinct was to draw away from the scene; avoid the uncomfortable situation. Tom, in the same way was at once repelled by the actions of a man who should, by all standards, behave in a manner more suitable to his position as a representative of their banking enterprise.

In short, he was embarrassed. Tom watched in fascination and disbelief that anyone could make such an ass of himself. Curry was shit-faced! But the topic of his dissertation became even more bizarre as he faced his audience. With inhibitions gone the way of alcohol, he was demonstrating the first tenets of misbehavior. He was quickly becoming a spectacle.

"You want to know how to pick the best wines?" he boasted. "Easy! Ask the guy who's selling it to the stores. Yeah! Really! And I'm the one who tells them which ones to push," he blustered, "and I'm always right! They ask for *my* suggestions, and *my* suggestions are invin…invincible." He nearly spilled his drink on the nearest listener as he gesticulated wildly. "When you're in distribution, all you have to do is set up as many wineries as you can. Then, you can control *all* of them *and* their wines. And which ones you want to sell…you sell! The rest can go to hell, no matter how much huffing and puffing and making nice they try to do." Words were becoming slurred. He took another drink. "Control. That's what it's all about. Control." His eyes bugged as he stood, swaying slightly.

Tom couldn't stand it any more. He stepped forward and took his co-worker by the elbow and firmly walked him away from the group that had gathered but were now recoiling, backing away. As they hastened out of earshot, he glared at Curry and said, "Howard, I'm not sure what that was all about, but you and I are having a long talk about a few things on Monday."

Curry looked sheepish. His small five foot seven frame was dwarfed by Hutchins' height. He cowered at the way Tom had taken hold of the situation and looked as though he were afraid of being whipped. It was a complete turnabout from the vociferous loud-mouth he had portrayed just a moment ago. The effects of the wine had made the high-water mark and suddenly he was buckling into an ebb-tide. He responded to Tom with a 'what did I do, and what do I do now' sort of expression.

"How did you get here?" Tom asked coldly. He could see that the responsibility of getting this idiot home without letting him drive would fall upon his shoulders.

"Car," was his mono-phrase. He acceded to the fact that he couldn't drive.

"Give me the keys and I'll drive you home. Go wait for me at the entrance...NOW!" He practically shouted not knowing if his command would be carried out or not. Curry was so fouled up he was likely to jump into anyone's car if they'd let him. But then, he couldn't conceive of anyone else providing Howard with transportation tonight. How did he get so drunk so fast? All he wanted to do was get him home, and the earlier the better!

He thought of how he would forfeit the rest of this enjoyable evening with Kara, but he had to do this thing. Frustrated and angry, he charged back into what was left of the party. He located her at the table where the Mountain View wines had been shown. Except for Kara her table was empty. She was wearing an odd expression.

"They're all gone! Everything left of the wines we were pouring are gone! I made a quick inquiry about Gary, our wonderful pourer for the evening, and learned that he had left...along with *my* wine. There had to have been several hundred dollars worth of product that just disappeared. Thanks a lot, Gary!"

"Surely he only took it away for safekeeping until you could retrieve it." Tom took the more positive attitude.

"But he's taken it upon himself to take everything without consulting anyone. Seems the distributors had arranged for the servers instead of the management. They said there was no way they could locate or return the wine. They even said he didn't wait around long enough to be paid the balance of what we owed him for the pouring. Not that he'd need extra money after absconding with that much wine," she added contemptuously. "Oh, Tom, I don't mean to lean on you with my problems, but this kind of injury is more serious than I can explain, and right now this wound is too fresh." Her words had come tumbling out like a water flow. Nearly in tears, she stopped herself and put her hand on Tom's arm for support.

"What a way to end such a wonderful evening," he commiserated. "I don't know what's worse, having to listen to Howard, or finding your wine missing."

"Howard?" She was confused.

He proceeded to tell her about having stopped Howard Curry from making a further fool of himself after she had left the scene. "I can't let him drive. I'll take him home in his car. He can pick it up tomorrow at my place or the bank. He doesn't live too far from there. It looks like our party is over for now anyway." At this point, he had placed his hands on her shoulders. He gave her a sweet kiss on the forehead and then lightly on the cheek. They were warm friendly kisses that held no promise of sexual overtones. He conjectured that right now Kara Tower could use moral support rather than having to field an insincere pass. This recent loss on top of her greater dilemma was just too much. He wanted her to know that he would like to stand by her as a friend.

Thinking of the evening that had started off so nicely, Kara was disappointed and understandably furious, first with that social disaster, Curry, and with the disappearance of her wine.

Still she wouldn't let on to her feelings. Instead she said in acceptance of the situation, "I can see what you have to do. That man was making an ass of himself, and I was glad to get away from him and that crowd. And you're right, this isn't the best way for the evening to end. Tom, thank you for coming with me tonight."

"You know I loved it! I'll give you a call tomorrow, if you'll be there."

"Of course."

She watched as he hurried off to get the car for Curry.

CHAPTER 12

❁

Following Hutchin's departure, Kara spent another hour just saying her goodbyes, making small talk, and thanking the people who were responsible for putting the affair together. After being at a public event where she was constantly under scrutiny, Kara was more than ready for some quiet time. It *was* work, the constant demand of 'on stage' performing for an audience that expected glamour and excitement along with sophisticated banter. All she wanted and needed at the moment, was a warm shower, a cup of hot hazelnut chocolate, and a cozy place to curl up with a good book. Reading was always her favorite means of exiting the world and tonight she needed it!

On the drive home, she was able to go over the evening at a leisure pace. Thinking over the more positive highlights, she was flattered and uplifted to hear the words of the media during their interview. They congratulated her for her success as one of the pioneers in an industry that was now producing a nationally accepted commodity. She enjoyed the appreciation most people extended. At times it was almost to the point of adulation, the swooning over the vintages, elevating the mysterious knowledge surrounding the ritual of metamorphosing grapes into wine. Educating the masses and good publicity were major factors in justifying her personal appearances.

Her mind ranged over the evening in vignettes, scenes of people and events that had taken place. The road ahead was in focus, but without her registering any conscious thought of driving. It was too dark to be distracted by the passing scenery, or the pick-up truck that paced her movements two vehicles behind her on the freeway.

She was musing over Tom's appearance at the wine tasting. He made a very attractive escort. She had overheard more than a couple of women making admiring remarks about the handsome banker. What more could be said about someone who could be labeled as Mr. Perfect? He was pleasant to be with.

He was certainly a departure from the group of men who made up her distributor's team. Their appearance reminded her of a cabal of spies from a really bad Hollywood budget film. They were an unfathomable lot, perpetually having the look of clandestine manipulators. Surely it was her imagination, but they always seemed to be discussing private issues that would come to a halt whenever she or another outsider approached. And it always seemed to her that their enthusiasm for marketing her wines blew hot and cold. Hot, when they were face to face with her, and cold the minute they turned their backs on her. Not this evening though. They were cold, cold, cold. Ah well! She sighed for the unavoidable frustrations that she knew came with the territory of the business. She yawned from the exhaustion that was creeping up on her.

So now, safely back at the house at last, her pulse was racing as she tried to calm herself. Of all nights for it to happen, there was a near-accident that took place on her way home as she exited the main highway. The close call was a more than just happenstance, but she made herself a promise that she would drop it out of mind the moment she stepped through her front door. Instead, as she stood there in the kitchen waiting for the hot chocolate to be ready to pour, she replayed the nearly tragic incident once again as she remembered it.

It didn't turn out to be anything more than a near miss, she tried to convince herself. The one-lane off-ramp ended at a poorly lit, four corner intersection. As she started to make the left-hand turn, in the rear view mirror there was a flash of headlights. She looked back at the road behind her. The pick-up was either out of control, or the driver was a maniac. It careened down the off-ramp heading for the left side of her Mustang as though it were aiming straight for the driver.

Kara's actions were swift and automatic. They were in defense of her life. She kicked back second gear and spun the wheels to a hard left. As the back-end tires broke away from the pavement with a scream, she swung the car around, pivoting on the front. The truck came within a hairs-breadth of hitting her.

With the screech of brakes, it catapulted off the road and landed unscathed, but stuck, into the far roadside ditch, the driver apparently still in one piece. That was enough! It frightened her and Kara wanted out of there. Not about to expose herself to further confrontation with the driver, she hastened on her way as she patted the dashboard of the car, saying over and over again, "Good little war pony! Good little war pony!"

The phone rang, bringing her out of her reverie that consisted of the earlier events of the evening; the good the bad, and the ugly. She was comfortably ensconced in her cozy bedroom, attempting without much success, to concentrate on the clenching drama of a Wilbur Smith adventure novel.

She reached for the phone.

"Hello?" she queried, wondering why anyone should be calling her so late at night.

"Kara," the voice said. "Are you all right?"

The question hit her like a blow to the pit of her stomach. It was Tom, and he was asking about her condition. Did he know something about her trip home, or was she just getting paranoid? She hesitated just long enough to calm the tremor in her voice.

"Yes, of course. I'm surprised you called." She was waiting for an explanation to be forthcoming.

"I just wanted you to know. I dropped that…Howard off at his place. He couldn't stop telling me how powerful he was and on and on with nonsensical hogwash. I told him we'd have a serious conversation on Monday to clarify what the hell he has up his sleeve. I doubt he'll even remember it though."

She said nothing, and he continued. "…No, that's not why I called." Her breath caught.

"Then tell me. What made you think of me?"

"I kind of missed the rest of the evening. We were having such a good time. If it wasn't for Howard behaving so outlandishly, we might still have been enjoying the event. If I remember correctly, there were plenty of leftovers."

"Food, yes. But not any wine," she pointed out.

"And speaking of wine, anything more about the missing bottles?"

"No, but Tom, should I remind you that it's nearly midnight? My bedtime, at least." She decided not to mention anything about the earlier incident on the road.

"I realize that. I simply wanted to apologize for the interruption and tell you that I intend to make it up to you."

"I appreciate that. Could it be that you feel badly enough to drive all the way over here tomorrow? I'll be busy in the morning, but I make it a point to take every opportunity to make Sundays special. Besides, we have plenty to talk about."

"Kara, me darlin'," a Scottish brogue lilting his voice, "warm up the old picnic basket and I'll fill it with delights for the stomach as well as the soul. And pray for good weather!" he added.

"Done," she responded to his rollicking mood with an accent of her own. "If the gods be of good nature, I shall be freed of this cumbersome load by one o'clock."

"Then gird yourself, sweet lady, your servant awaits the hour."

No good-by, just a gently disconnecting of the line. Kara was smiling at their silliness as she snuggled more deeply into the covers.

CHAPTER 13

❀

The beating on the window brought Kara out of a deep sleep. Beth was gesturing from the garden for her to get up and open the locked door.

"Hey, sleepyhead. Since when do you *veg* later than 8 o'clock?"

Kara was still stretching. "Since I have to do wine tastings till the wee hours of the night. What on earth have you got there?"

Beth was manhandling a large box into the front room. "Got any coffee? No, of course not. Well, guess I'll have to make it myself." She proceeded to the kitchen with Kara close on her heels, her robe, lufting behind as she shrugged it on.

"You didn't answer me. What's in the box?" Her curiosity was burning. Once she was focused on something, she wanted to persevere until it was resolved.

"Well, if you don't know, I'm not going to tell you. You'll just have to open it yourself. But first, we're going to have some coffee. I want to hear all the post-evening gossip. How did the tasting go?"

Satisfied that she would solve the mystery of the box shortly, Kara settled into taking the next best action. Bagels, lox and cream cheese, slices of melon, and a service platter for breakfast appeared. As they settled themselves in the parlor, Beth betrayed her own inquisitiveness by again probing into the activity of the evening.

"Did Tom enjoy himself? Did you see a lot of people you know?"

"The tasting itself, was a boilerplate event," Kara explained. "You know, the extravagant and very fattening food, all the guests gussied up to the nines. Naturally, it was the crowd that was the entertainment. Wish you could have seen some of those outfits! And I don't mean just the ladies! The people from that new winery near Roseburg had a table next to ours, and you couldn't help hearing their catty remarks about practically every person who walked by. Some of their 'asides' were so funny, I could barely keep my face straight. And some of their comments were so *scathing*, I was embarrassed to think they may have been overheard by the people they were talking about."

"It's hard to believe how people in that position could act like that. Besides giving a bad rep to anybody who they talk about, they don't realize how they look to the people they're talking *to*. Not very nice! Kara, I'm so glad you're not like that. It wouldn't look good for the rest of us."

"A point well taken. I'm glad you're aware that when one of us acts in a certain way, it reflects directly on the rest of the group. Gotta be a pretty good moral in there somewhere. You may have to pass this wisdom along some day."

While they had been talking, they hungrily attacked the food and sipped regularly at the coffee.

"Are you going to tell me anything about Tom, or is that classified information?"

"Bethany Chris!! Are you asking about the evening at the Club, or are you asking what happened after the tasting." Her reluctance was a sham.

"Moi? Would I pry?"

"Do you want to know more about Tom, or do you want to know what we did or didn't do?" she asked testily.

Now, it was Kara's turn to be teasing Beth. She sensed that Beth's inquiry was a little more than a casual one. She believed that Beth really wanted to know if there was any importance in her new relationship with Tom Hutchins. Well, there wasn't! At least, not importance in the way Beth was thinking. He was justifiably of interest because of their business connection at the bank. Surely, he was much too young for any serious interest.

At last she remembered how Beth had behaved when Tom had been at her home. Yes, Beth would definitely like to know more about Tom Hutchins. Well…why not? They would make an attractive pair, if that was where Beth's fantasies led her.

Beth looked at Kara with a big-eyed innocent expression. "Just wondered what was happening there. He does seem to be pretty nice…good looking…hung, no doubt like…well…good looking."

"Beth!" Kara's expression was a pantomime of offence. That broke the ice, and Kara settled in to give Beth the whole scenario of what had transpired on the night before. She included the climactic near-accident at the conclusion of the evening.

The incident, when it was retold, sobered the conversation as the facts were laid out.

"You're right, Kara. Either the driver was a maniac, or he was *trying* to bash you. Now why do you think anyone would want to hurt you that way.... Strange!"

"Well, that was last night, and today is today. Maybe something will come along in the form of a clue if the accident was really intended for me...like a bomb under my office chair. Meanwhile, I think we've been watching too many TV thrillers. Let's just drop it." she replied in an effort to lift them out of the dark mood. "And I still want to know what's in the box! Where did it come from?"

"Don't know. Found it on your doorstep when I arrived. I figured you might still be at the house after being out so late last night, so I came down here rather than going directly to the winery."

"I'm glad you did. What's that in the folder?" She pointed at the papers enclosed in the manila envelope.

"Festival info. There's work to be done on the final list of participants for the festival flyer. We'll include a map that shows the placement for the booths. Thought we could work on it here for a while before we go to the winery."

"Good Idea! But I'm not waiting any longer to get into that box." She took the remnants of their food back to the kitchen, and returned with a butcher knife.

"Don't do it! Don't stab me!" Beth dramatized. Kara ignored her and made no comment as she attacked the large package. Inside was a card. She read it aloud:

"Just so you don't think I'm a complete barbarian-
some treats for our lunch. Love ya', Turner"

Just beneath the card was a huge picnic basket. Further exploration uncovered a variety of foods, some of which could rival the gourmet tables of last night. She took a closer look at the message to make sure she hadn't been mistaken about the signature.

No mistake, it was from Turner. A token of gratitude for his new job. It was a kind gesture.

"Oh m'god!" was all she could say. She didn't move. She just sat there on the floor in suspended animation, staring at the thing.

"What's wrong? Are you all right?" The question was posed with both confusion and concern. "It's beautiful! Turner really did all this?" She was incredulous. "Didn't know he had it in him. Really creative!" Again she looked at Kara and had to ask, "What's wrong?"

"What's wrong is me!" Kara looked pained. "I have a date to spend the afternoon with him."

"So…this is a bad thing?"

"No, it's not a bad thing. The bad thing is that I went and suggested to Tom that he drive all the way out here to have a…guess what?…a picnic today. He called late last night when I was half-asleep…not thinking. I suggested it because I thought it would make up for the crazy time he had with Howard Curry, and damned all, I forgot Turner! Forgot I would be going out to lunch with him. Lord, how could I do that? What am I going to do?"

The two sat there on the floor looking at the gift while each of them sought a way out of this problem.

There were times before when Kara found herself in this kind of a predicament. Anyone with several irons in the fire was bound to have a line or two crossing unexpectedly. It could happen any time. Making more than one commitment for any given date was an inconvenience and often an embarrassment, as it was now.

True, the date she had accepted with Turner was informal…implied, rather than specifically made for a certain time. In fact, she realized lately that their activities were usually spontaneous rather than planned. This friendship between them was a comfortable development made possible by the circumstances of their proximity. They were easily available to one another. She felt badly that his friendship could have been taken so casually that a commitment could be forgotten.

However, apart from the need to acknowledge the beautiful gift he gave her, it would be a reasonably simple maneuver to postpone their date. And wouldn't it be more politically wise to encourage the budding rapport with her banker? Looks notwithstanding, he certainly could in the long run help to give her greater credibility in facing her financial problems. It was a proven fact that rubbing elbows with the elite was good networking. She thought of the adage that you are judged by the company you keep. Well, that would definitely depend on who was the judge and who were the players as to what would be a smarter move…politically.

Just as she felt the situation would be resolved to here satisfaction, she was unavoidably confronted with the bleak face of guilt. How could she, with any integrity, push away her devoted *aide de camp*; the one who was always there when she needed him. Thoughts scudded and reeled. What would she do with Tom?

"Hold on, Beth. Let me try to call Tom Hutchins before he leaves. Heaven help me, I made two dates for this afternoon and I don't really want to break either one of them."

She found the number and dialed.

CHAPTER 14

Already on his way to the winery, Tom was looking forward to seeing Kara today. It had been a while since he had taken the time to develop any kind of personal interest in anyone related to his work, especially a woman. He had found to his surprise that Tower was engaging, inventive and more important, he enjoyed her maturity. He also perceived that the industry she had created here could be of inestimable value to the area, or for that matter to anyone with the correct business acumen following in her path.

He admired and respected the kind of ingenuity that could create and maintain momentum for so many years. He had seen it before; successful people in new enterprises benefitting other businesses in turn. These were the builders. These were the pioneering entrepreneurs who held his admiration. Kara Tower was one of them.

The car phone buzzed, interrupting his thoughts. He answered, giving his number rather than the standard greeting, hello.

"Tom?" Kara tentatively confirmed the speaker.

"Kara! I'm about half-way to your place. Just making one stop and I should be there about 11:30. Anything you'd like me to pick up on the way?"

"No, nothing." This is not good, she thought. "Just a second." She quickly turned to Beth, covering the mouthpiece. "What are you doing this afternoon?" whispering.

"No plans."

"This is a situation. Can you cover for me?"

"You mean take care of the hunk?" Beth was overjoyed. "Yes, and you can tell him I want to talk to him about some money matters." She grasped immediately what was expected of her.

Kara didn't wait for an answer, but continued on the phone with Tom.

"Tom, I can't tell you how sorry I am, but something came up and I'll be away for the better part of the afternoon. But if you could come just as you planned...uh, because Beth, you remember meeting her at the house?...she mentioned she was anxious to get together with you concerning some personal financial matters, and if you two could lunch together..." She let her entreaty hang in the air. "Seems we're destined to have our plans interrupted."

Tom took the news without pause. Normally, he would have the resiliency of a rubber ball, but this time his reaction was stifled. He reverted to a businesslike tone.

"No problem, Kara. I realize things can come up unexpectedly." He couldn't help but remember the surprises of the previous night. "I'll look forward to talking with Beth and seeing you later."

"Great!" And in a small voice, "See you soon."

He hung up and continued thinking about Kara Tower as he drove. Was she trying to avoid him? Perhaps his unexpected departure with Howard Curry last night was niggling at her and in some convoluted way, this was pay-back time. But surely, she wasn't that shallow! He tried to read the signs. Surely this was no predetermined conspiracy to manipulate him in any way. No, he decided he still liked her, and he shouldn't be making any mental accusations.

He continued toward the road that would lead him to the winery and vineyards. It gave him the time to take yet a closer look at himself. He had always viewed himself as a 'careful' man, and it wasn't altogether like him to stick his neck out for an acquaintanceship as he seemed to be doing with Kara Tower. It wasn't like him at all to reach out to the unknown, but this time he really felt like he wanted to pursue this new trend. His self-preservation instincts had been catered to long enough, and this time he wanted to step through the door to the world of involvement.

Years ago, Tom was like most young men who's hormones controlled their lives. A bright, well liked collegiate type, he always wanted to improve himself and most of all, improve on what he considered his mediocre home life. He never understood how his dad, a blue collar worker could countenance the never changing day-to-day agenda that was his life. Nor could he fathom his colorless mother who he loved, and yet for whom he held little respect. His feelings for her bordered on pity. A bovine acceptance of the non-enlightened existence that she and his father led would not be the road taken by their son.

Early on, he decided he would never be commonplace. He would turn one-hundred and eighty degrees from his background and become a man of imagination, ambition, enlightenment. In the naivete of his youth, he envisioned himself becoming a mature man of unquestioned integrity, enviable wisdom, and above all, with the capacity for success in every endeavor. He would be all things to all men...and to all women, an irresistible suitor. He would live a life of perfection.

This was his own force-fed regimen of dreams. Later he discovered, it wasn't the real Tom Hutchins, at least not to the extent of his childhood ambitions.

So much for goals. One by one the dreams of grandeur were harnessed as choices were made in conjunction with opportunities and abilities. An appropriate adjustment of goals became a continuous predilection. Still, Tom remembered his ideals for attaining a more measurably meaningful and intellectually stimulating life than that of his family. By means of careful selection, his life had become steadfast and secure. Conservative? Yes, but infinitely more interesting he thought, than that of his forebears.

Stopping at the shopping center, Tom made a sweep of the grocery store, selecting the delicacies he had envisioned sharing with Kara. It was questionable whether or not he would need them now, but better to be prepared.

He tried to remember his brief encounter with Beth. He remembered very little about her with the exception that she was dark, adequately attractive and, come to think of it, pretty curvaceous. A flirt. Now, what do you suppose she wants to talk to me about? Finances? Well, he thought, as he made his way through the express check-out line, at least she'll be well fed!

Tom packed his purchases in the trunk of the car and, on an impulse, he returned out of curiosity to one of the stores opposite the parking space.

It was a cutlery shop specializing in kitchen implements and culinary accoutrements bordering on the out-of-the-ordinary. He lingered over the diversity of coffee makers and was tempted by the patterned crepe irons. Since he was in no hurry to arrive at Mountain View, he ambled through the store with moderate interest in the various sections. Until he arrived at the knife display.

It had not occurred to him prior to this moment that he would have any compulsion to purchase anything...but there it was. Laying with the single blade exposed was a beautifully crafted knife. It was hafted with fossilized bone, carved with an eagle in bas-relief. Neither large nor small, he knew it was a something he had to have.

"How much?" he asked the store attendant.

"One sixty-five. Would you like me to take it out of the case?"

"Yes." Tom took the handle of the knife as it was transferred to him by the salesman, who caressed the blade, sharp side facing away from the palm of his hand. Tom levered the blade to close it and then opened and closed it several times to feel the response.

He examined it carefully and said, "Very nice. I'll take it."

He walked out of the shop feeling good about the purchase without further consideration about why he made it, other than the thought that it was just meant to be.

CHAPTER 15

About the same time Tom was making his purchases, Turner had been mirroring these activities with less emphasis on the Epicurean aspect of food. His selections were more concentrated on supplementing the picnic basket he had deposited on Kara's doorstep. For Turner, abundance rather than gourmet selection was the criteria of any market expedition. The last thing he grabbed before leaving the market said it all. Along with a goodly supply of flavored chips and a variety of nuts was a half-rack each of ale, stout, and *Rain-doggers* as he referred to his favorite beer. Survival!

Turner had plans. The picnic basket he had sent to Kara was only one part of it. Now, there were enough supplies for two or three days.

He sailed out of the store nearly running into one of the better known locals.

"Hey man, looks like you're hustling an issue of food. In a hurry?"

"Hey Raven. How's it going?"

"Good, good. Turner, you got change for a buck?" He indicated the newspaper dispenser. You could depend on White Raven to be out and about absorbing the comings and goings of everyone in town, as well as anything acquirable in the way of gossip. He always had a quiet but unexplained sparkle in his eye that made him appear that everything was a game. Just another street person? No one ever bothered figuring out what he really did.

Turner dug into his pocket for some coin and took advantage of the grapevine to connect with any of the latest action around town.

"Anything happenin' at the river?" he finally asked.

People living in that area knew that the 'river' was the general area surrounding the winery. Telepathic news was often filtered down to the tall, handsome and well-informed Native American. He was a good listener. He was also a good source for unpublished information.

"Heard some pretties were traded for toot last week. Such a shame." He shook his head, looking at the ground in sadness. "So much for so little. Tradin' ain't what it used to be."

Turner wondered what the 'pretties' were and what the imbalance was, but he knew it was not politically correct even in this genre to push too hard for specifics. Instead he repeated sympathetically, "Pretties for toot. Some folks work hard for what they get. Some just piss it away. That's life!"

"Got that right! Heard you got a good job out at the vineyard."

"Yeah!" He was surprised. "News travels fast! You know, it's the first time I've had something to do where I can actually initiate the work. I like it. In less than a week I think I've planned out enough projects to last me about three years. The more I look around the place, the more I see what can be done."

"Well Turner, I think you've just discovered how inventive your mind is." As he departed he added, "I'd like to hear how you're getting along."

Turner was aware that this was a most unusual person and that the enigmatic Indian was better educated than people gave him credit for. Also, he knew far more about the workings of the town than he ever talked about.

And indeed he did. White Raven had not only heard of, but had seen some extremely nice pieces of jewelry. His well trained, Arizona reservation-bred eye had told him that they were a cut above the usual junk that was traded for drugs. He even had a pretty good idea where it came from.

It disgusted him to think of the fine workmanship of these pieces being given so little respect. He was not as offended by the fact that it was stolen as he was saddened that it would be traded for so little value. It discredited the spirit of the maker. It insulted the original owner.

Raven was curious about the recent appearance of several stolen items with a growing realization that more and more of the thefts were revolving around Kara Tower's winery. Turner's conversation was more pointed than he had first thought. There was a genuine concern there.

He needed to find a quiet place to ponder this further. Bits of information from here and there were starting to come together into a pattern. A seemingly random occurrence of articles turning up on the street. He wondered too about how many more things he had *not* heard about that might be floating around out there.

What really puzzled him now that he thought about it, was that as far as he knew, no whistles had been blown. There were no charges being made, or even reports of theft being filed with the police. The daily newspaper police blotter would have had these incidents listed as they took place. Except for a wine barrel, nothing at all was said about them.

And Kara was a nice woman.

He remembered when she had found him one late winter afternoon without a penny in his pocket; he seldom carried much money, credit cards being so much more convenient, and no coat to fend off the cold. She gave him a heavy jacket from her car and took him to the local Hamburger Hut, saying she was on her way to get a bite to eat. She managed to casually put some dollars in his breast pocket before she let him leave, thinking him destitute. The memory made him smile. Yes! She was a nice woman.

Again, he thought about the thefts. The one incident he read about just recently, maybe only a couple of days ago on the 'Blotter', was when a bunch of cellar rats were 'alleged' to have stolen a barrel of wine from Kara's winery. But Raven knew about quite a few other missing items. There was a small pump, an O-Haus balance beam scale, a five-gallon tank of gas, a bike, a calculator...and once, even a cash register. Lots of things. Why wasn't she reporting it? Did she even realize that all these things were missing? She must! Perhaps there would be someone, somewhere that fate would call upon to put these incidents all together into a meaningful whole.

It was not in White Raven's nature to interfere with the fate of people, whether it was their life style in question, or the destination of their belongings. He was normally indifferent to these happenings. What took place in other people's lives was their business. He considered himself an aloof observer...unless the victim was a vulnerable personality. It was then that his sensibilities kicked in. He could not condone the unnecessary pain inflicted on the innocent, but usually he would not concern himself further.

Yet in this case there was something gnawing about the consistency of things being taken from the winery woman. It mattered not at all that they seemed to emanate from different quarters, unconnected. This was a mystery. It was like a parasite...no, an animal chewing at her. A piece here, and a piece there. Yes! Like rats in the cellar. Chewing and stealing until...there's nothing left, and the insatiable cellar rats move on.

CHAPTER 16

Turner pulled into the driveway of the winery, making a mental note of even more projects to be addressed when he returned to work. There was a fence to be built between the crush area, where the grapes were delivered during the harvest season, and the outer rim of the driveway enclosure. It would improve the looks if the posts were replaced by stonework stiles. Inspired, he planned to build a stone entryway at the head of the drive that would ultimately enhance and create a whole new ambience as guests approached the winery.

Funny, he always remembered what he had to do when he saw these things, but out of sight, out of mind. How could he correct that, he wondered? He promised himself not to forget to make entries in a notebook to help him become more productive. Why, he could be the most organized son-of-a-bitch in the valley! Feeling that he was veritably on top of things, he approached the entrance of the winery.

Turner had another burst of creative imagination. At the door to the winery, he would pounce in, making a grand entrance. He envisioned himself posing at the door. Workmen would cease their toil and stare. The women would audibly sigh and swoon at his presence. He would sweep the most beautiful woman off her feet and carry her away in a swashbuckling wave of passion. Their destination would be the far reaches of the world, their love, phenomenal. He opened the front door…

"Oh, hi Turner," was the casual and slightly bored response from Shiron, the girl of the moment in the tasting room, as her red curls disappeared once again behind the tasting bar. It seemed as though this particular job required that the employees spend ninety percent of their time with their ass in the air and their heads under the bar. He was disappointed. No one else turned away from their tasks to give him any further attention. The grand entrance was a dud.

"Where's Kara?" he asked of the out-of-sight attendant.

"In the bathroom...I think."

"Swell." Took care of that fantasy. Turner had to prepare himself for another psychological buildup. These grand entrances weren't all that easy on a guy.

Before he could recoup, Kara upstaged him. "Turner!" She literally, as only as she could, swept in from the hall. There was something about this woman that attracted everyone's full attention without her even trying. This time, the workers did pause for a moment to observe Kara's physical momentum. "I just finished tying up some loose ends, but I left a little paperwork for tomorrow. I do that so I'll look like I'm indispensable for this job." She gave him a wink and a friendly pat on the shoulder.

"I must thank you for the lovely picnic basket. Let's use it today. I packed it with a few more things..."

But he didn't let her finish. "Never mind the basket, I brought the market with me. We're going to a special place today so don't expect to be back till morning...a couple of days from now, that is.

"Turner," she blanched. "What are you saying? I can't just up and leave here for that long! There are reports that need to be taken care of, and I expect to be here to accept confirmations for the festival entertainment. I was supposed to be seeing the fellow from the bank today, and I'll be putting him off as it is. There's so much to do..."

"Kara, stop!" Shiron interrupted. "When was the last time you took a day or two away from work? With the festival coming up next week a little rest and relaxation would do you good! Isn't it about time you gave yourself a chance to breathe?"

It was agreed. They would be back in two days, and in that time they could have a delightful adventure. This was one of the things that made life so great. Spontaneous activity was always the best. With most of her workload behind her for the moment, the expediency of having Beth...bless her heart and her constant animal hunger for men...take care of entertaining Tom Hutchins, her immediate problems were solved. She felt free enough to look forward to enjoying a short time off. This would give her a chance to stretch her cramped body and shake the cobwebs out of her overworked brain.

A sunny smile grew on her face when she said, "I do have to talk to Beth before we leave. She's still at the house. I can be ready to go in about fifteen! Throw a bottle or two of wine into 'Curley' and we'll be on our way!" She could feel the excitement generated by an unplanned journey. She hurried to the lab to let Digby the winemaker know of her plans, said good-by to the rest of the crew who gave her their benediction and headed for her place.

Beth was nearly as much at home in Kara's house as her own abode. She was often there for one reason or another. It was a convenience for both of them. Together, they shared the comfortable closeness of two people who were conditioned to each other's movements. After two and a half years working at the winery, Beth had become Kara's nearest friend in spite of being an employee.

When she learned that Tom Hutchins would be thrust upon her for the afternoon, Beth looked as satisfied as a she-wolf with a fresh kill. Kara had at first been apologetic about her scheme, but that was a ruse. She wasn't the least bit worried about Beth's being disenchanted about the arrangement.

"Beth, I'm not sure how to put this, but it seems Turner had extended plans for our outing and wants to be away until day after tomorrow. What do you say to entertaining Tom for the rest of the day and make my excuses that I won't be able to see him until Wednesday?"

"Kara Tower, is this a con? Are you trying to set me up with this guy, or what!"

"I'm innocent! It was a total surprise. I expected to be gone for an afternoon picnic, and Turner decided to whisk me away for a couple of days. Said I needed the time off. I've got to say, I agree with him. It couldn't come at a better time."

"So true, so true. You need this. And don't worry, the winery will be in my good and capable hands. Do you know where you're going?" She followed Kara to her room as they commenced to stuff warm clothing into an athletic bag.

"Haven't a clue. Well," she paused for a moment and came up with an idea, "he didn't say for sure, but I figure we're going camping in the great outdoors, and possibly we'll end up east of Roseburg. Anyway, that's my guess."

"And a good guess it is!" Turner peeked around the bedroom corner as they zipped up the bag. "Fish are bitin' and the water is high!! You about ready?"

"Nearly." She turned to Beth to say, "When Tom arrives, let him know that I couldn't avoid this change of plans. Remember...make it sound like serious business."

"Not to worry. I won't let you get busted. After I get though explaining how diligent you are about business, the man will be totally impressed with your decision to take care of your responsibilities. This way, I'll have fun, and you'll have fun."

"Glad you see it that way. We need to get out of here before I trip over him on the way out the door. See you day after tomorrow."

"Or the day after, if you're having a great time," she encouraged. "Bye!"

Beth waved and watched Kara and Turner as they pulled away. She thought, how lucky can one woman be! Kara has one of the most interesting lives and at the same time can have a great time with a really sweet guy.

Well, at least some of it is rubbing off on me. Tom would be there at any moment now, and she wanted to be ready to give him as good a time as she was told to do. She thought grinning…it's my job.

CHAPTER 17

It was a two hour winding drive into the mountain area, and another forty-five minutes to the remote campground. The scenery unfolded curve after curve into glorious compositions of cliffs, trees and a river that was in turn clear and deep, and then roiling with the conflict of rapids and their rock barricaded channels. Kara had an inkling about their destination but had not envisioned such beauty. At home, they had spoken about it on more than a couple of occasions.

"The rock formations are unbelievable, Kara! There's a place you can jump into the stream and let it drift you through smooth channels like a cork. Then you slide, and whump...!! You're sucked under a kind of big water tube and shot out the other end into another slide. They couldn't have designed a better ride in Disneyworld!...And the fishing! You want to catch *the classic* trout on a hand-made nymph? 'Tis the season! The area's designated as fly fishing only, so be prepared for that strike with your fish making like a flamenco dancer on the end of your line."

Turner's diatribe was accompanied by vigorous gesticulation and body language. One could, just by watching and hearing his descriptions, believe that this fisherman's paradise and recreation utopia was a dream-come-true.

Kara couldn't think of a more perfect place to back off from her work. Being out in the wilderness felt as natural and comfortable to her as it must be to her mountain man. It was the perfect place. She couldn't rid herself of the feeling of exultation. Ah the benefits of playing hooky!

Not long after noon, Tom Hutchins pulled into the driveway of Kara Tower's house. He noted only one lone vehicle parked in the front. This had to be Beth's car.

He wasn't exactly angry following their conversation, but the drive there had given him just enough time to work up a healthy aggression against what he thought was a rebuff from Kara. He became increasingly ticked off for allowing himself to be manipulated into this position of taking a substitute for his time there. Twice he had nearly turned around to return home. Was she ungrateful or just ignorant of what he was trying to do? If she was going to run him around, he simply didn't have time for that. He didn't care for last minute changes of plan. For him, a date made was a date kept. As reasonable as a change of plans could be made to seem, Tom's ego was undeniably suffering a setback. This kind of treatment was something he hadn't experienced for a long time.

Frustrated as he was, he reasoned that the arrangements he had made to meet with Beth could be some salve to his injured ego. At least he would have some entertainment until Kara returned. Beth might prove to be a healthy diversion. He pulled in to the front of the house, parked his car and headed for the door. His attitude was already improving.

With business completed for the time being, Beth had dressed herself carefully for the afternoon. In an ankle-length button-down, dark blue-denim skirt, the only under-thing she wore was a slim, thong-like bikini bottom. Her top was a light upholstery fabric, a chintz bolero that exposed the mid-section that *just* closed across her abundant bosom where glimpses of white, untanned skin underneath could be seen when she moved. Sandals on her feet, rings on her toes and a scarf in her hair, she resembled an upscale gypsy without the affinity for baubles and bangles. Her object was to get this man's attention!

There was a time, back when Beth first arrived in this part of the country, that it was Beth and not Kara who would have been seen at Turner's side. He was attracted to her soft South Carolina drawl and her east coast manner, both of which seemed to be switched on and off at will. The southern belle act was only an effectation. Her tenure in the South was a short one, but long enough for the ambience and southern accent to linger at times, and at other times, not! In truth, she had been raised in southern California. Little did she know, it was precisely those unaccountable transformations that caused Turner to lose interest. Some men preferred stability.

So now Turner was displaying an interest in Kara. So what! In a fit of devilry, Beth imagined a scenario in telling Tom the truth; that instead of taking care of business, the big boss went waltzing off with her hired hand into blissland for a couple of days, leaving her loyal employee to sort out the loose threads of unfinished work. But after a few moments of bathing in bitchery Beth returned to reality. Of course she wouldn't divulge their secrets. She would never be disloyal to their friendship. She would never jeopardize that.

The doorbell rang. Picnic time!

When Beth opened the door, she expected a grinning caller…at least a pleasant one. Instead, the man standing at the entrance looked more like an auditor from the IRS. Tom threatened to be as serious as a heart attack when he said, "Where's the body?"

"The what?" He took her completely by surprise, his usually very proper personality had taken a 180 degree turn. She had expected good manners, even courtesy. Instead, she was jolted by what appeared to be serious anger. Then, she could see that he was pulling her leg.

"She must have died. Why else would she miss the opportunity to have an afternoon lunch with yours truly!" He could no longer contain his ersatz demeanor, especially in the presence of the wonderful looking girl standing there. His face progressively changed into a beguiling smile. The period of angst disappeared and the dark mood gave way to a brighter one.

"You gave me a scary minute there, Mister." She recovered.

"Just kidding! You know we're going to have some time together this afternoon. I don't know if Kara told you, but I brought a few things along for us to munch on, even if we won't see her until later." He looked her over more carefully and added, "Perhaps we should find a quiet place for lunch where we can talk." His voice suddenly sounded a point more seductive than he intended. It was beyond his power not to respond to the way she looked.

Beth reacted. "I happen to know just the place." She knew where she wanted to take him, but she wasn't sure of the most auspicious time to be telling him that Kara was not going to be available for quite a while…like two days.

Beth and Tom found a spot not far from the streamside where Kara and Turner had picnicked not so long ago. It was accepted as the picture-perfect setting for a pastoral sojourn. After the appropriate words of appreciation for the tranquil beauty of the place, a car blanket appeared and had been spread, a bottle of wine opened, and a toast was now being proposed.

"To an intriguing afternoon." Tom sensed that this woman would possibly be open to personal overtures at almost any level. He would take his own sweet time though, in deciding just when and where he wanted to take this opportunity. For the moment, prudence was in the forefront of his mind. He in no way wanted to upset the delicate balance of his business relationship with Kara Tower. His respect for her gave him a reason for wanting to take a more discrete tack in his approach to this rendezvous with Beth.

Tower was important to him. He saw in her the opportunity to become involved in a way he had never been involved before. At first, he was compelled only to learn enough about her predicament to establish an educated verdict for the loan application. Now, it seemed he foresaw the opportunity for…what? He wasn't sure.

He could imagine himself going the distance in support of this woman's goals. She incited the stirring of his imagination. He would love to see her succeed, but how could she possibly fight the opposition? Without a doubt, she was working against a pretty strong adversary.

There was no question in his mind that the operation Kara had established was destined for success. He knew now that others could see this too. All the components were in place. Her property, the location, equipment, product, marketing; the only problem he could see holding her back was under-capitalization. The most visible thing keeping her from making the expansion she desired was her inability to convince the banks to back her play.

The underlying reason she had been thwarted from her goal was slowly surfacing. The powers that be were using their weight of financial leverage by preventing the much needed loans from being exercised.

And why? Why else would they withhold a perfectly suitable loan? It had to follow that Howard Curry was making certain offers to those people who could ensure a considerable kick-back. The enterprise was a golden egg to be bartered by those in control for those most able to return the favor. He wanted to somehow confirm these newly formed suspicions before he decided exactly what was to be done about it.

In the meantime, there was this lovely girl to be attended to, and an equally delectable meal to be eaten. Tom needed to stop thinking so seriously about Kara's problems.

"Are you going to sleep on me? You've been very quiet!" Beth brought Tom out of his reverie. "Don't you know, you're supposed to take a siesta *after* you have lunch? Anyway, I wasn't going to let you drop your wine glass. This Gewürtztraminer is lovely. Soft, compared to some of the very astringent whites. Very spring-like…floral. Sometimes I like it with a good Ementhaler cheese." She chattered on and on. Little Beth was acting as nervous as a fox.

"Of course, I might have known you would be pretty knowledgeable about wines." He tried the compliment to neutralize her disquiet. "You must like working at Mountain View...Been there long?"

"Sometimes I think maybe too long, but actually it's only been a couple of years. When I think back to the time I started, I realize how much I've learned about the wine industry. I should be grateful for that. Of course, Kara has been a wonderful teacher!"

Was there a hint of peevishness he heard? Perhaps not. He began to listen now. He looked interested in her every word. Without asking, he poured more wine, and prompted her to continue.

"What's really great about this work is that you aren't locked in to just one job. I mean, there are so many facets to the winery. Sometimes you have to be out in the vineyard either collecting data or even working on the vines, taking the place of someone who is out sick. Then there's the winery work itself. I've been asked to do everything from cleaning, to paperwork, to rolling barrels around for washing. I don't think there is a job description that would fully outline all the things that have to be done during the harvest. And last, but not least, there's the *festival*!" She finished by rolling her shoulders with eyes cast to the heavens to accentuate the gravity of the intensified activity.

"Tell me more about the festival. I wanted to ask about that."

"For openers, I don't know if it's a blessing or a curse. It's an unavoidable event that happens every year. We work like killer bees on a victim, party to the max on that weekend, and hope we can forget what disasters took place the night before while we're cleaning up the mess the morning after. All in all, a great party. The guests keep coming back every year for more, so I guess it's a roaring success."

"Do you make money on it?"

"How like a banker to ask."

By her own statement she reminded herself to guard her words. She held out her glass for him to pour and for a moment reflected on the color of his skin. The elegant tan that must have been accumulated in out-of-door activity looked healthy and altogether too touchable. In spite of the internal warnings, she could feel an arousal that stemmed partly from the wine they had been drinking. He was starting to look *verry* sexy!

"I really wasn't trying to pry. It just appears to be a sound source of revenue, that is besides being hard work and an enjoyable event at the same time." He too was starting to feel the effects of the wine. Perhaps this would turn out to be a better afternoon than he anticipated. He stared at her.

"Well, I don't know much about making money, but I definitely approve of enjoyable events. And I think it would be a sin not to take advantage of this wonderful sunshine." She stretched out on the blanket ignoring his stare. Her own soft skin glowed with a light tan and her legs were exposed as one by one she undid the buttons from the bottom of her skirt slowly to the top, exposing to the elements the hip that was encased only by the thong of her panty. Her arms and legs embraced the sunlight as she felt the warmth between them.

Tom was staggered by her suggestive movements. His body responded even before he could think. He really didn't want to think. But on the other hand, he didn't want to get in too deep with this girl. Interesting thought. Bad pun.

"Wha's up?" Amused, she was looking directly at the uncontrolled erection.

God! What else could he do now? He played it off, leaning over her with one hand holding his glass of wine and the other, with just the back of his finger stroking the exposed flank, teasing between her flesh and the elastic band of the undergarment. Finally, and with great delicacy and gentleness, he removed the folds of fabric from her already exposed legs and replied, "I think I'm about to over-extend my account here."

"You have ample credit in my institution." He was responding according to her plan. The spell was definitely woven as he tenderly slipped the thong from her body and tossed it into the sparkling stream. Beth went with the flow.

"'I'm famished! I've worked up an appetite." Tom was dazzled. He had never acted on such an impromptu turn-on before. His head was spinning to think of how quickly he had responded to Beth's witchery. Was he that much in need of a woman? Probably. It had been a while. All he knew now, was that he felt damned good.

They now directed their attention to the bounty of the picnic. The instinct of the provider surfaced. He wanted to ply her with food. Beth had no quarrel with that. She, too was hungry.

"Help me dig into the grocery bags and I'll put together a meal that will be suitable for a queen, and you can tell me what it was you wanted to talk to me about. Kara did say there was something on your mind you wanted to discuss. Personal matters?" he asked confidentially.

It was Beth's turn to become serious. Tom was stricken by the similarity between Beth and Kara. It was in the way they were able to conclude one situation and immediately focus on the next. They unpacked the food, and he could see that Beth was shifting gears before going into her story.

To his surprise, she was candid and forthcoming. To begin with, Beth disclosed how she had privately found a way to earn quite a lot of cash. More money in fact, than she knew what to do with, and now she needed to find a home for it.

The 'plan' started at about the time she commenced working for Kara Tower and the winery. The 'plan' came into being when she found that she could only afford to rent a cheap, run-down trailer on a secluded property. It was off a residential street, down a tree lined dirt road that was heavily rutted by time and weather. Anyone casually passing the entrance to the driveway could not see the residence from the street, the trees and bushes were so dense. She was especially pleased by the privacy this location imparted. She would have no visitors.

The owners of the property were from out of state, well to do, and had no interest in the rental other than collecting the small monthly payments from whom they considered was a caretaker for their unwanted property. These payments were merely a token amount, with the agreement that within a three-year period, Beth would have the option to purchase the property at a set price, the rental monies acting as her down-payment. It was a very good, working deal.

Beth said nothing about it to them, but proceeded to clean up the trailer, turning it into a comfortable retreat. By the time she was settled, it was a pretty little dollhouse where she could hide from the world, the perfect place from which to operate her clandestine 'plan'.

The first time she implemented this 'plan', it was anything but prearranged. The occasion arose when Turner had caught up with her in town, and since it was the weekend, they decided to visit a friend who was having a party. Musicians in the area often collected informally to practice there. Jam sessions were not uncommon at these garden parties of a Saturday afternoon. There was always plenty to drink and plenty of smoke to pass around. Turner and Beth took the usual half-rack of beer with them and settled back to enjoy.

It was an interesting melange of people, represented by all ages including children. The only common bond among the adult parents was their apparent disinterest in their grooming. She had never seen so many raggedy tots. It offended her. In fact, she had never seen youngsters in such close proximity to the drugs and smoke that were so obviously being used. God forbid the kids could get their dirty little hands on any of mommy and daddy's 'stuff'. How could these people be so irresponsible, she wondered. Sure, she knew lots of people did drugs; that was their business. She also knew that these kids were being exposed far beyond what was appropriate. She was so appalled, she forced herself to think of other things, like listening to the music and drinking beer.

As nature would have it after a while, Beth felt the need to make a trip to the powder room in the house. The exceptionally formidable sweet-pungent odor of marijuana struck the senses as she entered the area of the bathroom. It was like a blast of permeating atmosphere. It emanated from the back room. There was no one around. She quietly poked about until she found it.

The closet was *stuffed* with great, vigorous green plants hung upside-down. The valuable colas swelled at the bottom ends. Drying in that enclosed area, they were heavy with scent. Normally the plants would reach this stage of harvest during the autumn months, but at this time of year, these plants could only come from an indoor growing operation. No doubt, a large one! She closed the door, finished her business in the bathroom and went out to join Turner. She said absolutely nothing about the discovery.

It wasn't until the next day that Beth knew what she would do.

She experienced a heart pounding thrill as the first thoughts emerged from the farthest recesses of her mind. At first they were scenarios that came to her in *what if* situations. Like, *what if* the entire crop fell into her hands. Nearly everyone she knew, at all levels of social strata, indulged in a toke or two. How hard could it be to make connections with these people when she was out of town, disbursing the marijuana for money. At least this way, she knew it wouldn't wind up in the hands of kids, let alone their lungs. How hard *could* it be? *What if* she checked it out to see if anyone was watching over that stash of weed.

Without excusing herself, or letting anyone know she was leaving work on Monday, she hastened to her car and drove quickly to the house where the party had taken place couple of days before. At mid-day, no one was around. It looked like an entirely different setting without the action and the people there. She discerned no movement at all coming from within the house. Beth had confidence that this would be the case because everyone would be at work, or at least pretending to be involved in some sort of job activity, and with her heart beating like a turbo, she walked up to the front door and knocked.

No answer.

Her hand reached out and took the handle and opened it.

She was prepared to tell an unexpected occupant that she had left a sweater, a scarf, a tampon…Christ, she didn't know what she would say that she left behind the other day…something. But no one was there.

Beth made a dash for the closet. She snatched nearly half the plants there, stuck them in the big plastic garbage bag she had brought along, and rushed them out to her car. That was too easy! Should she go back for the rest? They would kill her if someone appeared and apprehended her 'in the act'. Take a greater risk of being caught?. Yes!! She ran back into the house. One more trip and she had it all.

When the plants were crammed on the floor and back seat of the car and safely hidden under a car blanket, a dozen items that had inhabited the passenger area were thrown on top. Camouflage! She jumped into the driver's side and got the hell out of Dodge. A vapor tail of scent following her.

Moving more quickly than she had ever moved before, Beth concealed the drying plants near her trailer on the rented property, and before anyone knew she had been missing from work, she returned. A *fait accompli*. No one knew she had been gone.

And that was how the most lucrative enterprise she had ever known in her life had first come into being. What a plan!

Beth applied herself to learning the subtleties of preparing the whole marijuana plants into saleable quantities, as well as which parts of the growth would be more expensive than others. She acquainted herself with the street prices of the product and was at once overwhelmed at the prospect of how much money could be realized.

There was never a time that she would establish herself as a regular 'connection'. She was careful enough to never, but never do business when she was on her home ground. Working for the winery gave her the perfect opportunity to move anywhere in the country selling her wares without a soul asking or suspecting where the pot came from.

Yes. She made money. And any time she could make a score like the first one, she took advantage of it. Beth kept her eyes and ears alert and was often rewarded by the knowledge of a stash or 'grow patch'. It began to thrill her incredibly when she went off to pilfer the 'magic weed'; a seductive enterprise. She came to think of it as her personal 'extreme sport'. Always, she worked alone.

This was the moneymaker she had never experienced before. It would be difficult to give it up, but part of her 'plan' was to discontinue the illegal activity when a certain ceiling of money was amassed.

This was the point at which she had arrived when she informed Tom without being specific about the details, that not too long ago, she had come into some cash. It wasn't a huge amount, she said, and she didn't want to let anyone know that it even existed. She wanted to invest in something, but at the moment she hadn't even opened a bank account for it.

"You mean this money is just sitting around in something like a sock?" he asked, chiding her. Tom could be courteous in the extreme when discussing money, but in this case he chastised her gently.

"Yes," she answered.

"I see." He really didn't see at all, but he intended to find out if he could. "May I ask, and this would be in confidence, how much are we talking about?"

She had no intention of sharing her private information about her money with anyone, even somebody supposedly as trustworthy as Tom Hutchins. Her compulsion to speak with him about it arose from her need for professional advise as to how to go about investing. She would only give him the barest of facts.

"Several thousand dollars," she said, wanting to distance him from the specifics of her holdings by her nebulous response.

"Well, unless we know the ballpark amount of what you have to work with, it may be difficult to point you in any particular direction. And Beth, I do understand that you may not want to divulge what it is you want to invest."

"Thanks for understanding." She was visibly relieved. "It's just that I've never done anything like this before, and I don't know who to go to." It was surprising that this girl, with her outgoing personality, could be faced with this kind of dilemma. Of course for him, the answer was so simple! He was struck by the lack of sophistication in someone who by all rights should have been far more intellectually creative.

"I think I can help you, so don't worry. I'll be back at the office tomorrow and I'll give you a call with the name of an investment broker we have used for some years now. He'll be able to not only answer all your questions, but assist you in placing your money."

"Oh Tom, thank you so much! Just one other thing?"

"What is it?"

"Please don't mention this to anyone?" She formed her request as to elicit a confirmation.

He gave a penetrating look at this naive, helpless girl-devil. "My lips are sealed!"

"Great! Now can we get on with that well-advertised lunch you've been promising?"

CHAPTER 18

❀

"I hope Tom Hutchins takes it all right. He thinks I'll be back to meet with him this afternoon."

Kara and Turner had just finished setting up their campsite beside the river. In a state that was known for exceptional scenery, the North Umpqua was among one of the most beautiful rivers in Oregon, including its surrounding watershed. The designation of the area as 'fly fishing only' set it apart from most other waterways inasmuch as the quality of fishing was enhanced to the point of being accepted as a world-wide Mecca for fly fishing enthusiasts.

Little time was spent on thinking back to the business of the winery while she was totally engrossed in helping with the organization of their camping gear. The trip driving up here gave her too much time to think as it was. Now, her attention was on locating the equipment. Even the barest necessities for staying a couple of days involved tenting, sleeping bags, clothing, camp stove, lantern, fishing paraphernalia, and of course the mandatory games, playing cards, and other superfluous items that were thrown into 'Curley' at the moment of departure. There was plenty to unpack and coordinate.

"You know that Beth will take care of Hutchins. Not to be disrespectful, but by the time she gets around to telling him you won't be back for a couple of days, he probably won't even care."

Kara was taken aback by this statement. It was probably true. Tom may have expressed interest in her business, but she couldn't, she admonished herself, expect him to take up his valuable time waiting for her to return…especially in view of the fact that she was off playing hooky with a co-worker. At the same time, she hoped that the rapport they were building would be of some positive consequence. The way things worked out, it was her hope that Beth would be the catalyst to act as bonding agent until her return.

In the hidden passages of her mind, Kara truthfully wanted him to care about what happened to Mountain View. It was touching that he had taken the initiative to act on his curiosity regarding her loan. She wanted Tom with his background of knowledge to be available to her at this precarious time.

"Isn't it fortunate that she wanted to get together with him," she countered Turner's jab. "Her timing was perfect for her to cover for me. Still," she went on, "I wonder what it was all about…her wanting to talk to Tom Hutchins. It doesn't seem in character for Beth to be courting the idea of having conversations with a banker type."

"Ours not to question why! Even then I would say that Beth would court the idea, as you put it, of having conversations with any guy…doctor, lawyer, or banker man," he intoned. "The only criteria that she requires, is that it wears pants!"

"Sounds like sour grapes, fella. Are you sure you haven't completely gotten over her?"

"Like the sore throat I had last month."

"You say she's a thing of the past, but I do sense a troublesome reaction to her extracurricular activities." She kept it light.

Kara was always careful not to make any of her comments too solemn. After all, she was a good deal older than Turner and would feel foolish if she took their relationship any more seriously than it should be. It would be silly for either of them to consider anything more substantial than a friendship. She could joke about Beth.

Looking realistically at her past associations with men, she was glad to have kept a certain dignity in dealing with them. Her propinquity for attracting men of younger years predetermined that there would be a limited length of time for any relationship, and inevitably a time when an affair, if it was an affair, would pale. In any case, brief affairs eventually became untenable and ended. There was always the point at which the most enlightened action was to keep your chin up and walk away from the situation. In this way, no one could be seriously hurt. It was a built-in safety factor that kept her from fruitless involvement in a serious relationship.

"For Christ sake, Kara. I got over her the first time I noticed her watching that scumball, Talbert; not that she ever dated him. He even creeps me out! God, what a perfect name for a dildo like him! Talbert!" He made a face.

They had paused, having completed their camp set-up. They perched on the river rocks for a moment of streamside conversation. Turner was casting flattened pebbles into the water as it rushed by, making them bounce. "Now, there's a marriage made in heaven...Think about it. Talbert sneaks around, sometimes here, sometimes there, but nobody really has a handle on the guy. Beth, on the other hand doesn't sneak. I think she has mega brain power compared to Talbert, but again, nobody really has a handle on her. She just disappears at the end of the day. An enigma."

"Turner, we're all entitled to whatever little privacy we have." He wondered at her ability to sympathize with so many people, half of whom he thought of as mindless cretins. She went on, "Think about what you're saying. Probably one of your *own* most precious freedoms is the ability to back away from people when you feel the need. No one else should want to know where you go, or what you do when you decide to make a retreat into your own world when you're looking to be alone.

"I guess what I'm trying to say is that everybody does things because they have a reason. It may not be a *good* reason based on your standards, or my standards, but others don't have to live by our ideas. If they're not hurting anyone, what people do and how they act is something that should be accepted, not judged. If it's possible to understand why someone does something...fine. If you can't understand, just accept it."

"Okay, okay. I'll admit I was out of line to talk about Beth. But what about somebody like Talbert. He *is* strange, and I know damned well he was behind the theft of wine out of the warehouse. Have you figured out what to do about that? I say, fire the guy!"

"I was thinking about it on the way up here. If we let him go now, I don't think we'll ever find out how he got away with entering the 'big' room and making off with a barrel. Think of it, a barrel would be pretty hard for one person alone to move. Even a small barrel is extremely heavy when it's full. There must have been more than one person doing this. Anyway, Digby acted like it was the end of the world when he found his precious wine missing."

"What a loyal winemaker!"

"He said he wouldn't stop until he learned who did this. Maybe if we work together...Turner, we have to help him find these thieves!"

"Yeah. You're right. Maybe if we stay quiet about this, whoever did it might try the same thing again since it was so easy to get away with. We'll catch him yet! Good plan!"

"All right," she agreed. "Except unfortunately, we have no way of consistently watching the place. With the festival coming up, all the available people will be too busy, including you. Nobody's going to have the time to physically keep an eye on the winery twenty-four hours a day."

Sitting there on the ground, with her arms propped on her knees, she dropped her head in a defeated gesture. She'd had her fill of problems. Turner had never seen her look so vulnerable.

"Kara...I hate like hell to see you have to deal with this. I want to be able to do something."

She raised her head. "I know." His concern was deeply appreciated. If he could help her with this one incident, she might be able to tackle the others, one by one. She hadn't told him about everything.

"How 'bout something to eat? Make you feel better. You rest there little darlin' and I'll rustle up some grub." He gave her his best John Wayne impersonation, attempting to lighten her mood.

"I'd love it! Go shoot a buffalo," Kara returned. This is how it worked when your partner was a strong, young man and aiming to please. He deferred to the age of his woman and 'did' for her as he probably would not 'do' for a younger girl. She took full advantage of the situation and had to enjoy every minute of it.

During this hiatus of activity, her thoughts drifted back to her winery in spite of her efforts not to do so.

"I need that balance beam!" Digby was irate at the disappearance of the scale. Having a weighing device at hand was a *must* for the winemaking technician, especially during the time after harvest when the grapes were being processed into wine.

"We'll get another as soon as we can." The Ohaus balance scale was there one day and gone the next. Who could have taken it? No use to call the authorities as they had in the recent past when the cash register had disappeared right off the bar in the tasting room. It was never seen again.

"Aren't you at least going to take fingerprints or something?" she had asked the police.

"With all the people going through here Ms. Tower, we just couldn't separate the prints. Don't you have any idea who might have done this? Surely you know who would have had access to the cash register. You said it was a new one. Can you think of anyone who might be suspicious?"

The police were polite, but not very helpful. Kara would not consider any of her employees as possible burglars. She depended on them, and they depended on her. She could not, by the furthest stretch of the imagination think of any of them as being candidates as perpetrators. The furthest it went in getting action from the police investigation was having her name and the winery mentioned as victims of a robbery in the newspapers. The headline read *"Mountain View Winery Targeted as Easy Prey".* Nothing like publicity, she thought cynically and decided then and there that in the future it was better to say nothing; and better yet, do something about catching the thief themselves.

It was constantly surprising how many small things kept disappearing. More and more, the employees were noticing tools that couldn't be found. Fertilizers that suddenly were not all there when they needed them. Gasoline from the supply tanks having to be replenished more frequently than ever. And the most personal items missing, hurting Kara more than she would ever express to anyone. Jewelry that was taken out of her home. Precious, irreplaceable gifts from loving friends and family.

There was no way she concluded, that one person or even a couple of people could have done the damage that was slowly being done to her and her business. It was like being eaten away from one side and then the other. A bite here. A nibble there. It had to stop or she would be eaten to death.

But what to do, she lamented. These were problems she could not tackle at present. Not at least until the financial needs were met. Finding solutions to those problems were all-important.

Until Mountain View received the loans that were compatible with all the viable cash flow analyses that had been made, her position would be precarious at best. Cash for operating was getting so scarce that she didn't want to face the fact that this year's harvest would be completely impossible. Storage for prior year's vintages was becoming untenable. There just wasn't enough space. They had to have a new building for storage of finished product, or the whole strategy for a successful expansion would be down the tubes. In this business you either grew, or you faded away into oblivion. From now on it would be sink or swim. God only knew what she would do if she failed. Or rather, when she failed.

Well, it was good to have a day or two to gird herself for the work ahead. She would return home refreshed and recharged. Meanwhile, Turner was returning from their camp with a comfortable looking ground cover and the most beautiful picnic basket.

CHAPTER 19

"I'm becoming impatient!" Francis Gillman put his fork down to take a drink from the claret glass. The red wine was even better than he remembered it when it had been sampled at the Club tasting. "Mmm." He continued following an appreciative nod, "Now that we're this close, I'm beginning to see certain projects I want accomplished with the winery, and you know I can't do a damned thing until she gets the hell out of there."

Dinner at the restaurant overlooking the same river that ran by the winery had taken a toll on Gillman's restraint. Normally he wouldn't have been so outspoken, but he was given the idea by Howard Curry that possession of the coveted property was imminent. Not only imminent, but since Frank had turned over 'earnest money' to that little weasel at the bank, he was given to understand that Kara Tower was no longer in possession of the property. Now it turns out, she was totally unaware that she was expected to step down. She was going on with some pretty gutsy plans. Impossible woman!

"I'm not sure what to do next," he added shaking his head and looking a little as though someone had just died.

His companion was a little less vociferous, but he sympathized. "I know. After all Frank, we were primed for action. I left Washington last Friday thinking that there would be paperwork to take care of. Now, it seems we can do nothing better than bide our time until the property becomes available."

A glint of amused cunning entered Gillman's eyes as he said, "Clark, I'll bet six ways to Sunday that when you created Pacific Land, you didn't just wait around for business opportunities and acquisitions to 'become available.'"

They both chuckled remembering the early days when they first worked together in California. A symposium concerning land acquisitions had brought them there in their mutual interests.

They met, and soon found themselves the recipients of information regarding a fairly large construction outfit that was heavily in debt and on the brink of toppling. Recognizing the opportunity, they immediately contrived to find two of the major creditors and factored out their positions, paying seventy-five cents on the dollar. Then, Frank leaned heavily on the construction owner for full payment which he knew could not have been met, and *voila!* within a month, the business fell into the hands of the newly created Pacific Land Development. They had been fast friends ever since that time.

Certainly Clark had been more than generous in his gratitude for that windfall by including Francis Gillman in further business. They not only did well together, but had accumulated vastly successful holdings by their own ingenuity. It was still their habit to keep their eyes open for other opportunities.

"We both know what was done in the past. What have your got in mind for now?" Clark asked.

"I want to think of something we can do to hurry this thing up. Carl Bradshaw has the power to cut off the loans at the bank."

"Yes, but do you think he'll play ball with us? Go for the touchdown? I'm concerned that he might be developing sympathy for this woman. God, I hope not! That *would* throw a monkey wrench in the works."

"What do you think of using our old system?" Their voices had gone down a decibel or two, not wanting other customers of the restaurant to overhear as the room filled up with dinner guests. Frank continued, "We could buy out the winery's liabilities and call the debts. Wouldn't Bradshaw be forced to do one thing or the other then? The old bastard has been straddling the fence about that loan long enough. Surely we could convince him that it would be good for the community as well as the local industry to have an aggressive group running the shop. With Curry advising him to do that, how can he not cut her off?"

"Simple." Clark finished off the appetizer of oysters Rockefeller, and took another sip of an oak flavored California Chardonnay. "If she has the know-how, all she has to do is file a Chapter Eleven bankruptcy for a reorganization, and if she does that, nobody can touch her for a hell of a long time. That would mean years before any take-over could happen. It's only a question of which racehorse gets to the finish line first. Either she files, or we take over."

"Shit! Is all of this worth it?"

"Damned right it is, and you know it or you wouldn't be here."

It was then that they recognized Howard Curry approaching. Late again as usual for their dinner meeting.

Clark took a jab at him first by saying, "If you hurry up and order, you might just catch up by desert!"

"Sorry I'm late, just a few odds and ends to tie up. You know how it is on Monday." He gestured to the waiter and ordered a scotch mist.

He went on commiserating, "I realize how frustrating this has been for both of you. I want you to know that I've been working on solving the problems that came up unexpectedly. I told you that Mountain View would be made available at an unusually attractive price and I intend to come through with the deal." What he didn't say was that he also intended to get more money out of these tightwads!

CHAPTER 20

❀

Howard Curry had been busy indeed. Since Saturday night he had been nursing the hangover of the century. Nothing like wine to make you swear off drinking for the rest of your life! Or at least till some hair of the dog was available. His head still hurt like a sonovabitch!

At the wine tasting he knew he was getting out of hand, but he couldn't help it! All that wine, and oh yes, the drinks they had beforehand. He didn't touch any of the grazing food that was available. Simply put, he was too excited. Even after all those years of being in touch with the industry, it was something he never quite got over. Being caught up in the glamour of the event was in itself intoxicating. Everyone was hanging on to his every word and he just kept going. He was on a roll for the whole evening. They loved it! They loved him! That is, until that goddamn Hutchins gaffled him up and took him home.

But that wasn't the end of the evening, was it? He fooled everybody! They didn't know he had the pickup parked a short way from his apartment. He had been trying to unload the second-hand vehicle for about three months now. It had been purchased from a friend of a friend who said he needed a couple of hundred dollars right away. The pink slip, he was told, was sitting in Boise, Idaho, and as soon as the guy got there, he would send it. It never got sent. But Howard was always there for a good deal, so…there was the truck, sitting reproachfully, running good and begging to be used.

He had the presence of mind to stagger up to his place under the watchful gaze of his fellow work-mate who followed him to the door to let him in. In truth however, at this late hour he was beginning to sober up just a little. From behind the lavelour blinds, he witnessed Tom Hutchins backing out and leaving the parking area in his Toyota. Come to think of it, he was grateful to Tom for his foolish act of kindness. He could proceed with the idea that was forming in his head.

At first, on his arrival at the Club, Howard was surprised when he thought he saw Tom and Kara at the same table. He didn't want Tom to interfere with Tower and his plans for Mountain View. How much better it would be if she was totally out of the picture.

Then, as the evening went on, he overheard Peterson questioning Kara Tower about her wines. Fearing that she might recognize him, Howard kept apart from their conversation. There were enough people there to cover him while he listened in. He did hear Peterson ask if she knew Tom Hutchins from the bank, because he had heard that Tom was a wine enthusiast.

"Oh, really?" she had replied, "I'm glad to learn he's here. I hope he has the opportunity to taste some of the Mountain View wine. I heard from Carl Bradshaw that he's quite the connoisseur and I'd love to hear his comments." She had just received the message from Tom via his lady friend. *'Don't let them know we've met!'* the messenger had said. Kara played it off, but the consequence of that exchange was to inform Howard that she was by herself. That was, after all, the only thing he wanted to know. He had no desire to just stand around listening to the bitch.

The coup for the evening turned out to be Tom's insistence on taking Howard's car to drive him home, telling him that he could pick up his vehicle in the morning. The bonus was that now he would have an alibi in the event one should be needed later. Tom would be certain to say that he had escorted Howard to his door and then took his vehicle.

Meanwhile, Kara Tower would have to be driving home. That was the most important part of his plan, that she would be driving home *alone.*

As soon as the door shut on Tom Hutchins, Howard went directly to his bedroom. The apartment was small. The strictly masculine furnishings belied the fact that he really wasn't that interested in his masculinity. If anyone even considered his persuasion, it would have to be ascertained that he was, for the most part asexual. For the larger portion of his life, money and the machinations of power play held his interest to a far greater degree than associations with other human beings on a personal level. In fact, the alliances he had with several attractive women were more cosmetic than earnest relationships.

He went about changing his cloths. Levis, tee-shirt, jacket, Nikes. He looked like any other Oregonian in these parts. Okay, so the tennis shoes were a bit more expensive than the average guy could afford, but they would do.

It wasn't at all difficult to jockey into the position he wanted in order to follow Kara's Mustang down the highway. He had simply waited for her car to leave the Club driveway and took his place, pacing the car colored midnight blue, at a discrete distance.

The old truck ran amiably along. At times, two or three cars separated them. Most of the time he stayed directly behind her. She would never suspect she was being followed. It was dark, and no one would recognize the old Chevy anyway. If he were any more ambiguous in this traffic, he'd be invisible.

Although he was not absolutely sure of the off-ramp she would be taking, he guessed correctly that it would be relatively remote, and according to his plan, would be obscured enough for him to do what he intended.

Her right signal was on. He maneuvered to the right.

As if in slow motion, the Mustang came to a brief stop at the bottom of the off-ramp. The left signal indicated the driver's intention to make a left, and the car started into the turn. Howard gunned the truck and it responded to his heavy foot on the pedal. He sped up instantly on the downhill and aimed at the driver's door of Kara's Mustang with the intention of ramming into it broadside as it swung to make the left under the freeway. If he did it the way he had envisioned, he would hit her car squarely in the center. The driver would be flattened!

Jesus Christ, his mind flashed, what the fuck was she doing! Shit!!

The other car had not continued at its slower pace. Instead, it seemed to do a pirouette around the front, swinging the back side out of the path of the pickup. After the evening's libations, Howard's reflexes were not what they should have been. Missing the target by a fraction of an inch, he careened into the far side of a ditch at the edge of the road at full speed. Foliage came tumbling around the truck as jolt snapped the hood up to meet the windshield.

He was brutally shaken from the abrupt halt. It took moments before he knew precisely what had happened. Still in one piece however, thanks to the mandatory seatbelt, he checked each of his body parts one by one to make sure everything was functioning. Arms, legs, neck. The neck was questionable. He'd know tomorrow.

Shit! Shit! Shit! I'd better get the fuck out of here. Somebody's going to call the cops. Leave the truck where it is!

Sober now, he struggled out of the cab, paused and leaned over the steering wheel to wipe it and the door handles with the jacket sleeve. No use leaving prints all over the place even though vehicle wasn't registered. There would be no paperwork tracing the pickup back to him.

Howard put as much distance between himself and the truck as was possible at that hour before he attempted to hitch a ride back to Medford. His adrenaline was rushing. He could feel it course through his system. His anger fed upon itself as he grasped how ineffectual he had been in his attempt at removing Kara Tower. She was an obstruction to his designs. And it wasn't the first time.

The long walk that night gave him plenty of time to reflect on the past. He needed a drink!

CHAPTER 21

❀

Howard Curry-Cottner had moved to Oregon in an attempt to flee the long arm of the law in the state of Florida. It wasn't like he was a criminal. No, he had simply taken advantage of what he knew he deserved, even if his boss, the owner of the business didn't know anything about it.

Howard was ambitious, carrying two jobs at the same time. He worked part time filling in as a night attendant for one of the larger hotels in Miami, but his main job was working as a paper pusher for a small industrial parts supply house. Actually, he was pretty happy there. The kind of activity that he excelled in was the hustle of buying and selling. It didn't take long for him to discover how really inventive he could be. If given enough slack to pull off some of the transactions, he could turn over a quick buck for himself, and who would be the wiser?

This of course went on until one day his boss, a harridan of a woman, presented some paperwork and shipping documents with a flourish, showing that a transaction had been made with Cottner's name on it. At that time, he never used his fully hyphenated name. "But where Howard, is the receivable? It clearly shows that the customer has paid, but no credit to our account is shown on the books. I don't even see a purchase order in the customer's name! So Howard, where the hell is it?" The owner knew perfectly well that the transaction was Howard's and that the money had been absorbed into Howard's own bank account.

Cottner had very little to say at the time. He was too busy being humiliated in front of his co-workers. He did have the presence of mind to extricate what few belongings he had accumulated, and by that afternoon he was out of there. Out of the city. He took the money and ran…to Oregon.

The journey across country was by bus. The ambling stop and go of the trip was, he imagined like being in prison where any and all schedules were dealt by the 'man', leaving no decisions for himself. This, he felt was his way of doing penance, not for embezzling money, but for being caught. Anyway, the old codger he worked for wouldn't bust a grape to try to locate him once he disappeared. It was in that week that he promised himself that from now on he would run his own show and design his own schedules. He even planned changes in his appearance to accommodate the new life he anticipated. Let his hair get a little longer and give his emerging beard a chance to grow. He thoughtfully decided he would express himself in a more casual demeanor, more appropriate to the west coast.

There was only one person he knew who lived in southern Oregon. This was a distant, very distant cousin. They had talked some time ago, and Howard was intrigued even then with the growing area. Someday he would go there, and that someday was now.

"How're ya doin?"

"Christ...Howard! I remember you talked about visiting this neck of the woods, but I never thought you'd actually do it."

They were sitting at the kitchen table, where a plain looking girl had poured them cups of steaming coffee. The house was old, and he could see was far from being loved. The furnishings were shabby and the dishes piled in the sink bespoke the acceptance of daily sloth. The morning light shone in the dirty windows with the fierce determination that only clear sky and clean air can render. It exposed any and all defects in the room. The air inside smelled like dirty laundry and stale beer.

"Sunny here was just fixin to go to work." He slapped her smartly on her generous backside as he hustled her out of the kitchen and then out the front door. "Bet you're beat after ridin all that distance. Sleep at all last night?" It was morning, and strange to tell, Howard felt curiously energetic. By all rights the trip should have left him feeling wrung out.

"Buddy, I could probably sleep if you hung me up on a hook on the wall, but right now, I'm so goddamn glad to be off that bus, all I want to do is par-tay."

They spent the rest of the day and the next, talking about the town and the kinds of work that might be available. He learned that his Oregon cousin wasn't exactly ambitious when it came to getting a job. Howard learned with growing disappointment that in fact, he was definitely a loser.

One of the first things on Howard's mind was to follow up any classified work ads. For the first week, he often went out for interviews in search of a new position. He was looking for something that would give him the freedom to work at his own pace, yet give him a dependable salary. A position in sales would be his preference. He would continue looking until he found what he was after.

The used car he purchased was the only other vehicle in the household besides Sunny's. And Sunny was usually at her job as a waitress. Before he left the house, he learned quickly to expect to be asked for one favor or another in the way of picking up a package, dropping off a parcel. It didn't take long to figure out that when they stopped at one of his cousin's 'places', it usually involved the purchase or sale of whatever might be illegal.

"Since we're goin that way, you mind we stop by a place? Oughta be right on the way to where you're goin." Howard couldn't very well say no to the guy. Especially when he was staying at his house.

Actually, it wasn't even his house. Cottner got the picture that this was Sunny's house! What a misnomer, he thought. Her disposition wasn't exactly what you could call real sunny. But he noted that the homely girl was grateful just to have a man to come home to…she was being sponged.

Thus began Howard's Oregon tenure. He at long last landed a job that took him from Sunny's domain to a more suitable as well as convenient apartment. He was more than glad to get away from their depressing low-life.

He said good-by to Sunny and his cousin Talbert.

Working as a distributor's representative was fun! Chameleon attributes were not only useful, but essential. Howard managed to fit his role like a typecast actor. Not only did he look the part, but he was energetic, and expressly resourceful in marketing development. His initial job was that of merely delivery boy. He quickly progressed from that function to taking orders from the established customers. Both jobs were field work which gave him a great opportunity to become intimately acquainted with the outlying area.

Braverly Wine Distributors was *not* a huge operation. There were under twenty employees. This accounted for the more than usual periodic changes of activity for most of the hired hands. In most of the larger businesses, an employee would be hired for one position and forevermore would be stuck doing the same thing day in and day out. Not so at Braverly. All of the Braverly people were expected to fill in jobs wherever necessity required. Answer phones, drive trucks, be a gopher. If Howard were asked to clean the latrines, he would do it. He may not like it, but he would do it.

Within the first year of association with the owners and the managers of the distributorship, Howard Cottner had proven his ability not only to move product, but gain the audience of some of the largest distribution centers and key people. He was becoming an integral part of the 'good old boys' networking. No doubt about it, he could wheel and deal with the best of them.

And how was this accomplished? Little Howard had a formula!

In order to sell, he concluded it was not the quality or uniqueness of the product in question that was of ultimate concern to the buyer. He could stand there all day trying to convince a storekeeper or restaurant manager of how superior his wines were. He would pour it down their throats if he could. Predictably the response from the prospective customer would usually be, "Very nice. We're not adding anything to our wine list at present, but you can stop in next month!" Sure, like they would have space on the list by then! Of course, Braverly represented wines that were more than adequate in quality. No need to worry about that. It was simply a point of fact that something *more* had to be done in order to have the impact to make the important sales that were necessary for success.

It was because of the brick wall he encountered in his first attempts at marketing several wine labels, that he formulated the tactic that always worked in the long run. Adding to the well worn stratagem of supply and demand, the element of *necessity* became the foremost tool in Howard Cottner's repertoire. His product, above all others must be *needed* for the shelves and tables of the purveyors of wine.

The first step Cottner took was to look at one of the larger market chains. They all carried the same brands in the beverage section. He would then determine which, of several wines, would need to be discontinued in order to leave an obvious vacancy in their customer's selection. The name of the game was 'available space'. He wanted whatever available space he could get for *his* product. Greed motivated him. Howard had a one track mind. His credo was to beat the other guy at the game.

He would then connect with the appropriate wineries, the ones he wanted *off* the shelves, reaching the sales managers to set up a meeting. Within a short time, an attractive offer by the owner of Braverly Wines would be made to the winery. It was a simple matter to court the winery, gaining their interest by making grandiose promises of large volume distribution and a mutually beneficial relationship. Tremendous growth of sales was the normal bait used for luring the companies away from their current distributors. These were empty promises at best. However, one by one, based on the Braverly presentation, each of the wineries would eventually express dissatisfaction with their existing distribution, and one by one they met with the principals of the Braverly company. New liaisons were created for the benefit of…who?

Once committed to the new distributor, Howard had *complete* control of the placement for all of their wineries' products. He could concentrate on whichever wines he picked to be successful, and on the other side of the coin, those wines that he picked to be overlooked. He was playing God to these businesses, and he felt damned smug about it.

Cottner went on to apply his 'formula' with restaurants and any other retailers he deemed of importance to his marketing plans. With this blueprint in place, it was a simple matter to promote the wines of his choice, with emphasis on the ones that returned his favors tenfold. He pointedly rewarded those entrepreneurs who were generous with him.

On the other hand, those who didn't know how the game was played were *out*! In particular, he remembered that the Mountain View label had, at one time, been a public favorite. As soon as Braverly had Kara Tower's wine tied up for distribution, he certainly changed that picture. Every time he went out to place his products in new accounts, he would replace the Mountain View label with another label of his choice. Little by little her sales dropped. She would puzzle herself about the reason for this. Braverly would inform her that her pricing wasn't favorable, or the public just wasn't buying her wines. She would be polite to her distributors. After all, they were doing their best!

Her winery was a thorn in his side ever since its early popularity was the cause of several lost sales. Worse, it was owned outright by this woman who in his estimation, didn't look as though she could count to ten. His experience with women in business he remembered had been less than encouraging. He wouldn't forget the one who humiliated him in front of other employees before firing him. Someday, he considered returning to Florida just to turn the tables on that bitch. She had a little punishment coming.

Kara Tower was so much like this other woman, he could puke. There was something about her nature that was intolerably abrading to him. He couldn't deal with it. It was only reasonable that he replace the wines from her winery with the ones of his choice. It would hurt her marketing. Hurt her. She deserved it. At least, he placated himself, he could avoid seeing her personally. No need to take chances of being rude to her when it was to his advantage for her to continue with their company. He made sure that any negotiations with Mountain View would be made by his superiors. They were always gracious to their suppliers. They would keep her hanging on.

For three years, Howard was the spokesman for his chosen clients, and he represented them as successfully as he ignored and overlooked the others. Some of his affiliate businesses grew substantially because of his promotions. Some could do no more than wither away. Howard was the controlling factor, and they weren't even aware of the power he wielded.

This state of affairs would have continued indefinitely had it not been for Dan Braverly's bad heart. One moment, he and his business were purring along smoothly and the next moment…nothing. Once in his grave, the organization was disassembled, their hard earned clients being cast upon the hungry waters of other distribution channels.

Only after the dissolution of Braverly Wines, and the eventual settling of the newly abandoned wineries into the hands of their new distributors, it was discovered on several levels that this Mr. Howard Cottner was not always operating on an even or legal keel. His many under-the-table manipulations, promises, bribes and intrigues were finally catching up with him. The time had come for him to become a chameleon again and change his colors. The current affectation of the young bearded, ponytailed, outgoing, flamboyant salesman would have to come to an end. He needed to become something different, quite different.

Clever, he thought. It was so easy to have made the change from a legally hyphenated surname. For simplicity he had always avoided its use. Now, to help him disappear, he would utilize only the one name that would render it difficult for anyone follow his metamorphosis into another new life.

He took on his mother's maiden name and Howard Curry was born.

PART II

❦

THE PRODUCTION

CHAPTER 22

Of all the busy times of the year, it had to be spring that was most demanding on the energies and patience of the people of Mountain View Winery. The work seemed to double and triple by the mandates of vineyard work, bottling schedules and the annual affair, better known as the *Festival*.

The concept was one that emulated some of the more artistic gatherings of earlier times preceding the development of the wine industry in America. Long before California became the colossus of producers, it was often the smaller, family owned farms and wineries that celebrated the first bottling of the prior harvest, honoring the new vintage with song, dance, art, and food. Legions of each!

In the trail of this well-accepted tradition, the members of the Mountain View Winery workforce joined together for an all-out effort to bring to their community an event carrying the flavor of those earlier times; in countries so far away.

For this Oregon winery, the days and weeks before the event were marked off as in a countdown. Both time and projects were itemized and checked off the master schedule as the days wore on. Whatever future plans were made by any of the participants beyond the weekend of the festival were obscured and took an unimportant back seat to the activities at hand. Anything personal or financial was postponed for another day. Do it after the festival was the unspoken hue and cry! At this point, the *world* came after the festival!!

With the tension growing long and time growing short, personalities clashed unavoidably at closer and closer intervals. Catastrophes involving last minute scheduling appeared to be more imminent by the hour. Those who were temperamental had license to amplify their inherent traits. It could be ugly or beautiful. At times it was not surprising to see all hell break loose, and a moment later, a surge of bonding with those involved. It was nothing short of a miracle to witness the whole undertaking come together into a meaningful design. And yet, since all the past annual productions had been successful, there was no need actually to stress over what might go wrong. No matter what transpired unexpectedly, what disaster or knotty problem, it would all be sorted out in the end, and the show would go on!

CHAPTER 23

❀

Kara had brought a great bouquet of flowers and greenery to the house. The basket and gunny sack she used for carrying them were full to the brim. She had smudges of dirt on her face, and her large heavily lashed green eyes appeared to have a smile of their own. For all the times she was expected to wear make up and dress for more formal occasions to look her best, she never looked more beautiful than now.

This was one of her favorite activities. She loved her garden and appreciated the truism that the garden was better for having been picked, and the house for having the bounty of the garden.

An assortment of glass and ceramic vases were spread out in the kitchen, waiting for their transformation into the casual little works of nature's art, later to be seen peeking out from a bookcase, adorning a corner, or presented in full splendor at the entrance table leading to the living room.

"I don't have your knack, but can I give you a hand?" Beth peeked around the door. She had been in the service porch delivering the paper goods that would be used on the weekend. Paper towels, napkins, water cups, tickets for the entrance. She had picked them up at the local discount store along with a car full of other supplies, all slated for the festival. She had listed every item, labeling where they all would go. Netta would disburse what they needed to each of the designated sites. Beth was a very good planner and director.

What she couldn't know was how many of those items in the past had disappeared into the homes and kitchens of others who helped themselves, using their 'five-finger discount'. Her system, she thought would alleviate some of those problems.

"Sure. I'd love some help. Somehow it just cheers me up to have flowers and greenery in every room."

"You need some cheering?"

"No, not really…well, maybe a little. When Turner and I got back from the mountains, I tried to make an appointment with those bankers. Beth, they haven't given me any answers yet and it's too frustrating. I wanted to see them this week, but I can't seem to make connections with them on the phone. They're not answering my calls."

"Do you think they're avoiding you?"

"No, not really." Kara didn't sound too convincing.

"When Tom left here, *he* didn't look like he would be avoiding any of us. He was…congenial." She downplayed his earlier enthusiasm.

Kara tried not to think about what had transpired between Beth and Tom on Sunday…but actually, she was dying of curiosity. She controlled the urge to ask for the details. After all, what Beth did was a private matter, and who was she to butt in? In truth, there wasn't time to think about that just now. Beth would tell her about it in due course. She contrived to stay on the subject.

"That's a relief. Since I was unable to reach Mr. Bradshaw or Mr. Curry, I made sure with the secretary that they would get an invitation to come here some time this weekend. I want them to see what we do at the festival. It would be to our credit that they see the operation in full swing. And Tom…now that he knows where the place is, I hope Tom will make it too. Did you say anything to him? I mean, did you ask him to come?"

"Of course I did." There was a smug smile. "And I expect him to be here too. Meanwhile, will you have time to go to Medford for that talk show on Thursday? The TV station called to confirm."

"And you said…?"

"'Oh yes, Ms. Tower is looking forward to being with you.' So you're going!"

"Thank you darlin' girl! I hate having to drop everything to drive all the way over there, but the publicity is too good. Anything else happen while I was gone?"

"Oh, there were the usual messages from people participating this weekend. Mostly confirmations. But there was one that was particularly strange. A guy. Almost sounded like a heavy breather. He had a really peculiar way of talking. Like, you couldn't be sure if he was serious or not."

"Well, what did he say?"

"He said, '…we're going to have a good time. Some of us are going to have a *real* good time'. Kinda' breathy like that."

"Did he leave his name?"
"Not even. When I asked, all he said was 'You'll see.'"
"Creepy."
"Yeah, creepy."

CHAPTER 24

❀

Later that afternoon back in the winery, Kara was with Shiron, refurbishing the tasting room decor. Every month they did a make-over, reflecting the season or holiday. May, of course was 'Spring Florals'. It gave the room a look that bespoke of the out-of-doors. Freshly planted flower boxes brightened the entrance, and ribboned flower arrangements surrounded the wines and related gift items. The effect was as always, stunning.

Kara looked forward particularly to that day, exactly thirty days after the semi-trucks came to the winery to make a pick up for some of the larger accounts. It was *payday*! Checks for these previous wine purchases arrived at the mail box and were greeted with profuse gratitude. This was where the winery made the bulk of their money. It was earmarked for the enormous overhead that accompanied the production of the wine and most of it was spent even before she had the time to enjoy it. The ongoing obligations were attended to first. But opposed to the less glamorous but requisite needs for running the enterprise, the monies spent on the beautification of the tasting room were a pleasure shared by all. Kara was especially pleased when the decorating was completed, and they could sit back to appreciate their creativity.

A few customers were already happily at the tasting bar, talking, sipping, laughing, doing what just about every person who came to taste the wines did. They moved about the winery room with unbridled appreciation. It made a very satisfying picture.

But the steps they heard approaching the front door now were heavy, thumping strides.

"Three days to go." Turner came bursting in from the field, boots clumping, chain saw still in hand, gaining every one's full attention. "I just finished putting up the signs. We're two days ahead of schedule. You know anybody with a little yellow 'bug'?"

"Well, what do you think?" Caught up in her own inventiveness Kara waved her hands around the newly decorated space, fishing for the expected complement on the room and then stopped, took a second breath and said, "A yellow bug?"

"Yeah, a Volkswagen bug. I was putting up the signs out on the road with Roger, and this asshole drives by and throws a beer can at me. Roger and I shine it on and keep on working. But the sonavabitch turns around down the road, and here he comes again the other way, and damn if his buddy doesn't throw another one at us. This is not just an empty can. I mean, he doesn't just toss the fuckin thing, he throws it!"

The customers cringed at the language while ineffectively trying to hide their discomfort behind their tasting glasses.

Shiron's eyes were wide as she stuck her head up from behind the tasting bar and mindlessly chewing on her extremely long, well manicured fingernails, repeated, "Yellow bug?"

"Easy boy!" Kara gently reminded Turner of where he was and just who was attending this outburst. "We have guests here and I'm sure they have little interest in our problems."

It troubled Kara greatly to have this kind of intrusion, and even more so to think of her people under attack by vandals.

An older man, grasping the situation stepped forward.

"Please don't worry. It's all right, we can handle it, and we understand. I don't think anyone is immune these days to being victimized, or at least knowing someone who's been victimized by pranksters. It's pretty maddening!"

"Thank you for your understanding," she said gratefully.

Calmer, Turner inquired if anyone was familiar with the offending vehicle. As expected, he drew a blank. No one here knew anything at all. It wasn't all that unusual for some of the juveniles in the area to pursue these kind of lawless escapades. It was something that would more often be ignored than reported to the authorities, but it was understandable that Turner would be angry. Of course, if it were possible *he* would find the perpetrators and like as not, *kick-ass*!

"Were they just kids?" someone asked.

"I couldn't tell. They had to be old enough to be drinking though. If I didn't have all the tools spread out by the highway, Roger and I could have jumped in

'Curley' and busted them. Shit!" he mumbled as an afterthought. "I should have left Roger and gone after them myself."

"Never mind," Kara said. "You know as well as I do, if they're in town for more than a couple of days, you'll either see them or hear about them. A yellow car couldn't be that difficult to locate. We can ask more people about it. Something will turn up."

She remembered her customers and turned to them, saying with a shrug and a smile, "Life in the country!" And got an unrestrained laugh from the collection of people. When they returned home, they would now have a good story to tell their friends about their visit to the winery.

What she didn't discuss, was that her instinct had told her it sounded as though Turner, or at least his project was a premeditated target for the vandals. It was beyond her to think of who would do this, but one thing was certain, she could turn the other cheek to violations on her own person, she had done that so many times in the past it was second nature to her, but on one of her own people? She couldn't abide that!

A temper that Kara seldom experienced was surfacing. Knowing full well that it was futile to anger herself, Kara still fumed deep inside. She had to get away from the tasting room, away from customers, and most of all away from the people she wanted least to witness the frustration she experienced. There were other matters that needed her attention and as an escape, she would focus on those.

She excused herself from the others to have a talk with Digby about the scheduling for the festival. He was expected to be available for socializing with the guests and to be left unfettered by the demands of normal winery operations. He would be the figurehead for the technical artistry in the winery and the public loved to fawn under the mystic aura shed by the master winemaker. It was an unexplainable fact of life that the mundane machinations of turning grapes into wine were swept into the potpourri of glamour and fascination.

Kara wanted to make sure that he had completed his plans to move the various wines for use on the grounds of the event to each of their correct places. They had discussed at length, the broad strategy for dispensing beverages. A light fruity blend for greeting people as they entered the designated party area. Luncheon wines, easily accessible for use with the foods that were being served. And for the leisure enjoyment of listening to music or merely having polite conversation with friends, a selection of after dinner wines.

After years of presenting an event of this kind to the public, the winery received tremendous notoriety. Each festival became larger and more involved.

From a mere two hundred guests in the first year, it had grown to accommodate thousands. Calls were pouring in from all points of the compass requesting more and more information about the activities and entertainment. Netta wasn't two steps away from the phone at any given time and could be seen pulling the cell phone out of her vast pocket for a brief communication.

It was surprising too, how many varieties of entertainment were offered up this year. In the beginning, it was a struggle to pin down even one music group to make a solid commitment for a 'gig'. Now, they were literally elbowing each other aside to have the privilege of performing. What a chuckle it caused Kara, to think of how they now had to 'jury' the selection of entertainers, and then to carefully schedule them in order to fit them into the time frames in which they had to work. So different than the old days.

The whole endeavor was awesome. It was one of the many reasons her employees looked up to her as their leader. She was the one who knew the answers to every aspect of the project. Having inaugurated the fledgling festival in earlier, less complicated times, she had grown along with the event in sophistication and know-how. Of course, they respected her for it. Her staff looked up to her as the professional that she was. They would do her bidding without question. On the other hand, a leader could not allow herself to fall into the abyss of negative thinking, on the negative aspects. There were too many details to be seen to, too much to do!. Nuisance phone calls. Juvenile pranks. Missing articles. She must ignore them for the time being.

For a leader, it was tantamount, especially at this critical time, that she hold on to her sanity with a positive outlook and undaunted spirit. Mostly the undaunted spirit.

Looking for her winemaker, she tried to block out the latest of her niggling problems. Yet, one in particular defied any solution, and Digby would be the first to be faced with the major issue. They were falling perilously short of operating cash and his salary depended directly on that. She had pulled most of their resources for the staging of the upcoming wine festival. Successful or not, without the prescribed incoming funds, the next bottling of wine would be in jeopardy to the point of impossibility.

The truth was, the distribution of Mountain View wines had hit some kind of unexplainable snag. The numbers were not adding up the way they normally should and there was no discernable reason why this was happening. Sales were falling. With the added strain of the plummeting cash flow, there was pressure for timely ordering of bottling materials as well as accumulation of added staff that would be required for containerizing the wines that were sitting in tanks and barrels. It was becoming a case of interrupted production. As long as the process progressed in a timely fashion, all was well. But any alteration in the scheme of things and the losses could be inestimable. Wine that was not bottled could be lost to spoilage. However, these things were at the very back of her mind, not to be something that should be addressed on the advent of one of their most important public relations affairs.

She found Digby in his office, sorting papers and computerizing data. They were forever thankful that so many of the winery details could now be set forth in a format by their new, upscale software.

"Can you imagine going back to the time when we had to do all of this by hand?" She had knocked at the open door, announcing her presence.

"Bloody right, I can! Like returning to purgatory, if you ask me." He sat back in his chair and spread his long, lean body into a much needed stretch.

"Brought you some coffee. Do you have time for a break?"

"Thanks, love. I've been at this for a couple of hours. Hey," he pointed at the cup, "don't you know any better? I thought winery people only drank beer!" he chided and then reached for it. "Coffee'll be lovely."

Kara chuckled at Digby's subtleties and handed him the mug, perching herself on the corner of his cluttered desk. "Did you get the receipt for our entry into the 'big one'?"

"Yes, and I get nervous every time I think of it."

"Why? It's only the *most* important competition on our side of the globe!" The Grand International Wine Competition was held annually in Cannes, and awards from it were probably the most sought after in the industry. Personal attendance was never required as thousands of wineries participated in the event, often with multiple entries. But the top winners were discretely invited, having been told of their placement prior to public announcement, to attend the awards ceremony. It was a hopeful but tense period of expectation for the principals of the wineries as well as their winemakers.

Digby was straight faced. "Because I believe we are very serious contenders for a major recognition of the Pinot Noir that we entered. *We* think it's exceptional, but until we have results from this 'blind' tasting, where we *know* there cannot be any bias, we won't have utter substantiation of the quality of the wine. This will be the official evaluation, and frankly, I'm sitting on pins and needles about it."

"You're right, Digs. It's an important competition, but think about it, we've usually garnered some award or another out of it. Maybe not the most important ones, but for a small fish in the pond, we haven't done too badly."

"Just six more days to wait and we'll know for certain. I'll settle down then."

"Good! I could use some settling down myself. Are you ready for the weekend?"

"To be sure! I wanted to try out a sample run of the off-dry Riesling though. You know, the one we wanted to use for the Monterey tasting? We haven't gotten to the Washington people with it yet, and I really think it would be a smashing success up there. They responded to some of the other dry whites so well. Anyway, I had been sitting here pondering on how we might best introduce it on the weekend. We could get a recorded response from here, and use it to take to Washington."

"Clever!" Kara appreciated the inventive side of her winemaker. He often dreamed up ways to present a new wine, ways that never would have occurred to her. His kind of input was immeasurably important. The industry demanded that the creator of the wines be an impeccable spokesman for their product. Added to his lovely English accent, his ability to conceive imaginative methods for presenting it was nothing less than frosting on the cake. She quietly waited to see where he was going with this.

"Couldn't we build on the crowd's expectation if we preclude the bringing in of the wine with some appropriate music, heraldry maybe? Let the guests know there is something special happening. Bring it into the area by a procession?" Digby was on a roll.

"Go on, go on." Kara was visualizing and in her mind, expanding on what he was saying.

"Trays of glasses being paraded around by the servers. Say they disappear from the wine bars for just enough time to dress themselves up with ribbons and flowers, something like what you have in the tasting room? That way, everyone will be ready for a fresh glass. They file in with a musical announcement that we all toast to the new vintage. Work it out with the band. Hell, work it out with the security guys, they could clear the way at the entrance and make it look like the Queen's sentries. Only no rifles or bayonets."

"Sounds super! After they've had the chance to taste the Riesling, we canvass the people for their reactions, making notes on everything. Maybe even have our publicist take some video shots to bring with us to Washington. Great stuff!"

"I am great, aren't I!" He all but kissed himself.

"Definitely! Now, is there anything else you can think of the we can take care of now, before the festival?"

"Well, my major concern is that we keep a close watch of the inventory. I know I'll be out among guests and so will you. The girls will all be assigned to various duties, and the extra hired help is already placed. I noticed last year that every bottle wasn't exactly accounted for, and I wanted to be on top of that this time, but you and I both know that I'll be tied up with the customers. What do you feel about having Turner doing it. I think he can count." This was a facetious remark. "Bloody hell, I'm not really sure what his function is supposed to be. Overseeing the muscle?" Turner was indeed a part-time body builder and did appear to be suited for the coordination of the occasionally needed bouncers.

"Do I detect a note of irritation there?"

"Oh, not really. It's just the way the bloody guy prances about. He's like a cartoon character! Doesn't he ever take anything seriously?"

She was thinking, *We all can't be as serious as you,* but she replied, "Digby, what you say is very true. But remember, what Turner contributes is work that's a lot less exacting than…say, what you do. Your job carries tremendous responsibility. It always has and you carry that responsibility to the limits. You do a great job. And well, Turner is placed in a more relaxed atmosphere. He's outside mostly. You and he are simply not cut of the same cloth. Actually, the two of you compliment each other very well when you think of it."

"True enough Kara. Do you think he'll be trustworthy enough to do that job?"

"Yes, and I know you've made the perfect selection for overseeing our precious inventory."

CHAPTER 25

❦

On Wednesday morning, Carl Bradshaw had asked Howard Curry into his office. He wanted to discuss some matters that had come up with respect to the linking of several associated businesses. Curry would have some of the answers.

Earlier that day he had been on the phone with Francis Gillman, personally going over a summary of his portfolio of accounts in the Medford-Ashland area. Several acquisitions were made by Gillman corporations that were handled by the bank. Bradshaw was only perfunctorily aware of the total number of enterprises in which Gillman was involved, many were out of state. What he didn't realize until now, was the extensive number of businesses that Gillman's holdings encompassed here, on his own ground. It was uncanny, he thought disbelievingly. How he could have missed seeing this before? Well, Curry was in charge. But how much was he aware of? He certainly hadn't brought this to my attention!

In his position at the Southern Valley Bank, it was incumbent upon Bradshaw to be acquainted with all things of this nature. It was therefore embarrassing at the least, to feel as though he were just learning about, and recognizing the 'big' picture. He recently researched Gillman, and found he was often the major force in several of the corporations that were represented as accounts at the bank. And because of the variety of names and associates that were listed in the corporate roster, it was not always clear that it was Francis Gillman, who was behind the helm. Clever bastard! Most people would never relinquish their names at the top of the list of officers for the sake of the ambiguity of ownership. It was now obvious that this was exactly what was being done. And it was Howard Curry, who was the bank officer that normally took care of the finite details. He had to be working with Gillman, not to have brought this to his attention before.

What triggered Carl Bradshaw into looking into the Gillman holdings more closely, was Gillman's latest insistence on obtaining more and more facts about Mountain View. It seemed as though every other day Gillman would call, gathering snippets of information. Not that he would come right out and ask what he wanted to know. No, it seemed he would beat around the bush before going deeper into the mechanics of the winery.

"Have they applied for a building permit on the new facility they're thinking about?"

"What do you think the production will be this year?"

"How were the crop levels for the last harvest? I've heard they weren't as good as the year before."

How the hell did he know, right off the top of his head? The only query that he didn't hear was, "Is Kara Tower going to get her loan, or is it possible that she might be subject to losing her business?"

It struck him suddenly that these questions were far beyond casual curiosity. It also struck him that Howard Curry was being strangely reticent about the loan applications that he was purported to have analyzed and which he summarily guided the others to turn down. Tom Hutchins was instructed to drop the bomb on Tower last Friday, yet he had asked to extend the time for consideration. Things were not falling into place as they should be. Come to think of it, Curry did seem to be going around looking a bit miffed every time the subject was brought up. He didn't want that loan to go through! Are Curry and Hutchins at odds with this? What the hell was going on? Whatever it was, spelled money.

The intercom buzzer announced that Howard had arrived.

"Good morning, Carl." He entered the office looking dapper in a three piece suit, manicured and freshly coifed. He was businesslike, with the appropriate humility. If nothing else, Howard knew how to play his part.

"Yes, have a seat. How did you enjoy the wine event Saturday night?" Obviously he hadn't heard about the end-of-the-evening fiasco.

"Very nice. I talked to quite a few people about a mutual industry account. Gillman, of course was there. He told me it gave him a great opportunity to familiarize himself with the local product. Said he and Clark Peterson may be interested in the wine industry business."

"Tell me more about that, Howard. I've been expecting it. Have they intimated anything more tangible than idle interest?" He asked, knowing what the answer should be.

"Well, I knew that sooner or later you'd suspect that there was more to it." Howard acquiesced, seeing that this was the point at which he would need to divulge at least part of his plans. "The answer is yes. There has been one prospect available that could be in the offing. These people are willing to put up a substantial amount in order to firm up an arrangement to acquire the property. I've been assisting them"

"Howard, I don't need to warn you that you are treading on thin ice. Insider information. Conflicting interest and all that. What you are suggesting is something that perhaps should not be considered a bank transaction. Am I to assume that monies have been proffered?"

"Ah…yes. In fact, I really didn't want to bring this to your attention until it was time to set up some kind of financial sequence. These people, as I was saying, are quite well heeled, so whatever leverage they want to go in with should be acceptable to you."

"And am I to take it that the property in question is the same property that we have been asked to fund?" Howard didn't perceive the subtle color rising from Carl Bradshaw's neck to the top of his balding head. He didn't recognize his incredulous reaction to this information. The fact that Howard had not disclosed his intentions *prior* to acting on them infuriated Carl. For all the guile and shrewdness it took to successfully maintain the position of CEO of his organization, Carl Bradshaw considered himself outwardly to have some amount of righteous integrity. On the surface, he wanted no one to question that. What happened beyond the limits of good conscience was something he did not directly want to be party to. It was with the greatest control that he interjected, "Don't answer that. I don't want to know…at least not yet. Please Howard, please be circumspect about these dealings. I want nothing, and I mean nothing to be traced back to the bank. Is that understood?"

"Yes Sir."

"I was on the phone with Gillman this morning and I agree that his clout is impressive. I can't deny that further association with him wouldn't be an advantage for us. However, I must stay publicly neutral until the dust settles one way or the other with that winery. I can't encourage you in your pursuit of this, nor can I prevent you from cultivating it. Just keep your eyes open."

"Yes Sir." Curry repeated.

"Then that's all for now." The discussion, as far as it went, was over.

As Howard Curry returned to his desk area, he was unbelievably relieved. When he was called in to see the boss, there was the oppressive feeling that he was going to be read out for his aborted attempt to offer the Mountain View property to Gillman and his friend, Clark Peterson. But Bradshaw hadn't actually known as much as he suspected. He certainly didn't know before, that Gillman had given money to gain the option. And surprisingly, Bradshaw had all but said that he would turn the other cheek while Howard masterminded whatever deal he could bring in. Bradshaw knew what side of the bread his butter was on...the money side! What Curry had to do now, was to make sure that he could make that property available.

Not too long ago, his first attempt to relieve Kara of her entire business followed the initial loan application information that ended up in his files. Coincidentally on the same day, he had lunch with his old acquaintance, Francis Gillman. It seemed the businessman was putting out feelers attesting to having interest in the wineries in the area. Did any of them appear to be in the precarious position of having the need to liquidate? Translating to terms that Howard could readily understand, were there any wineries in the area that were in trouble, and could one be bought for a minimum amount of money?

"Of course, if I was party to information of that sort, I realize that it could be very valuable to someone." Howard led with a statement that would illicit some response if the wealthy businessman was willing to pay.

"Should the savings on a purchase be substantial, a generous finder's fee would definitely be in order." The man was hungry and Curry was more than willing to lead him on to think that what he had in mind was currently available.

Gillman suggested further, that an initial payment to Curry for the promotion of such an offering would also be in order. Oh, yes. Curry agreed.

And so it came to pass, that when Kara had come to Southern Valley for the final solution to her problems, every minutiae of financial history on her business found its way to Howard Curry's desk. The loan was destined for defeat in his hands, just as her distribution for the wines was destined for obscurity.

There would be no bank bonus for him by consummating the Tower loan. But with Gillman, the rewards would be great. Dealing with her application by himself, he was very likely to get what he wanted. That is, until Tom Hutchins was told to butt in. So Howard reverted to plan 'B'. If he couldn't bury the loan, maybe he could bury the woman.

Early stages of the planned harassment involved a few, randomly placed crank calls. Actually, they had been amusing to make, and no doubt served their purpose well. He was sure that it upset the people he had reached at the winery. That would set the stage for what he hoped would be an atmosphere of tenuous insecurity. It also didn't hurt to have an insider within the ranks of Mountain View employees to keep him informed of the current status.

Just the other night he had tried more than crank calls. He attempted to eliminate the woman by creating a hopefully fatal accident. Unfortunately, that backfired. He only succeeded in nearly killing himself, and to add insult to injury, he had to leave his own truck in the ditch where it landed so hard the drive shaft broke. Thank God they couldn't trace it back to him. Worse, he lost money from the eventual sale of the pick-up. That pissed him off.

His mind dwelt on those disasters, the momentum gathering in him to force Kara Tower from her safe little world. He had to do something. He hated her now with a growing passion that overshadowed all other thoughts.

CHAPTER 26

❀

This is where I belong. White Raven intoned as he carefully picked his way around the trees and rock formations following the creek. After spending more than a day or two in town, the return to nature was irresistible.

Three or four days spent wandering the mountains required only a minimum of survival gear. A pack to carry a light blanket, skillfully made of hand loomed wool from the Arizona pueblo. A few light-weight comestibles. A small pot for brewing ground coffee beans, along with the emergency matches, a small concession to civilization. A large but empty carry pack. His carving knives.

These excursions were not idle, soul searching forays into the wilderness. White Raven had no need to search for, or assure himself of the sanctity of his soul. He found a sublime peace in traveling the mountains and streams in search of the stones that spoke to him.

In the hidden quarries scattered here and there in places known only to a few was the rare pristine white and green soapstone that Raven discovered was some of the finest he had ever used for his carvings. He would spend hours, and sometimes days in searching for a certain stone. Then there would be hours more spent on contemplating the piece. Only when an image appeared in his mind did he begin the process of removing the outer material in order to free the spirit within.

The selling of his artwork for Raven was secondary to the creation of it. It came from his mind and hands, as it would the birth of a child. Two elements nearly always found their way into his creations. It set him apart as an icon of his art. First, there was the human element—either a face or form of man, and second, the wild element—animal, bird, or reptile. It was a peaceful conjunction of man and beast executed with great detail. His hands were guided by an inborn talent for the sensual, dramatic and faultless reality.

He was returning now from having spent five long days of work on two magnificent pieces. One large stone said it wanted to be a man, who's eyes were averted upward into the eyes of a large predatory bird that seemed to spring from his hair. The bird's gaze was downward in a bonding connection with the man. The two were one.

The second piece, smaller than the other was only the blocking out of a sculptured hand. In it, the open palm would be holding a small mouse. The color of the stone demanded that it should be a mouse! This unfinished carving, he left hidden in a cache between two boulders overgrown with manzanita. There, it would be waiting for him for another day.

The larger carving was heavy as he carried it in the leather pack he brought along for that purpose. As he neared the area where he knew others had come for recreation, he was thankful that the people preceding him had thoughtfully left the area in the unsullied state of its natural beauty. It was in fact the very place where Kara and Beth had recently enjoyed their respective outings.

A good place for coffee, Raven decided, shrugging off the weight of the stone. He retrieved the pot from the backpack and filled it with stream water. It was a simple matter to build a small fire, made easy with the use of safety matches. Much easier than having to set up a fire using duff, dry twigs and a flint. He couldn't help but smile at this departure from the past. In no time he had a steaming cup of the brew.

And this would be as good a place as any to spend the night. Tomorrow he could box up the carving for shipping to the gallery in Arizona. There was no hurry. By mutual consent, he carved, sent in his art work by a reliable trucking firm, and in time an amazing amount of money was placed in his out-of-state account. It was long, since he had contacted or bothered his blood brother, a financial consultant, about the balance. He knew there was quite a bit of money being accumulated and subsequently invested, but how much it was, he neither knew or cared. It was as if it belonged to someone else. He didn't need it. At least, not now.

Reclining on the backpack he slowly sipped the hot black coffee, taking pleasure from the fragrance. He contemplated the circle of trees overhead from his focal point on the ground. Aimlessly one hand trailed over the earth, thoughts on nothing in particular, when his fingers touched an object.

He picked it up and looked at it. A knife. Nice. Very nice! And by the looks of it, fairly expensive. Beautifully crafted. Hasn't been here long, he thought as he added it to his belongings in the side zipper of the pack.

CHAPTER 27

The following day, Kara spent about two hours on the phone touching base with her friends and acquaintances to let them know she was looking forward to seeing them all this weekend, and how important to the event their attendance would be. Included in this list were some political figures as well as a few celebrities along with their entourages, who she had been forewarned, would be arriving together. Well, that was good! The more, the merrier!!

But now she had to get ready for the media! It was great that the TV talk show liked her on their show every now and then. Beth was close at hand to help her make preparations, as she always was when there was a public appearance. Once Kara had dressed, Beth would go over her whole 'look', fine tuning her make-up, jewelry, and accessories. She was expressly gifted in this subtle art of personal presentation.

Then they would put their heads together, conferring on what sort of prop they would introduce as a point of interest during the conversation on camera. Something of personal consequence, or perhaps some memorabilia from the winery.

This time they decided on one of the more important medals that had been won in the past.

"Perfect!" she said. "You're right! After hearing of so many awards, I think the audience would like to see the actual medals that we win. Be sure to bring me a gold and a silver to take along, and I can explain how important it is for us to win these accolades."

"Yes, and if you win one more award, I think the medal chest could be used as a Disney prop. It's beginning to look like a real treasure trove! Did you ever think when you started that you would win so many?"

"I told you before, I don't win the awards. The wine does. Anyway, it's Digby, who can take the bows. It's his babies that win them."

"Speaking of Digs, he's been nervous as a penniless addict without blow. Says he can't wait for the results of the Cannes International next week. Is it that important?"

"The *most* important! Where any of the major awards are disbursed, the media follows. The publicity is awesome, and the benefits to the winners can be compared to the perks of Olympic gold medalists. Digby knows we can win something, but he really makes *me* apprehensive with his agonizing."

Throughout the conversation, Beth fussed over Kara. She darkened the too conservative eye makeup with eyeliner, shadow, and more mascara.

"You look great!! Now let's go before the phone rings."

Too late.

"I'll get it. Probably one of your adoring public, and you haven't got time." She headed for the ringing instrument.

"Good morning, Mountain View Winery," she answered. "Yes…yes…no, but I'll ask." Turning to Kara, signaling with her hand over the mouthpiece she whispered, "It's Tom Hutchins. I told him you were doing the talk show and he asked if you had any plans for lunch afterwards."

A flush of apprehension ran through Kara, feeling the prickling on her skin. A moment of indecision and a mouthed 'yes'. For Beth's sake, she didn't want to seem to be too anxious, but she couldn't help the anticipation of speaking to Tom alone without interruptions. She just knew he must have information regarding her loan.

"Tell him I'll call his office as soon as I'm ready to leave the TV studio, if that's all right."

Beth relayed the message and hung up.

"Looks like it's your turn with the 'hunk'. He said he could drive over to the station and catch you when you were finished. Is that eager, or what? And I thought he was in love with me!" Beth was no longer worried about cornering Tom Hutchins' attention. After all, hadn't he expressed his interest in her in the most intimate, personal way?

They laughed and Kara gave her a hug. There was no feeling of competition between them. It was more like two sisters enjoying the activity of the game.

As the phone started ringing again, Beth urged Kara out the door. She rushed back to pick up the phone, only to hear the same odd voice as before saying, "We're going to have some fun." Only that, and it disconnected.

The studio lights were too hot for anyone wearing more than a bikini. The trick was to ignore it gracefully.

They were gathered in a conversation-oriented seating arrangement that was both as comfortable as it was attractive. The studio at the television station was not a large one, and as though two worlds were contained in the same room, apart from the central stage, the perimeters were conversely uncomfortable and congested with equipment and crew, wires, and the blazing hot lighting Even in a lightweight outfit of a loose cut, she could see the beads of perspiration on the upper lip of the anchorwoman. It pleased Kara that due to some phenomena in her genes, the excessive heat was not as bothersome to her as it was to the others.

"So what you are saying, Ms. Tower, is that when push comes to shove, it is a concentrated statewide effort. Maybe that will properly place the Oregon products as well as Oregon wines in every retail outlet. That would certainly be an advantage to our home-state produced items."

"I'm sure everyone here would agree that we have seen enough products from out-of-state and even more consumer goods from out of the country. What I am saying is that it's a matter of commitment that could be reinforced for the items that are produced here, in Oregon. It will take a consolidated effort throughout the Oregon based industries to effect a public relations promotion that would generate this loyalty."

"Well! That is stating an immense challenge for any of our viewers today. But Kara, if I may call you Kara," Kara motioned her assent, "I believe what our listeners would really like to hear about in the near future, is the more personal workings of what it's like to run your winery, and of even more interest, something of your personal life on your ranch. I hope you will join us again for another show."

"I would be happy to," she responded with warmth.

The interviewer turned to look directly at the television camera, resuming with, "And so, with that in mind, we look forward to another exciting interview with Kara Tower of Mountain View Winery and an in-depth look at the woman behind the business. We have come to the end of our show today...."

At that point, Kara had tuned out the announcer and made ready, with the director's assistance, to leave the set. It was then that she noticed that Tom was standing there, listening to the program. How long had he been there?

After making her most gracious thanks known to the show hostess, with a promise to return for another interview, she joined Tom.

"Ms. Tower, you make an excellent spokesperson for your industry," he said rather formally. "Are you sure you should be confined to representing only one winery?" He smiled.

"Once the public has heard the next segment on the life of Kara Tower, I'm not sure I'll be able to represent even my own winery!"

"Are you saying that it will be an exposé rather than an interview?" He mimed astonishment.

"I'm saying that they might find out that this winery life is not quite as glamorous as they thought." In her mind, she was remembering back to the time she took on the job of mucking out a septic line on a Sunday when there was no other help available. If the job needs to be done, don't make excuses, *just do it*!

"Maybe I can make up for that over lunch. I have reservations at Trianon."

"Lovely. I can't wait!"

For Tom, taking a female out to lunch was not normally a special event. It happened with a fair amount of regularity. Often, it was a question of making all the right moves and making an impressive show of how great it was for her to be in his company. Taking Kara Tower for lunch however, became a quest of fulfilling her every desire in order to be worthy of being by her side. He was humbled by this unfathomable, mature woman because of the aura that constantly surrounded her. In one respect, she seemed to be as down to earth as a family member, and yet there was always some untouchable quality of depth that set her apart.

He enjoyed her company. There was no end of conversation covering local events and adventures of the past. They carefully contrived to keep their dialogue away from business, and for that reason, they were often laughing and giggling about some story or another, shared over a wonderful meal and a bottle of wine.

For Kara's part, the brief respite of relaxation following the unavoidable tension of being on television, was just what the doctor ordered. Oddly enough, what she discovered that she liked best about being with Tom, was the almost sterile perfection of his behavior. He made her feel like they were moving through a movie set rather than in the real world. Their words and actions having been choreographed, as if written in a script. It was amusing for her. She was surprised in her discovery that this superficial play-acting could be therapeutic to the stress factors in her life. She was enjoying herself!

It was for that reason, a hasty departure following their meal was unwelcome although necessary. Tom understood, correctly that with only one more day before the festival, Kara would be consumed with last minute details requiring her personal attention.

Throughout the meal, no mention was made with regard to anything financial. It was a relief to both of them that this particular subject had been deferred. They each in their own direction, returned to work.

Back at the winery, Shiron emerged from her station behind the tasting bar and met Kara with the opening statement, "Well, which do you want the first, the good news or the bad news?"

Kara blanched, but not because she hadn't heard the ominous words before. It was just the premonition of knowing that something in the works had gone wrong and she was helpless to prevent it.

"I think I need the good news first."

"Remember the customers from San Francisco that were in here a couple of days ago?"

Kara thought for a moment before placing the group in her mind. "Yes, the ones who were all dressed in summer shorts and short-sleeved shirts."

"Those are the ones. They bought one bottle of every wine we had. Did a lot of talking about them and spent about an hour and a half discussing it."

"So…what about them?" Kara led Shiron into her office.

"They phoned the winery earlier today to ask you to return their call. Said something about a substantial order."

"Sounds good to me. Great! Now, on to the bad news." Kara settled herself into the swivel chair behind her black walnut table desk. Normally cleared of any superfluous paper, today it was scattered with the debris of tomorrow's event. "I'm ready!"

"Well, it seems Turner and good ol' Talbert got into a fight. I don't know exactly what it was about, but they said Turner didn't look too bad, but Talbert looked like he had been sent through the grape crusher." She looked apologetic in just relaying the information to the already burdened Kara.

"Good lord! I'll look into it as soon as I can. You're sure Turner is okay?"

"Pretty sure."

"Thanks for breaking it to me gently though. Dare I ask if there is anything else I should know about?"

"The bookkeeper took care of the monthly reports. Digby included the missing wine in the inventory, so he said we won't be paying wine taxes on it.

Wouldn't that be the frosting on the cake to have to pay taxes on something that was stolen? Oh, and the delivery man called to say he could bring in the twelve pallets of bottles next week."

"Thanks, Shiron. Did he leave a number where I could reach him, or did he want me to call the office?"

"Uh…here's the number," she confirmed after running through several slips of paper in her pocket.

"All right. From now until the festival is over and cleaned up, please tell *everyone* who is involved with the ongoing winery operations to please bear with us, and cool their heels. I will get back to them *late* next week."

"Will do. Anything else?" she turned an ear as some customers could be heard approaching the entrance.

"No. Go ahead with the tasting room."

Kara wanted to be alone. Enjoying a moment of quiet, to her own surprise, the spark of an idea was building inside of her. It was inspired by her conversation with Shiron, and it had something to do with certain operations that could be postponed for the time being. Elusive as it was, this idea required time to bite down and chew on it, drawing the flavor of the thought into her…slowly, in order to broadly identify all of its constituents. Details would be brought to mind one by one, as eventually she dignified each segment.

With considerably more thought and analysis, perhaps she was wrong. Her thoughts deflated. The only thing her idea could accomplish would be a postponement of the inevitable.

Turning to the phone, she commenced to dial the people from San Francisco.

CHAPTER 28

❁

Turner was sitting at the shop workbench up to his elbows in grease. What looked like a couple of dozen assorted nuts, bolts, parts and screws, were strewn around the carburetor which was the central figure of his attention. There were gaskets, spark plugs and a multitude of tools that had either been in use for the abandoned project, or could have been lying around for the past decade. Today in the garage/shop, it was a project that seemed to require one worker and three onlookers. The three spectators were taking what they called a cogitation break. From their respective positions of the audience they chugged at their brewskis, scratched and belched and made comments.

"Good thing you guys weren't on the payroll when this project was abandoned. You'd be outta here today!"

"Fuckin Talbert never did shit around here. He was a master at putting off anything he was supposed to do," Roger complained. "Look at this shop! I'll bet he never once cleaned it up. Good thing he's gone, the way he's been acting. The guy's weird!" To demonstrate his point he gave up his position on a fender to attack the corner shelves where he had indicated earlier that he would make a start at the much needed organization project.

Turner didn't make an effort to reply. He just looked around, hands on his hips, and calculated the progression of necessary cleaning and then replacement of tools and equipment. All of this had to be accomplished before the shop could be considered workable again. He felt sorry for Kara, who had her hands full with the operation and now the festival. There was no way she could have kept track of what was going on over here. He quickly discovered there must have been a human pack-rat doing his best to cart away whatever tools or supplies were of any value. He even knew the pack-rat's name.

Talbert must have been taking things for some time. It occurred to Turner that the shop would not necessarily be the only place that the shithead would be hitting on. There was the winery as well.

He knew it! Knew it had been Talbert all along, who was responsible for so many glitches in the operation. All he had to go on before were nebulous clues and tentative guesswork, but now he knew!

Because of these thoughts, he intended to get to Talbert again, even more thoroughly than he did earlier when he caught him putting the company chain saw and an electric drill into the back of his old beater car.

Turner knew something was up, because he had just used the saw the day before and it was working perfectly. The thing hummed like a worker-bee…as good as his own saw.

After keeping a watchful eye on the unpredictable comings and goings of his quarry, he noticed Talbert putting the constantly used tools into the backseat of his old Duster. No way they were going in for repairs. Talbert never took care of the tools. The sneaky way he had been acting was the tip-off, the bastard! Turner watched him rushing to his car huddling over the stuff in his arms.

He was hustling to get into the driver's seat to start the car and make a hasty exit, but just as the engine turned over, the passenger door was flung open. He turned to look. Turner was on him, reaching over to grab the keys out of the ignition of the running car. What followed would later be described by the work crew as the action of a maniac warrior. He then proceeded to drag the protesting Talbert out through the passenger side of the car, pummeling him with punches to the face and body, yelling in a rage, "Fuckin asshole thief."

"What're ya talkin about!" Talbert shouted back, his arms covering his face to ward off blows to the head. He swung back as soon as he saw an opening.

"Goddam puke! What else have you got in there?" He pulled the chain saw out and put it on the ground beside the car, took another swing at Talbert and went for the drill. There wasn't anything else in the car…now.

"Nothin', nothin'. I was just going to borrow 'em for crissakes. Goddamit, can't a guy borrow a tool around here?"

Turner ignored his whining.

"Get the fuck out of here, and don't come back!" were his last words, as he tossed back the car keys.

Once the deed was done and the tools returned, Talbert was allowed to slink off the property, his tail between his legs, where he knew he dared not return again.

Now, as he thought about it, Turner decided that a call to the winery with some questions would be in order. If there were some unexplained missing things there, he would bring their attention to it. He had seen this before. Articles that had vanished, or at least unaccounted for, were often thought to be misplaced…never stolen! It could be ages before anyone recognized a permanent disappearance, and of course, that would happen when the tool or implement was badly needed and it was irretrievably gone! Cellar rats at work.

Turner addressed the whole group. "Any of you fellas ever notice Talbert with any more a' Kara's stuff?"

No answer from the boys in the shop. More drinking beer and scratching. So Turner continued, sweetening the ante.

"Cause if ya did, ya get to come with me when I pay a visit to Talbert after work. Just going to check his place to see if I recognize anything from here."

Now that promised to be some entertainment.

"Hey, Turner." Chris looked reluctant to speak, but he went on. "I didn't want to get anybody in trouble, but I seen him take gas from the equipment tank and put it in his car. He almost shit when he saw me watching, but I didn't think it was worth gettin' anybody in trouble for. There might even be some more items we could recognize. I wouldn't mind going along," he added, hopefully.

Roger spoke up. "You know that bag of nails we looked all over hell for last week? Remember when we found 'em the bag was almost empty. Well, Talbert had grabbed most of them, but I thought it was for some project 'cause he took the hammer and vice-grips too. Coils of fencing wire were in the back. Could be he just took 'em home. Anyway, if there was anything at his place that looked like ours, I *would* recognize it. You could probably use me along." This obvious knit-picking was Roger's way of letting Turner know that he wanted to be there.

"Fellas, ya know this is just small shit. What about that big pump we had for stand-by that nobody can find. Any of you know anything about that?"

The new man, now an elder of the crew, had been sitting, quietly listening without commenting. Being labeled as a snitch was not what he wanted. Here in his current job his past was better left unknown. He preferred not to make waves. However, not to speak up now could mean credibility problems later. He wanted more than anything, at this point to be considered trustworthy.

"Now that you mention that pump?" He spoke up. "Seems that young man was mighty interested in a pump that was laying over by the irrigation equipment about two weeks ago. I noticed him doing something there, but I didn't see him take it. Figured somebody moved it, cause it isn't there now."

"Seems to me we ought'a have a look to see if we might find that too. You in, Mason?"

"If you don't mind Turner," the man said apologetically, "I'll leave the huntin' party to you boys. I'm expected at home tonight, so I wouldn't want to disappoint the missus."

"No need for you to go along. Think I'll have all the help I need. But thanks for the info. We'll be keeping an eye out for that pump."

They all talked at once. The conversation was moved from Talbert's thievery to the extent of Turner's injuries. They noted the small cut above his left eye, now a badge of courage, and then back to Talbert's injuries which were far more extensive, but surely more deserving as he had it coming to him. Before anyone could reach for another can of beer, Turner put an end to the rest period.

"Okay ladies, tea time's over. Whattaya say we get back to work."

CHAPTER 29

Carl Bradshaw was contemplating a phone call to Francis Gillman. He was deciding on just how the odds stood for absorbing those lucrative accounts along with the take-over that was being planned. And the take-over was to all events a done deal. Yes, he wanted that account to be placed at his bank. That would be the lure for Gillman's other holdings.

But he certainly didn't want to be primarily involved with the fall of Mountain View Winery as it existed. Although the only involvement for the bank at this point was to turn down the *only* possible loan that Kara Tower could expect. This would be traced back to Howard Curry and Howard Curry alone, not himself as the bad guy. Even then, Howard had kept a low profile in their dealings, relying on their dialogue by telephone or correspondence. It was surprising she hadn't been screaming to the rooftops to meet with the branch manager. Her own misgivings about her bargaining position were reflected by this very telling reluctance. He concluded that she was on shaky ground, and she knew it.

Unwittingly, Tom Hutchins was letting her down more easily than Curry would have. Tom, by pursuing the remote possibility of entitling Mountain View with a loan-on-demand account, was drawing out the inevitable. Oh well, Bradshaw knew it would never happen, even with all the digging into the loan application papers that Tom would do. Eventually, Tom would be forced to acknowledge that the project was dead meat.

On the other hand, it was perhaps the most auspicious time for him to get together with Gillman, reestablishing a rapport with the man, as well as his partner, Peterson. He wanted to get a better look at Mountain View, so what better time than this weekend at the festival. He reached for the phone just as it commenced ringing.

"Yes."

"Mr. Bradshaw, there's a Mr. Gillman on the line for you."

"I'll take it." He relaxed back into his well upholstered soft leather desk chair and answered with bonhomie, "Francis, I was about to call you. What are your plans for this weekend?"

It was five-thirty and in another part of the building, Howard Curry was tying up the loose ends of his Friday afternoon paperwork. When all was said and done, he played the part of the dedicated employee to the point of almost believing it himself. Not all employees however, while acting out this conscientious role, would take advantage of any and all opportunities that came their way in the manner that Howard did. If there was a deal to be cut where he could make an extra buck, he would do it.

There is a well known precept that bankers as men, contain the coldest of hearts. Although occasionally true, this adage was taken one step further with Howard. Furthermore, Howard lacked the normal integrity that was expected of bank executives. He looked upon his portfolio of accounts as mathematics only. Personalities had nothing to do with viability. The numbers were there, or they were not…and if it didn't make money, it wasn't in his portfolio.

Always, the first premise in banking was the potential of how many points (dollars) could be made in a transaction. But with Howard, a transaction usually meant an added fee (undisclosed in the final papers) that would go directly into his own account…an account nebulously named Trans-Oregon, Ltd. for anonymity.

Another of the too little observed criteria of acceptable behavior in banking, was the avoidance of divulging insider tips. Whereas some executives dealt with this small transgression as only a bone to be thrown to an occasional preferred client, Howard made a point of using this leverage to ingratiate his clients and connections to his astute ability, rendering himself as the favorable person to be handling their businesses. It was little wonder that Howard Curry had made his meteoric rise in the banking community.

Also, like any other institution with fiduciary relationships, gratuities in the banking system were considered a thing to be kept at arms length. Or to be on point, they were taboo. But for Howard, gratuities in the form of say, finder's fees, were a vehicle to be ridden as far as the fuel would take him. And whenever any opportunity arose for a client to grease his palm, he would take it.

Presently, his sights were set on Gillman *et al,* and he wasn't about to let go of the wheel.

The weekend fest at Mountain View was looked upon as an amusement as well as cultural event not to be missed. Howard was anticipating his enjoyment at several levels. The date he had made with Helen, the pretty girl who made daily deposits for her boss from the furniture outlet, was one of them. He had noticed her for weeks now. He liked the cute little bounce her tits and ass made as she walked, and her intense and competent style. In fact, it was she who approached *him* to ask if he would like to join her for an outing at the winery 'party', she called it. She had planned to go with her girlfriends, she told him, but their car was getting crowded so she thought of asking him if he would be interested in going.

Not only interested, but wouldn't have missed it for anything!

He knew now that Bradshaw, Gillman and Peterson would be going on Saturday afternoon and he was sure to see them there. Perfect. He had absorbed the reports from people who had attended prior festivals at Mountain View, and heard it was a tremendous success…a subject of conversation for months afterward. Having those men see first hand the operation in full swing, spelled the promise of whetting the taste for his prospective buyers. With himself as the go-between, the finder's fee would be awesome. So much so, he could probably quit the bank and go to work for himself, making five times the amount of money he was making now. He was sure of it. Gillman would get over his angst about having already paid out some money, as long as the property was ultimately available for him. And little Howard would see to that!

Gillman was the ticket to his future!

The achievement would be twofold. On one hand, he would be paid handsomely, and on the other, he could watch Kara Tower go down, squirming and pleading to save her precious winery. That would be a pleasure in of itself. If there was any further mischief that could be done, he would keep his eyes open at the festival for any ideas that came to mind.

He tapped the reef of papers on his desk into a neat pile and chucked them into a file folder, making a last notation on the computer before turning it off and depositing the file in his desk drawer. Another day, another dollar.

Saying good-bye to the now diminished staff straggling towards the outer door, and the security man, who would then lock the door after each person exited, he headed for his favorite bar for a drink. It was starting to rain.

"Hey, howya' doin'"

The tone of any bar at Happy Hour on a late Friday afternoon is always a varied melange of keepers and customers. The expectancy of the establishment for their part was to make the most of this occasion, the pacesetter for the weekend's lucrative business. The anticipation of the customers, categorically as those who are either looking for an audience to crow their various victories achieved during the week, or those comprising the audience. That would be the ones who are looking for entertainment, those on the prowl for a suitable partner, or others, just plain too depressed to do anything but drink with the desire to absorb the festive ambiance along with their alcohol. It was in all cases a warm, dry sanctuary out of the rain.

Howard recognized the voice at once. He headed for the bar and ordered a bourbon and water.

"Glad you could meet me here, cousin. It's been a while. How's it going with you?" Howard could see by his shabby attire and the black eye he was sporting that the man wasn't exactly doing well at all.

"Great man, great. We've been mushroomin' this winter. Christ, I can't believe the prices they're giving for 'em. Mazutaki, mainly, but Sunny has some friends who showed us where we could get morells and some of those real expensive ones...I can't remember the name. Good little worker she is, when she can get away from her regular job. Between the two of us we made over ten thousand for the season."

So much for appearances. Howard knew for a fact that his cousin made more money on the side, dealing. He guessed they were doing all right, that is until the money was spent on Talbert's habit.

"How'd you manage that? I had you fixed up with that job at Mountain View."

"Well...I didn't spend *all* my time at the winery. Hell, that bitch only paid me a little over minimum wage. I managed to slip away to do what I want. I gotta' say though, little Howard Curry-Cottner sure as shit looks like he's doin' okay for hisself." He backed away with a toothy grin to give Howard an appraising look.

"Uh...by the way, be cool. Remember, the name's Howard Curry. Just Curry."

"Sure, sure." Talbert saw the advantage immediately. "Could do with another drink," implying that Howard could buy. He did.

"Tell me what happened to your face. Sunny finally get back at ya'?"

"Fuckin shit! Just a little altercation with one of the assholes at the winery. My days are over there. Goddamn people!"

"Sorry to hear about that. You know I wanted you to be there to access information for me and stir up a little trouble. Well, nothing we can do about it now. Look, I thought you would like a little job on the side. Care to get back at them?"

The crooked smile reappeared. "I'm listening." He could feel the vibes of something underhanded in the air, something he would enjoy. He became more alert.

The two of them talked for more than an hour. So intent in their topic, they were unaware of the Happy Hour entertainment or even the close of that cultural segment of cocktail life. To the satisfaction of both parties, they left the bar, filled with thoughts of tomorrow's activities. This would be fun, fun, fun!

CHAPTER 30

Kara was still exhausted when she left her bedroom late that afternoon. "I thought a nap was supposed to be restful!" The soft evening pajamas caressed her glowing figure as she moved through the living room to the yet sun-filled kitchen. Clouds had been moving in from the south and it looked like rain was imminent. What she looked forward to as a revitalizing hour spent reclining with her eyes closed, relaxing on her favorite lounge chair, turned out to be a revitalizing romp with Turner.

It was a surprise to Kara to have had the desire to ask him to her home for a drink, especially in light of the upcoming meeting at the winery that evening. She knew Beth would be busy and had no time to spare. Normally she was so reclusive. It wasn't unusual for her to be content to be alone. But for some reason, she wanted company. After all, she and Turner enjoyed spending time together. It was for them, more in the line of a close friendship.

"Want me to bring anything along to the house?" he had asked.

"No, let's just have drink. Once we've had that meeting tonight, our time clock will be on high-speed."

He knew what she meant. With all the work to do during the weekend, they would all be on constant duty, and before they knew it the whole thing would be over. Barely time to think! Even today had been energy-charged with so much action surrounding the festival. He was understanding, inasmuch as this would be a good time for her as well as him to blow off some steam.

They had spent time intimately on a few occasions, and it seemed entirely appropriate now to help her clear her mind with a little physical pleasure. But it wasn't until they were readying to leave for the winery that Kara admitted, "You know, I think I'm going to wish I had taken a real nap."

"Now that you mention it, I could use a nap...again," he said smugly.

"Not on your life, you time bandit. We've got to attend the last meeting with everybody to make sure everything is ready for tomorrow."

"Kara, if we were any more ready, the festival would have been all over with last week."

"What?"

"We're ready." He said simply.

My oh my, He does look good in this light, she was thinking. Now, *she* felt pretty smug. What they had just been doing was reflected in his eyes, and he looked even more appealing than before. His body was gorgeous with a healthy glow and Kara thought she had better stop thinking about him or she'd want to turn around and go back to the bedroom to explore that slick body again. Wasn't she getting too old for this?

"I know, I know," she said distractedly. "This meeting is more a gathering for moral support than strategic information. Besides, we'll have goodies to eat and drink and everyone seems to like that. *And* best of all, it gives everyone time to talk and gossip together. You know, bonding! This is important for morale." Kara was a mother hen when it came to providing for her brood. "Besides, we're going to need a good-weather dance for tomorrow. Everybody is really edgy about the rain. Did you notice how it looks outside?"

She switched on the small television set that hung suspended in the corner of the kitchen. The local weather followed the news and she had to know what tomorrow would bring.

Turner turned up the volume, saying, "Listen!"

"And the weatherman tells us to be sure to bring our sunglasses along for the Mountain View Winery Annual Festival. The scattered showers tonight are expected to dissipate, and we can put the rain behind us as the forecast for tomorrow is clear skies, sun, and more sun. The highs expected will be in the upper seventies, and the lows tonight..."

Turner tuned the volume down and exalted, "Kara, you did it! You picked the perfect time for the festival! Did you love the way they put in a plug for the it?" They hugged, joyous with the news, even though it had started to rain. "Oregon fog," he gave title to the drizzle.

No one could deny that the rain was a continuing threat to the weekend's success. To speak of it was to entertain the consequences of it happening in reality. Although it was preferred that the skies be clear, there had been times in the past when periods of rain had caused the musicians to put away their instruments and run for cover, along with the guests. Out of doors by the river, there were plenty of trees to act as umbrellas, so the whole exercise became more of an adventure than an irritation. It was more like a shot of adrenaline that woke up the crowd. In any case, it usually didn't last for more than a few minutes at this time of year, and everyone was back at their respective activities, drinking, eating, playing music, or…whatever.

Nevertheless, no one at the winery would bring up the subject of the weather. Bad luck.

Kara had changed into her old comfortable jeans and an oversized sweatshirt. When she got to the winery at six-thirty, all of her employees were present plus a half a dozen more people, who would be filling in for the numerous jobs required for the event. Along with service people, a representative of the hired security company was accompanied by a member of the local police force. They were invited for this last tactical meeting so that they could coordinate in the event of any emergency. With as many people as were expected, it was not only necessary, but good common sense that all contingencies be provided for.

The decibels of conversation were uncommonly high. It should be expected, inasmuch as they were appropriately hyped for the work tomorrow. Glasses of wine and soft drinks were being poured to accompany and enhance the bountiful table of food that had been catered in. Even that project had been an in-house enterprise, accomplished by two of the girls, Gracia and her friend Judy.

"I snacked on everything while I was making it, and now I'm not hungry any more." Gracia took another sip of the blush wine.

Kara had automatically picked up a bottle, poured some Rose for Judy and was going from person to person, pouring their glasses to an appropriate level. Once again, by her action and without even a word, she established her control of the room as she made her way to the head of the tasting bar. "Is everyone ready?" she projected over the room.

The group responded with varied affirmatives and then quieted in expectancy of what would follow. Kara stood up on a case of wine, placing her a head above the others.

"We are about to have the largest and classiest event of its kind in Southern Oregon. I have seen the progress of work that all of you have contributed for its success and I want to thank you now for a job well done. We all know that the weekend and the clean-up are still in front of us, but the excitement will carry us all, as it has in the past. By Sunday night, we'll all be asking each other where the time went, and looking forward to a couple of paid days off from work." Tittering and agreement from the crowd.

"I have asked Beth to go through the main list on the duty roster. If you have any questions or comments, please *write them down*! We have several scratch pads made up of old labels…they can be found along with pencils all around the room. If there is something important to be addressed, we won't be committing it to our *very* imperfect memories. This way there will be a written notation to be acted upon. Beth, are you ready? Beth?"

Beth shook herself out of an abstract space of thought and immediately connected with what was going on. She carefully gathered her skirts and took Kara's place on the riser. She was attended by Shiron, who watched over the scheduling papers, handing them out one by one as they were needed.

While everyone's attention was on the speaker, Kara moved to the back of the room and approached the head security guard and the police officer.

"Could you come to my office? There is something I'd like to speak to you about."

They shut the door for privacy.

Kara always had a hard time doing what she considered, blowing the whistle on anybody. In the past she had given her people the benefit of a doubt if some transgression had taken place. She showed it in the forgiving way she treated them when the cloud of accusation was evident. Without proof of wrongdoing, she would take the word of the accused into serious consideration. And taking others at face value was something she expected others to do for her. It didn't always happen that way.

Not that Kara was entirely without sophistication. There were certain tenets she had arrived at through observation. For example, it was her conviction that one very strong human trait that could be thoroughly depended upon, was that of greed. But from her perspective, greed was no different than any other life preserving instinct. For that reason, it should not be classified as being either bad nor good. It should be perceived instead, as a fact of life. Something to be accepted rather than immediately condemned.

This was where Kara drew the line. In her judgement it was the degree of integrity that separated the good guys from the bad guys. Apparently one of her employees was indeed playing by his own rules and his integrity had fallen short. It was for this reason, she felt the need to speak.

"I appreciate your coming here tonight. Beth will be getting to your part in the event in a few minutes, so I won't keep you long. Are either of you familiar with Talbert Cottner?"

"I know who he is," responded the security man. "Don't know him well enough to talk to, but I know him from sight. Works here, doesn't he?"

"*Worked* here. As of this morning, he won't be coming here as an employee. He had a little run-in with Turner Ferguson about some property that belonged to the winery and was asked to leave and not come back. That's what I wanted to talk to you about. If it wouldn't be too much trouble, I would like you to keep your eyes out for him in case he decides to come in with the crowd tomorrow."

The police officer spoke up, "Do you expect him to cause any trouble?"

"I don't know what to expect, but it might be a good idea to let us know if he is here."

"We can do that. Is there anything else Ms. Tower?"

"Just that." She nearly mentioned the odd phone messages that she and Beth had been getting, but crank calls really could not be traced. Instead, she ended lightly, "We had better join the others so you won't miss any of the pep talk. We really are looking forward to a good weekend, and I do appreciate the cooperation we've had from your people."

"That's what we're here for. It looks like you've done a good job of forestalling any problems. Let me know if anything else comes to mind."

"Thank you, officer." She opened her office door and they unobtrusively mingled with the others in the tasting room. Each person was given their check-sheet as to their individual stations, what jobs they would do, the supply lists for administering their work, and their schedules for time off to enjoy themselves. Kara and Digby were at liberty to act as good-will ambassadors, and had no precise duties. Every one was in high spirits with the expectation of a great weekend.

CHAPTER 31

❀

At the same time that the meeting at the winery was winding up, and Beth was making her notations of a few changes in the schedule, a curious chance meeting was taking place at the local video store. Tom Hutchins had decided to stay at a convenient bed and breakfast inn, fairly near to where the wine festival would be and still proximate to town. Nearly all the hotel and motel rooms in the immediate vicinity had been booked. He felt fortunate in reserving a place for the night.

It was a rustic place aspiring to house six or seven units, upon which each had been designated a name to imply a character from Tolkin's The Hobbit. The gardens were a surreal jungle of vines and trees. Tom cringed at the thought of what kind of netherworld cuisine might be expected in the morning. He feared his cabin would be named Golem's World. It wasn't.

He had tried in earnest to call Bethany Chris wanting to see her again. Knowing that Kara would in all probability, not be happy to be intruded upon this night, he avoided calling there. It would have been nice to have some company.

He tried Beth's place a few more times. Her phone rang and rang. No voice mail. No one was home.

Tom assessed his situation and decided to make use of the VCR that the quaint inn offered at his disposal. He could kick back and watch a couple of movies that he had been wanting to see. A bulletin left on the machine, instructed guests that a large selection of videos could be obtained at the local video store, just a short walk from the B and B.

It was in the Comedy section of the Video Mart that he noticed the handsome tall Native American who was casting about for a selection.

He was dressed in Jeans, a tee shirt and loafers, with a lightweight Levi Jacket slung casually over one shoulder. He reminded Tom of an art piece that hung in the dining room of his parents' home...tall, lean, and muscular with features resembling that of the painting. The luck of the draw in genetics. Tom recalled the physique that ran in his family. Short, slightly overweight and, well...they didn't exactly call to mind the 'beautiful people'.

Shaking his head, the man noticed Tom and had to ask, "Got any good recommendations?"

"Wish I did! You know, it's funny," Tom responded, "Whenever I'm at home, I can think of a dozen movies I want to see, but when I get here, I can't think of a damned one."

"That's the way it is with me. I don't even know why I'm looking in Comedy. I don't really like Comedy."

Tom sensed a kindred spirit of the moment. His next move was on impulse. It must have been because he was at loose ends in a town where there should have been some kind of amusement, say in the company of an attractive woman. It more probably was because he had tried to reach Beth on the phone and batted out. Nonetheless, Tom offered, "I'll tell you what...I could easily forego a movie in my room if there was anything more entertaining going on around here. You know the area?"

"Sure." Raven looked around, giving up on finding any movie titles that jumped out at him saying *watch me!* "I guess when I can't find a video I want, I'm really not all that interested in watching a flick. My name is White Raven. Yours?"

"Tom. Tom Hutchins. Drove over from Medford to go to the wine festival. You going?"

"Who isn't?" He paused to look a little more closely at Tom. Figured him to be relatively prosperous, all dressed up with nowhere to go, as it were. It might be just as well to suggest another form of entertainment, and what better place than the Friday night magnet the locals referred to as the 'Body Exchange'.

He suggested, "Suppose we could get a drink at the local watering hole and check out the action."

"Sounds like a plan!"

Tom drove his car the short distance to the bar. He felt genuinely relieved at having an alternative to the prospect of spending the evening by himself.

You could hear the live music from the street. Country western, of course. A group of revelers came out of the door with the look that guys have when they've gotten off work, stopped in for a beer or three, and were headed home for dinner. They would be back at the bar within a couple of hours, spending more money than they earned that day.

The bar was small compared to the dance floor. It would be crowded later, with sweaty bodies moving to the rhythm of the guitars, fiddles, harmonica and drums. Cowboy boots would stomp and wide skirts would fly in the ritual line dance. Cigarette smoke permeated the air. The huge mirror on the wall in back of the bar stared down at the customers' reflections, like a godhead watching over his children in a communal ritual. White Raven ordered two beers.

It was during the break that they were able to get a word in that could be heard above the din of the loud music. Tom reordered drinks for both of them.

"How long have you lived here?"

"Long enough to get the lay of the land. Pretty interesting place if you're into getting past the surface. People here are mostly retirees and unemployed. Good thing there's some industry like lumber and vineyards to bolster the economy."

"Yes. I've learned recently that wine has pulled in a great deal of money into the area. Looks like it's here to stay." He went for a direct question. "Know anything about Mountain View?" Tom was curious about the local attitude of the winery.

"Like what?" The question was so probing that White Raven reticent to open up on that line of conversation. He waited for a more detailed question from Hutchins.

"Oh, I just thought about the people who ran the place. Seems to me they're pretty gutsy to start a business like that in a new area." He ordered another drink, then Tom went ahead and told his drinking partner broadly about his relationship with the winery via the bank business. Without becoming too specific, he wanted to show he had a legitimate interest.

Raven pondered Tom's story, not answering for a moment and then said, "Kara Tower is a fine woman. She works hard and deserves some success. I would like to see her succeed, but there is something missing. Something in her life. I think maybe this business of the winery is more than one person can handle."

"I get the impression that you think the business is too much for her."

"Yeah, something like that."

"Maybe what she needs is a partner to take off the pressure."

"Maybe. And maybe what she needs is a psychic to analyze where all her troubles are coming from…the cellar rats."

"Cellar rats? What do you mean?"

Although White Raven was more a listener than a talker, he did see that Tom looked genuinely concerned, and for that reason, he continued.

"I'm not talking about the rodent kind. I think the expression comes from the nickname for the workers in the winery, but I'm not sure I'm referring to them either. It's just that I hear of too many things going wrong in too many places for her. You know?...As if a pack of rats were attacking, biting and tearing from many directions. Sooner or later the victim will fall if the onslaught isn't put in check. What has been bothering Kara Tower is taking place without her even knowing or realizing it's there. I don't very often get around the place myself, but I've heard enough about things happening out there that I start to wonder how long she can hold out without some help."

"Then you think she *won't* last there for long?"

"Hell, I don't really know shit." Raven wanted out of this discussion. "Like I said, this is a good woman, and I wish her the best, no matter if she stays or goes."

He was obvious about ending their gossip, turning his attention to the action in the barroom. They both concentrated on drinking and perusing the mingling of the customers. Whenever an attractive woman entered the room, there was a noticeable wave of interest as the men took stock of the available inventory against the incoming goods. As a rule of thumb, the married men, or those with steady live-ins would be found at the tables, with or without their partners. The single guys were at the bar, where they would be more readily mobile.

"So where do you stand now. Are you going to be staying in this area?" Tom asked, thinking that Raven came from another area.

"I come here from time to time," he answered elusively.

"Forgive me for prying, I'm only curious. What keeps you coming back to this place? I keep wondering what the attraction is for different people."

They had come this far with their conversation, Raven could tell him about the work he did. "For me it's the stone. I'm a sculptor. There's good material in these mountains."

"Well, an artist. Have any pictures of your work?" Tom was beginning to feel high. The effects of the alcohol were making him overly-inquisitive.

"No, not here. Anyway, I send it all out of state. It goes through a gallery in Arizona. Not too many people around here even know I carve."

"Sounds like you're pretty successful." An alcohol induced statement followed. "Truth is, when I first saw you I wondered if you could really afford a video. I'm afraid I thought you might be a little down-and-out," he confessed with a guilty look in his eyes.

"Part of my disguise," White Raven said with a small smile. "Don't tell anybody any different. Just as soon they think of me as a poor dumb Indian."

"Nobody'll hear any different from me." Tom replied hanging his arm around Raven's shoulders.

Also, part of the woodwork of any bar were the regulars, to whom no one paid attention. One of these quiet types was sitting near enough to the incongruous pair, the American Indian and the White Collar Worker, to overhear snippets of their conversation. He was getting impatient to repeat the gossip to his buddy that there were other people who thought Kara Tower was on her last leg. He knew his friend was pissed off about losing his job at the winery, and there was more mischief in the air. He loved mischief! He got off on it! Better get to Talbert soon because Talbert had plans. Jeremy wanted to be part of those plans.

He left the bar shortly after finishing his last drink. Shit, he thought as he got into his yellow Volkswagen, I better not get stopped with this beer on my breath. He accelerated with caution. He would take care not to be pulled over by any cop.

If it hadn't been for the winery meeting, which lasted longer than any of them thought it would, Turner would have seen the yellow car that left the bar just before he and Roger arrived.

CHAPTER 32

❈

Kara helped with the tidying after the meeting broke up. The crew had been wonderful with their positive attitudes and energy. Once the tasting room was put to order, the others were scooted out the door and told to get a good night's sleep. Sure! Like they would do just that! They would undoubtedly go to town in spite of her admonishments, but in no way would she want to do anything to quash their enthusiasm. She felt obliged to be the last to leave, and so peered into the second office, where Beth was still working.

"Aren't you finished yet?"

"Just a couple of things, and I'll be out of here. You can go home and get some rest. I'll lock up," she said.

"Think I'll take you up on that. I'll need all the strength I've got for tomorrow. Well…good luck to all of us."

"We won't need luck, Kara. We've got a winner! Anyway, I know you always worry about the festival. In fact, sometimes I think you worry until it's been over with for a week. Face it! This year will be perfect. The weather, everything. So get home with ya'! See you in the morning at about eight."

After she finished making copies of instruction sheets and up-dated the schedules, Beth straightened her own desk before making ready to leave for the night. She tried to calm herself for the project at hand, but her state of excitement was uncontrollable. Oddly enough, the winery and the festival were the last things she was thinking about. More to the point, what was on her mind was the connivance of an excuse to be in town briefly tomorrow morning. Tonight, she was on her own time.

Had it not been for those customers today, she would have been heading for her own place and straight to bed. But now, her plans were definitely altered by their visit to the winery.

They had arrived early in the afternoon, following a burst of activity in the tasting room. More or less on their own, waiting while the other customers were being looked after, they strolled out and settled themselves on the deck chairs just outside the office where Beth had been organizing her unending paperwork. It was an advantage to have an attractive place for people to wait when the tasting room was full. They could have a glass of wine, cheese and crackers, and the ambiance of the beautiful view of the vineyard and mountains from the deck. They were not, however, aware of their voices carrying clearly through the window to the quiet office.

Beth tried to tune out the words as she worked.

"...said we'd *have* to wait till tomorrow morning. I don't like staying at a motel, but I guess it's okay this time. We'll pay cash. No paper trail that way. Plenty of people in town. Good cover! But we were goddam lucky to get a room. Everybody else is going to that wine festival, so we might as well go too."

The woman made a reply that did not register at first. They must have been seated directly outside the wall from Beth's chair, but couldn't see in the window because of the reflection. "We could have stayed with Stark. He lives close enough to Pottsman."

Beth's attention was immediately drawn to the conversation. She knew Earl Pottsman. Turner had roomed at his place for a short time and was lucky to get out of there and move to Mountain View. Pottsman was an unsavory character who was known around town as a sleazy dopester. Hung around a lot of young kids where he did maintenance work at the city park. How anyone like that could even hold a job there was beyond her. He was a real creep!

The woman was saying, "Anyway, I don't want to get anywhere near Pottsman's place if it's at all possible. We can't afford to be seen around him."

Beth thought, this is a juicy piece of eavesdropping. Her work was forgotten.

"We won't go near his house. He and I worked out the trade." This from the man's voice. "There's a utility box for tools by the shed at the park. I pick up the money there, leave the shit and we go out for breakfast. There'll be plenty of happy kids around these parts by noon."

"Not to mention the rest of southern Oregon."

They laughed and talked for a few more minutes before returning to the tasting room for wine samples.

That did it! Beth was compelled to act. But how? She thought it out for a moment before entering the other room to get a good visual on these people. She wanted to see what they looked like. Quickly she committed to memory, the most pertinent details of the conversation. The box at the park. Morning pick-up and drop-off. Before breakfast. Pottsman. He was going to sell the dope to kids at the park…that piece of shit was corrupting children right under the noses of the towns people.

She wondered further about the amount and the kind of dope they were talking about. She had a flash vision of herself walking into the other room, stepping right up to the couple and innocently inquiring, "Excuse me, how much dope did you say you were transacting tomorrow?" Hah! What would the expression on their faces be then? If it weren't so serious, it would be comical.

Instead, Beth kept busy for a minute or two as the couple accepted tastes of wine and conversed. She was careful not to stare, but she could see that they were well dressed, somewhat flamboyantly, and well groomed (not what she expected) and they wore heavy gold jewelry (what she did expect). They were a tad younger than Kara, putting them around fiftyish, she would guess. She had never seen them before.

Beth retreated from the room, heading for the parking area and after perusing the vehicles there, decided that their car must have been the dark gunmetal gray BMW four door. Conservative for their occupation, she thought. Boy, what she would give to see what was packed away in that vehicle.

What she would give to see how much money it was worth! Ooooee!!

It had been some time since the incident with the marijuana stash she had appropriated. She had since heard that the growers were flaming mad when they had lost that crop, but the following week when the police had set up a mega-bust, there was no weed to be found in the place. For that small blessing, the occupants were grateful and, unknown to Beth, had since then set up a larger 'farm' in what they had hoped would be a more secure location.

She had felt pleased because she thought that they would no longer supply poor families with kids by taking their last dollars for weed. Unfortunately, the growers were unstoppable.

Beth unloaded that crop for a substantial amount of money. She divided it into small portions trading it off to wealthy yuppies and professional people who were very discrete about their habits. But no children! Never anywhere near children!

What she suspected now, was no small operation if it netted these people the kind of lifestyle they demonstrated here. The quantity of the transaction was still in question, but could very clearly present a danger with which Beth had never before been challenged.

In the back of her mind, she played out a scenario of intercepting the exchange that would take place at the park. She thought about it. She knew this was way over her head, but the excitement of just thinking about it was nearly enough to give her a climax. What would happen if she could get her hands on those drugs after the 'shiney' people left the stash. Pottsman would have to be watching from somewhere nearby, and unless he could be distracted, no one else could get their hands on it.

What to do? She really had no desire to be in possession of any hard drugs. Would she merely take them, only to destroy them?

On the other hand, what if she could find the money before it was exchanged for the dope. Now that thought deserved some consideration. Again, Pottsman would be watching the cache once he left the currency, and it would be a question of distracting him in some way in order to get to it. If the money turned up missing when the couple came to make the trade, two things would happen. The supplier would be mightily pissed at being led astray, and dear old Pottsman would be in deep shit with his connections. He would also be poorer by the amount of the transaction. Serve him right. Maybe he'd get the message that he should get out of the business.

The second thing was, what would the supplier do with all that dope that he couldn't deliver. Leave it in his car? He planned on going to the festival. She heard them talking about it. Would he try to sell any there? No, no way!

Then his car would be a sitting duck for a sting. Wow! Serve *him* right. Aha...another angle to the plan.

Beth may have been devious in her thinking, but behind the perverse thoughts and actions was a mildly justified attitude. Without reasoning it out, Beth was getting back at the world for having done her an injustice.

She was young and innocent when her parents had been running the small hardware business. The trouble came like a dam bursting its gates when, during a wild and raucous party given on their partner's birthday, the cops were called in to subdue a fight between two of the guests. It was never made clear to Beth that in anger, one of the men had later planted a large stash of drugs in their house. In the end this was the catalyst for the loss of home and hearth, and finally her parents, who were incarcerated. It was her first lesson that life was not fair. Distraught and uncomprehending, at the age of fourteen, she ran away to some distant relatives to avoid being placed in a dreaded foster home.

From that time on, to her way of thinking, the world owed Beth a favor. Her distant memories would return one by one, year by year as her parents served their long prison sentences to term.

Drugs were the problem in the past. Drugs *could* be the solution to the future.

Beth decided to wait until after midnight to drive over to the park. At that hour, anyone still awake would be in town at the bar, not likely playing games on the teeter-totter. She parked her car a block away from the entrance and walked the distance to the now silent tennis courts. She was prepared, in the event anyone was out walking their dog or just walking where she could be seen, to take on some kind of disguise. Getting into the flow of the idea, she could have just had a horrible argument with her significant other. That was it, she would act like a despondent woman. All the while, she watched to see if there was any other person in the park. She was alone. There was no audience.

Making a circuit of the baseball field, the path took her to the shed and the lock box for tools next to it. Again, she moved her eyes to see if there was any movement to be seen under the amber night lights. No one.

Good. She wanted to check the exact position of the door to the box now, so that in the morning there would be no question of where the stash would be and how to get to it. All of the details were not set in her mind, but she would think of something to get Pottsman away from here. It would be easier to determine what her options would be by physically checking the interior. She tried the lock. To her amazement, it fell open.

Quickly looking around again, for if at this point she was caught, it would be pretty hard to explain what she was doing there. She held her breath and opened the door to the cabinet.

Inside was a canvass bag about the size of a large shoe box, one that boots would come in. She reached for it, her heart commencing to beat so fast she could feel it pound.

"Hot Damn," she mouthed. Retrieving the bundle and closing the door in one motion. She tried to bury the bulk of it under her coat, and hunching slightly, she moved away from the tool box and proceeded to work her way out of the park, hoping against all hope that no one would see or stop her before she got to her car. Her mind wanted to race, but Beth used the limit of her control to make a safe retreat from the area.

Back at her house, the first expedient was a drink. With ice and a liberal pour of Canadian whiskey, the sturdy drink was topped off with a splash of soda. On the low coffee table sat the untouched bundle of unknown contents. It was money. She couldn't imagine why it should have been there before tomorrow, but it was there. She didn't know how she knew it was money, but she *knew*.

Carefully she sat her drink down and tugged at the cord that closed the bag. Inside, indeed was a large box. Holding her breath, she opened it.

CHAPTER 33

Trying to sleep when sleep won't come is one of the most frustrating dilemmas that often takes place the night before an important occasion. No matter what plans have been made and carried out for scheduling a 'good night's sleep', insomnia can and will rear its ugly head with a vengeance, destroying all the good intentions for getting a much needed rest.

Sometimes worse than nightmares—the dreaded aspect of dreams, are the conscious thoughts that niggle and burn in the sleepless mind of the victim. Sleeping pills would do the trick, but who ever had those around when they were needed. Instead, the unrelenting meandering of the brain, like dreams, came and went, unsolicited and definitely unwanted.

Kara endeavored to keep her thoughts on the level of pleasant aspects of her present activities. What she wanted most was to sleep. She was exhausted from the day's events. Expecting that she would drift away to sleep in the arms of comfort the moment her head touched the pillow, she instead drifted in and out of imagined situations that would take place tomorrow; seeing friends she hadn't seen for an age of time, enjoying the foods and music, remembering the past years of entertainment, past festivals and the unforgettable occurrences that had taken place. In spite of herself, her mind sped backwards in time to days with her husband.

Gregg had been a real asset to the business when they first started the winery. Never one to follow in any man's footsteps, he was surprisingly inventive, and together they tackled the work as if it were a game and they were the team. There were no children in their marriage, which in turn allowed them to expend even more energy on their mutual projects. Children were not missed. They were busy and things were looking good for the Towers. They were happy, productive people. It was a tragedy when Gregg became terminally ill from cancer, and even more of a hardship after he died.

In particular, Kara didn't like to think of that period of time following his death. It was not a transition she was particularly proud of. Maybe it was the mid-life crazies, or perhaps it was a flaw in her personality, but the profound relief she felt after Gregg's death was indisputable. She was actually glad to have had the burden of caring for him at an end.

Her celebration of independence took the form of a liaison with a young man who passed through her life like a season passes in a year. There today, gone tomorrow. Passion and past. She would tell herself that he was the right man…for right now. The brief involvement had at the very least maintained her sanity. At the most, it satisfied her physical need and gave her the needed distraction from her loss. What was that boy's last name?

As she lay there in her bed, eyes closed, her thoughts continued with recollections of the onslaught of reality that went along with her newfound freedom. The work that had been executed by two, would have to be accomplished by one. With the expectancy that her spending patterns would differ from Gregg's, she had reviewed their financial position, part of which was in probate at that time. She remembered the horror of finding the debts that had been incurred by Gregg's signature alone.

Well, there would be no frivolous spending in the offing. Her purse from now on, she promised herself, would be tightly closed against any unnecessary expense. There were times she was certain that to walk away from the whole enterprise would have been the sanest thing she could have done. But Kara held on and muddled through with more grit than many had expected of her. She continued on as the glamorous head of Mountain View Winery.

And under her management, at least publicly, the winery enjoyed tremendous success. So much so, that as long as two years ago she could see the necessity for the current expansion. The balance of survival in this business was sink or swim. What were her options if she was going to sink? What would happen without the infusion of more money? What contingencies were being considered?

Kara had been anything but idle in the last few days. Because of the upcoming festival, she had been even more preoccupied than usual. What with the normal carrying on of activity, there were added phone calls made to various factions in the industry which went unnoticed by anyone, including her staff. No one was aware of the singular purpose when she made and received curious messages on the voice mail. Her *Plan 'B'* was now well past the formative stage.

It was starting to take on shape and substance. The question was, would it be enough?

No wonder she couldn't sleep! It was too exciting. The festival. The plans she was making. The business. Even Turner was an element of fantasized excitement. She thought of the possibility that he could return to her place in the early morning hours. In her mind, the picture of his body made her tingle.

Oh, quit it, Kara! she admonished herself, making a reality check. You really are hopeless! What you should look for is a more permanent relationship in your life. Someone solid. Or perhaps no relationship at all. Maybe I'm better off alone, she thought.

Lying there in bed was doing no good at all. Frustrated, she slipped on a sheer robe and headed to the kitchen for a cup of warm milk. Kara jumped in surprise. She wasn't alone!

"Good God, Beth! You scared me half to death! What are you doing here at this hour?" Kara was not the only one to jump at the discovery of someone else in that wing of the house. Beth was looking sheepish as she turned off the burner on the stove and wiped up the hot water she had spilled in her surprise.

"I didn't think you would be awake. I was being quiet so you wouldn't be disturbed."

"I couldn't sleep."

"Neither could I. I thought a cup of hot tea might settle me down."

Beth had wanted to speak to Kara, but she was also sure it should wait until morning. She was glad to have this late night opportunity to talk to her. She would not be disclosing her earlier activities in complete detail, but she had to say something. She could use a good alibi. She went on, "Look Kara, I know you have plenty of things on your mind right now, but could I ask for a favor in case it comes up?"

Concern crossed Kara's face as she responded, "Of course! Anything! I hope you aren't in any trouble."

"Well, not exactly. At least, we're not talking about the law being involved or anything like that. It's just that I'd like it to be known that I spent the night…all night that is, at your place. Any problem with that?"

"No problem. Dare I ask why?"

"You don't want to know." They both laughed. Friends did not push friends into explanations.

CHAPTER 34

For many people, the Saturday dawn broke with the insistent barrage of alarm clocks signaling in their various persuasive tones, an earnest call to arms to attend this beautiful day. They would herald the annual crowd of celebrants to gather at the local festival. Almost everyone in the town knew about the event, or were eagerly planning to attend. Nearly everyone.

Among the exceptions, Earl Pottsman woke with a whopping hangover. His eyes would not focus when he tried to open them, and he felt queasy when he turned his head to look at the clock. It was already eight-thirty in the morning and he remembered with a jolt, the important package he would be picking up for exchange of the money pouch. "Earl Boy, don't sweat the small stuff," he said to himself, amused that he could joke about what was a huge amount of money, just sitting there waiting for the transfer.

With a grunt, he sat up in his bed. Whoa, thirsty! What he needed most was a drink. Dehydration had set in and liquid was immediately foremost on his mind. Gotta' fix this thirst thing, he thought. He dragged himself to the kitchen and opened the refrigerator. Nothing but beer. His stomach did a turn. Oh well, why not? Better than water any time of the day, identifying the early hour. He collapsed in the living room, sucking up the liquid. Why didn't he grab two? Then he wouldn't have to move again for a while. Fuck, he felt terrible.

Taking his time to adjust to the light of day, his brain commenced to function in proportion to the amount of alcohol that reached it. Pottsman wondered if maybe it wasn't such a good idea to leave the money there last night. At the time, the hiding place seemed so unobtrusive, so out of the way, that surely it would be safe for the time being. Nobody'd be messing with it. Now, he started to worry. He needed to justify his actions of the previous night, one by one as he remembered them. True, he had regular contacts to make in town, it was part of his business. See and be seen, and hell, he knew beyond all doubt that Friday nights were always heavy drinking as well as heavy transaction nights. He prophesied correctly that he wouldn't want to jump up at dawn, bright eyed and bushy tailed to run out to the park to leave the money. So he left it there last night. So what! Nobody was going to bother with it there. It was a safe place. Wasn't it?

But the safety of the hiding place became less and less secure in his mind until the thought of anything happening to the parcel became an acute concern. Shit! What if something did happen to it? My ass would be…he didn't want to think about it. He dressed as quickly as his shaking hands would allow and left the house.

Arriving at the park utility area where he usually left his truck, Pottsman looked furtively around, attempting to be casual, not wanting to be noticed by any of the early risers who dutifully brought their children for a fresh air outing at the playground area. The sun glared hurtfully in his eyes.

His real concern was certainly not the children. When the drop was arranged, it was made very clear that under no circumstances should he be seen in tandem with the man who would be leaving the parcel. He was to stay out of the area until he knew that the drop had been made, and then approach the tool shed with its utility box on the pretext that he had come to carry out his usual work. What he couldn't figure out now was, if he was early or if the man had already come to the park and was long gone. What was in the box now…money or dope?

Earl swallowed hard. He recognized that he was in a bind. He should have gotten here a lot earlier. He could have messed around with the watering system. Anything, to look like he belonged here on a Saturday morning while he watched for the man with the package. That would have been easy enough, and at least he would know if everything was okay. He wanted more than anything to go straight to the shed and open the box.

He waited to see if anyone came to the shed.

A half an hour passed. The man still hadn't arrived to make the switch. His patience died. This is bullshit, he thought, and headed for the box. None of the children, or their mothers were paying him the slightest attention. He opened the door and looked into the toolbox.

The beer he had for breakfast rose to his throat as the impact of the empty space hit him. He lost it on the grass, impervious to the now disapproving stares of the parents shielding their children from the gross picture.

Giving himself a moment or two to compose his stomach, he forced himself to approach the shed and take another look into the box, knowing it would have no package in it. Empty! That sonofabitch took all that cash and ran!

Earl forgot about his hangover. He forgot about the people gawking at him. He even forgot about the promises of certain deliveries he was expected to make a little later that day. He thought only about one thing. Find the money and/or find the dope! But who the fuck would know where? Today, everybody was going to that stupid winery thing…the festival. So maybe there would be a lead or clue there. Where there was a festival there were usually lots of people. Where there were lots of people, there was usually dope available. And money, there would be plenty of money.

Earl Pottsman wasn't the only one who woke to the reality of a nasty hangover. Saturday mornings could be termed as the official time to separate the more innocent Friday night revelers from the real party animals. How was it that people, when they were drinking never considered what they would feel like the next day. Caught up in social conversation and entertainment, who counts drinks? And interestingly enough, when people were drinking, they did things that were surprisingly out of character.

Tom Hutchins woke with one arm and one leg hanging over the side of a narrow, cushioned space. There were two small pillows made with rough material that supported his slightly aching head. He raised it slowly, testing the movement and its results. So far, okay! The cushion he was on was nestled in the alcove of a cabin and he discovered further was the central angle of a large window seat. He looked around to establish his bearings in an effort to recall the preceding night and how it was that he came to be here.

He heard the clanking of a pot being replaced on the burner of a cook stove and turned to see White Raven approaching with two cups of steaming coffee.

"I see you have returned to the living. Sleep well?" He handed a mug to Tom.

"Apparently I did. But I don't remember how I ended up *there*." He indicated the window seat with a gesture of his head and winced slightly. The coffee was more than excellent, and now as his faculties returned with every sip he was able to progressively appreciate the surroundings. "This is a beautiful place! Where the hell are we?"

"Thanks." Raven ignored the inference that it couldn't have belonged to either of them. "It's not often I bring people here."

Tom continued to take in the rustic room. He noted the elegant deep green colored slate floors and heavy redwood beam ceilings. Occasional rugs with heavy deep pile complimented the hand carved furniture, giving the space a snug warm feel. He could almost sense the heat from the massive fireplace with its dual purpose cook section, although the logs that were presently laid down would not be in use again for several months.

"Yours?"

"Yes, it's mine."

"What you've done here is wonderful. Even with a hangover, it's so inviting and comfortable…so peaceful. Makes me want to go home and burn everything in my apartment and start over."

White Raven laughed, glowing in the complement. He appreciated it, but there was no explaining to someone like Tom Hutchins, who was usually so precise about his actions and life, that achieving the kind of habitat that bespoke of calm and security, was more than the result of quick and facile interior decorating. It was the accumulation of fine household accoutrements over a period of years.

They had taken the time the night before, to get to know one another more personally, giving Raven the insight as to the character of the man. He saw Tom as closed in. Intelligent and open to new concepts, but reluctant to break away from his established patterns. Not at all like himself, he thought. Interesting how two diametrically opposed personalities would connect in the way they had. It had to be because of the knife.

Prior to any 'in depth' conversation at the bar the night before, Tom and White Raven, like most other customers, had taken a few moments for absorbing the ambiance of the room and generally scoping out the patrons for their visual interest. It was a colorful, animated crowd, as diverse and interesting as they were boisterous. While they did so, Raven could feel the growing irritation and pain of a previously unheeded splinter in his thumb. Casually, he had pulled out a pocket knife and attacked the offending wound, squinting and working with concentration on his hand in the dimly lit barroom.

Tom had only just looked to see what Raven was doing, when his eyes narrowed and he stared in disbelief at the very knife he had purchased and was subsequently missing. It was all he could do to keep from shouting out, "That's my knife!"

Keeping a cool head instead, he asked, "Uh, where did you get the weapon?"

Raven looked up briefly from his self-imposed surgery. "Good looking pocketknife, huh? Found it by Beaver Creek not far from the winery. Fine workmanship. New. Sorry for the guy who lost it. Don't think it had ever been used." He put the finishing touches to his hand.

"It hadn't."

The tone of Tom's voice alerted Raven to the gravity of his comment. He looked questioningly at him and said, "You know this." It was more of a statement than a question.

"Yeah…I know this. I'm the pathetic guy who lost it."

"You?"

"Me!" He fished out his wallet and waved the receipt before putting it down on the counter in front of Raven. "I bought it the day I took Beth, the girl from the winery, up to the park for a picnic. Didn't notice it was missing at first, but once it was gone, I never expected to see it again. I didn't even know where I had lost it. Surprised the hell out of me when I recognized that you were using it."

White Raven wiped the blade on his jeans, carefully folded it away and offered the knife, reluctantly, to Tom. "Guess this is yours."

Seeing the pain of loss in the man's reluctant gesture, Tom came to a quick decision. As much as he wanted to repossess this quality object, he suddenly wanted very much for this quality man to have it, and said, "No, keep it. It seems the gods have decreed that you should have the knife, so…yours it is."

Raven looked lovingly down at the piece and for a moment Tom braced himself as if he were about to be given a great bear-hug by this tall and very grateful Native American. The moment passed as White Raven generously extended his right hand for a controlled and manly shake, his countenance stoic but his eyes radiant with gratitude. The tenuous bond that defines certain people as close friends was set.

"Have you ever considered attempting any art form as a vent for your own pleasure?" White Raven asked as they settled back to enjoy one more cup of gourmet coffee, the breakfast dishes pushed aside for the moment.

"Me?" Tom reacted in surprise. "I don't think I've ever been still for enough time to create anything let alone having the focus and concentration it takes. Although I must say that over the years I've come to appreciate artwork in its finished state. Now that I've seen some of your work, I'm inclined to place your talent at the top of the heap." Evidence of White Raven's exquisite work appeared throughout his home.

"Is this where I blush and say 'shucks'? Actually, I had the idea after talking to you practically all night. You'd probably like dabbling in creativity from time to time. It's a mind-clearing experience. Especially therapeutic for anyone so involved in their work."

"Really, my friend, I do manage to smell the roses once in a while."

"Sure you do. But if, and I only say *if* you were to choose a form of artistic expression, what do you think it would be?" He got up to clear the table while Tom thought out this ponderous question.

"Well, it would probably be silly to anybody else, but there is something I thought of before you asked."

"And?"

"Not the kind of thing you would think of as a true art form."

"I'm a judge?" He returned to the table and sat, giving Tom his undivided attention.

Tom looked embarrassed for a moment, bit at his lip and then said, "I keep looking at these logos and labels on wine bottles. Some of them are really dogs! Some of them are really great. I could see myself drawing and designing something like that. It would be fun!"

"You know…?" Raven was totally serious now, "I believe I'd like to see you give it a try. With the wine festival this weekend, you might even come up with some original inspiration that should be committed to paper. How about it? If you'd like, make yourself at home here for the next couple of days. I have drawing materials you could use. And this way," he added laughingly, "I'll have a ride to the Mountain View event."

"Don't you have a car?" Tom asked incredulously.

"Yeah, but nobody around here will ever know that I do. Like I said. I have a reputation to uphold." He didn't elaborate about the sleek Ferrari, securely locked away in the immaculate garage.

Together and simultaneously they nodded their mutual understanding.

CHAPTER 35

❀

Kara stirred as she focused in on the sound of distant clattering in the kitchen. She rose, wrapped a dressing gown around her still sleep-bound body and headed for the bathroom. It's going to be a long day, she thought while making the usual circuit of her morning ablution in about half the normal time.

Heading out the door, she nearly ran into the tray that Beth was carrying to the bedroom. It was set for two with a fresh coffeepot and warmed croissants.

"I was sure you'd like a wake-up jolt before you got on that non-stop conveyor you'll be on today."

"You sound like you're in a rare mood, yourself. Somebody bring *you* breakfast in bed? Or are you doing this to get us both energized? How did you sleep?"

"Great! And I never felt better!" Or richer, she thought.

Kara wondered what the reason for Beth's extremely high mood swing was. She wanted to ask about the need for an alibi last night. But Kara was discrete enough not to dig into the explanation for anyone's actions, least of all Beth's. She would merely wait it out, knowing that when the time was right, Beth would explain.

Sitting by the garden window, they sipped coffee and nibbled breakfast for a while without an exchange. Then, because she could not abide the silence any longer, Beth blurted out, "If you found yourself with some extra cash…hypothetically that is, a lot of extra cash, what would you do?"

Kara was stunned. This was not at all what she expected. And further, was she speaking 'hypothetically' about herself, or Kara? Knowing Beth, she had suspected that last night's behavior had something to do with one of her numerous flings. Beth was an attractive and very sexy girl, so it wasn't uncommon for her to find herself in some imbroglio with the entreaty for Kara to back her up after the fact with appropriate excuses and explanations. That had been done a few times before. But this was a new development.

She ventured, "You won the lottery?"

"Kind'a, but not exactly." Beth took a deep breath, sighed and then continued, "I don't want to distract you any more than necessary today, but if you get the chance I'd like you to think about it and tell me what you would do…hypothetically. We can talk about it some other time when we're not so busy. I really shouldn't have brought it up now, but I just had to say something. It was pretty much on my mind."

"You robbed a bank." Kara stated flatly.

"No." She couldn't help but smile. "And not to worry. I haven't been out selling by body either!" Beth was laughing now and they both benefited from a good joke between them. Except, Kara still wasn't sure what the amusement was about. She took a beat of time to consider the miracle of a sudden burst of cash available for the business. Certainly a daydream! A healthy injection of cash would definitely cure the problems of the moment. Wouldn't it be nice to be able to tell those tight-assed bankers to take a hike…that she didn't need them? Ah, the dreams of the poor and helpless!

They were interrupted by the chime of the clock.

"Lord, I've got to get some cloths on. Go ahead with what you have to do. See if there's anything we need to bring with us from the house, and I'll be out in a sec." Kara made for the bedroom.

CHAPTER 36

Turner had been assisting the staff in setting the tables and chairs according to the layout that was planned for the patrons to get maximum enjoyment of the scenery as well as the entertainment of the day. He and the others had been on the job since dawn.

This was more than just another pretty spot, he thought to himself. Just wait till those city folks get a load of what this country life looks like. They'll never want to go home. He stood back for a moment to absorb the beauty of the mountains and trees. The river beside them was crisp and clean with the soft song of riffles and rushes. The alders and cottonwoods were still the color of newborn growth, and the grasses were resplendent with copious arrays of wild flowers. Movie-set perfection!

He returned to his truck for supplies.

"I think we're ready! Let the games begin!" He brandished a checkered tablecloth from the back end of 'Curley', and sweeping the fabric through the air, gestured like a matador before a bovine adversary, in this case the unimpressionable hood of the truck. Netta plucked the cloth from him and placed it with the others to be spread on the tables.

The entire area was beginning to take on the look of a real party. Flowers were arranged in used wine bottles displaying labels from past vintages. They were stationed on every table. There were a multitude of booths with their decorations competing for attention. They were appealing to the eye and would be enticing to the customers and passers-by. The vendors were standing at the ready. Buy our wares!

As much as the day's activity had been pre-orchestrated, unavoidable glitches happened in spite of their efficient preparation. Roger had searched the winery for the tasting glasses, three thousand of them, and they were not to be found. How could *that* many glasses disappear? He was ready to either cry or kill. He learned eventually that they were delivered to the wrong outbuilding and found them with just enough time to truck them to the entrance for disbursement to their first customers of the day.

Shiron, who was in charge of the wine pouring stations, was trying to juggle the schedules for what she hoped would be the last time.

Beth and Kara had made their appearance with arms loaded down with bags and papers, schedules and money-receipt ledgers. They deposited each of the articles in their appropriate places, and continued on to speak to each of the various people participating in this production. The vendors, the chefs, the entertainers were made welcome. She complemented them on their displays, commenting on the auspicious weather they were fortunate enough to be enjoying, and thanked everyone for being there to insure the success of the event.

The musicians had been warming up for what seemed like hours. They suddenly ceased their discordant sounds and commenced with a polite up-beat swing that would heighten the convivial ambiance for the crowd as they filed through the gate.

For Kara, it was like *deja vu*, as it had all been done in the years of annual festivals prior to this. Each of her regular employees were accustomed to the bustle of preparation, and Kara was content that on the whole, her crew was performing this ritual in a professional and competent manner and she again felt a real pride in her accomplishments.

Her appreciation for the growing development of the festival was all the greater because it wasn't always like this. There was a time, when the winery was in its infancy, that it was necessary for Kara to pull the weight of several people. There were no qualified candidates as yet for the positions that were opening with every leap and bound of growth in the business. The weight of the extra work always fell upon Kara. This was manifestly evident for example when help was required in the 'big room' of the winery. She would be there at the winemaker's side. At the bottling line she could be found at the corking machine or hefting the empty bottles onto the conveyor, always where there was the need for an extra body to shoulder the job. At harvest she would blend in with the crew, picking grapes if an extra hand was needed. In every case, she was instructor and prompter to all those around her. There was no job she asked to be done that she wouldn't do herself.

The result of this involvement was the professional level that was reached by each employee under the watchful eye of their employer, as her staff was carefully honed for their respective positions. Indeed, Kara had a very personal investment and pride in 'her people', as she called them.

Shiron came running up with the exclamation, "The driveway is filling up with cars! They're backed up to the street already." She turned to Beth. "Shall we open now?"

Beth, who was in charge of the overall scheme, responded immediately. "Absolutely!" Her eyes flashed. She wasn't the only one who was primed for the action. They were all super-charged. "Like Turner said, 'Let the games begin!'"

The first groups filtering in were primarily families. They towed their resisting children with determined tugs, admonishing the little rascals to behave themselves. Expectation was in their faces. They could be seen casting about for a place to settle children and belongings on the grounds before making the foray into this world of food, wine, art, and entertainment.

Others arrived in groups of twos, threes, and fours. They were ready for a pleasant day's outing. It wasn't long before the festival area was alive with milling people as they went about their various activities, eating, drinking and browsing around the various craft booths. The instrumental music played on, interjecting a fresh rhythm every few minutes.

Beth was at the welcome-table when the first group of what they referred to as 'heavy hitters' walked in. She spotted them making their approach to the entrance. The men wore the prescribed attire of the 'successful businessman on his day off'; Dockers, golf shirts or button-downs, no tie, cordovan loafers. Their hair was uniformly short-clipped. They were clean-shaven and bore no visible tattoos. Definitely *not* any of the locals!

She tried to place them in her memory, but failed. If she wasn't so busy with the immediate details of securing the various serving booths with their needs, she would have dashed over to where Kara was taking care of her public relations image, to ask her about the new arrivals. Did she know them? Were they important? And on and on. Beth was not only a curious young lady, but she was known to be pretty forward about asking questions, whether they were appropriate or not. But reason and courtesy won the day. She drew back and watched the progress of the group in the crowd.

Of course, Kara knew and had indeed worked with these men. She had shared a close business relationship with them for more than seven years, first in the name of Braverly Wine Distributors, and now as Superior Beverage Distributing. Although Beth had never met them personally, these were the people who were the winery agents, and who now had control of the Mountain View product distribution.

Kara shuddered when she saw them. Although the relationship between supplier and distributor was expected to be viewed as 'congenial', during their last couple of meetings she had sensed a withdrawal in their overall behavior. Nothing substantive, just a cooling off in the atmosphere, and a notable reluctance to maintain the momentum of their past interest.

Even more curious, after examining the numbers in her own files, she had noticed a reduction of both warehouse and retail orders. That in itself was odd…and frightening. Normally, with the winery's aggressive marketing strategies, the demand for their wines would be escalated each month, and by the end of every year could be tracked as a healthy growth in the business.

However, in the last few months, the picture was changing for some reason. Orders had slacked off and in the last thirty days, had dropped considerably—another one of the several reasons for her acute need of a substantial cash infusion. Kara didn't understand the cause for this. Eye appeal and quality of the product had not changed in any discernible manner. If anything, they had improved on an already good thing. Public reaction was positive. Expansion was in the schedule, not reduction. She had discussed the problem with the principals of the distributing company and they assured her that the slump was merely a temporary one, due to a slow season, and that perhaps she should take some deep cuts in the pricing of her finer restaurant wines.

"I really don't understand how a price cut in some of our highest award winning wines could do us any good. Why would we do that?"

"Just an interim move to introduce new labels to the market. We'll have your wines moving again in no time. It would simply be easier to re-enter at a lower price, that's all."

At first she was disappointed and then furious to see the Mountain View label being replaced by other names on wine lists, and these, offered at even higher prices. Other wineries were certainly not being asked to reduce their pricing. It was uncanny.

Kara had personally visited about thirty key restaurant accounts only to find that her wine had not been merely sidestepped temporarily from the lists, but had been completely discontinued. Disconcerted, she dared not voice her complaints. That would not only be poor form, but the politics of the business demanded that confrontation did little other than to alienate the victim.

She had seen this before. She was aware that it was an ongoing hue and cry, and not a popular one, from nearly every winery in the distributor's portfolio. They all competed for more exposure and sales...absolutely necessary for the continuation of their businesses.

But neither pleading nor threats could melt the hearts of the powerful distributors. These constant hammerings were taken in stride at the distribution level and met with replies that sounded like recordings. "Of course, we are doing all we can to promote your product," they explained. "Patience! It takes time to establish the label." Oh yes, the distribution game is a hard job. After all, they are all doing everything they possibly could.

And the unfaltering path of their operations would continue to function as though no conversation had taken place at all.

What a crock, she thought at the time. It was obvious that distribution would become untenable when each and every year they added a dozen or more new winery labels to their roster. There was simply no way, backed by statistics, that so many varieties of labels could be crammed into existing retail outlets. Markets, wine shops, and restaurants were at maximum absorption. It was like trying to stuff a hundred-ninety pound woman into a size eight. Where did they expect to place all these new products? Impossible!

The reality of the problem was self-evident. Kara bit the bullet and reluctantly approached her visitors. They couldn't in fact, do as they promised for every winery they represented. No matter how perfectly acceptable a winery's product was, some were predestined to succeed and some relegated to defeat. It seemed that the outcome was totally controlled by the whim of the seat of power...the distributorship. It boiled down to who was calling the shots and what they were getting out of it. Most of all, what they were getting out of it.

"I'm happy to see you were able to join us today." Kara greeted as warmly as she could.

"Hello, Kara." Jerry Majors, Vice-President in charge of fine wines for Superior Beverage Distributors stepped forward. "We couldn't pass up the opportunity to enjoy the party this year. I'd like to introduce you to the new man in our group, Steve Hoag. Steve's been very active in the chains and wants us to do a drive for more facings."

Kara was aware of the need for centralized disbursement for the larger super-store chains and could see why this specialized field would require new personnel. Steve would be an incredibly important key addition to the company. And a very handsome one, at that. But what were his intentions with regard to the future of her winery? He looked like a man who could make miracles happen, until she looked him squarely in the eyes. The smile was pleasant enough, but the eyes were cold steel.

"I'm so glad to meet you. And I'm pleased you could all make it today. We'll have a surprise for you later, so I hope you'll all be here for the introduction of one of our new wines. You can see for yourself what kind of a crowd-pleaser it will be."

"Excellent, Kara, we look forward to it." And with that, the new man seemed to withdraw with the others as they exchanged polite smiles and murmurings. Slowly, they moved off.

Their first stop was at the wine bar where they were met with a cordial and friendly, "Hey, howya' doin?"

"We'll have the Cabernet Franc," Majors abruptly told the bartender in an authoritative voice.

"I'm sorry Sir, we have none of that varietal here for the festival. Would you care for a Merlot or Cabernet Sauvignon?" The reply and question took on a more formal tone.

"You don't have any Cabernet Franc?" His voice was truculent now. "That's my favorite wine!"

"I'm terribly sorry." Ryan tried to smile behind the thought that this was a great way to start his tour of duty today. The other helper at the bar turned away from the group in a pretense of activity, away from the uncomfortable exchange.

"Well hell, give me some Merlot," he pouted. What about the rest of you?" He addressed his cohorts.

This was not the first disagreeable customer that Ryan had ever handled, so the nonplused bartender poured a generous glass of Merlot and Sauvignon Blanc for the others.

"Will there be anything else?" He prayed not.

"No, that'll be all," Majors said. He was perilously on the border of being discourteous as he paid for the drinks.

"Customers from Hell," commented the other wine pourer, quietly.

Ryan agreed. "Whoever they are, I hope Kara doesn't have to deal with them. She won't put up with rude people."

Neither of them knew that this clan of businessmen was *never* rude to anyone who 'counted'.

Beth was interrupted by Netta's approach, a worried look on her face.

"Beth, when you brought out the money pouch and the receipt books, where did you put it?"

It was necessary to supply ample money for making change at each of three stations on the grounds, one at the entrance and two at the wine bars. Tills were kept full with supplies of coins and currency from the pouch as Beth would extract the larger bills when they accumulated, placing the 'stash' in a carry bag that she kept on her person.

"Under the counter where the guest book and the wrist stamps are. In the corner."

"Could you come back and show me? With all the extra supplies back there, I just don't see it." She appeared hopeful, but agitated. She could hear Gracia asking a new customer if they had correct change for their entry fee.

They advanced to the supply area in question and looked about. Turner and Shiron had been busily arranging glasses and bottles of wine.

"I put the money and ledgers in the corner. Turner, you've rearranged some things. Did you move a money pouch?"

He looked up from what he was doing. "No." He commenced to look around the enclosure. Nothing!

"Good God, there was a lot of money in that bag. We have to find it!" Panic had set in.

"Were you looking for a green bag?" across the counter, a small voice inquired.

Tuner replied, "Yes, have you seen it?"

"There's a green bag right here." The petite, plainly dressed woman pointed outside the entrance booth, between it and the adjacent vendor's station. She bent over to retrieve the bag from the grass and handed it to Turner. He expressed his thanks and pressed a free glass of wine in her hand.

He removed himself from the hearing distance of the other customers. "Jesus Christ, what the fuck was it doing out there. Beth, you'd better count it."

"I will." She produced the ledgers from her shoulder bag and computed the expected total of cash change on hand.

Of the money that remained, Beth found that only the banded one-dollar bills were missing. It was not a huge amount, but could have been far worse if the entire bag had been taken. Come to think of it, she wondered, confused, why *wasn't* the whole ball of wax lifted. Whoever did it wouldn't have had much of an opportunity to be selective. They might have planned to take the whole thing, but got scared off.

Undeniably, the culprit had to be one of their own. An employee. Beth hypothesized a scenario in which the bag had been lifted from its place behind the counter and pilfered in part. No one would miss a small amount of cash. Then, in a greedy impulse, the thief attempted to make off with the entire pouch, believing the others would only think it had been misplaced. But this maneuver must have been thwarted by the arrival of an unsuspecting witness. The bag was thrust between the two booths in avoidance of being caught with his—or more probably her—hand in the cookie jar…and back to business as usual.

Anyway, Beth thought to herself, that's the way I would have done it! It takes a thief to think like a thief!

So, who could have had this opportunity behind the counter? Sure Turner was there, but he had his hands full with the moving of wine and glasses. Wouldn't have even thought of it. No, it wasn't him.

One of the 'imported' help? Day workers, who were here only for the weekend. Not likely. They were neither inventive nor daring enough to do much more than their jobs by rote. She doubted they could find their own private parts in the dark, much less be instigators of any malfeasance.

Shiron or Gracia? No!…Netta!

What better alibi than to 'discover' the theft. She was clever enough to cover her ass. With complete control of the booth at intervals, Beth guessed she would pad her income if given the chance. She was known to be perpetually broke due to the peccadilloes of one guy or another. Netta it was!

She went to Kara with the bad news, omitting her suspicions regarding Netta.

"How much was taken?"

"Well, luckily not a whole lot. Just a partial bundle of ones. Fifty dollars. The point is, we didn't lose the whole pouch."

"Any ideas who did it?" They spoke quietly, not wanting others to overhear their conversation.

"Maybe. But let me check it out. I'll let you know. But for now, forget it and have a great time with your adoring public."

Kara gave a resigned shrug and just turned to make off for other parts when she nearly ran over White Raven…if a five-foot four female could run over a six-foot one man. The jostling took him by surprise. Raven wrapped his arms around Kara to keep her from falling.

"Was that a body-slam, or are you just happy to see me?" A twist on an old cliché.

"I'm *so* sorry!" Backing up for better focus, she exclaimed, "White Raven, it's been a while."

She took in a marked change in the man. Or was it really a change. Perhaps it was subtler than that. She studied him with interest. This man was handsome. Had he been hiding this more refined side to his looks? She couldn't remember why she had never taken more careful notice of him. Come to think of it, she had never really given him much more than a cursory glance in passing. He was someone she recognized; had even remembered a day last winter when she had taken pity on him thinking him destitute. She also remembered the intelligence of his conversation and wondered what he did for a living. He certainly didn't look destitute today! Now, he seemed…somehow totally different.

"Yes," was his simple answer, pregnant with undertones of meaning.

"Wow," Beth spoke up with her usual directness in a voice that no one could miss. "Raven, you're lookin' fine today! See Kara? Not all the things that happen around here are so bad. Like I said, have fun. Socialize! I've got a hundred things to do so I'll see you later." She acknowledged them and went off at a trot.

"Something bad happen?" White Raven questioned before he could stop himself.

"Just an incident. It happens when we have several things going on at the same time."

"That isn't surprising. Whenever people are gathered in numbers you can expect the unexpected. The best any of us can hope for is that the extent of damage control won't be too devastating in the long run."

He didn't dig any further into the issue. His calm assurances, however, served to placate Kara. She answered him honestly.

"It could have been pretty devastating. That's what unnerves me. Fortunately, the culprit in this case wasn't that successful. I hate these episodes." She didn't go into the details, noticing at the same time that it was so easy to talk to him, but added, "I hate to think that anyone cares so little of us that they would hurt us in any way."

"You only feel that way because you would never do that kind of thing to someone else." He managed in that one statement to neatly describe Kara's own regard for others.

"You're exactly right, I wouldn't. In fact, that makes it all the harder to understand." She was comfortable about talking to him this way, at a more personal level. His voice was deep and lyrical. Suddenly it was as though they had been old friends.

"This business you are in makes you a highly visible public figure." He went on, basing his reasoning on his knowledge of her public image. "Some people may think you have more than you need, so they take away from you. It may be money, it may be belongings, or even your influence; your power. But this banditry derives from one malevolent breed. For you they are cellar rats. They nibble away at anything they can when you are not looking."

Having listened to this mystic analogy, she was struck by his grasp of the situation. In so few words, he had captured the cloud that had settled over her. She had an overwhelming urge to continue their conversation.

"Again, you've made a good point," she replied. "I've learned recently that there have been occurrences that could be related in some way, and I'm trying to sort out some answers." She smiled. "I hope I'm strong enough to stand up to the task."

"Sometimes it's smart to listen to your instincts. That has saved more than one skin in the past."

As they conversed, they ambled over to the riverbank. Large stones bordering the water provided a multitude of selections for natural seating. Kara perched on one, her fingers trailing delicately in the water.

They talked about more pleasant subjects; the seasons, other scenic lands, music and art.

White Raven studied her as they talked. She was getting older, yes. You could see the character of the lines at the corners of her eyes and mouth. They bespoke of two diametrically opposed attributes; confidence and vulnerability, sophistication and innocence. He never realized before how really beautiful she was. There was an inner calm and utter confidence that was not obvious or overpowering. But the strength was there. He could see that she would never back down or break under pressure. A strong woman. Yes, he liked her.

For her part, the feeling was mutual. She was enjoying their unrestrained talk. It was nice to know that the festival would go on without her temporarily.

"By the way, did you know I came here with Tom?" he asked.

"No, I wasn't aware you even knew him. How did you two connect?"

"Long story. There he is, coming this way."

"What a beautiful setting! You two look like a painting by Fraggonard." Tom was jovial.

"So welcome to the scene." Kara smiled with the pun. "I certainly won't complain about the attractive company."

The men smiled politely at one another, each with a slight glint that could be construed as the eternal, but suppressed struggle for male dominance.

They agreed to have a bite to eat before participating in wine tasting. The crowd was building up as the morning progressed, and the art and craft booths were being enthusiastically admired.

"Quite a turnout," Tom remarked admiringly.

"I really enjoy seeing everybody having a pleasant time." Kara took a breath and added, "Although there are always a handful of people I could do without."

That surprised Tom. Somehow, the derogatory comment seemed out of character for Kara.

"What makes you say that?"

Kara considered how she could put it. After all, Tom was a member of the Southern Valley Bank. It wouldn't be politic to give him the impression of any dissension between her winery and its distributors. If there was to be a loan, there could be nothing in the wind to capsize the balance of probability. No suggestion of a problem. Yet, she had some instinctual confidence in their dealings, so following Raven's suggestion, she commented elusively, "Tom, have you ever met any of the people from Superior Beverage Distributors?"

She indicated the group of men standing apart from the others clustered around the wood carver's display.

"Let me see. The fellow wearing a blue jacket looks familiar. Jerry…something. I think Carl Bradshaw introduced us at The Club last week. Seemed to be always complaining about something."

Kara was disappointed to learn that the CEO of the bank was acquainted with the members of her distribution team, such as it was. Her heart sank with the thought that the winery's track record was being discussed behind her back, or rather right in front of her. What else could go wrong? She didn't want to think about it.

"That's the one. Jerry Majors. He runs the wine department at Superior. I've been with them for a long time, but recently," she had to admit, "they haven't been living up to their promises. They could be doing a lot better job."

"Another form of cellar rat." Raven spoke up.

Kara understood, but Tom was confused.

She answered before the question arose. "We have a broad theory regarding outside influences on business." A conspiratorial glance passed between Kara and White Raven.

"Oh." Tom took this in stride.

Earl Pottsman made his entrance shortly after one o'clock. He headed straight for the bar and asked for a beer.

"I'm sorry," repeated Ryan the bartender, for probably the twentieth time that day. "We are only serving Mountain View wine at this booth, but if you care for coffee or a soft drink, you'll find it just there by the yellow awning." His immediate thought was that this guy looked like he could use a strong cup of coffee.

"Gimme a glass of wine…anything you got."

"I'll pour some blush. It's neither sweet nor dry. That should be good for starting out. Should go nicely with whatever you choose to eat."

"Yeah, thanks."

Earl wasn't in the mood for anything to eat. That wasn't what he was here for. Through narrowed eyes, he scanned the crowd for anyone he recognized. Damn, he thought as he watched the crowd. No one was what you could call lively. What a bore! He knew he would be too early for any action. Maybe he'd leave and come back later. He slammed the liquid down his throat without tasting it.

At the gate, he asked for a stamp on his wrist so he could return without paying for another admission, and headed for the parking lot.

It was just as he was stepping into his car that he noticed the metallic gray BMW pulling into the slot about four cars ahead of his and to the right. The driver got out, removed his jacket, checked his wallet and said something to the woman, who was climbing out of the passenger side. They seemed to be deadly serious, and then burst into gales of laughter. What a trip! Pottsman continued to watch, fascinated.

The couple looked like something that made him think of a Hollywood version of Las Vegas. The woman was a stunner. She was stacked and had a behind that was well displayed by the sheer fabric of her printed summer dress. They both sported heavy gold jewelry.

He thought about who these people could maybe be. Like maybe this was the contact he had never met before. Maybe, these were the slick dudes who made the pick-up on his money and thought they'd pull a fast one, not leaving the delivery. Fools. On the other hand, maybe it wasn't them. How stupid could they be to hang around this area just for fun. Weren't they afraid of being caught? Maybe, they *wanted* to contact him by making themselves public. He couldn't decide what to do about it. He stayed in his car and watched.

They made an issue of locking up the car, but as they were leaving for the festival, it seemed the woman had forgotten something. She took the keys from the man and hurriedly opened the front door on the driver's side. Leaning across the interior she couldn't reach what she was after. Christ, Pottsman thought, now that's an ass! She got out, walked around the car, opened the lock on the other side, reached behind the passenger's seat and retrieved a broad brimmed hat.

With that accomplished, and with the man still at watchdog surveillance, she deliberately returned to the driver's door, where Earl could see as she pushed the door-lock button and closed the door. The two were joined again in their pursuit of the day's entertainment, disappearing along with other couples into the festival grounds.

Pottsman exhaled as if holding his breath had rendered him invisible. He didn't want those two to notice him. He was still wondering, were these the people he was supposed to transact with this morning? They never had met face to face, but he couldn't be sure that they didn't know what *he* looked like. It would be smarter to stay under wraps and play it by ear. Play it by Earl! He sniggered to himself for that clever piece of humor.

His curiosity guided his steps from his own vehicle, through the grassy parking area to the side of the Beamer. He peered from the hair hanging in his eyes, above dark glasses perched on the end of his crooked nose to check if anyone was observing his movements. No one was paying attention.

With his fingers twined at the bottom of his tee shirt, he left no prints on the handle as he tried opening the door. What he didn't expect was for the door to give. He had seen the woman lock it. She must have hit the wrong button!

Earl Pottsman nearly fell over backwards when the door opened so easily. He cast about furtively to check if anyone was watching and cringed to think there could be some loud alarm go off. But no, he was still okay. He reached to the back door, opened it and fitted himself into the seat, pulling the doors shut. He was safe, unseen in the back of the car with the tinted glass windows.

His initial shock of getting in the car so easily geared up the adrenalin and his heart was still beating fast. He looked about at the baggage and personal effects that allowed him so little space. The diverse bundles and packages challenged him. There was a hell of a choice as to which would be of interest and which would not.

He made a hurried search through this bag and that, finding food, books, and clothing. The usual accoutrements of the traveler. Jewelry! Where would they keep any jewelry? There was a small flat appointment/calculator, found in a side compartment of a locked carrier. He pocketed it. He'd have to pick the lock of the carrier or tear it apart. Something good in there! That would be work. He noticed an ice chest. He'd check it first, and treat himself to a cold beer if they had any.

He hoisted his body to reach over packages to the large container and opened it.

There was a layer of plastic wrapped sliced deli meats for sandwiches. He swept these carelessly aside. And there, in perfectly packed order, were meticulously wrapped packages. Pottsman knew beyond all doubt what the contents were, and now he knew exactly whose vehicle this was. Ka-ka-ching!

As he took in the volume of white powder in the container, he felt sick for the second time that day. There was enough to turn on half the state of Oregon for a month! He couldn't begin to compute the street value. It was too enormous. These fools were not to be believed.

Then his adrenaline really hit high gear. He grabbed a large grocery sack and dumped its contents on the floor. It would have taken too long to extricate the whole chest from the packed car. Package after package was stuffed into the paper bag, filling it. Hell, nobody would think anything about a guy carrying a paper grocery bag.

Attempting to calm himself before opening the door, he looked around for witnesses. None. He opened the car door. He was sweating.

He closed the door, again being careful not to leave fingerprints, and casually ambled over to his own car as if he were in no hurry. He could have peed his pants with the relief he felt when he drove away.

Tom was sitting at a shaded table finishing what had been a delicious paté en croute with fresh asparagus and an agreeable Merlot, when he saw Carl Bradshaw and entourage. There were three men and a woman with him; two of the Northwest Development Corporation people and Howard Curry, his favorite teammate. The young woman was unknown to him. Somehow, he knew that Curry was with the girl. They fit. Two nerds in a pod.

"Hello Carl, Mr. Gillman."

"Good to see you again, Tom," the large man blustered, looking pleased.

"Well, Tom." Carl Bradshaw cut in. "Glad to see you here, and you *do* remember Francis Gillman. Have you met his partner, Clark Peterson?"

"Of course, we were introduced at The Club the other night. Nice to see you again."

Handshakes were exchanged and a belated introduction to Curry's friend was made.

Tom guessed the reason for the presence of the four men. They were here to look over the viability of the winery. He opted to open a can of worms by saying, "Howard, I've been looking for you for the last couple of days. You promised to get the committee worksheets to me on Mountain View. You didn't happen to bring them with you, did you?" He knew this was an improbability. He was just rubbing it in Curry's face.

Curry sneered, "There won't be any need for any worksheets now. You can forget about still being a white knight to Kara's Little-Girl-Lost problems."

"What do you mean by that?" he said amiably. Prick, he thought.

"We've already discussed this at length, Tom. I believe the matter of the Tower loan has already been decided."

"And what, exactly has been decided, and why wasn't I told?" Tom was ready to swing on the guy. He couldn't believe they would come to any decision without advising him of it. This was an affront to his position as an officer at the bank.

Carl Bradshaw interrupted in his best *basso profundo*, "Now, now gentlemen, we don't want to be holding our office business at this festive occasion. I'm sure this lovely young lady would enjoy a more lofty conversation. Isn't that right?" He indicated the embarrassed girl at Curry's side. Until now, they had ignored her.

"Howard, I think I'll go have some wine and listen to music," she demurred. Without waiting for an answer, she fled from the group as if they were contagious.

"Well," Bradshaw was casting about for a winery employee, "I wouldn't mind taking a closer look at the facility. I was told there would be tours of the winery. What do you say, Francis? Want to come along?"

"I'd like that." He turned to Peterson. "Clark? Are you ready for this?"

"You know I am."

With a smugness born of insider's knowledge, they gravitated back to the entrance in search of someone who could take them to see the winery.

Tom was struck by the exclusion of both Howard Curry and himself from their touring party. There was so much going on that he didn't understand. Why didn't they invite either Howard or himself along on their investigation of the property? Of course, he had seen about all there was to see of it, but Curry hadn't. As far as Tom knew, Curry hadn't even met with Kara during her entire negotiations for a loan. That in itself was odd, though he had a pretty good idea why he had made himself scarce.

In any case, Carl would learn today that Kara's enterprise was a goose in the process of laying a golden egg. So to hell with the bank's committee report. At length, he couldn't possibly refuse her…or could he? Tom smelled a rat. Its name was Howard.

Screw them! He hurried over to attach himself, wanted or not, to the threesome as they arranged to leave on a winery tour. He wanted aboard, if for no other reason, to find out where these wolves were steering, and why Carl Bradshaw, CEO of the Southern Valley Bank would be leading the pack.

CHAPTER 37

Pottsman returned to his cabin at about eleven AM, his arms clutching the paper bag overflowing with drug filled packets. Still breathless and unbelievably charged by the successful liberation of the extremely valuable haul, he hastened to bury, literally, the bundles of contraband. Removing the throw rug from the center of the floor, he pried up the loose floorboards to expose his hidy-hole, as he referred to it in his mind. The paper grocery bag was deposited and the boards returned to their original position. He glanced back to check to see that the place looked untouched as he walked away.

Jesus! he thought, and he turned back to the spot in the floor, tearing the carpet away and digging the boards out for the second time. The rats would have a field day with this stuff if I don't box it up better than that. Too bad I got rid of the cats. Moving targets as opposed to static ones for target practice were great sport, but I shouldn't have wasted all of the them. Now, the place was overrun with rodents.

He found an old wooden container by the back door. It looked like the right size for the huge bag of dope. Emptying the trash out of it, he retraced his steps to the cache and loaded the contents of the bag into the box. It was a snug fit, even in such a large box, but he was able to cram all but a few packages into it. He could deal with those later. He congratulated himself on his farsighted wisdom for having so cleverly dug out a space before it was needed, and one that would accommodate such a prize.

Now he was exhausted. Needed a good belt with a beer chaser to bring him down from all that excitement. Having the kitchen in the same room as the bed had its definite advantages. He liked it even better now. At least he had more space since his roommate left. He took a long swig of some cheap bourbon and took the beer to bed, wishing he had some pot to smoke. Earl's last thought before he went to sleep was that this had already been a real long day at the office.

CHAPTER 38

❁

The festival was in full swing. Nearly two thousand people had passed into the main area where the decibels of conversations and music had risen perceptibly higher with every passing minute. Old friends were meeting new. New acquaintances were being established.

Howard Curry was more than a little pissed with the brush-off that he got from Carl Bradshaw and even more so with the two men with him. Until now, he thought he had them in his pocket. He knew that Gillman and Peterson weren't happy that the takeover hadn't been as easy as he had first led them to believe, but on the other hand, they were still eager to consummate the buyout. Now, it looked like Carl Bradshaw was taking over his position, filling his shoes, as it were.

They were clever, the way they had let him do all the footwork, ferreting out the buy of the century. He gave them access to an opportunity that didn't come along every day of the week. What he had to avoid was letting them put a deeper wedge between him and his generous finders fee. Perhaps old Carl could meet with an auspicious accident. Nothing serious. Just bad enough to get him out of the picture for the time being. It would surely give me time to solidify the deal, he plotted in his mind, and even imagined cutting into the profits that Bradshaw was now expecting.

Curry's nasty little daydream was interrupted by the unexpected arrival of his cousin, Talbert.

"Hey Cuz!" he blurted out, happily. Somewhat disheveled, he looked to have been drinking for some time now. He must have been or he wouldn't have had the balls to come back to this place.

"Not so loud!" Curry returned, his eyes darting about to see if anyone was noticing the exchange. "You know better than to let anyone know we're related."

"Yer ashamed of me? Come on Howie, whaa's happenin'?" He grinned idiotically.

Howard didn't want to confirm that he thought his cousin did, in truth look like a piece of shit. Talbert came in handy too often for that.

"Talbert, my man! We just might want to stay a little cool and collect in case the shit comes down."

"What shit? What's happenin'" he repeated glancing around like he was about to be ambushed.

"You remember the 'man' at the bank? You know, the one who runs the place where I work?"

"Yeah, sure. You've talked about him before. What about him?"

"He's here, and I just want to keep an eye on him today. You know, in case we see an opportunity to help him into some kinda' accident. Depending on what comes up, why don't you stick with me but loose like, and I'll make it worth your while."

"Sure Cuz," he answered in understanding. He loved dirty deeds.

"And don't call me Cuz."

"Sure Howard."

"That's better. Whaddaya say we get some lunch. Too much booze on an empty stomach and we'll both have trouble accomplishing anything."

Without speaking to one another, they split up to select their meals from the international foods offered at the many food booths. Howard converged on a large picnic table where several others were already lost in a culinary paradise.

"Howard?"

He turned to the speaker, surprised to hear his name, and then recognized a tenuous situation in the making. He had to be cautious. The voice belonged to his old friend from Medford, Jerry Majors, bigger than day. Jerry was just about the only person in town who remembered the days when he worked for Braverly Distributing, and the only person who knew his aversion to the woman who owned this winery, whose function they were now attending.

"Haven't seen you since old man Braverly died. Jerry, how the hell are you?" Curry cut in with the statement before Majors could say anything.

For a moment he was confused. Together, they had been conniving to control the volume of distribution for Mountain View wines with the promise of a fat piece of change. It hadn't been a week since he had seen Curry.

"Great, great! Been with Superior Distributors. I heard somewhere that you're a banker now."

Curry was almost visibly relieved when Majors caught on.

"Southern Valley. Loans," as if Majors wasn't already aware of this information. "Say, why don't I just authorize a loan for you, and you can pay your interest by buying me a drink."

They sounded just like a couple of business guys kicking back.

"Howard, you always knew how to wheel and deal something out of a guy. Sure, I'll flip for a drink." He turned to the fellows he had been sitting with. They seemed to be happy enough where they were. "Excuse us for a minute while we fill our glasses." They departed from the group.

Curry was uneasy about having this exchange. His nervousness was the result of having so many people banging on him to close the Mountain View deal, and time was growing short. There was Francis Gillman, Clark Peterson and his crew, and now Jerry Majors. So many promises to powerful people, and now he had a problem with getting that bitch out of there.

"I was worried they would find out we knew each other too well," Curry verbalized his concern. Majors ignored the comment and walked on as though nothing had been said.

Finally he spoke, "So Howard, the squeeze we put on the MV label must be working. She's been acting like everything is hunky-dory to the media, I saw her on the talk show, but word has it that she's hurting. What's happening on your side?"

"Carl's about to let the ax fall." He answered defensively.

"Carl, huh? I wasn't aware that he was cognizant of the plan to get her out, or is he? I hope you haven't forgotten your promise to me when we set this up. You know we've gone to a lot of trouble to accommodate you."

"I know, I know! It's going to work. Trust me!"

"You fail this, I'd hate to have to bring up any of your past shenanigans to any of the local law enforcement. You have far too colorful a past to be indiscreet about your commitments." His demeanor had become more menacing with every word. And just as suddenly, he transformed again to the congenial friend as they ordered their drinks and returned directly to their respective tables. The man was a Jekle and Hyde. He gave Curry no chance for rebuttal.

Little more was exchanged as the heraldry began for the grand entrance of the presentation for the 'new' wine. Returning to Talbert, Howard grimaced as they saw Kara mount the stairs leading to the stage microphone where she was introduced in glowing terms by the Master of Ceremonies.

"Thank you all for joining us here, today. I hope you enjoy being here as much as we have been enjoying your company. We want to welcome you by sharing some of our finest vintages.

"We have been complemented by your attendance in the past years, and look forward to having you return for the years to come!"

There followed an enthusiastic cheer from the crowd, as Curry and his friends smirked with the knowledge that Kara would no longer be the host of any such function again.

"And as our nearest and dearest would say, LET THE GAMES BEGIN!" As she pronounced the last words, she couldn't help glancing back at Turner to see his reaction to the use of his now-famous and often used expression. Her retreat from the podium was followed by a wave of more applause.

Shiron met Kara as she descended the short flight of stairs. She was breathless.

"Kara, you've got to come with me!"

"What is it? Is something wrong?"

"It's Beth…she wants to see you right away."

"Where?"

"Come on, I'll show you."

They made their way, weaving through the crowd. All Kara could think of was another disaster in the works. She couldn't tell by the way Shiron was acting, but the element of mystery prevailed in their journey to the enclosure, behind one of the large outbuildings.

The elephant! Of course, how could she have forgotten. Through the Wildlife Perceptions Association, she had procured the appearance of the behemoth, and there it was, in all its majesty.

"Beautiful!", was all she could possibly say. She stood, quietly in awe of the wonderful creature standing before her.

"Yeah, really great!" Beth replied facetiously with a peculiarly peevish expression.

Kara turned to her.

"What's wrong?" She could see that Beth was alarmingly upset.

"Kara, you won't believe this." Beth was now serious as a heart attack. "I was just out here admiring our large guest and I fed him some grass hay." Her voice stumbled as she tried to explain.

"Yes…and what else?" Kara was visualizing an accident…someone, or a part of someone being crushed under the tremendous weight of the elephant's feet.

"Kara, I'm sooo sorry! I didn't remember having the money pouch under my arm, and somehow, the elephant grabbed it. I guess he thought it was some of the grass, and…I could die…he ate it. I tried to get it back, but he ate it!"

The gravity of this statement wasn't lost on Kara. Some of the major proceeds from their sales were in that bag. It was the *bank*!

"My God, Beth! Do you realize what a loss this is to us?"

In all of her recollection, Beth had never seen Kara express such strong emotion. She was completely agitated.

"This has to be the biggest cellar rat to *ever*…I mean *ever* hit on us!" Kara, hands on hips, was nearly sputtering now. Those around her were rolling their eyes, believing her to be certifiable. They lacked any understanding of her use of the term 'cellar rat', but saw the humor in comparing a rat to an elephant. At least they thought they did.

She caught her breath and continued, "Beth, if it the last thing you do, you will be closely following this beast for the next twenty-four hours until you retrieve that pouch! Do you understand me?"

No longer able to hold back their laughter, the others in the crew surrounding the elephant pen were choked with amusement. Beth could no longer contain her self and broke into a guilty smile, handing Kara the money pouch. The meaning of their jocularity began to dawn on Kara and she immediately felt so foolish she could have sunk into the adjacent pile of hay and done a disappearing act.

"Oh God, I've been duped."

More relieved than embarrassed, she composed herself and addressed the owner of the animal. He had to be in on this charade.

"Just for that Sir, I'm riding our friend here into the festival, carrying a glass of wine and wearing a veil and a smile." Sinuously, she made like an Egyptian to the further amusement of the onlookers.

"Go, Kara, go!" Turner urged her on, as he approached them.

Her gyrations halted when she heard his voice.

"Get me out of here," she said to him. "Before I get as crazy as the rest of them. And Beth, you've got yours coming! I swear you do. Come on, let's get this parade on the road. The audience is waiting."

CHAPTER 39

❀

When he woke up later his hangover was gone but it was replaced by a growing anger. Pottsman was normally angry and cynical with life in general, but in this case his hatred manifested itself in one thing in particular.

That fuckin' asshole *meant* to rip me off. He was thinking painfully of the lost money and of course, the dope that was meant to be his. Well, now it was his.

But the near disaster filled his thoughts. He still couldn't believe his luck in retrieving that huge stash. He thought about the couple again with malice.

That guy fuckin' parades around showing off his woman, his car, his gold crap and anything else he can think of to strut his stuff. Fuckin' asshole. He left me to face the rap alone. Jesus! What kind of guy would take the money and not leave the dope? What kind of business was that? What the hell did he think I was going to use to pay off the homies I borrowed from? I could kill him. Come to think of it, if I couldn't make a timely payback, the bros would soon as kill me as look at me. Christ, why did I ever try to cover such a big buy?

He brooded about his greed and the near crisis he had just escaped, and then his thoughts turned to the bags of dope that didn't quite fit into the cache under the floorboards. They were stuffed into the back of the cupboard that held the pots and pans.

He jumped up to be sure that his memory wasn't deceiving him. "Sure 'nuff, there you are...you little darlin's."

When Earl Pottsman picked up the parcels and lovingly fondled them, he devised a plan. It involved the BMW at the festival. It involved getting back at those stupid people. Besides, it was nearly two o'clock and he didn't want to miss the parade. He loved parades.

He felt a whole lot better, now he had another plan. A shower would feel great and then…back to the action.

Earl arrived at the party at close to two. Everyone's attention was focused on the grand musical introduction that announced that something extraordinary was about to take place. Horns had been blaring their heraldry for some time now and the crowd was expectant.

Two sentries, ornately dressed in regalia took their positions at each side of the entrance. Following shortly, were a band of bare footed dancing young maidens, adorned with flowers, gossamer veils trailing in the air. The musicians had donned capricious hats and garlands of daisy and lupine as they took up the strains of Renaissance music to accompany the dancing girls. Their shirts were embroidered with floral design, with great billowing sleeves that closed at the wrist with more decoration and embellishment.

Next, and wearing clothing similar to the musicians couture, were the six men carrying the flowered braids that were tethered to the saddle of the elephant, leading him through the path that was being created by the dancers. He, too was decorated in the style of the event with flowers wound throughout the lace-like fabric covering his back. And atop the ornate saddle was none other than Kara, bedecked and garlanded with flowers, gracefully scattering rose petals from a large cloth basket, hanging at her side. Anyone looking at her could see she was having the time of her life riding this huge animal.

Following the pachyderm were eight more people carefully carrying an immense table adorned with not only flowers, but with carafes of wine. At the center of the table, and placed for all to see, was a beautifully designed painting with the words…Mountain View Riesling Fleurry.

Only when the table was placed on the ground, did the porters turn to their tasks. Wine was poured from the carafes into every outstretched glass. The dancers continued their terpsichorean antics to the music as the people toasted with the new wine in a truly Bacchanalian spirit.

Perfect timing, he thought. Pottsman ducked out of the party while everyone's focus was on the new wine. He headed for the parking lot. He noticed that even the security people had relaxed their attention to take in the entertainment.

Now where was that Beamer? No doubt the hangover had warped his senses, but he couldn't remember exactly where it had been parked.

There it was, sitting snugly between a parked van and a pick-up truck; the metallic gray car. He had to do this quickly, before anyone saw him!

Pottsman stepped to the space between the Van and the car and opened the driver's door. He removed the two packages of white powder from inside his shirt, twisted his body through the narrow opening and stuffed them under the driver's seat. They wouldn't be noticed for a while.

He was out of there as stealthily as he gotten in. By the time he returned to the festival, the parade was over, the audience proceeding back to their original places. Rock and roll music filled the air as dancers took up the rhythm. Pottsman was just another jaunty guest who was there to sample the product and enjoy the rest of the afternoon.

The only thing remaining for him to do was to watch to see when the couple belonging to the car departed. Then, he would make his call to the local police.

CHAPTER 40

"I promised I would bring the name of an investment broker for you, Bethany." Tom had courteously waited for the moment when Beth was taking a break from her work schedule. As he handed her an envelope with the information he had gathered, he watched the girl, appreciating for the first time the no-nonsense aspect of her personality. All of this was not just fun and games as their initial contact had indicated. The woman had a serious side that gave him an enlightened impression. The Beth of today portrayed a competent employee, knowledgeable and experienced. It dawned on him that what Beth had told him about learning so much from Kara must have been very true. It was Kara's training that had developed these professional assets.

Beth had just confirmed the work rotation schedules and made the rounds of each of the winery bars, collecting the higher denomination currencies and replacing them with smaller change. With money on her brain, she was happy to see that the 'take' from sales was so substantial. Now, with Tom handing her information on a broker, she couldn't stop thinking about the money that she had available for investment. What she was holding in her hand was peanuts!

She acknowledged that entering the domain of finance and investment was as alien to her as a society function to a street person, and she needed help. She was grateful that Tom was able to give her guidance on the subject. She was thankful she could talk to him so easily. Not only a trustworthy man with integrity to whom she could attempt to spell out her financial situation, it didn't hurt at all that he was handsome as well.

"I appreciate this so much! You know, after telling you about wanting to invest, I started to wonder if a broker will tell me how I could place my money…well…I mean, I needed to ask you something about it."

"I'd be glad to answer any questions you have. Shoot!"

Beth was stammering in her effort not to disclose too much about a matter that required the discretion of an international spy ring. She looked about her to make sure there was no one within earshot.

"Well, first of all, could we make this another purely confidential conversation? Again?"

"It will go no further than my own ears. Again! You can count on that."

"All right, but perhaps this isn't exactly the time or place to be discussing my personal business. Maybe…when this shindig is over? Later this evening we usually unwind after all of the customers and booth people have gone. Why don't you plan on dropping back by at about nine-thirty. Things should be quiet then and we can talk."

"Sounds fine with me. Where will Kara be by then?"

"Always worried about Kara, huh?"

"Not worried, Beth. Just thinking ahead. White Raven has been kind enough to ask me to stay over at his place for the weekend. I was just thinking that if I were to come back here this evening, he might like to come along. Not that he would be privy to our conversation. I just thought that it might make an interesting group composition, the four of us."

"An interesting group composition!" She laughed. "I don't think I've ever heard that one before." Beth was tickled by the straight edge to Tom's description though she preferred him in a less formal context…say like when they were at the park? Her instinct told her that informality wasn't one of his strongest suits.

"Yeah, that would be fine. I'll ask Kara, but I'm sure it will be okay."

"Great! I won't keep you from your work. Seems I'm going on a tour of the winery in a few minutes. See you later?"

Beth didn't answer, but as she left, she gave Tom a smile that couldn't be mistaken for anything but extreme pleasure. Although their conversation intrigued him, Tom was no longer thinking about business.

He was pulled from his lustful thoughts when Carl Bradshaw approached with the announcement that the time had come for them to be on their way for the grand winery tour. Together with Francis Gillman and Clark Peterson, he made his way through the crowd to the entrance, where a van sporting the emblem of Mountain View Winery was awaiting their departure. One or two other couples were already sitting comfortably at the back of the vehicle.

As he was about to embark into the van, Bradshaw halted so abruptly, the other men nearly ran into him. He reversed his movements and addressed the others.

"Anybody here have a camera?"

He searched for the answer from face to face, including their tour guide, who was still holding the door.

"Negative," Clark Peterson replied.

The others just shook their heads and simultaneously mumbled their inability to produce what he wanted.

"Tom, would you mind going back and asking Howard to run into town to get a camera and film? Here, take my keys to him." Bradshaw placed the keys on some bills for the purchase. "Tell him we'll wait for him at the winery. Shouldn't take him too long!"

"Yes sir, I'll be right back." He hustled away to carry through his mission.

Curry was heavily into a conversation with a group of men that Tom was not familiar with. Howard apparently had long since forgotten his 'date', who had amused herself too well with a group of young people more her own age.

Tom pardoned himself for his interruption, and delivered Bradshaw's message along with the money and the keys to Bradshaw's car.

"Sure…will do. He wants it at the winery? The old fart didn't exactly invite me along on the tour. Guess I'm good enough to be a delivery boy though. Hope he included a tip."

He was pissed off with Bradshaw, but counted the money as he took the keys.

Tom noted how two-faced this guy was as he viewed the other side to Curry's usually obsequious attitude towards the head of the bank. He was a consummate actor when it came time to make points with his superiors. It didn't surprise Tom at all.

"Just try to be back as soon as you can. And Howard, don't play Barney Oldfield with the boss' car." He couldn't help injecting the barb.

"What do you think I'm going to do, abscond with it? Take a side trip to Acapulco? Maybe I should. Or maybe I should find something really compelling to do in this burg that would take me away from all these fascinating people here."

"Just make it quick."

"Yeah, don't worry. I'll be right back so 'Carlie' can document the spoils of war for his little friends."

"Look Curry, I don't know why they want pictures. Just get the camera, okay?"

Curry had a nasty grin when he answered, "Just for you lover-boy!"

He marveled at Hutchins' naivete when it came to the motives of others. Tom suspected nothing. That in itself was unbelievable. If it were Curry, he would have ferreted out any unexplainable doings of his co-workers. He would be panting to get to the bottom of whatever was transpiring in order to cut himself into the deal. But not Tom. He seemed to simply go along with whatever was demanded of him without questioning the outcome. La-tee-da!

Howard relished the moment when Tom realized that his friend, Kara was going to lose everything. It was like hitting two birds with one stone…Tower and Hutchins. But now he had another adversary to contend with. Carl Bradshaw was trying to circumvent the fat finder's fee that rightfully should be all his. It was like divine intervention, Carl's wanting him to arrange for pictures. This way, he was forced to have Howard right there, shadowing his every move and hearing every comment. He could still salvage his position as coordinator for this deal.

As he headed towards the parking lot, he was accosted by his cousin, Talbert, and his buddy, Jeremy.

"Where'ya headed?"

Curry still had no desire to be seen with these two. He kept walking as they took up the pace alongside.

"Gotta' go in to town to pick up some stuff."

"Didn't know you had your wheels with ya'. We wouldn't mind going in for a bottle seeing as how we could use a little libation to tide us over till you need us. How 'bout you takin' us in with ya'?"

"Can't!" He didn't want to have to explain his reason. Didn't want them to know he was assigned to being an errand boy. Further, Howard wasn't thrilled with the idea of being seen with this twosome. Again, they were fine for taking care of dirty laundry, but socially…no asset! He continued to walk away from them. "You stay put until I get back and I'll let you know what we're going to do."

"No way. You're not going to dump us here. We're bored," Talbert all but whined. "Come on Howard, give us a ride!" They trotted alongside despite his rejection.

Curry knew better than to argue with these two. He knew they were as inconspicuous as two warts on a nose. He relented.

"Okay let's get it on, but hurry up!"

They walked swiftly to Carl Bradshaw's car and were rolling out of the parking lot before their seatbelts were in place.

"What's the frickin' hurry?"

"I told you, I'm on an errand and I've got to get right back, so for Christ sake, when we get to town, get your poison while I'm next door shopping." He finally admitted, "I've got to pick up a camera for the boss."

"Jesus," Jeremy interjected, "I thought you was some kind of honcho manager, not a gopher. Since when you're the errand boy?"

"Check yourself before you wreck yourself. There are a lotta' kiss-ass jobs when you work for the man. You wouldn't understand unless you were in my position, and rest assured, you'll never be in my position. So cool it, or I'll let you beat your feet back to the party. Now shut up, Jer."

Talbert held his peace until they arrived in town.

"How 'bout a couple of bucks for the whiskey, Howard? Jeremy and I are a kinda' short on funds, ya' know?"

Howard grimaced and dug into his pocket and pulled out a twenty.

"Gee, thanks, Howard. I'll get something good for all of us."

"Live it up, but be back at the car when I'm ready to go."

"We will…promise."

It wasn't long before Curry came back to the car with his purchases. He herded the other two into the back seat and took off for the Mountain View festival and his tour of the winery.

"So Howard, nice wheels." Jeremy was trying to be congenial while he opened the Jack Daniels and handed the bottle to Talbert after taking a long draw from it.

"Yeah, swell. May I ask why you didn't use your own piece'a yellow shit to do your shopping?"

"Aw, come on Howard. The place is jumpin' with cops and security people, and I don't want to be busted for no insurance. 'Sides, I'm low on gas. Hid it in the bushes in the parking lot. You know how it is."

"No I *don't* know how it is, Jeremy. The rest of the world pays the price, why the hell can't you get it straight? Don't you want to be a respectable citizen?"

"Yeah, I suppose I should. Here, have a respectable pull on JD." He handed the bottle over the seat to the driver. Curry couldn't resist the aroma and took a long drink.

"Suck up the whole thing, why don't ya.'" Talbert was already feeling the effects of the alcohol on top of the already digested wine. The small spillage from the open container being passed to the back seat didn't bother him.

"Whaddaya' got in mind for fun and games this afternoon?" Jeremy asked.

Curry wished he could toss an answer back to their question. He had to give these guys something to do, but as yet there was no definite game plan for what he had in mind for Bradshaw. The opportunity might present itself after they looked over the premises and the equipment that was in the winery.

The wailing of a siren interrupted their conversation. Howard scanned the rear view mirror and saw the blue and white, its lights flashing in his eyes.

Time went on hold and at the same moment he knew he would give anything in the world he possessed to be given the chance to take back and relive the last ten minutes. They were all instantly in deep shit.

"Get rid of the fuckin' bottle!" Curry snarled under his breath. He checked his rear-view mirror again and then the back seat to confirm that the other two had their seat belts on as the cop advanced on him. No doubt, the license number had already been run and checked. Christ! Even he could smell the alcohol.

"What's the problem, Officer?" Howard strained to convey the appearance of the respectful motorist, smiling, helpful. All innocence.

"May I please see your driver's license and registration for the car?"

Curry located and handed over the pictured card. The cop stooped to look into the back seat where Talbert and Jeremy were doing their best to play invisible.

"Your names please?"

"Jeremy French."

"Talbert Cottner."

"May I see your identification as well?" As he made the request, the wafted odor of the whiskey hit him. "Remain in the vehicle," he said, noncommittal as he took the three I.D.s and returned to his flashing car and immediately called for backup.

This was no ordinary motorist's detention. An anonymous call to alert the police of a probable transportation of drugs was usually taken seriously back at the cop shop. It couldn't have been more than a half-hour ago that the call regarding the gunmetal gray BMW had been received. Before stopping the three passenger vehicle, Sheriff Sloane had alerted his dispatcher with the information as to the license plate in question and its location. It was likely that another patrol car had already been sent to aid in the confrontation, but the Sheriff saw the need to confirm a backup, especially with two rangy men along with the driver.

Fumes emanated from the window. It wouldn't be difficult now to search the car. The stench of whiskey ensured that an open bottle was stashed somewhere in the interior, so given probable cause, that would present no problem. It was an open invitation to go through everything to support the accusation of drug trafficking. All he needed now was a little manpower. Drugs or no drugs, it looked mighty like an arrest was about to take place.

CHAPTER 41

"Mr. Bradshaw, do you mind if we go ahead with the tour and walk around the buildings? Forgive me, but we do have a schedule and some of these people are anxious to get started. I'm afraid another group will be standing by within the hour."

They had been bellying up to the tasting bar to kill time, waiting for Curry to return with the camera and film. Carl Bradshaw had done all he could within reason to hold up the group's dissection of the workings of the winery, and his patience was becoming short. They had tasted one or two small pourings of wines that were not available to the public at the festival, and had asked as many questions about the vineyard and the processes of making wines as they could.

The initial impression of the winery as they drove into the parking lot was the attractiveness of new landscaping. Some basic shrubs and plantings had been there for some time. Judging by their size and development, junipers and an established rose garden must have been there for years. It was the number of newly planted flower beds that bespoke of what would later in the season become a bountiful rush of color, and along with the freshly cut lawns, reflected care and planning. Gillman and his partners were no doubt thinking ahead. This gift of nature emanating from other people's work would be one more part of the whole enchilada. Nice, very nice.

As Bradshaw perused what he could of the lavish interior of the tasting room, Francis Gillman noted the unique potentials to be realized in the operation of such a business. The most enlightening fact was that having complete control of a product from its inception to its conclusive sale was to have total control of profit and loss. They had discussed the manipulation of assets, and

Clark Peterson opened Gillman's eyes to the limitless ways that altered bookkeeping could enhance their personal worth. Nothing they would ever do could be construed as untoward. Everything would be aboveboard…legal. It would be more a case of taking advantage of the loopholes—and there were many! Together, Gillman and Peterson questioned if Kara Tower had ever recognized this opportunity, or if she had ever made productive use of it.

Well, no matter now. Tower had her opportunity and instead of glowing in the radiance of success, she ran herself into the ground. Cash poor, she had a gun to her head. She would be forced to take what she could and get the hell out of Dodge. At least this is what Howard Curry had led him to believe. Howard had been paid for the information he had compiled, and he had better be right! Carl Bradshaw seemed to confirm it. In any case, this was a sweetheart deal.

Although he suspected the bind that Kara was in was not of her own making, it was nevertheless a fact of life. He felt no remorse for being a predator in an unfriendly take-over. It was, after all, the game of survival of the fittest. He and his group were unconditionally more fit to go forward with the programs that would eventually place this enterprise at the pinnacle of its peers.

"We've waited quite long enough. I agree, let's get on with seeing this fine place." Bradshaw was again in his congenial mode.

"Please come this way." Relieved of constraints, the young man representing the winery began a well-rehearsed outpouring of information.

Clark Peterson followed along with his note pad and pencil at the ready. Having been thoroughly indoctrinated into the machinations of the production of wine prior to their arrival, he made appropriate notes on their various points of interest. Should there be any selective comments, he would quietly take them down, enabling them to discuss things at length at a later time.

Questions with regard to equipment, size of average production, location of product warehousing and a multitude of others were posed and answered in turn by their tour leader. Notes were taken with close attention to detail…every answer, well documented in the partner's dog-eared notebook.

Gillman and Peterson refrained from making verbal expressions of interest. After all, Tom Hutchins was with them. They liked what they saw. The operation appeared to be tight and well run. Yet there was ample space for expansion on the property. Their marketing analysts had indicated an overwhelming recognition and acceptance of the Oregon product as being at the 'break-through' point of national distribution. Tower was justified in her intentions to expand.

Just to fill in that pipeline would take considerable increase in production numbers and would realize an incredible profit within the year.

Goddamn that Curry! Bradshaw now wished more than ever that he had the camera to get pictures of all that they had seen. Where in the name of hell was he? He should have been back an hour ago, and already, they had seen everything there was to see. The tour was at an end.

They found themselves standing about the exterior of the main building, some of them examining the immediate gardens and landscaping, and others gazing beyond the acreage of the vineyards to the stately fir and pine trees and the high mountains in the crystalline clear distance. They were now able to speak openly about the prospect of what they had just seen.

Gillman was asking, "What do you think, Tom? Ms. Tower did quite a job of bringing this winery along. Too bad. If she had a little better capitalization to back up her expansion, I'm sure she would have secured that loan…"

Until now, Tom had maintained a cover of silence until he could absorb the disposition of the other men. He wasn't sure if he was expected to make comment, and he certainly intended to take care not to overstep the bounds of propriety. Walking on eggshells for the time being, he opted for prudence and inconsequential murmurings of approbation. He was in no mood to give them the answer they *least* expected. Create no waves if it isn't necessary.

"It appears to be viable," he finally said. Then, unable to curb his curiosity any longer, he added addressing Bradshaw, "Am I to understand that the loan for Tower is no longer under consideration?"

"Tom, we're just being realistic," he placated.

"I don't think I understand."

"The operation got off to a good start as wineries go, but you saw in the balance sheets and profit and loss statements for the last couple of years that the distribution problems have become critical. The marketing fell apart. I know you looked over the paperwork carefully and wanted it to work for Ms. Tower, but the fact is, they're running out of money as we speak."

"But the festival, doesn't that bring in a considerable amount of cash profit?"

"From what we've been able to glean from the list of outstanding liabilities, it looks like she would have to do *extremely* well to break even and then some, just to pay off a few of her debts. Tom, I know you don't like to hear this, but when she applied for the operating loan, this business was looking for someone to come along to throw in a life preserver."

"What is she going to do?"

"That depends. We'll be negotiating an offer by Mr. Gillman and his partners, enabling her to 'escape' with all her debts paid."

"That's right Tom, and I believe it will all be for the best," Gillman said. "Think of what we could do with the existing enterprise with a real cash injection. We could put some serious meat on the foundation of this business."

Hutchins felt his heart drop when he pulled the meaning from that statement. These vultures were going to take a multimillion dollar business and property for a price of their choosing and offer the barest amount of cash to retire any debts, leaving absolutely nothing to the woman who had given birth to it. Great for the buyers. Hell for the seller. He wondered if Kara would have the strength to face her dilemma.

Tom kept his cool. He wasn't sure he wanted to know more.

"When will the offer be prepared?"

"I think we'll pretty well be able to tie up the loose ends by Tuesday. Maybe Wednesday. The preliminaries have already been typed, thanks to Ms. Tower's input."

Tom hoped he wasn't turning red in the face.

"Have you a ballpark figure?" Tom ventured.

"We're working on that, Hutchins."

Tom could sense that Bradshaw wasn't giving forth any more information than he had to. When he called Tom by his last name, it was a sign that further questions should not be asked.

Bradshaw looked about the parking area and asked anyone within hearing, "Now what do you suppose happened to Howard and *my* car?"

The four men and the other tour members were guided into the winery van by their host, who ended his presentation with a relentless dissertation, citing the historical and sociological aspects of the immediate area. It was both an entertaining and enlightening finale for the passengers who did not hail from that vicinity. It was a disagreeable diatribe as far as Bradshaw was concerned.

Tom absorbed the folklore and history, rounding out his knowledge of the 'big' picture. At the same time, there was the feeling of depression and distress for the outcome that Tower would have to suffer through when she learned the truth of her plight.

As they were driven back to the wine fest, he mulled over a budding idea. By the time they pulled up to the entrance to disembark, he was excited, looking forward to the rendezvous he had made with Beth for later that night.

CHAPTER 42

❀

The art displays were a cut above what might have been expected by the casual passerby. Commonplace landscape scenes or poorly conceived still-lifes were nowhere to be seen. Instead, there were painterly impressions, painstakingly laid down and set forth by experienced craftsmen. The artists of these paintings seemed less interested in pleasing the public at large than following their own momentum to express an artistic impulse. The bottom line was a sophisticated selection of paintings and artwork dealing with a full spectrum of genre, beautifully depicted and professionally exhibited.

Kara was very pleased with the overall presentation. For her, it called to mind the time spent during many a summer at Laguna Beach in her college years, honing her artistic tastes in that Mecca of creative endeavor.

Her parents kept one of the small, foliage covered cottages on Lombard Lane. It was a charming short little street, not too far from the heart of town without being too great a walking distance from the beach. She remembered how exhilarating it was to set off for the day to browse the galleries dotting nearly each and every block of the city, gathering in the flavor of the coastal area.

She greatly admired the proficiency of skillful expression and had developed a deep appreciation of solidly based art. Seeing that caliber of artwork on her own grounds here at the festival filled her with pride and awe.

Her concentration was focused as she deliberated on the color and technique of a particularly dramatic waterscape when the jostling from another admirer of art painfully interrupted her. He was equally involved in another painting. They collided for the second time that day as each of them backed away from the objects of their interest.

"Whoa, excuse me!" was his automatic reaction to the mutual blunder. Then he recognized Kara, marveling that he could have been so near to her without being conscious of it. He smiled warmly, breathing in her scent saying, "Well! Birds of a feather!" and then added, "Wonderful, aren't they?" inclining his head toward the pictures.

"Incredible! Who ever would have guessed that so much talent was hiding in this area!"

"You never know what's going on in these here hills."

His tongue in cheek delivery was lost on Kara. Raven's comment did not give away the considerable success he was enjoying in his own field of art. No one locally, save Tom, knew about it.

"I'm the first to admit how little I know about what's going on around me. Comes from keeping my nose too close to the grindstone," she replied.

"But you do seem to appreciate good art."

Kara wasn't sure if this was a statement or a question, but she answered enthusiastically, "Very much! I've studied art and its history from time to time. Someday, I'd like to get past that stage and actively try my hand at it...just for fun, of course. No talent intended." She was laughing at herself.

"You'd like to paint, then?" This time, a serious question.

"I think so. At least, as long as I don't take myself too seriously. What about you? Have you ever dabbled?" She watched him expectantly, genuinely interested.

He was formulating an innocuous answer when they were interrupted by Beth. She was in a frenzy, energized by her role in the festival.

"Come on, people! Let's get with it!" She addressed Kara gesturing with arms and body in a simulated ballroom dancing movement. "Why don't you and White Raven get out there where the music is playing and do some fancy dancin'? Let everybody see that you're having a good time too!"

White Raven was the last person there to flaunt himself on the dance floor, but he asked Kara with greatest courtesy if she would like to dance. He took note with relief that the tempo of the moment was more or less sedate. That would suit two old timers. Compared to the younger age group here, that was how he thought of himself and Kara. It had been some time since he had been moved to dance publicly. He could handle it if she could...if they had to!

Eyes sparkling, Kara accepted just as Beth touched her arm.

"By the way," she said, "you'll be glad to hear that I located the rest of the missing booth money. I put it back with your things in the house."

Kara stopped Raven from moving to the dance floor.

"How ever did you find it?"

"Long story. I can tell you later, so be happy! Have fun, go dance!"

Beth would not disclose any of her latest adventure until much later when they could speak privately. Even then, she doubted she would be mentioning all parts of the scenario. Truth be known, it was yet again one of those adrenaline-charged situations. She had pulled off another maneuver wherein the spoils of war had miraculously made their way into her growing nest egg. Yes, she had returned what was due Kara, but she kept for herself the amazing 'find' that accompanied the stolen money.

Anyway, Netta had always been a closet sleaze. Beth knew that. For this reason, it did her heart good to have caught the little cheat red-handed. What galled her the most was how Netta preyed upon decent people, who neither deserved nor could afford to sustain losses. And all the while, Kara disallowed the unprovable accusations…blind loyalty and the desire to protect her people.

Well, that was Kara.

Beth was a realist. She was sure that Netta was responsible when money or even wine was mysteriously missing. Netta and Talbert. The two of them could never be trusted. At least Talbert was gone now. Netta would be next.

Beth found Netta's belongings and purposefully examined them. It came as no surprise for her to find the remainder of the cash stolen from the festival. One dollar bills, neatly banded, were laying hidden under an array of clothing. The money would be returned to where it belonged.

The bonus was the collection of credit cards, driver's licenses, and IDs that fell free when she moved the money. The bag containing the cards also held an abundance of more cash.

Jesus! Beth thought, the girl was into selling! How bad was that! She could have been skimming cards from forgetful customers in the tasting room for God knows how long. But where would she have had access to the driver's licenses? This is even over my head, she thought.

It never occurred to her to call the police to accuse Netta of ID fraud. She had long since abandoned her trust of the ineffectual justice system. Instead, she gathered up the cards for disposal. If their owners were smart, they would have already cancelled out their accounts and replaced the licenses. She bagged up the extra money for her own use.

To tell the whole story to Kara wasn't in anyone's best interest. Already, she was editing the details to her own satisfaction in order to soften the story as it pertained to Netta. The important thing now was that Netta should be immediately and permanently extricated from the firm.

Meanwhile, her eyes still followed Kara and her partner as they moved to the music, and nearly laughed out loud to see Raven's expression when the band broke into a hot rock 'n roll number. He can't dance! She agonized for him in while at the same time laughing. But surprise, surprise! Raven matched up with Kara's motions, doing a cool Travolta imitation while Kara dazzled everyone by her underplayed, rhythmic movements. With all eyes upon them, they made a spectacular pair.

He sure looks darn good today. In fact, she didn't remember that he ever was quite so attractive. Oh well, too bad he's usually such a bum. He and Kara really made a fine looking pair.

CHAPTER 43

By the time the musicians had gone into their last set of the day, the couple was satiated from their consumption of good food, drink, and the absorption of local color. They watched the two dancers, who seemed to have caught the attention of the crowd.

"Darling, look at those beautiful people dancing. So graceful. I'm so glad we came. It turned out to be a great experience." Her voice had the trace of a Hungarian lilt. "The art, the music…what a treat! How do you like it?" Tentatively she squeezed his hand with hers, adjusting her wide brimmed hat with the other.

"Fine, fine." He answered distractedly. He was always preoccupied with manipulative thoughts. He wore the cloak of constant wariness for other predators, like himself. It would be out of character for him to be laid-back enough to enjoy the rural ambience.

"Do we have to leave now, before it's over? It's been such fun!"

She should have known better than to overstep her boundaries. His reaction was predictable. He was not a nice person.

"Quit your bellyaching. I can't spend all day here looking for that jerk! I thought I saw him a while ago, but I'm not sure. He should'a shown up at the meet if he wanted to transact."

"Maybe something happened and he couldn't make it."

"One of the biggest trades in this godforsaken part of the country, and he couldn't make it? Not on your life! He should have crawled on all fours to deliver the money for that trade. No money, no trade. He didn't make it. Simple. We cross him off the list for good!"

"Well, I sure had a good time anyway. I don't really care what happens to him. Are we going back to the car now?"

"Yeah! Pick up your purchases. We're leaving."

They joined the first of the trickling flow of people making their way to the parking lot. By the time the last set of music was over, about half of the vehicles would be out of the field, the crushed grass testifying to the abuse of traffic on the terrain.

The couple approached the BMW and he fumbled with the door lock. It felt funny when he turned the key, but then the door opened. Strange.

They entered the car and settled themselves in the leather and suede luxury. She turned to put her packages in the back seat with their other things when he said, "Hey, enough of the wine already! Reach back in the reefer and get us a cold can of beer!"

He sensed her astonishment when she opened the nearly empty cooler and looked in.

"What the hell's the matter?"

He was unprepared for the answer.

She was whining. "The cooler! The bundles are gone! Did you move them?" she asked hopefully.

"The fuck they are!!" He was over the back of the seat, looking for himself into the nearly vacant box. All that met his gaze was a couple of beers and some lunch meat.

She watched fearfully as the color rose like a thermometer from his neck to his face. For a moment of suspended animation, there was no movement on his part or hers, no other verbal outburst to indicate his anger. He composed himself, sitting back into the driver's seat. The only evidence of his frustration was the white knuckles of his hands grasping the wheel. They were twitching slightly. It was more terrifying than any movement he could have made.

"Come on," he said finally as he checked his holstered gun in an automatic gesture to his side, and moved to leave the car.

Angela followed him meekly. There was no way he could use a gun with this crowd of people around, but she could see that for now he was beyond reasoning. She followed, praying that the whole situation was just some crazy mistake and that it could be resolved without creating a dangerous public scene.

At first, Earl couldn't figure it out. Maybe that hangover this morning had addled his brain, but a couple of glasses of wine was supposed to have helped him over the rough edges. There must have been some mistake. Why would someone he didn't know, approaching from behind, be telling him to come along with him.

"Better come with me, Pottsman." The guy sounded like a cop until he said, "Where's the money, punk?"

Earl turned and attempted a boyish expression of innocence. It converted his face into a caricature of pain. He knew exactly who he was answering to, and he wished he were anywhere else but there. Why did he think he should stick around anyway? He had watched them leave in that gray car, and once he had made his call, he could have boogied on home.

It was all wrong. Somehow these people had escaped the cops. He couldn't figure it. The tip was valid, he had seen to that. He had called the cop shop anonymously to tell them that a known dope dealer would be leaving the Mountain View Winery festival going East on the highway in a gunmetal colored BMW. The car would have plenty of dope in it for a bust. What more did they need for chrissake?

But here these people were, asking him where the money was.

How the hell should he know! It was gone and he had been sure *they* had it. Now, he wasn't so sure of anything except that he had the white stuff.

The only thing that came out of his mouth was one stuttering word..."Money?"

"Angela, take the keys." He handed them over with the implication that she would drive. "We're taking our friend home."

"My car..." Pottsman protested.

"We wouldn't want our friend to be picked up for drinking and driving, now would we?"

His smile in no way concealed the hard implacable glint in his eyes. The threat in his voice convinced Earl, as did the casual hand motion indicating the underarm holster inside the sports jacket, that it would be futile to resist.

Pottsman was still confused as they ushered him into the car. After rearranging some of the baggage, he was placed beside the man in the back seat, the ice chest ominously separating them in the center. It sat as venomous evidence of his burglary.

"Beer?" the man asked, torturing the captive victim.

"I think I've had enough to drink."

Earl couldn't bring himself to look at the chest. His eyes darted around, taking in the interior of the car, hoping it would all disappear. He felt sick. He just couldn't figure why the car was still here.

"Aw, come on, help yourself! It's right here in the ice chest!"

"No thanks." He started to sweat again.

"Tell Angela the way to your place. I think we should get to know each other better."

Pottsman wanted to extricate himself from this situation, but he didn't know how. He wished he was back in the protection of the crowd at the festival. Stupid, stupid, stupid! Why did he leave? At least there he would have witnesses. He realized that his situation was becoming desperate.

Maybe he could talk to these people. Reason with them. After all, it wasn't his fault that the money disappeared. Forming in his head was the idea that they possibly were *not* the people who had robbed the cache at the park. Maybe together they could find the person who did.

But where to start? The only people who knew about the transaction on his side, were the ones who provided the cash. He would never have had the leverage personally for a purchase this size. Now, as in the past, he had gone to his pal, who had gone to *his* pal, who came up with enough unmarked bills to turn a quick profit within the period of a couple of days. And they wouldn't have queered the deal by taking their own money...or would they? Could this have been a double-cross? A set-up?

His confusion was turning to anger and he had to ask, "But the money...didn't you pick it up? My instructions were to leave the pouch at the stash place in the park and I could pick up the trade this morning. I got there, and guess what?" He tried to sound as indignant as he could. "No goodies! You ask me where's the money? Well, what I wann'a know is, where's my trade?"

No answer. The man had little to say, making Pottsman more nervous than ever. He directed the woman to his driveway where they cautiously approached his cabin, and parked on the gravel driveway. Like so many places in that area, his house was obscured from the road by an overgrowth of bushes and trees.

"Wait for us in the car, sweetheart," the man requested of the woman in a solicitous tone. He indicated with another head gesture for Earl to lead the way up the path to the house and then said in a conversational manner, "You live here alone?"

"Yeah, now I do. Used to have a roommate, but he just moved."

The man was confident now of their privacy. "We won't be long," he said over his shoulder.

He followed Earl Pottsman closely as they entered the unkempt building. "Where is it?"

Earl almost asked, "the money?" before he realized that he didn't know what the guy wanted. The money or the dope. Which?

"Where's what?" was all he dared to say, fishing for an answer to his dilemma.

He wasn't prepared for the lightening blow across the side of his head from the butt of the gun. It cut his temple and a burst of blood seeped down his shirt. Now he was seriously scared. This cold monk would kill him if he didn't give him something. Shit! It wasn't worth his life!

"What're ya doin'? Jesus! You hurt me!"

"Dumb fuck, I'm losing my patience."

"Christ! I don't know where the money is. Honest. I put it where I was told."

"So, who else knew about it?"

There was no hesitation as Pottsman explained his 'arrangement'.

He would tell Talbert Cottner, a local dude, about an impending deal and Talbert would get to his cousin, who supplied the cash. And no, he didn't know who the cousin was or where he got it, but he was cool, seeing how he made quite a few good bucks on the *vig* after the transaction came down. Nobody would have any knowledge about where the trade would take place.

Pottsman went on to say that in fact, this was the biggest trade he had ever done and he just didn't know what went wrong. The money was in place, he put it there himself, but after that…he shrugged, not knowing how much more he could tell.

Talbert and the other guy were supposed to be at that festival, he suggested to his captor, so why didn't he ask them what the hell was happening.

The man was turning over this information in his head and decided that whoever took the cash would certainly not be the ones who would profit by it. They would be better off if the transaction was consummated. That took Pottsman and the cousin off the chopping block.

Which left the Talbert dude. He must have it.

Fine. So much for the money. But what about the dope that was burgled from his car? There was a fortune involved here and somebody had to pay for it!

"Okay, moving on," he said, "I guess we go after the guy who took the product. Somebody had to know I still had the dope in my car since it wasn't delivered, and the only person who could know about that was *you*, asshole!"

"I don't know nothin' about it." Earl tried to sound sincere and look convincing. He thought he could gain some confidence.

The shot ringing in his ears and the piercing pain in his foot were one in the same. It obscured everything in the room. Pottsman yelped in disbelief. He rolled onto the floor.

"You shot me," he sobbed when he focused on the gun in the man's hand.
"Where is it?"
The gun was carefully pointed at his other foot.
"Jesus, don't shoot! I'll tell ya', I'll tell ya' anything ya' wanna know!"
"Where's the fuckin' dope?"
Pottsman was on the floor writhing in pain. It was only a matter of reaching toward the throw rug to pull it free to expose a corner the trap door underneath. He started babbling as dragged himself to the place.

"It's here. I just wanted to find the money first. I swear! I was just keeping the dope safe till Talbert came up with the money. I don't know what the deal was, but he must have re-po'd the cash. Maybe they was marked bills, maybe he was going to explain it to me. Christ, I don't fuckin know!" He finally gave up, sobbing in despair.

The man pulled the carpet away and hoisted the cover, its hinges squeaking softly. His sideways smile was more of a grimace as he looked at the contents of the hole doing a mental inventory. He stood then, looking coldly at his target as he raised the gun to Earl Pottsman's head and pulled the trigger.

CHAPTER 44

"It took them long enough!" Carl Bradshaw said to no one in particular.

The limo floated smoothly up the driveway and parked at the entrance to the festival, inviting curious stares from everyone within sight. The chauffeur went directly through the gateway without interference to contact his passengers as instructed.

"I'm here for Mr. Bradshaw and guests?" He queried the attendant at the welcoming table, expecting a more formal venue. He was Italian, small with a clipped manner. His dark, thick hair set off his handsome features. He had the profound impression that the pickup location was one where he would have greatly preferred to have been a customer rather than an employee. It looked like fertile ground to his attractive eyes.

"We're ready." Gillman stepped forward commanding attention as only a man of his size could. He strode to the car with Bradshaw and Peterson in tow.

"I guess we should consider ourselves lucky to have any transportation this far out in the sticks."

"Better than a hay wagon," Peterson chuckled at his own joke. He settled himself in the car and dove immediately into the enclosed bar. "Drink?" he offered the others.

Riding along in the plush comfort, they downed shot glasses of Crown Royal. Carl Bradshaw abstained. His gut had given him a bad time ever since Curry failed to return with his car. Something had gone wrong and his stomach rebelled.

Early on, when Howard hadn't shown up, Carl had made little of it to the others. Their trip through the winery had impressed him greatly, and seeing first hand what was being put on the trading block, he decided to make as few waves as possible that might divert the buyers interest.

Curry was absolutely right. There was a great deal of money to be made from the transaction of sale and even more from the subsequent expansion and operating loans. It was to their benefit that these people could take over the place for a song by offering just enough money to cover the current liabilities. It would be far more reasonable for Kara Tower to get out gracefully, paying off her debts, than to face a messy bankruptcy where she would lose everything anyway. Even entering a Chapter Eleven reorganization would be a painfully intolerable if not impossible solution.

No, bankruptcy was not the answer. The woman had a gun to her head. Bradshaw just hoped she recognized the cold facts and would be reasonable about it.

He thought about calling Kara on Monday morning with the news.

On second thought, better that she be informed of an offer if he could solidify one from Gillman by tomorrow morning. He would have it presented to her in writing immediately with the stipulation that it must be signed by midnight on Monday. That would foreshorten any protracted negotiations, forcing her to capitulate to his offer. It was take what was being offered, or lose it all. He was satisfied that he wouldn't lose, whatever her decision.

And now he didn't need Curry to close this deal. To hell with him. He would pay dearly for not returning when he should. Bradshaw was incredulous that Howard would disappear *now*! With his car! He was as good as fired.

The afternoon evolved into the inevitability of the end of the first festival day as happy people made their way home, many of whom came to Kara to thank her for such a wonderful time. Community leaders and politicians, business men with their families had made the most of the food and entertainment, vowing to return the following year.

She smiled graciously, even with the knowledge that there wouldn't be a next year. Kara had reconciled herself to her fate.

The distributors had left without a word, something she expected. They should have been confronted with her questions regarding their lack of active support. Not that it would do any good. They never gave her a chance, slinking off like a bad act.

The bankers too had disappeared without giving her any hope for continuing. That was something she had not expected. They could have given her some courteous gesture to give her some indication of their decisions. From their reluctance to converse with her, it was plain that they had no intention of playing ball. It appeared that even Tom Hutchins had been excluded from their network.

As sand through her fingers, the last of the guests departed, bringing to a close the first day of the finest event she had ever directed.

"Some of them are coming back tomorrow."

Tom could see the let down in her posture before she straightened and presented him with a sweet smile. He noted the courageous attitude in the face of impending financial disaster.

"Some of them have been coming back for years. So many are old friends."

"Kara, you look like you could use a rest. Will you be up to seeing Raven and I later tonight? Maybe a couple of other people? Beth suggested it. Seems she thought you would appreciate a diversion before facing tomorrow."

Kara's face lit up at the idea. "I'd love it! We can have some of the food catered to the house. Tell the others to save their appetites for later. And what about some extemporaneous music? Maybe Turner could be talked into bringing his guitar if we ask a couple of the musicians to join us. I know he likes to sit in on the music when he has the time. We'll have our own performance."

"I'll find him and ask while you scout out the others, if that would help."

"Good idea, Tom."

It wasn't the diversion of having company tonight that occupied her thoughts now, nor was it the fate of her business. It was White Raven! He seemed so…changed. He fascinated her. Having known him only slightly before, he had certainly emerged as no longer being a street person. He was now a self assured and confident figure. A metamorphosis to say the least. Had she missed some important signals in speaking to him in the past? She wondered.

CHAPTER 45

❦

Turner Ferguson was by nature comfortable with himself and whatever life might throw his way. He was a happy individual. Still young and strong, he could give his all to work and life, and walk away unscarred by the passing of time and unavoidable changes. These, he recognized were his best years. He regarded himself at the apex of his productivity. In his new position he was feeling a sense of accomplishment and personal growth with every completed project. More importantly, he felt a gratitude he wished he could adequately express for Kara Tower's confidence in him.

Until this time, he and Kara shared a lighthearted friendship. Because she was so much older than himself, he held her in deepest respect while enjoying her company. The admission that there could never be a permanent relationship was an unspoken agreement. And so being a feather in the wind he was not dismayed to see White Raven suddenly displaying his interest in Kara, nor for that matter, to see Tom Hutchins doing his waltz around the inimitable Beth.

Tom had extended the invitation to join the group who would be gathering at Kara's home later in the evening. Turner was tired, but the thought of jamming on his guitar with the guys in the band was too tempting. There was always some kind of party following the first day of the festival, and he wouldn't miss his first invitation to it. Suddenly his energy level hit another high.

He saw Beth as she collected the last of the signed schedules. Each member of Team Mountain View, as they had come to refer to themselves, had signed up for the next day's agendas, and would receive their copy of the entire work schedules in the morning.

"How did I miss you, big boy? I don't see your name on the list for any of the grunt work."

"Haven't you heard, I'm an executive now. What would I be doing on your peon list?"

"Executive huh? You ought to put a white collar on that tee-shirt. That way everyone else can recognize your lofty position."

"Couldn't do that! Everybody would think you were my secretary."

"I don't know, Turner, maybe it would be fun if you were my boss!"

"Never mind, I'm too used to taking orders from you…it would never work. How about tonight, what time you think I should get there?"

"Not too late. Eight-thirty? You bringing your guitar?"

"Yeah, but I have to get it. I left a couple of things back at old Pottsman's place when I moved. Left it there for safekeeping. Won't take me long to get it. Just want to finish moving these cases of wine for tomorrow."

"Get a move on, then. See you later."

The longer he accustomed himself to living in the guest facility at the vineyard, the more Turner appreciated the change of address. The burden of poverty was lifting from his soul. He wasn't accustomed to living like a pauper and now he found that it galled him to think he would put up with it, even as a temporarily milepost. For the time that he spent 'camping' at Pottsman's place, he paid little attention to the squalor. He had existed in a thoughtless lifestyle. That phase was gratifyingly behind him, thanks to Kara.

Thinking at this level put him in a euphoric mood as he approached the old residence that he had shared with Earl. This would be the last of the things he had left behind, his guitar and a box of books that had trailed him through life in a constantly growing collection of titles and subjects that would no doubt reveal his innermost personality more accurately than any heart to heart talk with a psychiatrist. It would be the last time he would have to come here.

He was at the point of hoping that Earl would be home to let him in when he wondered why he hadn't tried calling first. Silly, the place would probably be locked up and he couldn't get in. Damn! Did he see Pottsman at the festival? He couldn't remember. Too many people, and he had his mind on his work.

Ferguson was turning the corner to the street leading to the cabin when he saw a new vehicle come out of the driveway that he would be entering. It was a upscale BMW, very classy and much too dark with the tinted windows to see exactly who was inside. There was something ominous about the slow speed in which it passed 'Curley' that made him decide to continue on down the street without turning into the same driveway. He drove to the end of the block and turned right, slowed down, and pulled over to a stop.

What the hell was that all about, he thought to himself. He didn't have to hide when he was in his old neighborhood. What made him continue on as if he had been merely another passing vehicle? Where did this paranoia come from?

Well, enough! I'm going back. If he ain't there, he ain't there.

The pick-up nudged into the driveway, making sounds of crunching rock and spitting stones in the dirt. The sound of the tires seemed louder than usual for some reason. Turner realized this when he killed the ignition. The place was too quiet. No breeze, no birds, no music emanating from inside as it always had when he was living there.

Walking to the front door, there was the uncomfortable feeling that something was wrong. Everything appeared to be as it always had. Debris circling the house, every imaginable type of litter lining the entrance. Normal. But there was an unaccountable taint to the atmosphere. He knocked.

Much to his irritation, no answer was forthcoming. Goddam it! He ran through a series of expletives under his breath in frustration. He wanted his stuff, and Earl wasn't here to let him in…notwithstanding that his car wasn't in the driveway. Pottsman was often seen walking here and there because his vehicle was sitting on the street somewhere, broken down or out of gas. Car or no car did not define whether the man was home or not.

He tried the door. It was unlocked.

So, the guy was probably still partying after the festival like the rest of the people from town. Turner let himself inside to retrieve his belongings. He didn't get far.

The body of Earl Pottsman was sprawled across the center of the floor, his head a mass of bloody pieces, some of which were spewed across the room. He seemed, in his death to be clutching the edge of the throw carpet as though caught in the act of attempting to cover himself with a blanket.

Turner had never seen a dead body before. It had the unreality of a puppet-like quality, immovable until someone pulled the strings.

With a firm and unruffled presence of mind, he took care not to touch anything in the room, moved to the phone unhurriedly, and dialed 911.

CHAPTER 46

Kara and Beth sat back in their chairs, astonished with the story as Turner unfolded the events both before and after his call to the police.

The small group of people who had gathered at Kara's for a private party to celebrate the success of their first day of the festival had already partaken of food and drink to the point of near saturation. Until his entry into the house with the heart stopping story of his late-afternoon experience, bodies were draped about the living room in a near stupor. The partygoers were exhausted. If ever there was a time that Turner could make his blockbuster grand entrance, this was it!

Their wake-up call was greeted at the door by Shiron who just happened to be up at the moment, refilling her wine glass. It nearly spilled as Turner rushed by her to announce, "Hot news-flash in the valley!"

At first, the response was languid until he embellished further.

"Earl Pottsman is dead! Shot to death! I found him at the cabin when I went to get my guitar after work." And so, having garnered their rapt attention, he told his story to the now willing audience.

He prefaced that in a small community where the local people are nearly all known to one another, it is a fact of life that some citizen's are better known than others. Especially in matters of the law, there are those whose activities are perpetually in question and others, like himself whose stature in the community was never questioned. He explained that he was now to be considered a pillar of the community, and would never again a member of the trouble-making crowd.

"For chrissake Turner, get on with the story!" Roger complained.

Turner gave up the golden opportunity to blow his own horn. He continued with the facts.

It didn't hurt when the authorities found that he had been seen working for the entire day and would have had a hard time crowning his afternoon with a crime of this magnitude. They never considered him as a suspect. He was released from questioning at the scene by the local police with only the admonition to stay available in the event that any further information was needed.

"What do you mean you were held for questioning?" They were prodding for more of the juicy story.

"Why did it happen?"

"Who did it?"

They wanted to know everything all at the same time.

"The police really only wanted to know more about what time I saw the car leaving Pottsman's place. I wasn't *held* for questioning, Beth. In fact, they thanked me for not…how did they put it? I didn't contaminate the crime scene."

"Yeah, well you probably watch enough television crime programs. You're practically trained for duty. So what was it about this car?"

"Something about it being their day for this gray BMW. I told them I saw a gunmetal gray Beamer leaving Pottsman's driveway and thought it was peculiar the way it was moving so slow. Didn't look like the kind of people who would be associating with Earl. I waited till it was out of sight before I went in and found the body. Then they told me somebody had already called in a report about the car earlier and there was some confusion before they decided I couldn't have seen it exactly when I did. The timing was all wrong."

"Well how could your timing be so far off when we all know when you left the festival. There was no question of that." Beth interjected.

"You know that, and I know that. They just kept insisting that I had the wrong time. They finally admitted that somehow, the car was being impounded exactly when I called in. They said I must have been wrong, but I know I'm right." He looked bewildered.

Kara looked at Tom and White Raven and they all looked dismayed. Turner never lied.

Beth piped up with, "So what you're trying to say is that you're sure about the car you saw. And the police had impounded another one just like it. So, why couldn't there be two cars answering the same description?"

"Sensible! They should have an APB out for the one I saw, as we speak. They *could* both be involved in crimes at nearly the same time. Why not?"

"That's it! Why not? The *perp* is getting away. They should have an APB out for the car Turner saw…as we speak!" Digby piped up. He was clearly excited about the incident.

"APB on the *perp*, indeed!" Roger laughed at the Englishman's surprising use of the vernacular.

"Come on Rog, I'm still rattled about finding Earl like that. Granted, I didn't care for him all that much, but finding a dead guy just isn't on my list of top favorites. Besides, now I won't be able to get my books and my guitar back for who knows how long."

"The guy's dead and he's worrying about his guitar!" Shiron said.

"That guitar could contaminate the crime scene!"

"All right!" Kara cautioned. "It's time everyone gave Turner a break. He really has been through quite a lot today and could probably use some serious sympathy." She turned to him and said, "Don't worry about your guitar. You'll get it back. I suggest we call the detective on the case and let him know what we've guessed about there being two cars instead of one. We all can certainly back your statements about the time. I think this is something they should know."

CHAPTER 47

❦

"Pretty exciting stuff", Tom Hutchins was saying. He had been gazing out the window of the cabin, watching two young deer feeding on a treat of cracked corn and barley, their large innocent eyes drooping as they chewed contentedly. "You never know what's being wrung out of the wash when you put so many people together." As he said this he was reminded of his conversation with Kara at the festival.

"Have some more coffee, Tom?"

It was Sunday morning and White Raven had been up at an early hour despite his late arrival home following a satisfying night getting to know Kara Tower and her close friends. He had been working on one of his sculptures in the well-lighted upstairs studio for several hours before he heard the movements of his guest in the room below.

Tom helped Raven as they laid out strong coffee and freshly baked rolls with homemade elderberry jam.

"What really defies all description is the improbability of Carl Bradshaw's car disappearing with my co-worker Howard Curry, and then another car exactly like it being seen leaving the site of a murder scene. It's about as real to me as a TV plot. I'd love to call Carl right now just to see what he has to say, but I don't relish having my head bitten off."

"Good decision. Who knows what his frame of mind is at this hour. From what I gather, your Mr. Bradshaw was ignorant of anything going on around the time he left the festival."

"Well, I can't exactly say he was totally unaware of *something* going on...."

Tom's voice tailed off. If he was going any further with this conversation he would have to plug in some of the background of the Mountain View saga in order for Raven to understand. At this point he was losing his dedication to keeping the bank's secrets. It was now a matter of placing his trust in his new-found acquaintance with whom he shared a mutual respect. Tom relied on his good instincts.

He sighed. "Do you mind if I confide in you? There's been something on my chest for some time now."

"Sure Tom, shoot!" He was genuinely interested.

"I know you have no vested interest in any of this, so I think you might be the kind of sounding board I need."

Tom explained as briefly but as fully as he could, the story of the Kara Tower loan application and its ramifications. He took his time and tried to reveal the most pertinent facts and in doing so provided for himself a more vivid picture of Mountain View Winery as a clearly marketable product, thanks to the hard work of its proprietor.

"What I find so hard to understand, is how, or why anyone would attempt to take this away from her by putting her in such a financial squeeze."

"Someone is trying to take her business now?" Raven asked.

"That's exactly what I'm saying!" Tom rose and paced the room to both collect his thoughts and shed the band of frustration that was closing on him. "I researched this guy Curry, and found out he had been a part of the wine industry some time ago, only under another name. There's been no explanation, but he has harbored this hatred for Kara that goes beyond the pale, and from what I've gathered, he set up a takeover of her business for the consideration of a finder's fee, a fat one. And all of this was through the bank."

"Your bank? I thought you were an officer there. One of their chosen."

"I am."

"Then how is it that you are just learning about this?"

"Because these damned people hid the facts from me. They knew I wouldn't put up with this kind of maneuver. It's cruel and unnecessary. Howard Curry was the architect and I'm amazed that the rest of them are going along with his outline. They deliberately shut me out. That is to say they shut me out until it was time to tell Kara that there wouldn't be any loan. They left the dirty work for me. It's been a gall in my side ever since. She doesn't deserve the treatment they're giving her."

"But why are they doing this? What would they get out of it that would justify this action?"

"The bank would generate a fair amount of money indirectly. They would be scratching the backs of their investors by giving them an equity-heavy asset at an extremely low cost. In return, the investor would use the bank for further operating and development loans. A win-win situation…for both parties…for them!"

"I see, and screw over the woman who's lost everything for not being a member of their good old boys network."

"Exactly."

The two men sustained a pensive break in conversation while they contemplated the topic over hot coffee. For the moment there was enough said. White Raven sat quietly letting the words that had been spoken to him wash over his thoughts giving him a clearer picture of the chasm into which Kara had been falling. There was a lonely sadness in seeing someone who had shown so much spirit in following her dream, a dream that was being chipped away from too many directions.

All this time it had appeared to his uneducated perception of her, that here was an enterprising woman, successful in bringing to the community a clean industry that would benefit more than a few people. The trickle effect of having such a strong agricultural boost for the local economy could be enormous. All facets of the thing that she had accomplished appeared to be an extremely positive endeavor. And yet, looks not only could be, but in this case were deceiving. Kara Tower's winery business could be viewed as a dismal failure.

On the other hand, take his own situation as a reverse example. He had always thrown out the message that he was nothing more than an itinerant and vastly poor inhabitant of the area. A failure, according to most perspectives. To the general public he assumed a nearly invisible persona whereas most people would not give him any more attention than was absolutely necessary. The aura of poverty had a way of alienating others. In reality however, the reverse was true. Raven had accumulated untold amounts of wealth and would have found himself the target of a number of shallow acquaintances had they only known.

It was a scenario that was at once as amusing to him as it was a sorry commentary of human behavior.

"Ummph." He let out a sound of distaste.

"Was that a comment, or something untranslatable from your ancestor's language?"

Raven smiled at the reference to his Native American heritage.

"Give me a break. I was just thinking."

"Well, what do *you* think of Kara's dilemma?"

"Does it have anything to do with the killing that Turner found, or the puzzle about the two BMWs?"

"I couldn't tell you. At least, I don't see any connection there, other than the fact that someone from the winery was the one to find the dead body."

"Ummph."

"Come on, Raven! Is there something I should be understanding here?"

"Tom, your people should have taught you long ago that when a comment is forthcoming, you should have the patience and respect to wait until the answer is formed."

"In other words, you don't know what to say."

"In other words, I don't know what to say."

"That's what I thought. Well, back to square one. Kara's in a tight spot and I'd give a month's ration of wine for a way to foil the villains."

Raven smiled at Tom's unique turn of phrase. "Pretty much along the line of my thinking. Helping Kara. What about Beth? Think she would have anything to add to this?"

"Beth? What do you mean?"

"Well, if there was anyone who was closer to Kara *and* the business, I couldn't think of who it is. It could be that Beth would know more exactly what it was in dollars and cents that would put Mountain View right. What I mean is, between you and I and Beth, I'll bet we could figure out what it would take to pull the winery out of debt and maybe even have it up and running…without the banks."

It was at that point that Tom began to fathom the depths of White Raven's proverbial pockets. It should have occurred to him previously, but this came as an unexpected surprise.

"Good God, Raven! It would take an awful lot of money to do that. But you're dead right! I have nearly all the information contained in the loan apps and with what Beth knows, we could sure take a detailed look at the feasibility of it."

"What do you say? Let's go find Beth before the festival starts today."

"I'm ready," Tom replied, thinking at last about Beth's provocative 'financial' situation.

CHAPTER 48

❦

Sunday would be a replay of the day before. The pleasantries would remain the same, but for Kara, the gratification in carrying off such an event had lost its luster. Hard as she tried to ignore it, there was always the knowledge that her future with the winery was short lived. It created the feeling of a weight centered somewhere in her midsection. A heavy brick that felt like the guilt of failure!

Sooner or later she would be faced with letting her people know of the uncertain status of their position in days to come, and it played on her conscience. Now, there was a growing sense of omission…that she had not done everything in her power to accomplish her success. There was no way of knowing where her errors lie, but it had to have been her fault. She just knew it! If it wasn't for the need to take care of the festival, she would have gladly spent the day in bed with the covers drawn up over her head, hiding from the truth.

She gave herself a shake and headed for the shower.

Beth had stopped off at the winery to check in with Digby to see how the wine was flowing, so to speak. He, along with an assistant were loading cases in the van for replacements at the festival area.

"Go through much wine yesterday?" she asked.

"More than we anticipated. People were complaining that they couldn't bloody find our wines at some of the local stores, so they were buying cases to take home with them. It took Roger practically full time to take care of the orders. We had to come back to the winery twice to restock."

"I think this is a good thing! Looks like we more than doubled sales from last year."

"Yeah, and my back feels like it. Did Kara say she wanted anything special brought in for today?"

"No. We'll go for the same ratios that we used Saturday."

While they were speaking, Beth became aware of movements in the tasting room. It was early. Didn't she lock the front door? Please, don't let it be some tourists wandering by for a taste of wine for breakfast. God help me! Shouldn't they pick up on the signs telling the world there was a festival today and it wasn't here at the winery? What was it about 'Closed for the Day' that they didn't understand?

She had so many other things to attend to, it irritated her when she heard the voice.

"Hello!" The visitor called.

Bother! She despaired. Pa Kettle is probably dragging his wife, Ernestine with a fierce grip of his hand to relish the delights of this wine *thang*. She expected they would say something like, "We don't know much abou'chyer wine…heh, heh, heh…you got anything sweet?" Then they would go on about how they used to make the *best* watermelon wine, back t'home. Her thoughts harkened to the delights of Carolina moonshine and her disposition softened. Now that *was* a good thing!

The tenets of the tasting room demanded good manners, but sometimes…Beth headed for the voice that repeated, "Hello again!!"

This time there was something familiar about it, but it was difficult to tell. There was always a distortion of sound traveling from one end of the building to the other. Messages bantered from room to room by workers were often lost either by design or by the muffling of words which, no matter what the degree of effort, were never very clear.

"Hey Ken, mflem…fle."

"What?"

"I said, mflem…fle."

The exercise of communication from any distance within the winery could become a lesson in frustration.

Upstairs, Tom was starting to pace the room.

"I think someone's coming," White Raven said to his friend in his patient manner. He never seemed moved to hasten things along. His inclination was to watch others in a hurry-up world become agitated in their need to have things happen…now. Conversely, his temperament would have him wait for the results that would inevitably take place in the course of time.

"Good. We can find out where she is," Tom responded.

For his part, he was anxious to locate the girl. They were unsure where she might be this morning, but Tom and Raven were intent on locating Beth, and this was as good a place as any to inquire as to her whereabouts.

"Can I help you?" It was spoken automatically as she entered the room, at that point of time, unprepared for the sight of someone she knew.

"Tom, Raven, what a nice surprise!" Her broadening smile evidenced her pleasure in seeing Tom again, even though they had spent hours together the previous evening.

"It's been a long time since I've been here." Raven cut in, commenting graciously without having said so much as a hello. "I forgot how attractive your facility was."

Beth was stunned. Again she wondered, was this the Raven she knew? For the second time that week, she took note of the metamorphic change from street bum to articulate presence. Up till now she would have expected something more in line with "Nice digs!" coming from his lips.

Absorbing this difference, she merely fumbled her words saying, "Well, I'll be…"

"I've been calling. Sorry. I hope we didn't interrupt anything." Tom apologized, suspending her discomfiture.

"No…I mean, I was just finishing up with Digby. I didn't know it was you," she said in a genuine attempt not to seem patronizing. Actually, she was flustered at seeing Tom again so soon. She willed herself to stay calm as she waited for him to continue.

"Yes…well, we were actually hoping to find you with a few spare moments. I know that's a long shot today, but there's something very important we'd like to talk to you about."

The warning lights went on in Beth's head, and she shrank from his words immediately wanting to distance herself from embarrassing questions. What did they know? The fear of this made her wary. More to the point, the origin of her ill-gotten monies must never be discovered. She was concerned that her earlier talk with Tom could lead to more astute probing, something she was not at all eager to pursue, especially in front of Raven. Her confidence was leaking in the presence of a witness.

"Is there anywhere we could talk privately?" he added.

She felt a sweat coming on. Her pulse took off in flight again.

She demurred, "Sure, okay let's go in Kara's office. Everyone will be down at the river, so it will be quiet in there."

Reluctantly, she led the way, taking her place at one the chairs facing the desk. Kara's chair remained empty. No one would usurp Kara's domain even in her absence. She indicated the other seating and waited as they got settled. Raven shut the door.

The redwood paneled walls hung with fine paintings of vineyard scenes. In one corner stood a pedestal with an exceptional bronze depicting a field peasant picking grapes into a wicker basket on his back. Raven admired the sculpture as he did the selected array of medals which were displayed along with the bottles of the vintages that had garnered those awards. It was a warm, inviting room portraying comfort in a world of chaos.

"Well?" she challenged, maintaining as much control as she was capable of at the moment. She fussed with her clothing, straightening the lace ruffles under her jacket sleeves before sitting. Having dressed for the cool morning air, now it seemed to be getting too warm.

"Beth, I want you to know first that White Raven and I have been discussing Kara and her involvement in a financial crisis with the winery. We are both deeply concerned for her. Have you been aware of any of this?"

Beth relaxed, seeing that the direction of the conversation was veering away from her.

"Crisis?" she replied questioningly at length. "I knew she was seriously strapped for funds. That was why she applied to so many financial institutions. Besides the banks, there were investment companies, savings and loan companies…she even went out of state looking for money. Those avenues turned out to be dry for her purposes, and that narrowed her choices to her application with your bank. The others all turned her down. But crisis?" she looked at Tom expectantly. "I thought she found the answer to her prayers, and the loan from Southern Valley was going through. What's going on?"

Raven sat there composed, listening. He left the talking to Tom.

"Mmm…the picture isn't completely clear, but I know enough at this juncture that it frosts my usually impervious hide. It seems our Mr. Curry from the bank has taken it upon himself to offer up the fatted calf before the slaughter."

"Say what?"

Tom expected the confusion that was growing on Beth's expressive face, and continued by explaining, "Okay, I'll try to make this as clear as I can. What I have just learned recently by sticking my nose where it wasn't wanted, is that Howard Curry entitled himself as loan officer for the Mountain View account. It was premeditated and underhanded which seems to be this guy's specialty.

In other words, he purposefully did this to place himself in advisory control of either passing or rejecting Kara's loan request.

"Meanwhile, Curry does some fishing and reels in two heavy hitters for an investment deal on the winery. Theoretically, by paying a top dollar finders fee, the marks are rewarded by snapping up the property in question at an extremely low entrance price. Why would the winery come so cheap, you ask?

"The answer is that Kara is up to her ears in short term debt, and because at the eleventh hour, they plan to deny Kara her loan, spelling out instant disaster with no lifeline. In the same breath, they offer her an escape from debtors' prison by paying off the indebtedness with absolutely no profit for Kara, who has worked her ass off lo' these many years. They take control not to mention ownership of the property. Simple, quick and you have a *fait accompli*."

"They planned this all along? Planned on Kara losing Mountain View?" Her expression was incredulous.

"You've got it!"

The three of them sat in silence for a moment as though experiencing the demise of a good friend.

"Even then, Curry slipped up," Tom finally continued. "His timing was thrown off when I was given the job as axman just last week. They, and I mean Carl Bradshaw, who is the head of the bank and Curry had given *me* the nebulous distinction of setting the wheels in motion by officially denying Kara's loan. Instead, fate seems to have stepped in and directed me to personally go to see her. They never counted on me having any real concern for a customer. Certainly they never expected that I would see such potential in Kara Tower.

"In any case, I just couldn't deliver their message. And the more I procrastinated in delivering their message, the more I found problems with the whole loan picture. Long story about why I first suspected there was something fishy about the way they were handling her account." Tom took a breath and shook his head with incomprehension.

Beth listened with silent fascination. She waited for him to continue.

"Once I saw that the business was perfectly able to stand on its two feet and further, was in the position to inaugurate an expansion program, I was willing to keep the hounds at bay as it were, in order to give a little more time for the winery to recoup. Unfortunately since then, I learned that with the existing liabilities along with a major plot that was in place to take over her ongoing accounts, even with another week or two, she'll be completely out of operating money. Quite a gal, playing her cards right to the end. She should have been given the money she needed."

"Isn't there anything you could do for her?" Beth asked forlornly.

"Not a thing with the *powers that be* seeing the advantage of placing the business in the hands of the good-old-boys. Too much money under the table would be lost if they chose to let Kara remain here, and too much gained by putting their own people in."

Beth was contemplative. "My God, and she's kept this all to herself. That poor woman!" She looked up at Tom and said accusingly, "That bank must be some place to work for!"

Raven spoke up at last, addressing her, "The bottom line is that now Tom wants out."

"You mean that?" Beth asked suspiciously. She couldn't believe that a man like Tom could up and leave a prestigious and well paying position for any reason. Her understanding of integrity in others was hazy at best and never in her experience something that could be counted upon.

"Quitting the bank?" she repeated for confirmation.

"Exactly. It's about time I woke up to the darker side of my profession and made a firm decision to distance myself from it. But that isn't what we wanted to talk about."

"And what is it you did want to talk to me about?" She looked from Tom to Raven and back to Tom again, her hair tossing as she moved. "You know I'm going to be busier than a one armed bartender later today. Give!"

"It's about the future of the winery and just how much it would take to really continue with Kara still heading it up. I'm not talking about the expanded projections that would take mega-money to perfect it, but how much would it take to get things back to a viable base…looking at slow and steady growth over the years." Beth knew broadly what Tom was saying. "It should in fact be a simple matter for you to gather the information we need in order to know how much it would take to run the winery from day to day. The operating costs. Add to that, I could take the figures I have in Kara's loan papers and we would have a pretty good picture of what she needs to continue."

"But where would she get that kind of money? She sure hasn't been able to get it from the banks, or anywhere else that I could see. Have you talked to her about this idea?"

"Before we get into that, let me ask you one other thing. Do you think Kara would settle for a partnership?"

"Wow! It never entered my mind before, and probably never entered her's."

Raven interjected, "You know her better than anyone. Don't you think she would find a partnership more acceptable than letting those bankers squeeze her totally out?"

"Yeah, I guess you could assume that. But I really think that if Kara was involved in a partnership she would surprise everyone by stepping aside to let the others help her run the show. More than once she's told me that there were more things in this life that she wanted to do besides being so completely tied down to a business. So yeah, I think she'd welcome a partnership. That is if the partners were worthy!"

Again, Raven spoke up asking Tom, "May I ask how much these liabilities amount to?"

"A ballpark figure. My guess is around four-hundred thou, according to the papers we have at the bank. And Beth, that's what we specifically wanted to talk to you about. We want to try to see if there is anything we can do to help Kara and the winery...that is without raising any false hopes on her part. Do you think you could fit in the time to locate a list of operating costs to see what we're looking at?"

"You mean this week?"

Tom was shaking his head. A negative. "I mean between now and tomorrow. I'm afraid that these people are going to make a move on the property in the next couple of days, now that they've seen the operation first-hand."

"You're talking about the men who took the winery tour with you yesterday afternoon, aren't you?"

"The same. But they wouldn't even let me in on their conversations. The head investor seemed to be warming up to me, but somehow, they knew I would never take part in their plot."

"All right. Let me get my head on straight and I'll start on the paper chase before I go down to help organize for the festival today. I have nearly an hour before everybody will be screaming for the schedules. Why don't I plan on meeting you at the festival grounds at...say two o'clock? That is if you were planning to attend again today."

"How could we not?" Raven said. "The machinations of Mountain View become more and more interesting by the hour. Now, we have to see what the outcome for the future will be."

CHAPTER 49

❀

After a quick call to Kara, she was free to commence taking notes on selected paperwork. Beth was as thorough in her investigation into the winery's operations as time would permit. She not only knew exactly where to find her targets, but how to copy the most pertinent figures. After years of working closely with everyone in the winery she couldn't help but have a secure grasp on the requirements.

Also, she was fast. She had to be.

Digby had dithered around in the big room for so long that finally she had yelled at him to get the hell down to the festival,...didn't Kara need him to organize the wine supplies? It was always like pulling teeth to get that man to leave the security of his domain, and this day was no different.

With relief, she watched the truck bearing barrels and wine pulling out from the loading area. It gave her satisfaction to be alone in the building, a feeling of control. She liked that and felt comfortable with it. Now she could really get down to business.

Just as the files were lined up on the desk for a final methodical check into the figures that Tom would be needing, the phone rang.

She picked it up.

Nothing! She put it down.

It rang again.

Again nothing.

Goddam pranksters, she said to herself. Whoever had been calling the winery with the deep breathing was going to hang by his yang. Didn't he ever hear of caller identification? She was about to hit the new *star-69* to record the offending caller's number, when the phone rang again.

"We're going to nail your ass!" And as she was about to lay out some well chosen threats, she heard a small voice in the background.

"*Allo, Allo!*"

"Allo, allo to you," she replied mimicking without patience.

Then, in a strained accent the voice said pleasantly, "Allo, we are calling Madam Tower of Mountain View Winery. Is she there, please?"

My God, Beth realized this was a legitimate telephone call. The accent was French. She was all politeness.

"I am sorry, but *Madam* Tower is away from the winery today. This is her winery manager speaking, can I help you?"

"Ah oui! Yes! I am calling from Cannes, France with regard to the Grand International Wine Competition."

"Yes. I…We sent out our paperwork to you on time, and the wine was shipped for judging. Did you receive it in good order? Is it all right?"

"Oh yes! It is fine. We are calling you to wish our congratulations on your award."

"Award? We didn't know we won an award!"

The voice laughed softly and continued in the heavy French accent, "Of course you didn't know. The ceremony for announcing the judges decisions was only last night. We could not call you until today, and then we had to wait until it was late enough for someone to be there. Your time is nine hours earlier than it is here, *non*?"

"I understand. Thank you for being so considerate."

"You are welcome. Now, would it be possible to give Madam a message?"

"Yes, of course."

"On behalf of the Grand National Wine Competition committee, we would like to invite Madam Tower and her assistant as our guest to join us in Cannes for the Fete being held in honor of her winning wine."

"Winning wine?"

"The Mountain View Pinot Noir. I am very happy to inform you that this is the winner of the highest award of the year. You have won the coveted Platinum Challis."

Beth was speechless. It couldn't be true! There were the best vintages in the world being shown at this competition. How could their little winery be the winner. It was too much to even hope for.

"*Allo?*" The voice was insistent.

"Yes, I'm here. It's just…it's just that I'm so…." She couldn't finish the sentence.

"I quite understand, Mademoiselle. It is a very 'appy time for you. If you would like, we could place another call to you tomorrow afternoon in the hopes that Madam Tower will be in attendance. Would that be convenient?"

"Yes that would be fine, and thank you, thank you so much for your call."

"Until tomorrow, then. *Adieu*"

"Adieu…good-by," she had said weakly. She wished she could say more in the way of thanks, but the connection had gone dead.

Beth fell back against the chair, immobile, the wind knocked out of her. In waves of various emotions she slid from a state of shock, cresting through astonishment and awe and then evolving into a trough of skepticism and disbelief. She recorded the conversation again and again in her mind and wondered if she had heard it correctly. Maybe she only *thought* the woman told her that they had won the Platinum. She couldn't remember having gotten the woman's name. Stupid! Was this all a mistake?

She had the greatest desire to immediately put in a call to France to confirm the information she had received, but stopped when she thought of how that would look. "I just wanted to make sure nobody was lying to me. Did we really win the top prize of the…" No, she was sure that just wouldn't wash.

And what would she say to Kara? "I *think* we won the most coveted award in the industry?" No, she couldn't repeat a momentous piece of information like this until she confirmed it. Another tack must be taken.

She considered the timing. This was Sunday. If she waited until Monday morning, she could call a friend in the media. There was a wine reporter in New York who had expressed an especially keen interest in the progress of the Oregon winery. What was his name? He would certainly be one of the first people to get the results of competition for his Monday morning deadline. His bi-weekly column *Wine About The Town* was famous!

This writer not only could comment on the most successful vintages that appeared during the weekend, but could direct his readers to the most advantageous buys on wine, and the most glamorous places to buy them. A Guru? Yes, but at least a sympathetic one.

She would keep this call from France to herself and phone him first thing on Monday morning…early, and test the waters.

Meanwhile, she gathered the papers she had prepared for Tom, copied and placed them in a folder. She stopped to think if there was anything else of significance that would be appropriate to provide as a factor in the operation of the winery. Of course, a brief list of the major suppliers would be helpful in negotiating purchasing limits and credit terms. So many things to remember!

At that moment, Beth recognized and understood in surprising detail, the patience and training that Kara provided her in the form of demonstration and explanation over the past years. She pictured the many times she had been called in by Kara to be told how this or that worked, or for that matter, let her provide her own answers to problems where a learning curve could be experienced. Without actually saying that she was being groomed for the job that would potentially cover the big picture, Beth realized in a flood of gratitude that she now had a philosophical as well as technical grasp on the whole operation of this business, and it was all thanks to Kara.

She was determined to help Kara in every way she could. An idea was already forming in her head as to her participation.

After locking the winery door, she turned her back on the building and headed for the festival.

CHAPTER 50

Not all news passing through the telewaves that morning was good.

At home, Carl Bradshaw was still waiting for the return of his car and thinking that it was part of a youthful if foolish prank on the part of Howard Curry. He was becoming more and more pissed off and had to take it out on someone. He didn't want to call the police if he could avoid it. That would amount to bad publicity for the bank. Curry hadn't shown up yet to provide a whipping boy for him to vent his anger, so the next best thing he could do was personally call Kara Tower at Mountain View. He would feel better just telling her that the loan she had worked for so arduously would have to be turned down due to lack of ongoing income history.

He thought of how he would explain it to her saying, "You can try again in another few years after you have established your income as being more consistent." This he would say, with the knowledge that by the end of the week, there *would* be no business for Kara Tower.

The tray set for his coffee and breakfast rolls had been placed on the delicate inlayed table he recently bought from Italy. It always pleased him to have the ability to purchase and have use of such finery. He basked in the elegant comfort of his home. *He* would never have to worry about where *his* next meal came from. He was President and CEO of the bank. He was set for life.

The telephone was on the table by his favorite easy chair. With coffee in one hand, he punched the speaker button on the console and, with the electronic pocket memory turned to the Mountain View number, he dialed and then made himself comfortable for the pleasure of this call.

The phone rang several times before there was an answer.

"Mountain View. How can I help you?" Shiron answered.

"Good Morning," he said pleasantly, "May I speak with Kara Tower?"

"I'm not certain where she is at the moment," the voice at the other end said hesitantly, and then explained. "We are having our annual wine and food festival today, and I'm afraid no one is where they're easily located. We'll have to find her. May I take a message?"

"I don't think so. Is there any particular time she might be near a phone? I could call back when she's available."

"I think we could do that, say in about an hour from now?...Unless you'd like to leave your number."

"No, that will be fine, I will call again in an hour. Will you please tell Ms. Tower that Carl Bradshaw would like to speak with her."

"I'll do that." Shiron was juggling a pad of paper and a pencil to get the name correctly down and the time the next call would be coming in for Kara. Instinct told her that it was an important message, so she would get it to her as soon as she found her.

"Anybody seen Kara?" She asked a group of her co-workers.

"I just saw her over by the art displays. She was with Turner," the one answering voice responded.

Shiron cruised the booths, now busily gearing up for the second day of business. The dozens of intricately hand-made sale items that so laboriously had been laid out on Saturday and then placed under wraps overnight, were once again being arranged in elegant displays found on tables, hanging from rafters, frames, or curtains and backdrops. It was a carnival of good taste, she thought, wanting more than once to stop and admire the workmanship.

Turner was listening intently to one of the artists discussing his work with Kara. Being exposed to the intricacies of painting was completely new to him. He was fascinated with the conversation and found himself nodding agreeably to the comments and conclusions they made.

"So what you're trying to say is that the focus of light, not color or even the subject of the painting itself is the theme of your work."

"Exactly." The artist was delighted to be able to expound on his work. "Notice the differences of light on the subject matter, and yet it's the light source has become the main subject."

"Yes, I see that connection. Wonderful! You've really captured great intensity in all your paintings. It's inspiring!"

"Thank you," he said humbly. The enthusiasm for his art did not bring out vanity. Kara appreciated his humility. Refreshing, she thought.

"They're beautiful!" Shiron said from her vantage point standing between Kara and Turner, craning her neck to see between them.

Kara stepped aside to give her a better view.

"Here, look for yourself. We have some great talent here."

"Actually, I came to give you a message. You had a call from Carl Bradshaw."

Kara's reaction was evident. She paled. What could he want to talk to her about…today?

"Kara," Turner said, "are you all right?" He could see her change of demeanor.

"I'm fine," she replied, her mind racing. Yesterday, Bradshaw had left with his group of men without even saying good-by. And now he calls? "Shiron, did he say why he was calling?"

"No, but he said he would call again in an hour, and if you could be at the phone he'd like to speak with you."

"How long ago was that?"

"About twenty minutes ago.

"I'll take it at the house. I need to go there to get some things. Thanks for the message."

Turner trailed along behind Kara. He had seen the look on her face when the name Bradshaw was spoken. If she hadn't been in public, he was sure she would have shown even more distress. If there was ever a time when she needed some moral support, it looked like now. He was glad to be there to help in any way he could. Whatever it was, he would be there for her. He was a good friend and he would be there.

Turner opened the door to her car for her saying, "Kara, if you want me to go to the house with you, I'd be glad to. I can tell this call is really bothering you."

"Am I that transparent?"

"I know you, that"s all. And besides, it's not that often I see your hands shake!"

She glanced down to compel her hands to stop their quivering. "Well, if you think they can spare you for a while. I do appreciate your concern, thanks."

Beth passed them on the driveway as they were leaving. In that fleeting moment, Kara could see the amusement in her expression.

So could Turner. "She thinks we're going somewhere to play!" He was laughing.

"Isn't that just like her. But you know, in spite of her playfulness, Beth is very valuable to me. She's become so responsible! There are times I think I could retire and let her run the show."

"Ain't nobody as good as that!"

"You could lose the 'hick' talk, but thanks for the complement."

They reached the house and still had plenty of time to have a light breakfast before expecting the phone to ring.

Kara was just pouring a second cup of coffee when the call came. With a clatter of cups and putting the coffee pot back in it's cradle, she dashed for the phone and picked it up.

"Mountain View Winery, Kara Tower here."

"Ms. Tower, I'm glad I could reach you. This is Carl Bradshaw."

"Yes Mr. Bradshaw, I got the message that you had called. Did you enjoy your visit to the festival yesterday?" She decided that it would be best to be congenial.

"I did indeed. We all did. Sorry we didn't have a chance to say thank you for inviting us. It was an afternoon well spent."

"I'm glad. What is it you wished to talk to me about?"

"Well Ms. Tower, we have reviewed your loan application thoroughly and have come to a decision with regard to your account."

"Yes?" This was *it*. He was finally going to give her the results. She tried to keep from wondering why he would be calling on Sunday and at the same time keep the anxiety out of her voice.

"Yes, and we would like to see a longer track record of income before we could make that loan." Her heart fell to the ground. "That isn't to say that it wouldn't be possible a few years down the road, but for now we will have to deny your application."

She said nothing, but thought, *the bastard is enjoying this!* He sounds as smug and self-satisfied as a Christian bible society.

"Ms. Tower, I hope you understand that we wish you the best of luck."

"Thank you for your call." Thanks for nothing! And with no more to say, she hung up.

Turner saw the tears of anger and defeat in her eyes and had the presence of mind not to ask what just happened. He merely stepped forward and took her in his arms to give her whatever comfort he could. He guessed correctly that the issue was of greatest importance and would no doubt be told in time to those who needed to know.

The rest of the day would flow on its own momentum, the event very like a replay of the day before. Saturday had been like a dress rehearsal for Sunday, and on this day, each of the players were acting out their roles as prescribed by scriptwriters, or perhaps even experiencing episodes of *deja vu*. For guests, it would be an extravaganza of ultimate self-gratification and enjoyment as perceived through a wine filled haze. For others however, the parts they played would be rote performances, given without great concentration to the moment at hand.

Kara, was hard put not to think of anything but the loss of her loan and, ergo her life's work. She went through the motions of being congenial hostess to the crowd, but she would say nothing of the outcome of her conversation with Carl Bradshaw to anybody. She would keep that bad news to herself and wait for the right time to let the others know.

At the same time, Beth could no more keep her mind on business than she could knit a sweater. She was bursting with the news about the award, but didn't dare to say anything until she was absolutely certain. All she could think of was bringing this happy announcement to Kara.

The bundle of information she had gathered for Tom was sitting, safely locked in her car. The business of the festival was picked up where it was left off, as she melded with the crowd in pursuit of her duties.

CHAPTER 51

❀

Howard Curry's world had become a narrow channel down which his only thoughts were the factors that had placed him in this present and untenable predicament.

It was unbelievable! It couldn't be happening to him! Jail!! He had never been *caught* doing anything illegal, not that there hadn't been a few times that he had risen above the law. But he had never been *caught*! And he had *never* been in jail before. It was humiliating. He was innocent…this time!

Sure, they had been drinking a bit, but if it hadn't been for that asshole cousin of his and his buddy, Jeremy wanting to tag along, he wondered if they would have been stopped at all. They had merely been cruising along on their way back to the winery. What in God's name *had* they been stopped for?

What he really didn't understand was the substantial stash of cocaine found under the seat of Bradshaw's car. He was dumbfounded, to say the least. The boss wasn't a user, he was sure. So why was the stash there?

At first, Howard accepted the commonality of road checks on the route to the wine festival, and he figured that being pulled over was part of the drill for that weekend. It was when the pig had sniffed inside the car and noted the pungent odor of whiskey, that he ordered the passengers out of the vehicle. By then, the second cop car had arrived and the report was returned that one of the passengers had priors, and had broken probation…cause for immediate incarceration there. Fuckin' Jeremy!

So the car got searched and the powder was found. The word *setup* came to mind. And who would be clever enough to set him up like this? Who had the manpower and the police at their fingertips at just the right moment to bust him?

Nobody!

Unable to pin the blame on anyone else, his mind strayed to the person he hated the most. Kara Tower. It had to be her. Somehow, it had to be her! She found out about his moves against her and she retaliated. The bitch! The desire to destroy was overwhelming and now there was absolutely nothing he could do.

Howard sat there, stewing in the clammy cell as he waited to hear from his attorney.

At that same time, Carl Bradshaw was about to leave the house for a scheduled golf game with his buddies, Gillman, Peterson and…another guy, he never could remember his name for God's sake. He made a mental note to be alert and catch that name again.

He was irritated to distraction what with the BMW missing. Now he would have to use his wife's small sports car, and it was a stick shift. Goddam woman! He hated stick shifts.

Just as he reached for the front door, the phone rang. He stopped, frustrated at the further inconvenience of having to put up with another phone call. He didn't want to be late for the men who were bringing in so much money to the bank. After a beat of deliberation, he opted to take the call.

"Yes, what is it?" he barked in a clipped manner.

"Mr. Bradshaw? Mr. Carl Bradshaw?" came the answer.

"Yes, what can I do for you?"

"Are you the owner of a 1999 BMW, license plate number SVSAVE?"

Bradshaw was taken back with the fear that his car had been found in some mutilated condition.

"Yes, yes. What about it? Is it all right?"

"Sorry to inconvenience you sir, but the District Attorney would like to have a word with you and is sending an officer to pick you up at your home…say in about ten minutes. Can you be ready to leave by then?"

It was more of a command than a request, and Bradshaw knew better than to argue with the law. He knew most of the top people in the Police Department and they wouldn't have asked him to come by, especially on a Sunday, unless they were serious. Serious enough to send a squad car to bring him in. And the DA in his office…on Sunday? That worried him. Now he might have to call the golf course to leave the message that his foursome would necessarily be a threesome today. Drat! He could catch up to them later.

"I'll be ready." And with that he hung up.

Gillman, Peterson and his associate were having coffee and a hardy breakfast in preparation for the eighteen holes they would be challenging. From their breakfast table, they could gaze out the clubhouse window and see that the sun was shining on the crisp untrod morning golf greens. A filtering light through the trees was a glorious play of yellow and verdant movement. It created a beckoning appearance for the weekend warriors.

The meal was leisurely as they waited for the arrival of their fourth partner. As the enticing scene paled in proportion to their need to keep things on schedule, their conversation turned to the practical.

"I thought Carl would be joining us for breakfast, Francis. I'm surprised he'd miss a meal like this!" Peterson had just received a fresh poured cup of fragrant coffee as he was holding his belly in appreciation of the good food.

"Usually, he's not one to be late. Said he had a couple of calls to make this morning, but if you ask me, I think his wife coerced him into some project."

"With his money, you'd think his wife could hire some cute young studdly guy to help her with the chores around the house."

"She could. I think she just likes to know that she has Carl around to pay a little attention to her once in a while. I know he spends most of the time on his business and damn little on his family."

"Yeah, well maybe he had his own reasons for wanting to meet us after we ate. Example: Maybe he wanted us to have a final opportunity to hash over the deal he's offering us on Mountain View."

"That's a thought, Clark, a good one." Gillman was thoughtfully stirring his coffee. "He's already made the entire proposition and we've agreed to the bottom line, but the deal isn't signed, sealed and delivered." He looked up at the others. "You know, my guess is that something could go haywire. How about you, think there are any last minute surprises? I'd hate to think he's dicking us around. What do you boys say?"

Gillman was always one to listen to all sides involved in a deal. Better to learn of any snags that could and often do occur, prior to sitting down with a buyer or seller.

Peterson looked to his partner for a reply and a confirmation of their personal summaries. He relied heavily on the good common sense and intellectual expertise from this man. They had been together on so many deals they were beginning to think alike, and even laughed about the possibility that after all this time, they were beginning to look alike.

His partner was serious in his reply. "The only thing that troubles me now, isn't the deal. The deal is sweet. Almost too good to be true as it were. No...the thing that keeps gnawing at me is the lack of direct communication with the principal owner, Ms. Tower. I don't know what's happening there. From what I saw yesterday at the festival, there was no indication that she was aware that we, or anybody else would be taking over. It disturbed me that she was carrying on just as though nothing were wrong. Either she's a consummate actress, doesn't have a clue, or is the most courageous person I've ever seen. No matter. The point is, whether Carl has this property in his pocket or not, this should be a done deal before the middle of next week...say Wednesday. I've been studying the paperwork and I go along with all the details we worked out. If we can swing it, my side's go."

Overhearing only the last sentence as he approached, Carl Bradshaw took his comment to mean that the group was ready to get on with their golf game.

"My side's more than ready to go," he blustered. "Sorry I couldn't join you for breakfast. There always seem to be one or two odds and ends to take care of before I can leave the house. Looks like we've got the classic weather! What do you say we get to it?"

Their party of four went jauntily out of the clubhouse. Not a care in the world...Carl was not about to screw up the day by mentioning his early trip to the Courthouse and the DA's office.

The necessary cover-up to his business associates had been the disaster that awaited him when he arrived at his destination with the police officer. It was fortunate that the whole debacle took no longer than it had. He would have been hard put to explain missing an entire golf game with prime clients.

At the same moment that the police car he was riding in pulled into the official parking area outside the Courthouse, there were three impatient people surrounding the door before he could push it open to get out. Bradshaw was astounded at the probing questions that were immediately fired at him and he was dismayed totally when the flash from the photographer's camera rendered him temporarily blind.

"Mr. Bradshaw, how long has Howard Curry been working for your bank?"

"What?"

"Mr. Bradshaw," the other reporter asked hurriedly, "is this the first time you have been involved in the transportation of drugs?"

Shocked and confused, Bradshaw tripped and nearly fell over the curb, when the officer said, "Okay, fellas back off. I don't think Mr. Bradshaw is quite prepared to make any statements at this time." He trotted his passenger hastily to the side door of the building, closing it firmly behind them. The gesture discouraged the reporters from following.

The DA's secretary directed him immediately into the inner office.

"Hello, Carl." A distinguished well dressed man with carefully coifed wavy gray hair, Stephen Waterbrook stood at six-foot three. He gave Bradshaw a brief handshake. The familiarity stemmed from the fact that they had met before at several social occasions.

"Not sure if I should say nice to see you. What the hell is this all about?"

"Well Carl, it's some pretty serious business and I'm sorry we had to pull you away from your Sunday activities. You probably know that I don't always come into the office on weekends by preference. Have a seat. This shouldn't take too long."

He went on to tell Bradshaw what had taken place on Saturday afternoon when his car was detained and then impounded. He explained about the illegal substances found within the automobile and who exactly it was in the car at the time, as well as who was driving. A few pointed questions followed, several pertaining to Howard Curry.

"Damned fool!" Carl blurted, "Getting pulled over with an open bottle, and then this…dope? In my car? Incredible!"

District Attorney Waterbrook remained silent for a long while, watching Carl Bradshaw for any telltale reactions of guilt or perhaps unguarded remarks. None were forthcoming. He guessed correctly that if he were to learn anything pertinent, it would not come from the lips of this acquaintance. He knew Carl Bradshaw to be a well controlled businessman. He would have to be, in order to attain the position as the head of the bank. After a few perfunctory questions, he stood.

"I don't know as yet how we will be resolving this one, Carl. I hope you aren't planning on leaving town in the next period of time…in case we have any further questions?"

"Yes, of course."

"Larry will take you back to your place. Enjoy your game of golf!"

"How did you…?" Then he looked down at his clothing and smiled. "Guess I'm busted, huh?"

But for the churning in Bradshaw's stomach, they parted agreeably enough. The ominous incident was foreboding. There would be a cloud over the l deal he was working on with Gillman and the others. In fact, now he'd have to hustle his butt to the golf course to catch up with them. Wouldn't look good if he was ate for tee-off.

CHAPTER 52

❦

"Have you heard?"

Town gossip was on a fast train ride from mouth to mouth.

"The car carrying the dope belonged to a big-wig banker. Is that what they do with our deposits? Buy dope?"

"Three guys were picked up for that murder! Somebody said they were locals!"

Few of these utterances were factual.

The festival, as a gathering place for a great number of the local populace, provided the vehicle to implement both facts and fiction with regard to the incidents of yesterday. Word would have it that anywhere from two to twenty persons were involved with a drug-bust/gang murder. The people involved were not named, after all, it hadn't even hit the newspapers yet! But so-and-so had heard the police reports on the scanner (no names were ever mentioned), right as it was coming down, so the information passed along *had* to be accurate!

Kara weathered the onslaught as the arriving guests continuously zeroed in on her, asking probing questions in badly veiled attempts to unearth any complicity on her part in the as yet unpublished crimes.

"There is nothing and no one involved with Mountain View that could be connected with the crimes that were discovered," was her pat answer.

Drugs! murder! Tongues were wagging.

It was another blow to her now frail disposition. What more could go wrong, she asked herself with the fear that indeed something else *might* end in disaster. Was she in some way to blame? She was at a loss as to why or how this latest debacle could be affecting her.

Now, Kara was reduced to going through the motions of hosting when in truth she felt little more than like a zombie making an public appearance and at the same time wishing against all hope that everyone would just go away and leave her alone.

Tiring of the constant gossip, the back of her head was aching with the expectation of further questioning when she turned to see Tom and Raven walking toward her. With a fixed smile and a stilted greeting she let them understand her relief that there was no need for another explanation that her winery was uninvolved with the crimes *du jour*.

"A wonderful day for a sip of wine, a loaf of bread and Thou." Raven mused, discarding his usual restraint. Unlike Kara, he and Tom were looking forward to the day's entertainment.

Her dark mood immediately disappeared. She marveled at the ability of anyone to be in such a good mood on such a bleak day. The hint of a smile appeared as she carefully appraised them.

"Well, there's no need to ask if you two had a good time yesterday. You look like two kids on the day before summer vacation."

"That we are, and we're going to make the most of it!" Tom responded happily.

Not one more word of the incipient disasters.

"Care to join us for lunch today? Surely you'll have the time to break away and try to enjoy yourself for a little while." Raven suggested.

Okay, I can play at that game Kara resolved, and once again displayed the backbone that it took to keep on truckin'.

"I wouldn't miss it for the world," she smiled gaily.

On that note, Kara spent the remainder of the afternoon with her best public image in view for all to see. She responded to her customers and friends with flair. This was her last hoorah and she girded herself for the days to come by savoring this one day as though it would not be the end of an era. At first, the ponderous difficulty of this facade took a good deal of stamina and psychic prodding. But little by little, the more positive attitude consumed her and only occasionally was her mind distracted back to her problems.

In particular, she was glad to see that the mood of the staff, in general, was not only agreeable, but they seemed to be putting forth exaggerated efforts to be courteous and helpful. Was this her imagination, or was everyone else going through the motions as she did in a well rehearsed plot to sustain this year's success. No matter! The important part was to get through the day as best they could.

It was well past two o'clock when Tom ceased his 'people watching' and commenced seeking out Beth for the promised paperwork. He found her at one of the tasting bars, resplendent in action as she sorted out an argument between a customer who was insisting on another glass of wine, and a bartender, who was insisting that he would serve no more alcohol to the man.

It started as a face-off with neither party budging from their opposing positions and ended in a quiet *détente*. But in this case, peace had been reclaimed with Beth's promise that she would be glad to sell a bottle of their finest vintage to the man tomorrow afternoon. Of course having Turner there at her elbow giving discouraging glares to the customer with his hardest 'don't fuck with us' expression, helped make the decision to submit to the management. He tried his best to ignore Turner and deal with the pretty girl. No loss of face there. In the aftermath, both guest and server were on a far more congenial level.

"One for our side!" Beth exclaimed, restraining her volume while rolling her eyes in disbelief at the customer's behavior. She turned to see that Tom had been quietly observing the drama.

"Don't you love the cute little way she irons out the tough creases," Turner spoke in an aside to Tom. And then to Beth, "You really have a way with those big, bad alkies, girlfriend!"

"Her special talents never fail to amaze me!" Tom agreed with a touch of humor.

"She brings out the best in all of us, don't you Beth?" In his gratitude for seeing a confrontation settled, Turner was now being over-flattering.

"Yes, but I'm just as glad that Kara wasn't here to see it."

The three became silent as they communicated their mutual agreement without words, each of them with their own thoughts about how Kara might be spared another chip in the wall.

"How often does that happen?" Tom queried, breaking the momentary pause.

"Once is too many, but not as many times as you would think," was Beth's ready answer. "Most people will back down, or acquiesce as they call it. The laws are strict when it comes to serving alcohol, and if a customer even starts to look like he's had enough, he's cut off. Once in a while you get somebody who objects hard-core. The ones who scare me are those guys who may wait for the party to end and then they try to take their revenge."

"Good God! Doesn't that make these ordeals just a little bit scary?" Tom asked, thinking twice about a business that could create situations like this.

Turner answered, "Not really. Not much worse than the local taverns have to deal with. And remember, we aren't a bar!"

Beth added, "Turner's right. Most of the people we serve are at the tasting room and for the most part, the volume of alcohol consumed there is negligible. Still, we'll watch over the place very carefully for the next week or so. If nothing happens by then, it probably won't."

"I must say, my hat's off to you. You seemed to have taken care of the problem as easily as opening a bottle of wine. Very professional."

"We *are* professional!" Beth snapped back, and then after a pause added, "I believe you wanted some information? I do have that ready for you if you'll follow me."

Turner was left standing there wondering what was going on between these two. They acted like they had *real* business to attend to.

"So, how much did we make?"

It was early evening by the time Kara and Beth were able to bring out the final figures for the weekend's efforts. They changed into their baggy, 'let"s get comfortable" clothes and sequestered themselves with a pot of coffee and turkey and Swiss cheese sandwiches at the kitchen table. The money, checks, and receipts had been removed from their respective bags and spread out in front of them. It looked more like a game of Monopoly using play money than the real thing.

The sight was gratifying.

There was no doubt in anyone's mind that this had been a lavish entertainment, and the public would be looking back upon it as a highlight of the year. There was glamour, recreation and as an added bonus, intrigue for the curious, and all of the above took place on a sun filled weekend with the promise of spring.

Yes, an unforgettable time had been had by all…one way or another.

"We made over twice what we did last year. Sunday was a blockbuster!" Kara was more than a little surprised with the final outcome.

"That ought to pay a few bills," Beth suggested helpfully.

"A few, but not nearly enough for all." She took another sip of hot coffee. "Which brings me to a subject I've been avoiding for the last couple of days." Then she sighed, "There's something very important I've got to tell you. It's about our finances…"

"Kara," Beth stopped her in mid-sentence. She had no intention of letting Kara get into her serious problems before it was necessary. "Let me suggest that we dispense with the shop talk tonight and face this some time later tomorrow. We all need a break, even if it's for a day. Mondays are usually a day of rest after an event, but we can meet for a while later in the afternoon. I know you've had a lot on your mind and decisions to be made, but you should know that there are plenty of us ready to back up your decisions and give you the moral support you deserve."

"Then you…"

"I don't know the full extent of your problems, but Kara I do know that you've been going through some tough bullshit. Like I said, whattaya' say we just drop the subject for tonight. Relax and we'll face the down and dirty tomorrow. How about a slug of Kahlua in that cup of coffee?"

They were both licking their lips as Beth poured.

PART III

The Fall

CHAPTER 53

❦

While the rest of the population was still wearing the heavy cloak of slumber, the suited men in the well appointed conference room of Superior Beverage Distributors, Inc. were bright eyed and attentive for their early sunup gathering. Sunup! For most people, Monday morning was a less than pleasant expediency. Mondays could be cancelled as far as most people were concerned. At Superior, this early jump on the distribution market would be made every Monday. By the time the rest of the world opened its stores, the representatives of Superior would have their paperwork completed, their day scheduled, and their butts out the door and headed for their first customers.

To these men, the staunch team of the 'company', after a relatively short but intense time of training, recognition of the importance of having an edge on the competition was inbred. Early morning activity was the *most* important ingredient of the week. The promise that is implied in the 'early bird gets the worm' simile was among the significant quotients in their operation and it was unanimously met with unfettered enthusiasm.

Jerry Majors usually arrived at a reliable five-thirty a.m. each week at the main office, just off the Interstate in Eugene, Oregon to head up the meeting that would consist of the management as well as the complete staff of sales representatives of the company. Reports were made by each man and reports were duly noted. Information that was gathered by the staff during their forays into the world of their clients was included, and would be thoroughly compiled at a later date for the general development and disbursement of the product labels.

These were the mighty distributors. This was where the art of the business of distribution was demonstrated in its highest form. The precarious balance of supply and demand was the finite issue between prosperity and failure, and the attaining of success depended upon a cold blooded aggression and not a small amount of insider manipulation. These attributes were carefully honed and were in place at Superior.

As Vice-President of the fine wine division of this organization, Majors would lay out the accomplishments of the preceding week and move on to discussion of the game plan that would be used for the following time frame.

It was during this phase that the question was blurted out.

"But we're doing a reset for the whole market chain on Wednesday! Are you sure?" One of the salesmen spoke up. He was astonished at the odd proposal for the new layout of the wine shelves.

"Like I said Freddie, we have to pull all the Mountain View labels to make space for the new Idaho stuff."

"You won't get an argument out of me sir, but according to the computer data feedback, the consistent movement of the MV wine has really been acceptable compared to some of the other labels we could get rid of." He asked again, "You're sure?"

The salesman didn't want to come right out and say that what he was being asked to do didn't make any sense at all. You don't argue with the boss.

The other salesmen also covered over their disenchantment, and mumbled quietly. Some of the restaurant reps had difficulty in hiding their consternation in being expected to introduce a new label where an older, more recognizably established label was an easier sell. They didn't understand the change of policy, but they knew they would have to eat it.

"Not to worry Fred, it'll only be a temporary move to introduce the other wine. Mountain View," he said confidently, "will be back on line before you know it.

The salesmen groaned inwardly.

After the general order of the day was dispensed with, the representatives were promptly excused in order for them to pursue their respective accounts. This concluded the first phase of the meeting and commenced the 'no holds barred' section of the conference. It was now seven thirty. At this point, the management was left alone, free to open up and express themselves in more candid discussion.

Majors occupied himself with the ream of papers packed systematically in his briefcase. He removed the folder marked Mountain View and quietly looked over the now smaller group. He said nothing, but instead waited for them to start.

"You've got balls, Jerry!" One of the managers said admiringly.

"Yeah, well I hope those guys get the job done right away. My side of the bargain says cut off Mountain View for one month starting now. It won't be long and we'll have it back again, cutting the price per unit by nearly half. We can pass along part of the savings to the customer and keep the big pot for ourselves."

"Don't know how you do it, Jerry. You're talking about big profits on that account."

"That's what it's all about!"

What he didn't add was that as soon as he could possibly get to it, he would be making a call to Kara Tower to give notice that they would not be representing her product any longer. Howard Curry, with Carl Bradshaw's blessing had mapped out the strategy that was being used to oust Tower in favor of the new regime that would be taking over the winery. He was confident that what Bradshaw was backing would be one-hundred percent dependable. Hadn't they done business of this sort before? And wasn't it as profitable then as it would be now, as Curry had forecast?

"I understood 'Mr. Big' would be here this morning Jerry," the advertising exec was digging hopefully. He wanted to pitch an expensive promotion idea to their money man and was anxious for the opportunity.

Majors took another sip of his decaffeinated coffee and said, "He'll be here. When Nick says he's coming, it's usually gospel. I've never known him to be precise about it, but he normally does what he says he'll do."

"Funny guy." The comptroller had been enthusiastically chewing on a bearclaw. It was his third helping of pastry since the meeting began. His slim physique didn't reveal the incredible appetite that confounded his workmates. It led to many a raucous joke regarding the probable destination of this abundant intake. "You know, he's always been a kind of a mystery to me."

"Now, now Stanley, we all know that Mr. Brocci has been a great support for all of us here. I don't want to hear about any of that mystery stuff just because he comes and goes whenever he pleases. He's a busy man. You know that."

"Of course I know that Jerry, and I accept it. Gratefully, really. There have been times when he has pulled us out of some pretty tricky buy/sell positions."

"He's always there when we need him."

As comptroller, I probably shouldn't question it, but it kinda makes me wonder. I don't know how he's come through so *fast* every time we needed a sudden cash demand. No matter what the amount. It's uncanny, like having a fairy god-mother with a bank…straight out Las Vegas."

"Okay, enough about Mr. Brocci. Besides, he should be here any minute now." Majors shoved himself away from the conference table and said, "Look, if you'll excuse me for just a minute, I think I'll have time to make a quick phone call. Be back before Nick Brocci arrives."

Fred, the salesman was gazing out the window towards the parking area next to the building. "Too late boss, I think that's him pulling up in his classy car. The flashy way he dresses, you'd never guess he'd drive such a conservative machine. Gunmetal gray," he said, nearly salivating. "Boy, BMW sure knows how to build 'em!"

The call to Kara Tower indeed took not longer than two or three minutes. Because of the early hour, Jerry Majors had dialed her home phone.

"Ms. Tower," he had addressed her formally. "Glad I caught you in. I needed to speak to you personally about the Mountain View line."

"Yes Mr. Majors, what is it I can do for you?" Kara had met his tone with the same cold, condescending manner. She intuited that whatever was wrong in the past weeks with their relationship would be brought to light in this conversation.

"You know I hate to be the bearer of bad tidings…" He wasn't sure how he might continue. He waited for her to say something.

She didn't.

"Well, to make a sad story short, we find that we can no longer represent your label. The brand is doing all right, but we have found ourselves to be overstocked at present." A shallow excuse. "I'm sure you'll fare better with another source of distribution."

He couldn't help but smirk as he said this. Who could do a better job for anyone than Superior.

He waited again for her to react to his announcement.

"Ms. Tower, are you there?"

"Thank you for calling," was all she could utter. She hung up the phone.

Stupid! she thought. That was all she could come up with? Not "thanks for nothing, asshole," or "maybe if you tried harder you could go fuck yourself." No! Maybe Beth could say that, but not Kara…just "thank you for calling." Stupid!

I'm beginning to hate Monday mornings she thought, as alone she walked the distance to the winery. Driving the car in this state of mind seemed an implausible act. Kara looked ahead with full knowledge at the unpleasant work that was cut out for her today. She dreaded the task.

If anyone could see her at that moment, they would have noticed the heightening of her remarkable coloring and how Kara Tower resentfully gave up to the tears that were brimming in her beautiful eyes.

The executives did everything but bow and kiss his hand when Nick Brocci made his appearance. He now walked with the aura of power and an untouchable quality from the wealth that sprang from his pocket. The sincerity of their greeting may be circumspect, but the underlying obeisance in manner could not be questioned.

"So what are we doing about Mountain View?" He paused looking accusingly at Majors, his statement pregnant with purpose.

The men hung on his every word. Jerry Majors looked embarrassed. He didn't understand the tone of the question. It came so unexpectedly, he wasn't sure how to answer.

Finally he gave a nebulous response with as much charm as he could muster.

"Well Nick, they had a really nice presentation at their week-end 'do', but you know that. We saw you there with Angela…looking beautiful as she always does. By the way, I hope you noticed that the guys have all respected your request to leave you two alone when you're out together, so we left you lovebirds to yourselves." He chuckled conspiratorially as though part of a mutual and secret understanding. "But to return to your question about Mountain View, we have agreed to make some changes on a temporary basis."

"What changes, and what basis?"

It sounded like a challenge.

"We're looking at a major reassessment of the management." Majors was hedging about a complete disclosure of all of the particulars of the current takeover. His part of that maneuver was solely between himself and the officers of the Southern Valley Bank. He tried for a generalized answer. "The conditions of the changeover have been completed and should be finalized this week."

"Meaning?" His eyes narrowed. Brocci wanted more.

"So…meanwhile, as of today, in fact as we speak, we're pulling the Mountain View product line off the shelves and discontinuing the line."

There was silence in the room. Somebody dropped a pencil and even that muted sound could be heard on the carpeted floor. They watched the change of expression and the color that visibly enflamed the face of Nick Brocci, and although ignorant of the cause for his agitation, they shrunk back in fear.

The chief manager of wine sales became defensive without knowing why. He babbled, It'll be back on, bigger and better and cheaper that it ever was before…in no time at all. We'll be moving more cases…" His voice dwindled.

Brocci was livid!

"You dumb piece'a shit!" he shouted. "Don't you even know what's going on in your own fuckin' back yard?"

"What are you talking about?" Majors was at a loss, as was everyone else at the table. He was hard-put to maintain his dignity with the harsh language being hurled at him.

"Haven't you heard?" Brocci asked incredulously. "They just won the biggest fuckin' prize known to the wine industry!"

Immediately upon its utterance, the truth about the award, as it could only be known to those in the industry, appeared over the group like the picture of a cartoon lightbulb in an animation.

"The Platinum Challis?" was intoned reverently by half the men through jaws that had gone slack in amazement.

"You can't mean it!" Majors was dumbfounded.

"Where the fuck have you been? Doesn't anybody read the fuckin' papers around here?" He stomped from man to man, waving the New York Times front page.

As an apology to this oversight, Wayne the advertising man replied as though his heart was breaking, "We get here for our meetings so early in the morning, it's a wonder we have the time to get clothes on let alone sit down to read a paper."

"This is an excuse? Maybe you outta' go out'n excite the neighbors in your skin suit and get the fuckin' paper before you get dressed so's you can find out what's goin' on!" Brocci's voice rose in decibels with every word he spoke.

Majors had suffered the worst of the shock. He alone had been on the telephone just moments ago with Kara Tower, personally telling her she would no longer have the representation of their company.

Oh God! He had to think fast. There had to be some way to reverse the damage that was done during that phone call. His common sense told him that whatever it was, had to be accomplished post haste!

He pulled himself together to meet the crisis.

"Look Nick, no need in kicking ass with all the guys," he offered sensibly. "I just got off the phone with Kara Tower. Maybe the news of the 'Challis' hasn't reached her either. She didn't say anything about the award, and she would know that it would put the winery on the map…Jesus! More like the world map of internationally recognized wines. I'm certain she would have said something about it."

"Oh, that's interesting!" Sarcasm.

"And that's what I'm thinking. Why don't we call her right back and tell her that there had been some gigantic error in the computer reports and that all's well with our relationship, and aren't we going to have a great year, and maybe even tell her again what a great festival she just had. Get her to agree on coming in for a look on our new advertising campaign. Wayne," he gave a terse order to the advertising manager, "work up a new gimmick fast. Anything!"

Wayne jumped as though he was on a spring and left the room.

Jerry Majors decided then and there that he wouldn't be playing ball with Curry and Bradshaw. Who needed them. Their little scheme was dead. It couldn't hold a candle to the golden egg that Mountain View just laid.

Majors felt like he was once again on a roll until Brocci, who was pulling at the cufflinks on his French custom made shirt made a succinct sound that could have been "bullshit".

All eyes turned to Brocci.

He stood before them saying, "Go ahead and call the fuckin' broad you assholes! See what repairs can be made. Meanwhile, I'll drive back there to make sure her decision is the right one. We don't want to lose this gold mine."

"What are you going to do? Stick a gun in their face and force 'em to sign a document?" This from the normally practical comptroller.

"Come on Stanley," Majors reprimanded. "I see his point. I call Tower to put things right and our back-up meets with her to sweet-talk the issue and make sure she's happy. Good plan! Is that about it?" he asked Brocci. The plan sucked and everybody knew it.

"Yeah, sure. You talk nice. Convince the lady. I'll make sure she understands how serious we are if I have to get down on my fuckin' knees!"

Brocci wanted to get out of that place. The room was suddenly stifling. It was the atmosphere of losers.

This was not the way he should be feeling about one of the best money making laundry machines he ever had the good fortune to be involved with. Up until now, he would have been ready to back their play with practically any amount whenever they needed an influx of cash. He could always make back ten times what he gave them. Their operation had been run with Jerry Majors' astute ability, and there was never a time that he wouldn't have gambled on the group as a sure bet. Now, he wasn't so sure.

So nobody's perfect! But this faux pas was unforgivable. Until the problem was rectified, he vowed to extricate himself from this partnership…at least with Majors. Jerry was expendable. Brocci needed a means to place his illegal money. On the other hand, this wasn't the only laundromat in town. Maybe he could do better someplace else.

CHAPTER 54

❦

Carl Bradshaw entered the bank about a half-hour before opening time. He noticed with pleasant satisfaction that quite a few customers were already queuing up outside for the morning's business. Quite a few! A little early, but they could wait. Weren't they teaming up with the best bank in the valley?

The security guard, his official uniform clean and pressed, passed the scrutiny of the most senior bank officer. He greeted Bradshaw and unlocked the door to let him through and again closed the massive portal against intrusion by anyone other than the employees.

Bradshaw clip-clopped his way through the nearly empty room, thinking that his footsteps sounded more commanding this morning. They had the striking cadence of a metronome. He felt powerful.

This was a far cry from what he had been faced with yesterday at about the same time. But following the initial bad news about the BMW and Curry being in jail, the rest of the day proved not only to be a salve to his displeasure with Howard, but had evolved into a fruitful afternoon with Francis Gillman and his partners. Besides showing them how to play golf and winning their friendly bets, he had closed with them, a tangible contract that would soon give them full operational ownership of their very own winery. The negotiating for the offer was complete, prices agreed upon.

And Curry? Let him solve his own problems. Bradshaw would get his car back eventually. The incident no longer worried him. He was too far removed from it personally to have any effect on him.

Upon entering his office, his first move was to disembowel the heavy briefcase he had brought from home. He had worked up the information and figures for final printout and signatures. All that remained was to call Kara Tower for the last time to advise her of the generous offer that had been made on her property, enabling her to escape her indebtedness without the shame of filing for bankruptcy. She should be grateful!

Actually, he thought, after that last phone call they had, he hoped she would talk to him. Well, he considered again, after all, hadn't he been polite in telling her they would be glad to examine her application at a later time? He did leave the door open. He was smart enough to do that.

It was only nine-thirty, but he needed to get this show on the road. Gillman was getting antsy and Peterson said something about tying up loose ends by Wednesday because he was leaving town.

Bradshaw had to get in touch with Tower…*Now*!

He dialed her number.

Kara, who was to be the only one working in the winery today answered the phone.

"Good Morning, Mountain View Winery. How can I help you?" Her heart wasn't into the canned greeting that came naturally after having used it probably more than a thousand times.

"Good Morning, Kara. This is Carl Bradshaw," he said in his most congenial voice.

She noted the familiarity in using her first name. She instantly recalled that in the last phone call that it was 'Ms. Tower'. It surprised her that he would be calling her in the first place.

"Yes?" She wasn't about to give in to congeniality.

"I hope I'm not disturbing you at a busy time, but I have some very important news that I think you'll like to take the time to consider."

"Yes," she repeated noncommittaly.

"I'd like to be candid with you Kara, and please take no offense. We are at this point trying to help you in an untenable situation."

Kara thought she knew exactly where he was going with this and said nothing. No doubt the bad news that her distributors would no longer be carrying her brand had probably traveled to the ears of Carl Bradshaw. She didn't know and didn't care which direction the cutting blows would be coming from next. She was already numb from disappointment. All she could do was listen.

"It has come to our attention during the processing of your application papers that certain indebtedness by your winery has matured, *and* we noticed the absence of means by which to cover that indebtedness."

"Now we all know how hard you have worked in developing your business," tears were starting to appear again in Kara's eyes, "and the good news is that I believe there *is* a way in which you could completely dispense with those debts."

Kara was interested.

"I'd like to hear what you have to say," she replied carefully to hide any clue to the emotion she was feeling.

"We just happened to run into some clients, a group of investors, that would be interested in assuming your liabilities."

"And what would they want in return?"

"Well, it would be expected that they would take over the property. I'm sure that without this kind of solution, you could be faced with an ugly bankruptcy proceeding within a very short time."

If the truth hurt, this last statement was the cruncher of all time, and the painful reality was that she really had no other means of escape.

"So if I were to entertain such an offer, you would be able to expedite it?"

"Exactly what I had in mind. None of us want the extra expense of filing for bankruptcy," another threat. "We would in fact, have the paperwork in your hands this afternoon…that is if we could receive an answer from you by…say noon today?"

For the first time, Kara saw the wisdom in taking the first tangible step in letting go. This was a way out, one she would have to accept however repugnant.

The solution that was being offered had an unexpected twist. It never occurred to her before that she would ever be in the position of having no immediate means of support in the future. A sale like this would leave her destitute. Never had she padded her future with hidden savings or numbered bank accounts to sustain herself for the balance of her life. Everything she could lay her hands on went into the winery. It now entered her mind that for a period of time following the closure of her ownership of Mountain View Winery, she could very well be found in the nearest soup kitchen.

Tentatively she contemplated the other side of the coin. She imagined what it would be like to be free of indebtedness, while at the same time, having the assurance that all of her creditors would be paid in full.

"Noon," she repeated. "I will give you a call at noon with my answer."

Carl Bradshaw couldn't wipe the smile off his face knowing that he would be getting that call promptly at twelve o'clock. She was not only agreeable, but he could hear in her voice that she would give in to his offer. He was ecstatic and wanted to get on the phone with Gillman right away.

"Gillman here." The big man had returned to his suite at the Red Barron to collect his papers before going out for the day. The telephone made an ironic noise of repeated bleating, surprising him by not only the sound, but that someone would have caught him in his room.

Bradshaw was a little surprised himself to find the man so easily.

"Oh good…I thought I'd be leaving messages all over town before I reached you. Glad I caught you, Francis. Have you got a minute?"

"Certainly. Do I guess correctly that you have news with regard to the winery deal?"

"That I do. The little lady will be giving me a call at noon today with her answer to your proposal. Chances are very good that we'll have the deal in the bag and could possibly be looking at late this afternoon for signatures. What do you say to that?" His voice beamed through the telewaves.

"I say, good work Carl. Peterson wasn't sure you would be able to pull this off before he had to leave, but I can see he was just getting the jitters. Too much at stake for the price. Like you said, it's a sweet deal. I knew you would be able to do it."

"All we have to do is wait…"

There was a disturbance on Bradshaw's side of the connection. Someone had entered his office having knocked only once and passed in through the door in a rush. The door slammed open hard against the inner wall.

"What's the meaning of this?" he asked the intruder, and back to Gillman he shot, "Let me call you later, something's come up."

As soon as the phone was on its cradle, Bradshaw had risen from his chair, alarmed at the disconcerted appearance of the bank clerk who had burst in on his conversation.

"Mr. Bradshaw, I think you'd better come to the front. We have a major problem."

Some of it had to do with word of mouth rumors, but the media set the woods on fire. On Sunday, the news was known only by those people who were there first hand and learned about the arrest and drug connection relating to an 'executive' of the Southern Valley Bank. Anyone in the police department that day, arresting officers, dispatchers, clerks, or anyone listening to a scanner would know something of the incident. A comment here and a divulgence there, put the story into a long slippery-slide down the dirty laundry road.

It didn't take long for the reporters to make the most of this juicy aspect of the weekend…one of those incendiary stories that was too good to be true. Death, drugs and general mayhem. It was played up on the front page of the Medford Trib newspaper…in living color.

Later, Carl Bradshaw would be asking himself how he could have missed looking at the paper this morning! Or…how could he have been in that position in the first place?

But there he was, exiting a 'black and white', the officer helping him out of the car, as the photograph was shot. And the thousand words that this one picture showed was the CEO of one of the most prestigious banks in Southern Oregon in some kind of terrible and serious trouble. The consternation in his face made him *look* like a convict.

The bold print stated that Bradshaw was "*alleged to have been involved*", as the owner of the vehicle transporting illegal substances. Murder most foul was also heralded as an ingredient in the stew. Of course if one had read further down in the article, it would have been noted that it was "Mr. Carl Bradshaw's assistant and officer of the Southern Oregon Bank, Howard Curry" who was now being held for questioning in the case.

The reaction that was caused by the newspaper headline and the accompanying picture was a 'slam-dunk'. By eight o'clock that morning untold numbers of husbands and wives were discussing their plans that would take them to the doors of the bank as soon as it opened. By ten o'clock, when the bank opened its doors, there was a line out to the parking lot.

The first procession of customers who requested their savings or checking funds be presented immediately and their accounts closed, was orderly and gave no hint to the bedlam that would follow in the next half-hour.

By the time Carl Bradshaw entered the main floor only fifteen minutes later, voices had been raised to decibels that would forevermore drown the echoing footsteps that at one time sounded so pristine in this room. No longer were the customers polite. They were demanding! No longer were the tellers complacent and helpful. They were snappish!

People were pushing and shoving. A woman tripped over a man's bag of papers and whatnot on the floor and landed in an unseemly position with her skirts exposing her less attractive parts. The papers and whatnots were exposed as well. A loud and unsavory argument ensued. Children were crying. Someone in the crowd pointed with an accusing finger and yelled, "That's him!"

With perfect clarity, Bradshaw's world suddenly housed the reality of a new experience. Disaster! Even in his wildest thoughts he could never imagine the day would ever come that *they* would make a run on *his* bank. Unable to move, he gazed past the crowd and out of the window. More people were stacked in the street attempting to elbow their way in through the door.

Bradshaw turned to the clerk who was skulking at his elbow as if to hide from the onslaught.

"Sandra!" he barked, "Don't just stand there, call 911!"

The doors to the Southern Valley Bank were closed to the public one hour and a half after they had opened. It had to have been the worst day in the life of Carl Bradshaw.

A few hard-core customers were still knocking at the door an hour later, but the beating it had taken when it was first locked tight against any further entry had slackened off and only a dull rapping could still be heard from time to time. The phones were ringing unceasingly and the fax machines were scattering papers unheeded for lack of attention, as they operated at full bore. No answers were forthcoming from the members of the bank. Not today!

CHAPTER 55

Beth was not expected at the winery this Monday, but that was not to say that she wasn't involved with her work. Since early that morning when her wine columnist friend had called her with confirmation of the international wine competition awards, she had been gathering her resources, deciding just when to announce the good news. It so excited her, she thought she would wet her pants.

She was going to meet with Tom to go over the fine points the two of them had put together and they could come to some decisions with regard to the winery. This would take place at Raven's home. After all, Tom said *he* was involved as well.

Once again the question of Raven's new role came up. Now he's interested in the details of business. Since when? She resisted the impulse to say 'see ya at the pow-wow'. This was time to be serious. There were some big decisions as well as some big money at stake.

On her way to the address she was given, her attention was split between watching the road signs and rechecking the directions.

After about the fifth time when she looked up again to the tree-lined street there suddenly appeared a handsome buck. He made one leap into the center of the road and stood there unmoving at attention, his eyes on the car, daring her to enter his domain without permission.

"Okay, buddy. I give."

She pulled up to a stop within twenty yards of the animal before he turned and sauntered away in his own good time.

It was then that she saw the small road sign that proclaimed 'Dancing Bird Way'. Had she not stopped for the deer it would have blended with the leaves of the surrounding foliage and she would have missed the very sign she was looking for. And to have missed it would have been criminal. It was beautiful. The hand carved wooden sign was actually made up of three different kinds of lumber, laminated to appear as different shades of color as the carving went deeper. The effect of the detail was dramatic. It showed a starling in frolicsome flight with the name of the road peeking from the carved foliage below the bird. Good thing that it wasn't too conspicuous. Things like that didn't usually last a week in this country. If it wasn't stolen, it would have been buck-shot to splinters.

She turned into the drive and continued for a quarter of a mile.

It wasn't until the car was standing at the front of the house that Beth wondered if she was truly at the correct address.

There was a garden filled with native plants as well as ornamentals facing the driveway that would be spectacular later in the year. A portion of a kitchen garden could be seen in its development stage being planted off to the side of the house. The front door to the rustic cabin was an oversized work of art. An open Dutch door beckoned, as did the occupant. It was Tom.

"I thought you'd never get here."

"Am I here?" Beth asked. She still wasn't sure she heard right about meeting at Raven's 'place'. This place? Was he caretaking someone else's home?

She mounted the sturdy risers leading to the cozy balcony that surrounded the lovely cabin.

"Are you ready for a cup of Raven's spectacular coffee?" Tom opened the door. "Looks like you could use an eye opener."

"That I could, that I could," she said, looking about at her surroundings.

She entered the living room area just as White Raven came through the kitchen door with a tray bearing a coffee service, brioches and the accompanying fresh butter and homemade jam.

"You're timing is good. We have warm pastries to go with the Kona." He placed the tray on a burled table. It looked delicious and she was hungry. "Help yourself. I think we're going to need some sustenance to get us through this homework."

It was some time before Beth adjusted to the wonderment of the 'new' White Raven. She thought, this was a side of the man that nobody, but nobody knew about…here in town anyway…maybe some place else, but not here.

Eventually they got down to business. Beth had been anxious to get past any kind of wasted time in order to make progress in their communal undertaking. The others were as eager as she was to formulate their ideas into something workable. Once the three of them commenced to pour over their information, the contrast of their separate personalities was forgotten as they perfected their plan and how it would be introduced to Kara.

"So, it *can* be done," was the final analysis. The three conspirators agreed at last.

After hours of grinding out the numbers and the examination of possibilities that had until now never been put to use, the data had been placed on a computer disc file and was conclusive. They had conceived a good and viable package based on the ongoing history of the company. The reorganization, if it needed a label, could be made to the benefit of everyone involved.

"I think we should take this to Kara as soon as we can. God knows what she is going through today. Getting past this weekend had to be one burden off her shoulders, but now she's faced with an even bigger problem. I can't believe that she's trying to handle this by herself. Got to be going through hell," Tom said with his complete understanding of the big picture.

Beth added, "True enough. This plan we came up with may be a wonderful solution for all of us, but until she knows about it, I don't think we could say she's a happy camper."

White Raven completed the line of thought. "You're right about getting this to her as soon as possible. She won't be so unhappy when we present this package. What we've come up with is sure to be something she would like…very much."

Beth cocked her head looking at Raven curiously and asked, "Since when were you such an authority on Kara Tower?"

Tom picked up on the new vibes and the suggestive concept that Beth was now intimating. He added, "Yeah Raven, what's going on?"

Tom and Beth watched together in mirth as the usually stoic man became uncomfortable and then embarrassed. He had the definite look of someone getting caught with their hand in the cookie jar.

Smiling, Raven admitted, "Okay, so I've been more than a little interested in Kara Tower. But I'm not letting that get in the way of sound judgment. I still would place my vote for the solutions we've worked out for the winery problem." Then his voice softened as he said, "I've been aware of a lot of the things that have happened to her *and* to the winery, and if anyone deserves a break in their favor, it's that woman."

Tom and Beth couldn't help poking fun at Raven.

"I'm serious," he retorted.

"We know you are, big boy," Beth responded, "I can just hardly wait to see what Kara thinks about all this." She was laughing hysterically. "Shall we make a quick stop at the store for some champagne and flowers to make it a special occasion? It is, you know!"

"Good thought, but we can make it special without going to the store. I have a small wine cellar here. I'll get the bubbles. Oh, and here's a pair of shears. You and Tom can pick the bouquet out of the garden. And try not to get lost playing in the back forty! We have work to do!"

The growing interest that Tom and Beth were forming for one another had not escaped Raven's notice.

CHAPTER 56

"There's no one there!"

They were pulling into the driveway of the winery, headed for the parking lot. Odd...Beth had expected to see at least one car there, Kara's.

"I thought you said she would be working at the winery today," Tom said with some concern.

"That's what she told me." Beth responded. For the moment, she was at a loss as to what to do next. They had departed from Raven's home, taking advantage of the comfort of Tom's Taurus, the consequence of which left Beth without her keys. Without needing them for her own car, she had left them on the table next to Raven's front door. The fact that she was without them struck her as they pulled up to the building.

"Bother, and I didn't bring the key to the winery. I thought we could at least set up the celebratory flowers and champagne."

"Maybe she's still at the house," said White Raven. "You know there could be any number of reasons she wouldn't be here first thing today. Shall we see if we can intercept her there?"

Tom agreed. "Sounds good. I'll just keep going."

"Wait!" Beth nearly shouted. "I have an idea. Tom, go ahead and park there."

Tom cruised the quiet running car past the new flower beds, now starting to show their first flush of bloom, and sedately pulled in to the place where Beth indicated he should park.

"This is good," she said and got out of the car. "I think I know how we can get in without a key today."

"I get it, we're going to do a B and E." Tom said humorlessly.

"Like you really know about that kind of thing." Her own first hand experiences would have shocked him to the bone. If she could have done it with impunity, she would have loved to tell him. Instead she said calmly, "No, Tom. We used the cargo door for moving wine after the festival and if we're lucky, it'll still be open. If we could get to the office before Kara, we could give her a real surprise. Got that champagne handy?"

They approached the cargo door. Beth caught an unexplained atmosphere about the building. Something was strange here! Was there someone inside? She felt the hair stand up on her arms and the back of her neck was prickling. A gesture with her finger to her lips cautioned Tom and White Raven to tread softly and maintain quiet. They responded by nodding and remaining silent as they came closer to the door.

With no handle on the outside to accommodate entry, an initial groping for a purchase on the large sliding doorway was necessary before the panel sprung free from the closed position. At that point, Tom motioned for Beth to move out of the way so he could flex his muscles for her and wrench the door open. He curled his hands around the edge and pulled. It slid slowly open with a prolonged grumble to a space just large enough for the three of them to gain entry.

"So much for being quiet. If anybody is around, they sure know we're here now!" Tom said hopelessly as the three of them stepped one by one into the big room of the winery.

Beth still had the strange feeling that something was amiss. Nothing stirred in the building that she could see, but there was something alive about the air. She could almost hear breathing.

Stopping in mid-stride, she silently pointed a jabbing finger towards the tasting room, indicating the possible presence of an intruder.

Saying nothing, White Raven nodded in agreement. He placed his offerings gently on a table nearby, then fearlessly he held up his hand indicating that they remain where they were, and he took the lead. There was no sound in his stealthy footsteps as he approached the door leading to the next room where he stopped to pause, reconnoitering, listening. He could hear nothing now.

But then, just as he took a precautionary look around the corner, Tom and Beth saw the swift movement, and White Raven backing off and ducking with lightening speed. There was a crash at contact with the doorjamb, of glass and liquid spraying Raven and the immediate area. It looked like there was blood! Everywhere! Was Raven injured?

In no more than a heartbeat of time the avenging Kara appeared at the door, righteous arms raised with a second bottle of wine between two strong, steady hands. Her eyes were glazed with justifiable bloodlust. She was ready with all her strength to take a second swing at the offender.

Their eyes met.

The moment was held in a freeze frame.

Tom and Beth observed, but no one spoke. Odd sounds emanated from the bodies of the two adversaries.

And then with an exhaled sound of relief by all present, it was over.

"You give great bottle!" Raven broke the spell, trying to sound unruffled, casual.

"You give great target!" She tried to relax, but Kara could not measure up to his aplomb. It was embarrassing for her when she realized the destruction that the first broken bottle made, and observed the poor condition of his clothing. She felt shaky.

"So now we know what hand-to-hand combat's all about," Beth said as she and Tom came closer. "At least this one! My God Kara, I don't believe I've ever seen you so ferocious. You sure know how to make a guy feel welcome!" she added facetiously.

Hutchins couldn't contain his amusement in Beth's tirade and at the spectacle in general.

"Quit laughing Tom," Raven admonished. "Just because you haven't done battle with the Hun." He was making a perfunctory attempt to brush the red wine off his shirt and pants.

"Raven, I am so sorry." Kara gushed, coming to her senses. "I don't know what I can say. You know I would never have done that if I knew it was you. I simply didn't expect a break-in, and I certainly didn't expect it would be you,…you three, that is. Whatever are you doing here?" She scanned them in puzzlement.

Tom repeated, "Yes, what are we doing here?" He looked circumspectly at the others until they cumulatively focused on their objectives.

"I think what Tom is trying to say is…" Beth started. She didn't know how to approach the subject.

"Well?" Kara prompted.

White Raven took the lead.

"My clothes are wasted. Maybe we could deal with that problem first. Are you too busy to take off from your work for a little while? These things could use a quick rinse…at the house?"

The others caught on to the implication. It would be far more comfortable, not to say private, to make their presentation away from the winery. No chance of interruptions there. Their body language urged her to say yes.

Kara was all too relieved to argue, especially after this last episode. She would be more than glad to postpone the hated details of tying up the loose ends of her business. She'd also be more than glad to postpone thoughts about making her announcement to Carl Bradshaw that she would indeed, forfeit her business in order to satisfy the total of her debt. Tough as it was, that was the only avenue that held any integrity on her part. She had made up her mind to go along with his offer to let his investors take over the winery. It would be better for everyone, suppliers, employees, everyone. She would do it at noon.

But the other chores, the closing of her books…she would, if she could, put them off indefinitely. Of course she would go to the house with them. At least by going there and taking care of Raven, she could make amends for the mayhem she had created.

They all agreed to the change of venue.

Beth locked the cargo door affecting the impossibility of any further unauthorized entries into the big room. White Raven reclaimed the bag containing the champagne and flowers. They proceeded to the front door to lock up the building. It was just as they were about to make their exit, that Nick Brocci's car came gliding up the driveway.

"Damn! It never fails when you want to get out of here. A customer!"

"Beth, why don't we just go on to the house and you can take care of them. It won't take long and you can lock up and come and join us."

They were too preoccupied to notice the make or color of the clients' car.

CHAPTER 57

With her mind on the things that would transpire in the next hour or so, Beth also didn't recognize the dark car or its passengers at first. She figured she could give these people the quick *spiel*, sell some wine and have them out of there and on the road in about twenty minutes. She wouldn't miss too much of the conversation that would be taking place at the house if she jogged over to Kara's place as soon as they were through.

The customers had passed Kara's group on the path as they headed for the winery. Beth could see them hesitate, taking a second look at White Raven and the condition of his clothing. She could also see that they made some comment to one another before they continued determinately toward her. Her mouth dropped open as she stared at them, wishing she could put the scene in rewind and get them to go back into their car to drive away.

It was the 'Las Vegas' couple! Aghast with disbelief and fear of being alone with them, she nearly called out to Tom and Raven to come back, but she didn't dare. Did these people somehow connect her with the disappearance of the hidden money? How could they? How could they suspect her of any involvement? She couldn't believe that they would know anything, but she was ready to pray that they didn't!

"Hello," she said tentatively when they were too close not to expect some established pattern of courtesy.

The man grimaced for what was supposed to pass as a smile and said, "Are you the owner here?"

"No, that would be Kara Tower and she isn't in today." Beth realized that in passing White Raven on the pathway, their attention was on the sopping stains on his clothing and not on the woman who was walking with him. Perhaps they *didn't* notice that it was Kara. These people had to be trouble and she just wanted to get rid of them. Now, it was more than a question of the displeasure of having untimely customers. This couple could be a seriously dangerous problem for her…but they were asking for Kara!

"Is there any way she could be reached? I have some very important news for Ms. Tower, and we would like to speak with her some time today."

The natty man's overdressed wife was meandering around the tasting room, fondling the gift items as they spoke. Her hands glittered with heavy gold and a diamond and emerald bracelet that was color coordinated with her outfit. Who were these people? If Beth was agitated beforehand, she at least was now feeling the relief of no longer being on the chopping block. He wanted to see Kara, not her. Still, she was cagey in her response.

"Well, I could try to reach her a little later," she said hesitatingly. "Is there a phone where I could reach you in say, an hour or so?"

"Sure." He voice became soft spoken. Controlled. "We could wait for a message at the Woodlands Restaurant. We'll get some lunch there and let them know we're expecting a call. Please tell her to ask for Nick Brocci. This is regarding Superior Beverage." He almost sounded threatening.

"Fine," she said as she grabbed a note pad and wrote the information. She made no effort, however to make the admission that she even knew what 'Superior Beverage' was. "I'll get the restaurant number from the book and I'll phone as soon as I've located her."

When they left the winery, Beth puzzled over the reason for this flamboyant couple to be searching out Kara, and she wondered as well about their connection with Superior Distributors. It was then that she saw Turner bounding up the field on foot toward the building. He arrived panting and out of breath from the effort.

"Nice sprint! Couldn't wait to see me?" Beth jested now that the Broccis were gone and her immediate fears were allayed.

"That was the car!" he blurted breathlessly and pointing to where the vehicle had retreated down the highway.

"That was what car?" she returned, ignorant of what he was getting at.

"The car! The other BMW. Remember? I saw a gunmetal Beamer leaving Pottsman's after he was killed. I saw those people from the field and I'm certain it was the same couple I saw that day!"

Beth's eyes opened in surprise. She was conscious of it now, as she remembered the image of the gray car that had just been in the driveway. It gave her a shiver that coursed her whole body.

"Yes!" she hissed, putting two and two together. Those people were the ones who provided the dope connection with Pottsman. She *knew* this as she recollected their conversation at the winery that day. She knew with certainty, that those were the ones that had murdered Earl.

Before she could blurt out her knowledge, Turner turned on his heels and was on his way to the office phone to call the too familiar 911 number.

"Turner," she called to him, "they told me they would wait for me to call them at the Woodlands. You can tell the police they'll be there for another hour."

"Cool. I'd rather see them arrested there than here. That way, I hope, the name of Mountain View won't come up as having anything more to do with it. Kara's reputation is precarious enough without adding more spice!"

He was dialing.

"Precarious? A four syllable word escaping the lips of my old beatnik friend? Cool is good, but *precarious*?"

"Never mind my vocabulary! You know what I mean, any time you're in the public eye…you know how it goes!"

"You're right! It's better to be careful of how things look to outsiders."

She could hear that someone had answered the phone when Turner started giving them his name. It gave her a moment to rethink her own position. Beth decided prudently not to say anything further about the people who had just left. There was no need to incriminate herself by telling everything she knew. Now that Turner could identify them as being at the scene of the murder, there was nothing left to do but let the police take care of it. One of those glitzy people would be nailed for murder. No doubt! Unlike her prior position on the subject, she suddenly had confidence in the processes of law enforcement.

Turner was still on the line with the police dispatcher, but the conversation had taken a turn, and Beth noted that the subject wasn't on the Broccis, the gray car, or the murder.

"Yes, on the street in front of the winery. It looks like a derelict to me…"

His conversation with the dispatcher was curious. What was he talking about? She listened to what he had to say.

"That'll be fine. We'll be here and you can find me in the vineyard. I'll be working near where my green Ford pick-up is parked. You can spot it easily from the road…Yeah, you're welcome." And with that, he hung up.

Beth was on him immediately with questions.

"What were you talking about? What's derelict?"

"Remember the yellow bug that was giving me and Roger trouble out on the highway before the festival? The assholes who threw beer cans at us?"

"Yes, I remember."

"Well," he said smugly, "they're about to get their cute little piece of yellow shit towed away."

"You do have a way with words. Now, can you translate?"

"I was driving out to the vineyard when I noticed something yellow on the far side of the festival parking area. It was nearly covered by shrubbery 'cause it was parked so close to the bushes. You almost couldn't see it at all. Anyway, I drove over and discovered that it was the same 'bug' that we saw that day."

"Do you think that the owner forgot it was there after the festival?"

"I don't know why it was there, but yeah, it must have been left there after the festival…so I'm having it towed away."

"Wait a minute! I didn't know they would tow a vehicle off private property, at least not without charging you for it."

"Well, it isn't exactly *on* private property."

"So, what do you mean by that?"

"I sort of moved it."

"Moved it?" Beth was becoming exasperated having to drag the information from him in bits and pieces.

"How hard could it be? I just hooked it up to the tractor and dragged the sonofabitch out to the street! Now, the guy who owns it will be stiffed for the towing, and penalties, and for leaving trash on the highway. Poetic justice, huh? Oh yeah," he added, "I sort of told them I thought it had been there for a few days. It isn't legal to abandon a car on the highway for that long."

"Cruel!" Beth was smiling.

"Yeah, ain't it?" Turner smiled.

CHAPTER 58

When Beth walked into the house, her visual impression deserved a sub-title or caption. It was 'domestic tranquility' at it's finest. Kara, with her feet tucked up under her in the plush armchair was leaning towards and listening with rapt attention to a interestingly robed White Raven, comfortably ensconced in the overstuffed couch.

At the front door she noticed Raven's imposing paper bag, still waiting with wine and roses, sitting there on the floor. Tom entered the room from the kitchen with the well-used tray and tea set, filled to the brim with beverage and snacks.

"You make a very handsome butler." Beth quipped.

"We needed sustenance. What took you so long at the winery?" He ignored her barb.

With precise detail, she related the past half-hour, adding that they shouldn't be surprised if they saw or heard the police paying Turner a visit out in front of the field. They would no doubt be confirming his information and requesting him to come in later to the station and identify the people at the murder scene.

"Do you think Turner was worried about you being in danger?" Kara asked.

"I think he ran up to the winery so he could alert the police as quickly as possible...Oh, my God!" Beth stopped in midstream.

"Beth, what is it?" Kara asked with concern.

"I almost forgot to tell you. That man had come to see *you*!"

They stared at her in shock and confusion, waiting for her to go on.

"He said his name was Nick Brocci," she consulted a scrap of paper that appeared from out of her pocket, "and had to speak with you about some very important business. Said it regarded Superior."

For the life of her, Kara could not think of any connection she might have with this man, or for that matter, Superior Beverage after their conversation of that morning. As much as she had needed them for her business earlier in the game, it was time now to tell them to go to hell! Still, she was curious.

"Have I met this Nick Brocci before? I don't remember his name."

"Not to my knowledge."

"What does he look like?"

"Straight out of seamy side of Las Vegas. That was my first impression when I saw both him and his woman. Dressed like central casting's idea of what Mafiaites should look like. Slick, with lots of gold showing."

"I noticed a couple that fit that profile at the festival," White Raven said.

"Really? Are you sure?"

"It could have been the same two. Wasn't anybody else around there that would have fit that description so accurately. They stood out like alligators in a flock of ducks. I'm surprised you didn't notice them yourself."

"I noticed a lot of colorful people there, but not those two specifically. Do you remember which day that was?" Beth asked.

"I think it was Saturday...yes, it had to be Saturday because I remember seeing the woman buying a pair of small paintings from one of the artists. The next day, I saw that the paintings had been replaced by two others that were similar, but not quite as well done."

"Well, that does it! That puts them here, in the vicinity of Pottsman's on the day of his death. Raven, I think you should let the police know that you saw them here."

"Yes," he said thoughtfully. "I could do that. Clearly, that would be good evidence." He stood. "Kara, I'll give them a call. If it's all right with you, perhaps they could send the officer who is seeing Turner over here. I could give him a statement."

"Of course. Go ahead and make your call. I'll see if your clothing isn't ready to be put in the dryer. We can't have you talking to the police in that cute little piece of fabric you're wearing." She looked with amusement at the slightly feminine cover that fit her so well, but that barely came to his knees. She wondered vaguely about the masculine body that the cloth was so intimately touching.

When Kara returned from the service porch, Tom and Beth were deep in the midst of a whispered conversation. With good taste, it didn't occur to her to ask what it was precisely that they were discussing. Instead, she made for the food tray and helped herself to a fresh cup of coffee and a small blueberry muffin. Something was up, but nobody was talking. She decided she would wait for them to come to the point of their visit. All in good time, she thought, all in good time.

Finally, after White Raven returned to the room having made his call to the police dispatcher, the four of them settled back into the comfort of the overstuffed furniture and each of them waited for the other to start the conversation.

This is it! Kara thought as she fidgeted with her muffin, picking out the blueberries one by one and delicately placing them in her mouth. Now they're going to tell me what's on their minds. Patience was one thing, but she was beginning to think of the work that was waiting for her at the winery, becoming anxious to return and get it out of the way.

Beth was fidgeting as well. Her nervous fingers gave her away as they fussed with her hair, her clothing and the fabric of the chair. She was bursting with the news of the award, and at the same time was being gagged by the current happenings. But now, they could get to the reason for their being here.

The phone rang.

"Would you like me to answer it?" Tom offered.

"Thank you, but it's probably for me. I'll get it."

Kara stood and crossed the room to the kitchen where the cordless phone was hanging.

"Hello?" and for a brief moment of unfocused attention wasn't sure for the first time if she should even make the effort to say Mountain View.

The caller, not waiting for any more of a greeting said, "Have I reached the correct number? Is this Mountain View Winery?" The voice had a clipped but soft-spoken English accent.

"Yes, of course. This is Kara Tower. How may I help you?"

"Ah! This is Clive Cornwall here, calling from New York. I represent the International Wines Corporation portfolio in the United States. We would very much like to discuss your line of product with you for the purpose of distribution."

Kara was taken back. Mr. Cornwall was not only well known to anyone in the wine industry, his prestigious firm was probably the most sought after representative for only the most world renown wines. Cornwall was a celebrity. His distinguished good looks were easily recognizable due to the number of television and magazine articles in which he was featured.

She didn't know what to say. She certainly didn't know what prompted him to be calling her. Her winery held an excellent reputation, but so did many of the other wineries of her size. It didn't make sense.

In any case, she replied vaguely through her confusion, "I...don't know if there is anything I *can* do for you at this time." Sadly, she thought it was too late to be hopeful of establishing any kind of relationship with a distributor, no matter how well respected they may be.

"I understand," he said, translating her response to mean that for the moment she would be tied up with other matters. "You must be very busy at this time, so I won't disturb you any further today. Would it be possible for you to reach us later on in the week...say Thursday?"

"Certainly." She was unsure as to why he would be wanting her to phone.

"I'll give you my number. It's area code 212, 779-9000. Ask for extension 335. Have you got that?"

"Yes, Mr. Cornwall. I have it."

"Thursday then?"

"Thursday."

In a daze of disbelief, Kara made it back to her waiting guests.

"Beth, you'll never guess who just called."

"No, I guess I won't. That is unless you tell me."

"Clive Cornwall of International Wines in New York."

"Oooo-la-la! Did he tell you why he called?"

Beth was aware that neither Tom nor White Raven could possibly know anything about this grand distributor, known, loved, and respected, not to mention coveted by the industry. The implications of his call were all too clear to her. But her immediate thought was, did he spill the beans about the award?

Kara answered, "Not really. He said he knew we must be busy today and asked me to call him on Thursday. Isn't that odd? I mean a call coming from him...today?"

"Yes," Beth assented with an enthusiastic nodding. "Odd!"

Kara plumped down into her chair like a despondent teenager.

Beth could stand the delays no longer. She started the ball rolling by leaning forward to Kara and asking in a concerned fashion, "Kara what is it?"

"Oh, Beth! I don't know how to begin." She felt so utterly at a loss.

"Then begin anywhere. You know we're all friends here and we want to help."

"There is no help possible. You see...I feel so ashamed,...this will be difficult."

"Go on," Beth prompted.

"Kara, we're with you." Tom consoled her.

White Raven said nothing but by his attentive silence, conveyed his support.

"Yes I know, and it does make the whole thing a bit easier. But the hard truth that I have to tell you is that I will be closing the doors to Mountain View. That's the long and the short of it."

She paused to review their reaction.

There was no immediate reaction so she continued.

"For a long time now, you all…and especially you, Tom, were aware that I've been seeking financial aid. All we needed was a boost, not a hand-out, just an infusion of money to place the business on a secure footing and at the same time, enabling us to make a necessary expansion. Unfortunately and for reasons unknown, that help never congealed. The banking circles denied our every assurance that the winery was viable and refused to make the needed loans. It left the organization short on operating capital.

"The problem until recently hadn't been in the sales or promotion of our label. The problem was the number of outstanding liabilities, and the *strange* part of it is that *all* of our creditors demanded full payment at about the same time. It was as if some unknown channel of communication had spread the word to lean on Mountain View Winery. Prior to this time, these accounts were content with the knowledge that they were receiving regular payments and on top of that, were receiving a substantial interest on their outstanding money."

"Kara," Tom interrupted, "About when did this start taking place?"

"It really started a couple of months ago. Why?"

Hutchins had an idea that this was about the time that Curry had received the loan apps and had the resource information to have initiated the crippling movement.

"Just curious." he kept his reply concise, not wanting to go into the reasoning for his question. He was interested in hearing more about the odyssey of the winery's last days of life, according to Kara.

She continued. "In an effort to placate at least a few of my outstanding debts in order to continue operating, I've reduced our available cash and credit to the point that by next week there will be nothing left at all. Our normal sources of income through our distributors have been suddenly depleted and now, I'm afraid, there is no help to be seen on the horizon. Naturally, this is not the finale that I originally had in mind."

"What were you planning to do?" Beth asked without expression.

Kara took it as a challenge to her intentions and responded acidly, "The only thing I could do. I'm pulling the plugs and having another group take over the winery. They will be able to retire any and all liabilities and continue running the business with their own staff."

She took a deep breath and continued. "In fact, I think that's what hurts me the most. That they could replace any of my valuable people." She looked directly at Beth. "The team that we've developed here has become one of those entities that is far greater than it's individual parts. I've seen all of my people working together and witnessed their accomplishments. You've been phenomenal!" she was looking directly at Beth. "The winery has become a smooth running machine that fairly hums. It's almost criminal to think of placing someone else in the positions that all of you hold and fill so well."

"Thanks, Kara." Beth was humbled, thinking of Kara's anguish over this seemingly untenable dilemma.

"I guess that's why it seemed so implausible that the International Wines group would call now, today, expressing interest in our label. Only now, it's a little too late. Oh yes, and the other blow to our futures was the call I received from Superior this morning. They advised me that they would no longer be carrying our brand! It's like open season on Mountain View and the shots are coming from all directions.

"Those assholes," Beth could not contain the expletive.

"Yes, aren't they? But the *coup de grace* is yet to come. My deliverance from this complete fiasco came from the lips of Mr. Carl Bradshaw, CEO of the Southern Valley Bank, who also called this morning to convey his very 'generous' offer from his covey of investors, to settle all debts and liabilities for the consideration of entitlement to the winery."

Her words hung in the air.

White Raven almost choked on his coffee. He said, "You mean to say that with no compensation to you, they would take over this place?"

"*Generously* take over the place."

"Jesus Christ! What did you tell him?"

"He has asked me to call him back today at noon to give him my response. It occurs to me that he knows I have nowhere else to go. In any case, I don't! Isn't that right, Tom?" She couldn't help directing the cynical question to him because of his supposed attachment to the banking firm. She completed the diatribe with the final statement, "I'm prepared to tell him that I will take his deal."

"That's preposterous!"

"Perhaps, but it's the only thing left for me to do. I'm so sorry!"

White Raven stood, prepared to submit the second option to Kara. He could see plainly that she had endured all that was humanly possible to endure in these circumstances. For her, a poor present could only turn into a worse future. It was time to offer some light in a bleak world.

The doorbell rang.

While White Raven made a dash for the cloths that were only slightly damp by that time, Tom made the move to answer the door. As they suspected it would be, the young officer had arrived to take the statement that would eventually further connect Nick Brocci to the local homicide case.

"Mr....er...Raven will be with you in a moment," Tom said. "Would you like to have a seat? Something to drink? We have tea." It all sounded like he was flustered and nervous, a boy being intimidated by the grandeur of the uniform. Actually, his hang-up was on White Raven's name. Just what was his last name? Did he have a last name? He was startled to realize that he really didn't know.

"No thank you, I'll just wait. This won't take long."

They waited.

It wasn't long before White Raven reappeared. He looked a good deal more himself.

"Thanks for getting here so soon," he said. "It doesn't seem like it was more than a few minutes since I called."

"I got word from the dispatcher that both you and Mr. Ferguson were on the same property. Since I came to see him too, it saves me quite a bit of chasing around," he said this honestly, as though he were grateful for the respite. "Turner told me he'd be out in the field for some time, so I could get to you first."

"Fine," White Raven said, and then picking up on the casual use of his first name asked, "Do you know Turner?"

"Sure! We started a couple of the same night classes at the community college together a while back. Civil Procedure and Criminal Investigation. Turner's a real kick in the...Oh, sorry. I mean to say that he's an interesting person. I heard him talk about his new job here and he's really enthusiastic about it."

Beth couldn't contain herself. "Civil Procedure and Criminal Investigation? Turner? He never said one word to any of us that he had done anything like that. I am amazed!"

What amazed her further, was the realization of how quickly, yet subtly Turner was making the change of posture from itinerant wanderer to responsible citizen. How long had it been? Only a matter of a short time since he took on this job as managerial foreman. Kara really knew how to pick em'. Was it the job or the person himself that brought out the better side of his character, she wondered. Beth had no knowedge of his previous career experience.

But her thoughts were not of Turner alone. They were of herself as well. She recognized the changes that had taken place in her own perspective of life and her serious determination to do the best she could in her own job. It had to do with Kara's guidance. Maybe it was *having* to deal with the responsibility of performing well in the eyes of others. Whatever the case, she suddenly recognized in herself, the warm feeling of positive self-esteem and worth.

The officer went on to say, "Yeah, he's a pretty good guy. I notice he's smarter than he lets on. Got a good head on his shoulders. I believe he is interested in these classes and down the line, they could be a good security measure wherever he's employed. You're pretty lucky to have a guy like that working for you, Ms. Tower."

The only thought in Kara's mind was that his position wouldn't be a very long-lived one. Better he uses some of that college education to look for a new job. Smiling politely, she kept her mouth shut.

"Where would you like to start?" White Raven prompted.

"I was told that you were able to place Mr. Nick Brocci at the Mountain View festival the same afternoon prior to the homicide of Earl Pottsman. Would you like to tell me about it?" He held his pad of paper and pencil at the ready.

White Raven repeated the details of his sighting of the couple at the festival and the approximate time they could be placed as being in the area. He agreed to come to the station later to give a formal statement as well as make an identification.

"Does this mean that you have these people in custody right now?" Kara surmised by his words.

"Yes Ma'am. Thanks to Furguson's information, they were picked up at a restaurant in town. Their vehicle will be impounded and searched as soon as the paperwork catches up."

"Should be interesting to see what they find in that car." Beth wanted to say more, but she could hardly attest to the fact that she had knowledge that these were mega dope pushers. She had to keep her mouth shut. Anyway, their felonies were rapidly catching up with them. They would be facing up to their sins without benefit of her added input. She concluded, "I can already see the headlines going berserk with the news of an arrest. Some excitement for around these parts!"

"You got that right. And now they got themselves *another* headline," the cop said with his hand still moving across the notepad.

"Another news headline? What do you mean?"

"Oh, you haven't read about it?" He looked up from his task to answer her.

"No!" she said. The others were listening expectantly.

"This morning's newspaper! Had it all over the front page,…there was a drug bust on Saturday that incriminated some big wigs of a bank and according to the headline, it was thought that they had something to do with the homicide…Anyway, I heard on the radio that there was a gigantic run on the bank just this morning by customers who lost confidence and they had to close the bank. Big news! Looks like that branch is finished in this area."

Tom asked, "Do you remember the name of the bank?" He could scarcely contain his excitement.

"Sure, it was Southern Valley. I know the place! Used to have an account there a long time ago. Glad I don't bank there now!"

Glad I don't work there now. Tom cringed at the thought. He at once felt badly for the people who would be out of jobs. At the same time he gloated righteously over the retribution that was being served on a platter to the culprits who would bend so low for their own self-seeking gratification as to cause the ruination of a perfectly good organization. He guessed at how many other businesses must have been challenged by the banker's underhanded practices.

Kara, turning a pale white, collapsed back into her chair. The fall of the bank would mean that they would be unable to put through any kind of deal for the bailout of Mountain View. Bankruptcy loomed heavily in her future.

"Are you all right, Ms. Tower?" the officer asked solicitously.

"No…I mean, yes I'll be fine." She wondered. She could feel the actual beats of her heart throughout her body.

Raven, seeing that their business was finished for the time being, escorted the policeman to the door, conveying his willingness to assist in any way he could. The parting was brief and he hastily returned to where Kara sat in a near catatonic state. He crouched in front of her, taking both her hands in his. He would have her complete attention.

"Kara, look at me," he said with more authority than she had ever expected from him. Her focus was drawn to his eyes, although the crushing blow of the policeman's last words had altered her ability to think clearly. The loss of the bank became the loss of their proposal for a buyout, no matter how unpalatable it was. There would be no way now to settle her debts.

"Kara," he repeated. "There is something very, *very* important we want to talk to you about."

"All right," she answered listlessly. There could be nothing of great importance to her now.

"First of all, understand that Tom no longer works for the Southern Valley Bank. He has already documented his intention to sever his relationship with them. His decision was made this last weekend when he saw what was being done to you. We all know what you have been going through."

The others were nodding in agreement. Kara's eyes traveled from one face to the other.

Raven paused to rearrange himself in a more comfortable seating position. He never let go of Kara's hands as he sat cross-legged on the floor before her looking up into her face, forcing her to look at him.

Kara said nothing.

Tom left his chair to join White Raven beside him on the floor, placing his hand on Raven's shoulder, indicating solidarity. Beth followed suit, taking the other side of Raven. They were now a family...a force.

Raven continued.

"Kara," he repeated her name in order to capture her attention to the import of his words. "There *is* a way out of this! Tom and Beth and I have carefully gone over every aspect of running the winery, and getting you out from under your liabilities. Can you understand what I'm saying?"

"Yes."

She still looked confused.

"Forgive us for being so blunt and also for digging into what you must feel are very personal concerns. It's just that we could see that you needed some help, and needed it quickly. That's why we are here...to let you know that combined, the three of us, Tom, Beth and myself, believe we have more than enough money to do away with your immediate problems and eventually you could continue the expansion you had planned."

Kara blinked. This wasn't possible! They had no conception of the magnitude of her problem.

"Do you have any idea how much money this would take? The commitment?" she said disbelievingly. "You don't have that kind of money," her tone was to discount this unrealistic offer.

Tom spoke up.

"We know very well what it will involve, Kara. We've been researching this thoroughly and we *can* do it!"

Coming from Tom, this declaration had the weight of his professional understanding.

Kara looked again from face to face for confirmation and found the others nodding in agreement.

Tears filled her eyes and spilled over as she absorbed the impact of what they were saying. She uttered, "I don't know what to say." Her voice was husky and deep with an emotion she didn't know existed.

She could see the love emanating from these three people who were there, willing to support this cause with their astonishing and unanticipated resources. Beth too, was taken up by the emotion of the moment, her sympathetic teardrops ran over her cheeks.

"You needn't say anything Kara," she said. "Just be grateful that you no longer have any need for the Carl Bradshaws of this world."

"And for that matter, the Howard Currys of this world," Tom interjected.

"And the Jerry Majors," Beth added.

Kara brightened, remembering the earlier phone call.

"So just maybe we *will* have need for the International group for our distribution?"

"Yes, Kara," Beth was wiping her tear dampened face with the back of her hand, "now for the *really* good news."

"There's more?" was Kara's surprised response.

As if on cue, the telephone began its insistent ringing.

Tom rose from the group, offering to take the call, giving Kara a moment's respite. She needed a little time to absorb the welcome burden that was created by the avalanche of good tidings.

"Tom Hutchins here," he answered. "How can I help you?"

"Tom," the voice blustered. "I didn't expect to hear your voice! This is Francis Gillman. I suppose you've already heard about all the hubbub at the bank?"

"Yes, but only smatterings. It seems the newspapers have blown this into quite a scandal."

"Scandal indeed! That why you're not in town? Things getting a little too hot for you?" This was said with overtones of a friendly manner, not with rancor.

"Actually, the reputation of Southern Valley no longer interests me. I wrote a statement of disassociation yesterday. It entered the mails this morning."

"Good timing, Tom. Good timing. You're not the only one pulling out of there. I had our attorney make electronic transfers of all of our accounts to our banking in Washington. I'm glad to hear you're out of there as well. I felt you were much too promising a young man to be caught up in their convoluted difficulties. Yes, glad you're out. Have any plans for your immediate future?"

"Yes sir, I do." He was thinking of his involvement with the winery.

"And considering your presence there, I suppose it has something to do with Mountain View?" He took the words right out of Tom's thoughts.

"Yes sir."

Gillman paused, carefully formulating his next remark. "And…I suppose you are aware that my partners and I had a special interest in that operation."

"I did." Tom didn't elaborate. It angered him not a little to think of the attempted takeover.

"Hmm. My call here today was to discuss this with Kara Tower, but do you mind if I do a little guesswork while we're speaking?"

"Go ahead Mr. Gillman."

"You can call me Francis."

"Francis."

"I get the distinct feeling that you have already made some proposal to Ms. Tower that would put her on a more financially secure footing. How am I doing so far?"

"Not badly."

"But even with your proposal, there *could* be the need for further capital involvement."

"Francis, why don't you just tell me what you have in mind? Ms. Tower is right here with me," he indicated to Kara that she hear what he was saying.

"Fair enough! We, my partners and I, have reviewed the Mountain View operation carefully enough to know without a doubt that it is indeed a valuable as well as a viable one. Tom, I realize that the time for our effecting an immediate and complete takeover is now history, but I would like to offer whatever aid I can for the future of this business.

"And please, don't get me wrong," he continued quickly before he could be interrupted. "Don't jump to any conclusions before I finish. Please hear me out. Before we became involved with this deal, Howard Curry had lined up the business as one of the dead-enders that could be pressured into an untimely demise. Curry knew how to do that. He scouted around for buyers to glean a big finder's fee and easily found us since we were old-time regulars at Southern Valley. What he didn't include with his information was the personal involvement that was really supporting the operation. What he presented to us was simply a substantially profitable opportunity that would otherwise be terminally crushed by outstanding liability. The place was a jewel, and we were definitely interested in controlling it.

"But Tom, now that we, as well as yourself, are disassociating from the bank and the people who were setting up this deal, we've had time to take a longer look at what they were proposing. We feel that rather than entering at an owner's level, it would be equally satisfying to be a part of the operation by offering constructive participation and monies in the form of very low interest loans."

Tom was incredulous. "Low interest? But why would you do this at a low interest rate?" It didn't make sense to him. What ulterior motives could be hiding behind this seemingly generous offer now?

"Because, where else could we have more fun?" Gillman's enthusiasm was transmitted clearly by the phone line. "Think about it Tom! Being associated even in a tangential way with a winery would have so much more glamour…more clout than, say being associated with a pipe fitting manufacturer. We could have a good time! I've thought it over and at this stage of my life, I could use some fun. Besides, with you *and* me involved, I'm pretty certain we could dream up even more ways to make money for this enterprise. I'm good at that, you know."

"Yes, I'm sure about that!" Tom had to laugh. "Look Francis, you're offer is very generous and will no doubt be considered very seriously. But first, there are a lot of details that have to be worked out. Ultimately, you know, this will all be up to Kara."

"I understand. You'll talk to her and let me know then?"

"You bet." They spoke for a minute or two longer and then Tom was saying, "Good to hear from you."

"I'll be in touch, Tom"

They disconnected. All eyes were on Tom.

He addressed Kara, explaining the content of the call and what it would mean to their future. Gillman was extending capital in an open-ended offer. It was everything that she had been hoping and working for. And all Gillman wanted in return was to be able to participate is some small way with the winery.

Tom wound it up by saying, "So, whatever else we do, there would be enough available funds and then some, to carry over our expansion needs."

"Wonderful!" Kara responded.

"Oh no," Beth piped up. "You haven't heard wonderful yet!"

"Nothing could be more wonderful than what's been happening."

"Well brace yourself, Kara because what I have to tell you will knock your socks off."

CHAPTER 59

❁

For Kara Tower, the announcement was a moment never to be forgotten, a moment that could only be described as somewhere between euphoria and spatial vertigo. For her it was a form of ecstasy, similar, but not to be confused with the 'high' induced by drugs and mind-altering chemicals. Nevertheless, it was exactly in this state of mind that Kara floated as a leaf, and allowed herself to be tossed and propelled as in the current of a stream.

She willed herself to savor the moment, yet she was constantly unable to keep from drifting into a mental limbo. The whole time-frame took on a dreamlike quality of unreality. Whereas before there was nothing but failure in her future, now she felt like she had won the lottery. She was living an impossible dream.

Mountain View had taken the Platinum Challis!

They were all ecstatic!

"The bag!" Beth was nudging White Raven.

"Bag?" He didn't register her meaning at first, until she nearly pointed to the paper bag by the front door. "Ah, the bag!"

Flowers and champagne were produced with a flourish when the first of the congratulatory phone calls commenced. The news of Kara's award was hitting the industry in an explosion of publicity and instant attention. "Was it true that Mountain View had won the highest honor at the world's largest wine competition?" and "How does it feel to be on top?"

Beth took the calls and barely had time away from the phone to drink her champagne.

Wine writers, television stations and newspaper correspondents were calling for appointments. The marketing and distribution moguls literally were sitting up and taking notice of this small winery that had cornered such celebrity overnight.

"Can you believe this, Kara? After the way they treated you, Superior is calling. Didn't they just fire us? Can I tell them to screw off?" Beth was holding out the phone to Kara in a reluctant gesture, her hand covering the mouthpiece. She was champing at the bit for the job of telling off that distributor.

"Let me take it," Kara said, and with monumental self-control, she addressed the speaker sweetly. "Yes, we received the faxed copy of your cancellation of representation…and I can't thank you enough for sending it."

She listened to the voice on the other end of the line and then said, "If I'm correct, that was your signature on it, was it not?…Let me see…" She ruffled the pages of a magazine into the speaker and then paused as if looking at the document. "Yes, Jerry Majors, I see that it is. I'm sure you recognize that due to your timely notification, we'll have to be searching for another representative. Oh, I do hope we can find one." She paused once more while Majors floundered about with his explanations.

Finally she responded. "No, I haven't spoken to a Mr. Brocci." She gestured to Beth with a 'who was he?' shrug. Beth returned with an innocent expression and a shake of her head.

"What's that?" Kara was saying. "You would like to re-examine our account? Well, I don't think so. Thanks to you, I believe our business is quite finished," she said politely and then added, "Have a nice day."

She hung up to a resounding round of applause from her friends.

"Nothing like getting rid of dead wood. It's interesting how politely you manage to do it." White Raven thoroughly enjoyed sharing the experience of sweet revenge being served on those who deserved it. Smiling to himself, he took another taste of champagne.

Beth took another phone call.

Kara looked interested in White Ravens statement although she didn't completely understand what he was talking about. They were interrupted by a knock on the door. She got up to answer it and was nearly bowled over by an energetic Turner, who entered in a tidal wave of movement. He picked Kara up in an exuberant bear hug, pivoting her in a full circle. She was laughing by the time he put her back on the floor.

Addressing the others as well, he explained his excitement. "I talked to Alan a little while ago."

Beth looked up from her conversation on the phone, the instrument still at her ear. Without verbalizing, she indicated the question, who was Alan?

"The cop. We're buddies. You know, the guy who came in to talk to White Raven! Anyway, seems like all hell broke loose Saturday when they arrested one Howard Curry, an employee of the Southern Valley Bank, for trafficking in drugs. Not only did they find the stash in his car, well actually it was Carl Bradshaw's car, but the guys with him were arrested too. And remember the yellow bug I had towed away? Well it turns out that one of the guys who was with Curry owned it. He had priors with a warrant and they slammed him in jail instantly."

"So that takes care of your yellow bug mystery." Kara said.

"Yeah! What comes around goes around. I feel kinda' vindicated now for having the slob's car towed. Show him who not to throw beer cans at."

Beth mouthed the word *'vindicated'*, in awe of Turner's easy use of the word. She, still with the phone in her hand.

"So guess who the other guy was, picked up with this Curry?"

"I can't guess," Beth interjected as soon as she had dispensed with the last caller.

"Who was it?" Kara and Tom asked in a chorus. White Raven waited patiently for the unstoppable account of the story.

"Our very own and much loved…" he paused for the effect. "Talbert! Seems they were related in some way, Howard Curry and Talbert. Cousins, or something."

"Well!" was all Beth could say. The banker and the bum, was what she was thinking.

Tom still didn't get it. "Who is Talbert?" he posed his question to anyone who could enlighten him.

"One of the cellar rats." Raven said. He knew Talbert from town and had learned of his sleazy character.

"He used to work here. His full name is Talbert C. Cottner." Beth said in explanation. "Like White Raven said, he was one of the bad boys who was doing damage while he was supposedly working here, and probably thieving whenever Kara had her back turned. One more piece of deadwood, and good riddance."

"Right!" Turner agreed. "That 'banker' dude seemed to run with the scum."

Tom snapped his fingers when he came to the realization that he recognized the name that Beth had spoken. When she had said C. Cottner, it was as if a bell had gone off in his brain.

"That was the name that Howard Curry used when he was working with Braverly Wines Distributing some time ago. He called himself Howard Cottner then and I knew I'd eventually find out why he was hiding a past identity by changing his name."

"I remember you telling me that." Kara commented.

"Right, I ran across it in an article when I was doing some research at the library archives." He didn't mention that the research was for the benefit of Mountain View. "It was written some time ago and there was a picture in the paper of a group of men. That's what gave him away. I recognized him. No wonder he had zeroed in on this winery business as a target for his scheme. He knew more about it than anyone guessed."

"I vaguely remember someone with that name now that you mention Braverly." Kara stated. "They represented Mountain View for a short time, and if I remember correctly, they made a lot of promises without fulfilling them. In fact we had to separate from their distribution because our sales were falling off so badly then! I think that Cottner was the name of the person handling our account there." She paused for a moment to think about this. "Good work, Tom. I would never have remembered that connection unless you mentioned his old affiliation."

"Makes it feel all the better to know that he is sitting in jail as we speak, held without bail. Guess the nasty guy is finally getting what's coming to him."

"Knowing what she knows now, he's probably better off where Kara can't get her hands on him," Beth joked.

"You're right about that!" Kara could hardly contain herself. She had another flash thought about the humiliation she had endured and then being hurt twice by the same person. The recollection of her near accident coming home from the wine tasting sprang from the far reaches of her mind. It seemed so long ago that it took place...still, it occurred to her for the first time that perhaps it wasn't just a fluke accident. She would not bring up the subject about it now, on this happy day. Maybe never.

"Hey, if and when he ever does get out of the mess he's in now, he'd have to get by me before he even came close to Kara or anything that's hers." Turner said magnanimously. "And that goes for his cousin too!"

The phone was ringing again and again, Beth obediently doling out information to the callers. She handled the media people who continued to request a future audience with Ms. Tower. She carried out the task with politeness and speed telling them that they would be reached within three days to schedule a personal interview.

"Speaking of this mess," Kara needed to clear up one or two points and get them straight in her mind, "I must say I don't understand the connection between the downfall of the bank, your ex-bank Tom, and this mysterious Mr. Brocci, who was supposedly sent by our now ex-distributor. It's pretty confusing!"

"Brocci was sent by your old distributor?" Turner showed his surprise to the question.

"That's what Jerry Majors just told me on the phone a little while ago. He explained that one of their most important partners, this Mr. Brocci, was expected to be here in order to talk over their new and aggressive position in representing the winery. As if I'd ever let them represent me again. I had to tell him that his Mr. Brocci had never arrived, and then you all heard me dismiss any further dealings with Superior."

"Did you know him?" Tom asked Turner, surprised that he knew the name.

"Ha!" Turner exclaimed. "Wouldn't want to know him. Brocci was the guy in the other BMW that I saw leaving Pottsman's place just before I found Earl's body. The police picked him up in town as a prime suspect for the murder."

"This is getting more interesting by the minute!" Tom said.

"What am I missing?" Beth wanted to know after placing the telephone back in its cradle.

No one explained.

"I am dumbfounded!" Kara exclaimed. "And this man…who I have never met before…was supposed to come here to talk his way through for Superior? Incredible!"

Tom reflected, "Then not only is the bank up shit creek, but my guess is that so is your desperate ex-distributor!"

They all were shocked and pleased at what appeared to be retribution being generously disbursed.

CHAPTER 60

❀

The individual details in the weekend's crime were a puzzle nearing completion. Every effort was being made to establish any and all connections between the parties. A tangled skein of misdeeds were unfolding with every clue.

It was found to be a sheer coincidence that the cars in both cases, the highway arrest and the getaway car at the scene of the murder, had been the same make and the same color, but the coincidence didn't end there. When the police made their search, both vehicles were found to contain unlawful chemical substances. A solid, if provocative connection could now be made between the murder of Earl Pottsman and the drugs that were found in the car that belonged to Carl Bradshaw. The wrappings on the white powder were so tellingly similar in each car, that they could have had the name of the manufacturer stamped on them for product identification. Just how this could be possible would not be fully described by the officials at this point of time. Actually, on this point of evidence, they were at a loss.

However, the car bearing the Nevada license and belonging to Nick Brocci contained a cache of neatly packaged bundles of cocaine. Of this there was little to ponder. The street value of this newsworthy bust was estimated and duly noted for the record as in excess of six digits.

By the following day the dust was settling. The excitement of the previous twenty-four hours had taken much energy out of everyone. After the momentous events of the day, when they had finally separated for a night's rest, it was agreed that further examination and solidification of immediate plans would need to be accomplished at the earliest possible time. The following morning would be soon enough…"as long as your booties are in high gear," as Beth had put it. Things would be moving quickly now that the doors of opportunity were flung open.

Nothing feels quite so good as coming out on top, Kara decided. With new life being pumped into the business, she felt the surge of new life flowing through her whole body, and it gave her not a little satisfaction to have been able to fling her good fortune into the faces of those who would bring her and her business down. Truth be known, Kara was devilishly glad to feel the release that came with autonomy in handling her own business. Leaving her message of refusal to the bank for their offer on her property, (no one seemed to be answering the phone today), was as close to the feeling of sweet revenge that she would need for the rest of her life. Without dwelling on that reward, however, Kara's thoughts moved on to what was in store for the future.

They had again gathered at Kara's first thing the next day. Coffee and warm muffins warded off the post-morning hunger, enabling them to dive into the business at hand. Tom arrived with White Raven, a ream of papers spilling from their hands. Beth too, having stopped at the winery office to pick up any last minute thought-of items that would be of use for their project, came in bearing a box of printouts from the computer.

The paperwork was spread out neatly on the dining room table in order to categorize each and every aspect reestablishing the operating line. Having secured a source for a new and more affluent construct, it was a whole new ballgame. Tom, in his methodical manner had simplified the process of organization. The expertise he had developed over the years could now be put to use, pulling together the elements of priority and placing on the back burner, those of less immediate importance.

"And now," his inflection suggested summarizing, "the question of how our various talents might be best used?" Tom addressed the group after two hours of pouring over the updated information. It had been a grueling exercise of mathematics and material manipulation, which happily they confirmed was going to work.

"Well, Digby will continue with his work like he always has, but it would increase his productivity if he had his own working assistant." Beth said with the knowledge born of previous experience that whenever a good technician was relieved of the 'grunt' work, his labors usually exceeded expectations.

"Beth is right," Kara added. "And if we look at the new budget with an eye for the increased production, I judge that a proportionally increased staff will be required. The beauty of that, of course, is that the larger the output of the winery, the major increase in staff will be in the marketing end, rather than the production. No major changes would have to be made in production employment."

Kara sounded as though she had gathered her thoughts and was now getting back to business. Instead, once the words had left her mouth, she sat back in her chair assuming an aloof attitude.

"Good point," Tom took the lead again. He addressed Kara, "but you're missing what I was getting at. We all agreed that with the involvement that White Raven and I, and of course Beth too, would be having in the growth of the winery, we could actively contribute to the operation. It's what we want to do. Now, Beth is well versed in her job and already knows her functions backwards and forwards. But Kara, I'd like to use my expertise in the maintaining of the books and balancing the production figures if there's an opening where I could be placed."

"Mmm hmm," was her answer.

"And White Raven has more of an artistic bent than any of us had imagined. I can't help but feel that when he is able to spare the time, his input as to the market imaging would be invaluable."

"Mmm." He was rewarded only with her pensive nod.

"Kara, under your direction, we'll bring off the biggest, splashiest reentry to the industry that has ever been made."

Kara looked amiable but said nothing.

White Raven had been listening to everything all morning. Since eight o'clock, during coffee and a light breakfast, he absorbed the conception of the new plans for the continuance of Mountain View. He actually was starting to enjoy seeing the business aspect of an operation. It was new to him. He had always been spared the cumbersome details of managing his own personal work in the past.

Also, he was fascinated in the manner and style in which Kara Tower ran her personal life and her home. It became another source of his growing admiration for her.

There was nothing pretentious about her or her surroundings and yet there was the unspoken quality of good taste. It was conveyed in the careful selection of her life style. He had an appreciation for the home she lived in, her personal selections that made up the ambience; paintings on the walls, books, and knickknacks of various kinds, the fresh flowers on the tables. There seemed to be no discernible attempt to methodically match up the decor, but the entire presentation as a whole bespoke a singularity of purpose, comfort and beauty.

This, he decided was the spirit of the woman. In spite of the pressures brought upon her, there was an unspoken serenity. She walks in beauty, he thought. He could see it in the way she would hold herself, just a heartbeat, before a moment of action. First, the pensive thought, and then the complete giving her all to the matter at hand. He replayed the vision of Kara swinging the bottle of wine at him in the winery and decided it would be a good thing to stay on her good side.

Studying Kara in this way, White Raven was the first to notice.

"Kara, you're not saying much. Are we getting too far ahead of ourselves too quickly do you think?"

"No," was her answer. She didn't embellish. Somehow she didn't seem to be herself. Quiet. Withdrawn.

"Is there any part of this that you don't go along with?" Tom asked.

"Mmm, no, it all sounds fine."

"Well what is it?" Beth was perplexed. "Kara, we don't want to do anything you don't approve of or want!"

"I know."

There was confusion on their faces. It had all been coming together so smoothly that there had never been a question that Kara wouldn't be pleased with the outcome. All they wanted for her to do was state her desire and it would be attended to.

"Would you excuse me for a moment?" Kara asked.

"Sure Kara, anything." Tom was willing to go along with anything Kara had in mind.

"She's sure acting strange," Beth said as soon as Kara was out of earshot. "Do you suppose she's going into shock, what with all that's happened?"

"Not like her to be bowled over by circumstances." White Raven said. "Maybe she just needed a little time to absorb all this input. She's not likely to make any hasty decisions, but I agree, she's got something going on in her mind."

"Probably wants to just freshen up," Tom suggested without conviction.

More coffee was served along with polite conversation. It wasn't more than a few minutes before they heard the door to Kara's room opening.

To their surprise, Kara appeared dressed in a baggy pair of cotton trousers and a loose fitting sweat shirt. A chiffon scarf binding her hair pulled it into a tumbling cascade of curls and silk down the back. Her clothing now appeared to be more suited for puttering in the garden. There was a discernable change in her countenance.

"Well ladies and gentlemen, I guess you've been wondering what happened to the old Kara Tower?" she asked happily.

"Well, yes." Tom looked at her innocently, expectantly. He could have been answering a child, going along with the game.

"Well she disappeared! Went away on vacation! And I'm here to tell you that I am taking her place to give vent to all the wonderful things she would have wanted to do if she *only* had the time." Kara was radiant.

Was she going mad? This turn of events didn't make sense to them.

Kara started laughing. It was their expressions of disbelief that set her off.

Beth was the first to make the break-through into understanding Kara's actions. She started giggling at first and to the consternation of Tom and White Raven, was soon laughing as hard as Kara. Their laughter fed upon itself and became an uncontrollable fit.

"What's so funny?" Tom demanded.

Beth couldn't answer him. She had picked up a box of Kleenex and they were daubing at their eyes before they were able to speak again.

"Please, sit down," Kara implored. The palm of her hand outstretched before her in a gesture of promise for an explanation. She wiped her tears and took a seat with them. She waited for the correct moment before she made her announcement.

"I won't be continuing with the winery."

The reaction was predictable. The moment of silent disbelief, the stirring of thoughts, looking for answers in each other's faces, and then the reaction to what could be termed as betrayal.

"You can't do that." Tom said as reasonably as he could, given his desire to speak out and out tell her it was impossible to stem the flow of events.

"Yes, I can."

"Kara!" No longer laughing, Beth was pleading, "why in God's name would you say such a thing. In the face of nearly guaranteed success, why would you cut yourself, not to mention everyone else, off? Why?" In a matter of seconds, from laughter she had been reduced nearly to tears of grief. Beth unreservedly displayed her emotions as they struck her.

White Raven waited for Kara to clarify her thoughts.

"I know you deserve an explanation and I'll get to it. But first let me say that what you three have accomplished in such a short time is nothing short of a miracle. You can't know how much I admire and respect your tenacity in finding such difficult solutions. I don't know how you did it, or even when you did it, but I'm both impressed and grateful. I especially want you to know that I am truly grateful.

"You see, ever since I recognized the possibility of losing the winery, I had to imagine how I might reconstruct my life without it, creating scenarios in my mind if you will, of what kind of life style would be possible to step into. It became a multi-dimensional exercise. It interested me.

"My first consideration was that there would be no available money, so whatever I entered into would necessarily be at a modest level. On the other hand, I still had my intellect, no one could take that away, and I thought about the adventure of learning a new trade. Anything was possible. I would certainly have the time! Little by little, the avenues for the future *were* looking brighter. When I studied my choices, I channeled my ideas for what areas of career work I would like to apply to first."

"But you don't have to…," Beth started, but Kara waved her off, wanting to complete what she had to say.

"What I'm trying to tell you, is that even when I had the responsibility of the winery, I could see that I truly entertained an interest in other things. But with the winery, there was no free time. Now, I would dearly love to back off from the demands of the business. Let it go!

"Beth, you have been groomed for this job and I believe you can now fly on your own in the management of the winery. We've proven through Digby's expertise that it is possible to produce world quality wines that will, from this point on, have no difficulty in garnering their place in the elite portion of the market. Also Beth, you have the aggression and energy that it takes to back up the momentum that will drive this winery. I want you to do just that! With Tom's help in the routine of plotting production tables along with keeping an eye on new supply demands, the growth of operation will be in capable hands.

"Which brings me to you Tom. Now that you've become a member of that vast number of unemployed, an opening in what you would probably call a growth venture should be attractive to your needs. We'll need a comptroller. Do you think you would be amenable to this position in a full time capacity?"

"You know I would. This is like a dream come true for me, Kara."

The three of them saw in his intense expression the subtle change in Tom. He was actually expressing a deep hunger for what was being offered to him.

"And White Raven," she turned to him, "After you have found the time to give your attention to the question of our public image, I would appreciate it even more if I could persuade you to dedicate just a small amount of your busy schedule to indulge me."

"I could say your wish is my command, but Kara, quite simply I would be happy to indulge you." Tom and Beth noticed that he didn't pursue the terms of this indulgence.

"So now you can see the truth when I say I won't be continuing the winery.... You will!"

Everyone started talking at once. The dam of pent up conversation had been broken and the expressions of relief were roiling in a cascade of self-propelled statements, the most vociferous being Beth.

"Kara, you had us going!" she admonished. "You had us believing that you'd let the whole thing fold. I love the idea of taking on the responsibility of running the show, but you are *not* bowing out of *every* aspect of it." She stood her ground. "You can expect that demands will be made by the public and most certainly the media that would require your presence for upcoming promotions."

"I was hoping to avoid all of that."

"You can't avoid it Kara. I can do only so much, but the only one who can quench the public blood-thirst, is you. They'll want to see you, Kara,...not me!"

"I suppose you're right. It's just that I've gotten myself into a frame of mind where the public's opinion no longer interests me. I guess I've fought the good battle so long, I've lost the point of the war. Now, I've decided that all I want to do is live quietly, apart from what I've done too long and venture into the fertile fields of leisure creativity."

"This is good for the spirit, Beth." White Raven was supportive of Kara's position. "She has a valid argument." He turned to Kara. "And Beth has a valid argument as well. It would be wasteful not to have you continue your involvement, even if it is in some small way. For example, wasn't there an invitation to France awaiting your answer? It would be a shame, not only for the people at the conference, but for you as well if you didn't go. Think of what a wonderful experience that alone would be. No Kara, turning your back now on the winery's needs would be a great mistake for you *and* the winery."

"And what do you think, Tom? Am I being too selfish about wanting my time all for myself? Haven't I paid my dues?"

"In my opinion, this isn't a question of paying dues, it's a question of reaping the rewards! With Beth and I running the business, you'll be able to see that it will take two of us to accomplish what you were doing alone. It should come as no surprise that you may *want* to keep touch with our progress. You may *want* to do a little PR work from time to time. Most of all, we want you to be there to share the continuance of what you started."

"Well, I see it's unanimous. I guess my life just wasn't meant to be my own," she dramatized. "I bow to your wishes."

Tom was the first out the door as they disassembled in pursuit of their assigned jobs. Motivation was palpable in the air in which they moved.

"Isn't that Turner coming up the drive?" Tom said with his hand on the handle of the car door.

"Yes, and you might as well learn it now. The name of that green bucket of bolts that he drives is named 'Curley'!" Beth informed him.

"Curley?" he posed it as a question.

"Yeah. He bought it from a guy who had really long hair. The guy had his hair permed and it looked like his head exploded. Everybody called him Curley. Doesn't live around here any more, but the name carried through with the pick-up."

"Cute!"

Turner approached them in a huff.

"Where's Kara?"

"She's on her way out the door. There she is."

Kara was carrying the paperwork that had made its way to the house, and was taking it back to the winery. Her arms were full.

As she came closer, she could see that Turner was distraught.

"What is it Turner?"

"We've had a break-in!"

"Oh no. Was it the winery?" she asked incredulous that the building could have been burgled. They had all just been there and Beth had locked up.

"Somebody got into the tool shed and took my favorite pair of clippers...Goddamn it! Are we going to have to weed out more of these asshole thieves around here?" In his fury, his powers of description ran a little to the rank.

"Cellar rats." Tom said, warming up to the use of the vernacular.

"I don't know, Tom, maybe too many predators." White Raven corrected. "I don't think they'd have a chance around here now."

Kara was unweighting some of her paper burden onto Beth. She was shaking her head ponderously.

"It looks like we'll never rid ourselves of those pesky rats." Kara spoke with amusement in her face. "But in this case Turner, I confess! I borrowed your clippers early this morning to get a few fresh flowers for while I was working in my office. I neglected to return them. I'm sorry," her voice was remorseful and petulant with an absurd gravity. She reached into a canvas carrier on the front table and retrieved the 'stolen' shears and handed them over to Turner.

White Raven was smiling.

"Okay, okay! I was just worried we had another *incident* to handle." Turner looked from face to face, examining their reactions to his blunder. Why did everybody look so smug? "What's the joke? You guys act like you never had a problem in the world!"

"We don't," Kara admitted. "At least not now!" She didn't explain.

EPILOGUE

❀

White Raven had been sitting in the sun working a carving on an intricately burled piece of wood with deep concentration. Sweat was running down his back. The bandana tied around his black hair, now speckled with gray, was damp with perspiration. Kara Tower was only a short distance away, but standing there in the cool of the shade tree, she felt comfortably warm as she studied the angle of his arms as he worked. The sketch she had made was beginning to come to life with color as she painted in the contours of his body. She stood away from the easel to get a better perspective of the study.

"You make a wonderful model," she admitted out loud.

He looked up from his work.

"If you're comparing me with the figures you painted in Italy, I'd say that's quite a compliment. Some of them were beautiful young men. Who would have thought you'd have such empathy with your subjects?"

"Admiration of the human body is something I think we all have, at least to some degree. Empathy has nothing to do with it."

"Are you sure this isn't some kind of Freudian transference? There's a close bond between admiration and desire."

"Get away with your psychoanalysis. I have to concentrate too hard on what I'm doing to get emotional about it as well."

Their banter was the easygoing give and take of a relationship that was established during their tour of France and Italy three years before, and developed during the three years that followed.

Beth, her hands full with the functions of the winery, had been unable to accompany Kara to the International Wine Competition gala. It in fact, greatly pleased Tom as well as Beth to see Kara and White Raven off at the airport when they decided on an extended visit to Italy for the purpose of both absorbing and producing artwork on their tour. Most of all, it was satisfying to discover that the two of them had a penchant for enjoying the same things as well as each other.

The winery expansion had been even more successful than any of them had envisioned. Their entrance into the international market had put the wines into a class of their own, owing to the uniqueness of the newly developed winegrowing area, and Turner, with his battery of vineyard laborers was now able to allot even more time for what had become his new obsession, the development of superior fruit in that area.

The combination that Beth and Tom made in the administration of every detail in regard to the production and marketing for Mountain View was as a marriage made in heaven. Beth was the taskmaster for the management of the winery, and Tom, making use of his talent, became comptroller and the public representative for the enterprise. This workable team, together with Digby at the helm of the winemaking, completed the balance of authority for the growing numbers of employees that made up the crew.

Kara, as she wiped the turpentine from her hands took special care to towel the area under the gold ring, carved with the grape leaves circling her left finger. Of all the decisions she made in her life, she contemplated that this was probably the most satisfying of all. The manner in which she now lived was serene compared to the hectic days prior to stepping down from actively participating in the winery.

A life so changed. Although she had to admit, her name wasn't *that* radically changed. She liked the sound of it. From Kara Tower to Kara Hightower. Yes, as she drank in the picture of her husband at work. She liked it very much.

THE END

978-0-595-38569-0
0-595-38569-9

Printed in the United States
51857LVS00003B/1-51